Gunny

Rebel Wayfarers MC
Book #5

MariaLisa deMora

Edited by Hot Tree Editing

Cover design: Melissa Gill @ MGBookcovers and Designs

Front image: Sara Eirew Photographer & Designer

Back image: Mandy Hollis Photography

Copyright © 2015 MariaLisa deMora

First Published 2015

ISBN 13: 978-0-98635262-2-3

DEDICATION

These towering walls you have built to protect your heart do nothing more than imprison your spirit. – Dean Jackson

For the wounded among us, no matter the cause, may you find solace and refuge, and live your life in peace.

Contents

ACKNOWLEDGMENTS

This book began its life folded into the pages of another. In the midst of the whirlwind that surrounded writing *Jase*, with dismay I realized another strong voice had made his presence known, taking over whole sections of the book. In many ways he derailed the story I wanted to tell about Jase and DeeDee, because Lane Robinson had a very different agenda.

So, over the 2014 Christmas holidays, that is how *Gunny* came to be brutally ripped from the manuscript of his birthplace. When I had cut all the scenes that didn't have a place in *Jase*, there were nearly fifty-thousand words in a cheekily titled document sitting off to the side called PushyBastard.

I had assured him his own book, and now I had to live up to that promise. Another few weeks and I fell into a comfortable rhythm of rising from bed at 5:30 a.m. to write on *Gunny*, then heading to work, and going home to labor on *Jase* in the evenings. Advancing both manuscripts in parallel was challenging, but some aspects of their stories were so intertwined the words flowed easily.

Then...one day, I suddenly recognized Gunny the character. I realized who had inspired my mind to imagine this damaged soul. And once I knew who he was, I understood there was so much more of his story to tell than just about his relationship with Jase's sister, or his part in the Rebel family. So much more, because his tale is one of loss and pain, tempered by redemption and love.

Who is he? He's a combination of people, the genesis of which can be found in a chance meeting, deep in the woods in southern Indiana. In the spring of 2014 I hiked Knobstone Trail. While on trail I met a hiker, a young man who called himself Jackrabbit Joe.

Joe was an Army veteran dealing with severe Post Traumatic Stress Disorder (PTSD). You'll likely recognize that first meeting in a scene in this book, and I sincerely hope, since told from Gunny/Joe's viewpoint, it does not convey the alarm felt on waking in the early morning to find my campsite had been invaded during the night by a man who seemed damaged in ways that seemed both dangerous and frightening. I would never want Gunny to feel how terrified he made Peepers with his outbursts and angry language over trail conditions and other random things, or how alarmed she was by his very presence.

Over the next few days, I was blessed to get to know Joe. And fortunately for me, over those hours and days, the comfortable familiarity we developed stripped the veneer of fear from my interactions with him. Even now, more than a year later, I retain an ashamed memory of those first minutes, and a belated recognition of how differences can make people frightening. Men like Joe and Gunny need understanding and acceptance, not made to feel ostracized even more than their disorder already makes them.

As the writing of this story progressed, as I typically do, I sought out experts on a variety of things. Through my connections, I found a veteran closer to home who was willing to talk to me. Sharing the challenges of living every day staring at the world through the patina of stresses and scenes left behind in his mind by war.

Mikael, an Army vet, suffers from PTSD. For him it has stolen much of the life he led before being deployed overseas. His job—no longer suitable. His family—fearful of his outbursts, have removed themselves from the equation for now. His friends—staunch and supportive, protect him in ways he doesn't even recognize, such as chaperoning his interactions with me to ensure everything went smoothly. Mikael reassured me that he feels his service had meaning, and he will never regret his decision to enlist and serve. He is hopeful things will all work out in the end, and I believe right alongside him that they will. I am humbled in his presence.

Many other people were essential in ensuring this book made it to this stage, where you, the reader, can hold it in your hand or read it on your tablet. And, by the way, I don't want to forget to say *thank you* for reading, for wanting, for loving these characters as I do. Without you, none of this would be possible. <3 *Muuwah!* In no particular order, here are the 'thank yous' for my peeps:

My ever-lovin' critique partners: Kristen, Hollie, LeeAnn, Kay, Brittney, and the intrepid MirandaPanda. Your honest opinions will forever be treasured. Thank you.

Sara Eirew, your photography is amazing, and I am blessed that you had this shot embodying passionate possession in your portfolio for this oh-so unexpected book. The model, and your art, are remarkable, and the cover by Melissa Gill builds on the intensity captured by your lens. Mandy Hollis, your images are no less stunning, and the dancer picture on the back cover conveys all that is Sharon in ways that mean words are unneeded. Thank you.

Kayla, Becky, and the HTE betas, I am so grateful for your hard work. As always, you make these stories, and my life, better. Thanks!

I can't forget to thank my personal motorcycle men, members of clubs across many states including Michigan, Indiana, Ohio, Texas, and New Mexico. Love the feedback, and I love you all so freakin' hard. And, Dino? I hope this book is filled with everything you've been asking for, babe. Pucker up!

I do hope this story respects the dedication and sacrifice of the veterans and others I met during this journey, and if it brings to light even an iota of the struggle PTSD brings to their lives, then all their work with me to ensure I got it right is worth it. I'm honored to have met these men, and thank them for their assistance, and in so many cases, for their service.

~ML

GUNNY

1. FUBAR

Hiding in the back of the truck, he wiped across his face with his sleeve, dragging the cloth slowly and carefully, only moving a bare fraction of an inch at a time. The fabric wasn't clean, but at least it cleared the stinging sweat and fresh flow of blood from his eyes. One of the wounds near his ear had opened again and was persistently weeping blood. With the truck bed covered as it was by a tarp, he knew it was unlikely anyone could have seen his movement, but he believed in playing it safe...always. That was how you lived through the things he had been through over the past weeks, and was one of the primary reasons he was still breathing, when many of the jarheads who sauntered onto the base from stateside, clean duffle in hand, weren't. *Slow and steady*, he thought, *just as Kincade taught you*. Men's voices were approaching the vehicle from the side, and he tensed, listening to their chatter and conversation growing louder, if still unintelligible.

The truck's suspension rocked as the springs on the driver's side sank down slightly, accepting the weight of the person climbing behind the wheel. A creak of the hinges just before the slamming door signaled what he hoped was the impending departure of the vehicle from the roadside. Spreading his legs wider on the floor of the truck bed, he braced himself against the motion of the ride to come. He had chosen this vehicle with care, paying close attention to the color of the dirt dusting the sides, knowing from the shade of ochre it had come up from the south, near the area to which he needed to return. After sitting in the bed of the truck for several hours, waiting, holding himself still and immobile, the damaged muscles in his back and chest screamed in pain as the vehicle jostled into motion. He gritted his teeth, telling himself he merely had to endure the ride and it would bring him that much closer to home.

The monotony of the blind ride, the edges of the tarp fluttering in the wind only enough to let in flashes of sunlight, allowed him to sink deep, mining his thoughts and memories. Not for the first time, he racked his brain, trying to decipher exactly what had gone wrong with this mission. The failure behind the reason he was in this truck right now.

They had planned and executed the insertion flawlessly, conducted the surveillance demanded by brass, gained the necessary Intel, and then began their trek to the extract zone. Few people had known about the mission, fewer still had known the details, and only the men with boots on the ground, just the team, had known everything, and much of that only after they were en route. All checkpoint transmissions had gotten through and obtained a normal response from base. Right up to the end, everything looked to be on target; all signals were five-by-five.

They were not thirty minutes from scheduled exfil when disaster struck, unfriendlies overrunning the LZ as they made their undefended approach. He saw his team of men downed by enemy fire, one after the other. All of them, down. Kincade, his longtime friend and mentor, fell without a sound, obscene craters of red splintered into his flesh. Keffiyeh askew, the fabric obscuring Kincade's face as he crumpled to the ground, and he watched in disbelief as giant blooms of blood on his torso marked where the bullets had found their mark on his friend.

When the bullets finally found him, each had held the weight and punch of a sledgehammer, knocking him from his feet to his knees, and then taking him down, sprawled on his belly. Sucking hard gasps of air, it was from that position he took in the surreal sight of blood from his wounds soaking into the thirsty sand, the splatter rapidly darkening to black as the desert accepted the offering.

From where he lay, he saw Eklund, their communications specialist, frantically trying to contact base, and he watched in horror as the SAT phone Eklund was holding disintegrated in his hand. Then their radioman had slumped backwards from where he crouched, blood pouring from a yawning wound in his neck. He watched as the man's mouth opened and closed like a fish freshly yanked from the safety of the water to the alien surface of a dangerous and airless dock. At the time, as well as now, nothing about the attack made sense. How would the enemy have known how to find them, when to strike? Where was the leak? Who was the leak?

These men had been his friends...his brothers. His DRP had been detailed to Al Anbar province, sent past the DMZ time and time again, doing deep recon and bringing back much needed information and details about population and group movements, weapons caches and supply routes. Now, he thought bleakly, they were all gone. *After the initial attack, he and the lieutenant had made it to a hollowed out area in a hillside, seeking shelter behind a boulder, both men wounded and exhausted, exposed to the unrelenting heat of the sun. Then, three short hours later, he had been alone, the last surviving member of his team.*

That was nearly three weeks ago. He stole loose-fitting pants and a long, cloth coat to cover his bloody and torn uniform, and progressively made his way south ever since, most frequently opting to travel at night. He used his keffiyeh to conceal his too-pale features, but nothing could hide his size, so out of place in this land of sand. His only weapon was his military-issue knife, because everything else had been lost in the firefight and flight from the killing field.

Now, as the evening wore on, the steady, never-ending motion of the truck relaxed him, lulling him into a sense of security. As long as they were on the move, he judged he was safe. *Safe*, he thought, snorting soundlessly. *I won't be safe until I'm back at Chesty. That's if I can even find the fucking camp. Maybe I'm already dead and this is my Hell, wandering forever, lost and surrounded by enemies.*

He sensed rather than heard when the truck first slowed, the vibration from the engine and transmission slacking slightly just before the wheels steered the vehicle to the right, where it bumped off the road. There was the unmistakable sound of people from ahead, likely a farm and homestead, and carefully he worked his way towards the tailgate. He was still attempting to read the sounds and anticipate how much farther the truck had to go, trying to prepare to slide out from under the tarp and over the gate to drop away when the truck abruptly stopped, rocking him in place and halting his progress, effectively trapping him. *Fuck.*

The truck door latch made rough metallic sounds as it worked, the hinges creaking loudly as they moved, and then, to his horror, came the sound of children's voices racing towards them from the side. *Fuck, I left it too late*, he thought, watching as a man's dark brown fingers wrapped over the top of the tailgate, assuming the other worked the handle. *Head first, take the plunge*, he thought and moved as the gate dropped. He rolled out from under the tarp, off the surface of the truck, and onto the ground with a pained grunt, a puff of dust visible in the air from his hands and knees landing.

Pushing himself upright, from his full height, he looked down into the shocked eyes of the man he assumed had driven the truck, seeing three children freeze in place only a few feet away. He hunched over, trying to make himself seem less threatening, but with his size and bulk, knew it was an impossibility. Drawing on the few phrases he knew in Arabic, mixing English in his haste to communicate, he held his palms up to show he was unarmed and told the man, "Peace. *Salaam a eleikum.* Peace. *La bas.* No harm. No harm. *Ar juuk.* Please." The man nodded and made a quick motion with one hand, silently sending the children back towards whatever building they had come from, but neither of the

4

two men looked to watch them go, instead each maintaining focus on the other.

"No harm. *Ma'a salaama*. In peace, go in peace. *Laa a rif ar juuk*. I don't know where I am, please. *La bas*. No harm," he repeated, and the man nodded again, rattling off a sentence, which likely held critical information, but he would never know. Languages had been Eklund's specialty, not his; he and the rest of the team knew only the most rudimentary, mandated phrases. "Chesty," he said in English, hoping the man knew of the forward camp, and was pleased to see a flash of a smile, white in the dark face, followed by a nod. Another sentence of Arabic came in response, but this time the man held his arm out, pointing towards a glow in the near distance.

"Chesty," the man said, and moved his arm, pointing again.

No way was he so close. He knew, based on experience, his current run of bad luck wouldn't support it, so he skeptically repeated himself, seeking confirmation "Chesty? Camp Chesty?"

The man widened his eyes and nodded exaggeratedly, making rapid motions towards the glow against the sky and saying again, "Camp Chesty. Yes."

Shaking his head in disbelief, he said, "Fuck me. Okay." He took a breath, wincing at the pain accompanying his movements. "Thanks." He slowly walked away, because even this close to rescue—close enough to see the lights of the camp—he was really too tired to care. So he unconcernedly turned his back on the man, not even wincing at the thought of taking another bullet. *At this point*, he thought, *who fucking cares, right, Kincade? I think we're both already dead anyway.* There was a burst of Arabic from behind him as the man caught up, long strides easy over the unsteady surface of the sand, speaking quickly. He shook his head in response, barely catching his balance as he staggered sideways in exhaustion, trying to focus on the man's face. "I don't understand. I just need to get to Chesty."

Nodding, the man again said, "Chesty," this time pointing at himself, and motioning back to the truck. "Camp Chesty," he said, and gestured to the vehicle.

"You want to drive me? You're going to drive me to Chesty?" He made steering motions with his hands when he asked the skeptical questions, knowing his southern-laced English wasn't going to help him communicate.

The man nodded and smiled broadly, hand motions urging him back to the truck. When they were stopped at a challenge point twenty minutes later, he quickly exited, shouting his name and team information, painfully dropping to his knees, hands raised defenselessly. He submitted to the initial questions as patiently as he could, waiting while the men unwound his concealing clothing. When they realized he was American, the soldiers quickly surrounded him, urging him up. After making certain they would be letting the man with the truck go, he allowed them to help him to their vehicle, stoically suffering the pain from bouncing through the rutted and cratered roads. *Oorah*, he thought. The distinctive and oddly comforting sound of tracked vehicles filled the air as they drove around and through the camp, and he smiled when he realized the only other sounds he heard were English words. They might be spoken in a thick Australian accent, but they were English questions hammering at him. Against all odds, he made it back.

The patrol radioed ahead to the camp, and so there was a welcoming committee when the truck drew up before the temporary med unit, tent sides flapping in the sand-filled breeze. He laid back on a stretcher with relief, letting his eyes drift closed, reveling in the knowledge he was finally back among friends...he was safe.

He listened to the voices of the docs and med team discussing the injuries they could see as hands sat him up, cutting his cammies off with blunt-tipped scissors. Fingers pressing into his head wounds caused a muttered, "Fuck," and he flinched before he could school himself to stillness. Then came a hushed, "Bloody Hell," and the horror in that low tone registered as the hands returned, gently flipping him to his stomach while gloved fingers explored the painful wounds on his back.

His eyes flickered open when the CO's voice pierced the haze of fatigue threatening to drag him under, and he dreaded passing on this news with every fiber of his being. All he could do was shake his head when asked if there were other survivors, pressing his cheek hard against the canvas. He had not been in a position to go back and check, but knew there was no way any of the men who fell during the initial attack had lived. The scenes he still saw every time he closed his eyes were a testimony to the brutality of the attack. Gaping, ragged holes piercing bodies from wounds that were not survivable. Blood spilling into the sand in amounts too profuse to allow for continued life. Then, huddled behind that boulder, he had watched as his LT died in his arms. Their CO pushed harder, probably hoping for a different answer, but all he could do was shake his head again and again as each man's name was recounted. Eklund, Schwartz, Odenoski, Kincade, Lieutenant Porter—all dead.

Six weeks later, he was stateside, on his way out of the Marines, healing physically, but having been told he was no longer deployable. Gunnery Sergeant Lane Robinson would receive a medal for his wounds, but no answers for his questions. No one wanted to talk about what had happened, but after seeing the Intel sheets for the mission, he knew in his gut the reason for the losses. *Wardah*. His desire for a girl met in-country, the sister of one of their trusted translators, had cost his brothers their lives. Never again, he swore. Never again would he let lust place him in a position of compromise. Never again would he allow a woman close enough to hurt him or the ones he cared about.

2. Brotherhood

Lane Robinson sighed. They were only five minutes into the meeting, and he was already bored. They were all standing around and talking about fixing things everyone in the room knew would either never get fixed or be jury-rigged only well enough to get them by for another season. He looked around at the rest of the city crew, shaking his head. These were all good guys and wanted to do well, but restrictions from the city and state tied their hands much of the time. The city's principal summer festival was only a week away, and yet here they were, still arguing about the best detour patterns for both residents and festivalgoers. Shit that should have been published on websites and in the paper two weeks ago was still in the discussion phase of this hopeless committee.

Raising his hand with a wave, he drew the crew boss' attention away from the clipboard full of papers he was holding. The man stared at him with narrowed eyes for a moment, and then nodded brusquely, granting permission to offer his solution. Standing, Lane walked to the map they were projecting on the wall and touched a point with his fingertip. "Festival parking is here," he said, moving his finger several times. "Also here, here, here, and here. We need to keep those streets accessible, because as long as people can drive into those areas, they can walk to the park where the stages and vendors will be setup." He glanced over, seeing his boss nodding in agreement, and he continued.

"If we shut down these three streets for the run,"—he traced lines on the wall—"we'll need to keep these ones open for residents, especially if we close this bridge." He indicated another three streets. "So let's run the detour from here, to there. It's a good corner, plenty of room for even big trucks to make the turn. Everything else should be okay, unless the city decides not to run trolleys for mass transport, and even that only changes a couple of things. The baseball game isn't until Sunday, which means we don't have to worry about the run at that point."

He looked around the room, cataloging the responses. "I know it's different from what we did last year, but those arrangements didn't work. Hell, we had a shit ton of people trying to drive through the fun run to get to parking. There were some near misses, and the last thing we want is having folks get hurt when they're just trying to come out and have fun."

His boss nodded, catching his attention and said, "Looks good," then glanced down and made a note before looking back up. Lane caught his gaze, and they looked at each other thoughtfully for a moment before the man nodded again and said, "Robinson, wanna follow me over to the bar for a beer? Gimme five minutes."

Deke, his boss, rode motorcycles with a group of men belonging to a club called the Rebel Wayfarers. Lane also had a motorcycle, which for him was because it was a gas saving convenience, so he typically only rode during the summer and then into the fall, as long as it was comfortable. Deke was something different. Last winter, even when there was six inches of snow lying thick on the parking lot, he would see Deke come riding in on his Harley every day. The man was hardcore, and he respected someone who lived their life like that, by their own rules. He shrugged and said, "Okay," before turning to walk to his locker, putting up his gloves and tools.

He finished putting his things away and stood near the doorway, waiting. His alert gaze swept the area again and again, looking for a threat he well knew did not exist here. But, the knowledge that nothing was going to happen did not lessen his need to continue watching. He knew his obsession of vigilance wasn't reasonable, because he was no longer at war, hadn't been for years, but staying alert helped calm his thoughts, so was all the reason he needed.

Nearly twenty minutes later, not the promised five, Deke sauntered out from the office, giving Lane a chin lift and a gruff, "Come on." They walked to the fenced parking lot for city workers and mounted their bikes. Lane took his cues from Deke, following his lead as they started their bikes and rolled them out the one-way gate into the after-work traffic. Traveling on the surface streets, he hung back about twenty feet, staying to one side of Deke's bike, the two men taking up the width of the lane. Soon, they were pulling into the lot beside a local bar and restaurant, where he knew a lot of Deke's friends hung out.

Backing his bike in next to Deke's, he stood, setting his helmet on the seat then looking a silent question at his boss. "Yeah," Deke responded, nodding, "your stuff will be okay here. No one fucks with shit on Rebel property."

His eyebrows drawing together, Lane asked, "Rebel property?"

Walking towards the front door, Deke glanced over his shoulder at him. "Yeah, we own this bar and some other places in town."

"We? As in the guys you run with?" Lane was intrigued; he had never thought about a group of people going in together to buy something like a bar. The logistics would be interesting, and he briefly considered percentages, responsibilities, personalities, all the pieces that could make it challenging, then discarded the thought as trivial, not a puzzle he needed to solve tonight.

Deke responded, "My club, yeah. The club owns everything. Our national president, Mason, he has it all tied up in a legal corporation or some shit. Profits go to the club, and every active member works for the club in some capacity, so we all get a cut." He pushed the door open and stood for a second, seeming to take the measure of the room before heading towards a booth along the back wall.

Lane saw there were already a couple of men seated in the booth, and his footsteps faltered before continuing. Somewhat reluctantly now, he shook his head as he slowly followed Deke across the room. *He might not realize I'm not good with strangers*, he thought, and then saw Deke glance over his shoulder at him again. He frowned and stopped, waiting for Lane to catch up, then quietly said, "Robinson, come on, these guys are all right. I wouldn't fuck with you, man. It's all good, okay?"

Nodding stiffly, he followed, taking the remaining half-dozen steps to stand at the end of the booth alongside Deke. Each of the two men seated acknowledged him, one with a chin lift and the other with a raised hand, two fingers flicking gently against the man's brow. *How did he know I'm ex-military?* he wondered, and looked towards Deke as he began introductions.

"Robinson, this is Winger and Bingo. Bingo is the chapter president of the Rebels here in town. He's my club boss, if you will." The man with the thick gray beard laughed loudly, red lips framing his white teeth, and gave another chin lift. Lane nodded at him and turned his attention to the other man, the one who had saluted him.

Deke said, "Winger here recently folded his club into the Rebels, which I happen to think was a good move. Handed us another fifteen solid members, and seriously strengthened his position in the Fort." As Winger held out his hand to shake, Deke continued the introductions. "Robinson rides, a pussy six-fifty, but he rides, not a weekend waxer." Both men laughed at that and moved slightly in their seats, making room for himself and Deke to sit next to them.

Several hours later, he had met another dozen Rebel members and had a better idea what kind of group it was. He liked the comradery and ease they showed with each other. Then, later in the evening, when one man mentioned he had to go take care of what was clearly going to be some kind of uncomfortable business, four men had risen to their feet without a word and followed him out. Whatever it was he had to take care of, he would not be alone.

Sitting on his bike in the quiet of his home garage, he watched as the overhead door slowly closed, shutting out the night. Glancing behind him at the door leading into his house, he realized both spaces were equally empty of company and snorted at himself when he stood, saying aloud, "Kincade, you think I'm nuts? One night with those guys, and I want what they have, man."

The next day, he approached Deke right before lunch, asking, "Did you bring a box, or plan on eating out?"

"Wish I had a bitch's box to eat out." His crude comeback was humorous, but even as Lane laughed, a sudden vision of Wardah's soft, brown thighs flashed through his head, twisting the tone of his laughter to harshness.

"Yeah, me too, buddy," he muttered, then shook his head, "Limiting the answer to lunch today, think you could be bothered to respond to the question? I'd like to talk to you about the Rebels, if you have time."

"Always make time to talk about my brothers, man. One of my favorite topics of conversation." His response was quick, but seemed sincere. "Let's grab some dogs at Coney Island, take 'em to the park. Have a convo. Bear with me, though. I gotta answer a couple of emails, be right out."

Nodding, Lane walked to his bike and straddled it, waiting patiently.

***

"You were a Marine?" Deke's question didn't surprise him; the information was in Lane's personnel file, and Deke would be a stupid boss if he didn't pay attention to details, especially important ones such as this. They found seats on a retaining wall surrounding a large, open space set aside for foot traffic, somewhat away from the rest of the lunchtime crowd. The area, adjacent to downtown, was an office worker favorite, because it allowed for an easy stroll to and from a couple of good lunch places.

Lane took a drink of water before he answered, taking his time to push down the anger that always swelled when he talked about leaving the military. "Yeah, put in a good few years, a couple of back-to-back deployments. Did you do any?" He took a bite from his dog, loaded down with his favorite toppings, taking care not to get kraut all over his clothes.

"Yeah, Army. Sappers don't live long, so I stuck out my enlistment and then walked." Deke cut his gaze over at him, and Lane endured the weight of the stare like a physical thing. "Was my decision, not theirs. Hell, they wanted me to stay, but I was absolutely done. I was wandering, had been out about a year, when I met a Rebel member. The rest, as they say, is history."

"I caught a couple of bullets," Lane said, running his palm over his shaved head, fingers rasping against the short stubble there. "They didn't want me anymore or I'd have stayed in, I'm sure. I was Force Recon in Iraq, and it was all I knew. There aren't any desk jobs in that outfit, so when I couldn't go back into the field, I got dumped out. Probably for the best."

Swallowing a bite of his own dog, Deke asked, "Why couldn't you go back into the field? You seem healthy, and I don't remember any restrictions from your paperwork."

"PTSD." He felt sweat break out across his shoulders simply saying those letters. "I had a mission go south, total cluster." He sighed and turned to look away. "Needed a couple surgeries to dig out the bullets." He shook his head, his gaze ricocheting around the plaza out of habit, as he noted the places an attacker could hide. "So that bad one turned out to be my final one, because in the opinion of the white coats, it took me too long to get past everything."

"But you're good now?" Lane was glad Deke wasn't looking at him anymore, just eating lunch and calmly watching the people walk past, like any ordinary person.

"Yeah, pretty good. I have some...habits still. You already seem to know some of my quirks. I saw you pick up on a couple last night at the bar." He laughed softly, saying, "Was interesting, because, for a change, I didn't feel anxious, which is pretty unheard of for me in a new setting with new people."

"We're good people, though." Deke laughed, crumpling up his paper wrapper and tossing it hand-to-hand as Lane watched. "My brothers are all good people. I wouldn't hang out with them otherwise."

"Yeah, about that," Lane began, and then stood abruptly, interrupting himself. For a single frozen moment, he thought he saw Kincade in the crowd, but the face was gone as quickly as it had appeared. He shook his head and sat, pulling his thoughts together and hoping Deke didn't think he was nuts. "How long have you been part of the club?"

"You get points for calling it what it is, a club. I fucking hate when people ask me about being in a gang. Stupid, bigoted motherfuckers." He shook his head. "I've been with the Rebels for several years. I patched in after Bingo started this chapter, but I've been back and forth between here and Chicago quite a bit. I work closely with Bingo here, and our national president, Mason, and I help coordinate shit with our other chapters, too." He stared at Lane. "Why the interest in the club, man?"

"There are other chapters? You said last night you were a member of the Fort Wayne chapter; do you know how many members there are in all? How many chapters?" He would sidestep Deke's question for a little longer, if he could.

"Why the interest in the club, Robinson?" Deke's face was set in unmoving lines, and Lane knew he would have to respond before he got anything else out of the man.

He decided to answer honestly, because there was nothing to gain by hiding his interest. "I don't know, really. Just...last night, sitting with you guys, seeing the back and forth between the members..." He swallowed. "It was easy...comfortable, and reminded me of the military. My team. That was one thing I could always count on, was the fact they had my back. Last night, that same kind of loyalty seemed so strong among the men you ride with. It simply went unsaid, but everyone knew it. It was there. They all know it, and even unspoken, not one of you doubted it. If you had needed something, there would have been a dozen men holding out whatever it was, no questions asked. They've got your back, so you don't have to always be watching your own six."

"That's right enough," Deke said. "We got our fair share of dickheads, but the membership as a whole helps keep them in line. Distributes the load so no one person has to do everything. Rebels have four chapters; I think we're standing at about five hundred members right now."

"How do you become a member?" he asked, glancing nervously at Deke.

"We have a couple of probationary periods guys go through. They start as a hangaround, learning a little about the life and getting to know the individual members in different settings. They attend parties at the clubhouse, spend time with us, and see if it's a fit for everyone. If that seems to go well, and they can find a member willing to sponsor them, the chapter members vote on them based on their interactions.

It's an important reason for the man who's interested in the club to put the time and effort into getting to know the members. At that vote, if they receive a majority, we'll partially patch them in as a prospect. Club responsibilities will get assigned to 'em, nice and easy to start with, but we watch carefully to see how they perform under different situations, evaluating them, if you will. Performance under stress."

He laughed and looked at Lane under his brows with a grin. "Some guys call it the torture time, but we try to make sure it's never more than the man can handle. If they don't cut it, it wasn't a fit, ya know? But, if all goes well, they'll be given the main club patch to wear, our colors. We hold those motherfuckers tight, because they mean everything. When a man wears our colors, his actions are ours." He took a drink from his water bottle, recapping it slowly while Lane waited impatiently for him to continue.

"That generally lasts a while longer, and some prospects don't earn their next patch for months...sometimes years. Down the road, if the chapter officers are unanimous in their final assessment of the prospect, the man'll be fully patched in and their prospect rocker replaced with the chapter location. Hangarounds and prospects don't get a voice in church, our club meetings, but because a patched prospect has more responsibilities, they sit in at least, have a say on some things." He looked at Lane. "Once guys hit the patched prospect phase, we'll generally try to find their job fit at that point. Lots of members work outside the chapter, like me, but there are still roles to fill within the club. My brothers need me to pay my dues; plus, I contribute in other ways." He paused, and then laughed. "Shit. I'm fucking long-winded sometimes, man. Does that answer your questions, or you got more?"

Nodding, he asked, "What do you have to do to start the process?"

Laughing again, Deke said, "Hang around. Kinda like you did last night."

"Oh." That sounded easy, too easy. He paused a minute, then asked, "You said members vote on the prospect, how does that happen?" This secret society idea was interesting; it was like a subculture hovering along the edges of things. Like secret fraternities, with dress standards, behavior requirements, and secret handshakes. *Oorah.* For a moment, he thought he heard Kincade, and glanced around with a frown as he listened to Deke.

"All full-patch members have an equal voice. We might give a long-time member the courtesy of speaking first...or longest, unless they're a bastard." He laughed. "But when we sit for church, all members are equal. Officers are drawn from the member ranks, and they have a different set of responsibilities." He paused again and stared at Lane. "Tell me why you are so interested."

"Like I said, the connection between the members I met last night was...it felt comfortable. That's the only way to describe it. I was easy in a way I haven't been since I stepped foot off base nearly two years ago. What is the clubhouse?" He had many more questions, but already experienced an eager excitement at the idea of trying to join this group.

"It's our base of operations in town. The Fort Wayne chapter has the one; some chapters have two or more, depending on the size of their territory. The clubhouse has rooms for members to crash in, or for some to live in, depending on individual situations. There're a kitchen and a meeting room or two, business offices, that kind of thing. We have parties nearly every week." He shook his head, crushing the paper from his lunch in one hand. "There's one planned for Saturday night, in fact. Are you thinking you want to explore this?" Deke pinned him with that stare, again making Lane uncomfortable.

He thought about it for a minute. Did he want to go down this path? This was his boss, and if things went south outside of work, he could lose his job. *Fuck the job,* he thought. *I want what they showed me last night.*

"Yeah. I am," he said with conviction, and Deke nodded.

"Okay. At the end of today's shift, come find me." He stood, and Lane copied his actions, grinning as Deke looked up at him, chuckling. "You are one big motherfucker, aren't you?"

***

"Kincade." He laughed, tossing the canteen over to the man seated on the cot opposite him. "Keep your gear straight from mine."

The big, blond Swede grinned back at him, his sky blue eyes glinting humorously as he reached up, grabbing the canteen in midair, inches from his face. "But Robinson, if I keep my things to myself, what would a Cajun boy like you have to complain about?"

Bending over to lace his boots, Robinson shook his head. The two of them had been side-by-side since Parris Island, climbing on and off transports together and working as a team. Lane could track patterns and puzzles; he could look at things and see the path through the obstacles. That was his gift. Kincade? He noticed things. He was a watcher, and he got off on seeing what people didn't want him to see.

It made his day when he could uncover a secret. Like Lane lying to the Staff Sergeant that first night of basic on Parris Island. Not wanting to admit how alone he was, he had told the man in charge he read the scripted announcement about arriving safely to his loved ones, when in reality, he didn't have anyone to call back in Houma. Kincade recognized his panic when the Staff Sergeant had paused, smelling a lie, and had distracted the man with a question. From those first moments in the Corps through the last day of basic, Kincade had taken him under his wing and tried to buffer things for him.

Basic had been hard as hell, because the drill instructors all seemed to take his size as a challenge. It was Kincade who first explained something he should have already known: as long as he continued to react emotionally, the instructors would keep digging and pushing and *pulling at him, working to break him down. So, the two of them had conspired to train Lane to an impassive expression, staring patiently straight through the DIs, even when they were nose-to-nose with him. 'Sir, yes, sir,' the only phrase passing his lips.*

It had done the trick, and soon, the two of them were excelling, successfully leading their ranks through tough and competitive exercises. After the Island, their continuing education took them both into Recon, and then eventually to Camp Chesty, their current deployment in the sand wars.

He straightened, stamping his heel firmly down into his boot, and looked back to see Kincade lying crossways, draped awkwardly across his cot. "Come on, man. We got to get a start on this one," he said, reaching down to slap the bottom of his friend's boot. Instead of a solid thump, there was a softer thud, and he looked up in time to see a quarter-sized piece of Kincade's cammies high on his left shoulder swell outwards and then fall back in on itself.

He stared, waiting, filled with the sense he had walked into a rerun of a frequently watched scene. Lane had paced through this particular puzzle before, treading to the finish, and he knew what was coming. After a few seconds, a small, concentric ring of red appeared on the right side of Kincade's chest. He nodded in recognition, watching as the ring quickly grew until it covered half the visible area.

Squeezing his eyes shut, as he did every time, he tried telling himself it was a dream, but the scent of blood was thick in the air, dark and rich, underscoring the reality of what he was witnessing. Shaking his head back and forth, he muttered, "Already asked and answered. Radio is sharp and clear, five-by-five." Bending over to lace his other boot, he stoically listened to the steady drip of a thick liquid, sounding crimson as the splintered sun rising over the mountains in the east. The dripping echoed, sounding as thick as the roux his granny done made for gravy a month ago, gelled and covered by a thick skim of cold, cooked flour, plopping by starts and fits into a sticky puddle. Even with his eyes closed tightly, he thought he could see it growing, covering the floor. "Standard and routine. Lace 'em up, boys. Roll in five," he said to the room in general.

He lifted his head, startled by a rapidly growing loud whine. Instinctively looking up at the ceiling, he stared at the metal-covered planks and beams firmly holding the walls together, stalling what would be an unavoidable collapse if the concealing roof were removed, exposing the contents of the room to inspection from above. Closing his eyes, he tilted his head from side to side, attempting to get a bearing on the noise. It seemed to be coming from close by, but where...

With a start, he sat up in bed, reaching out to slap his palm down on the radio alarm, pushing the button to silence the strident sound. The air in the room was chilly on his sweat-covered shoulders and back, and he realized he was panting for breath, struggling to stay in his own skin. The nightmare brought emotions and fears swelling to the top of the dark water of his memories, and he fought to free himself from them before they pulled him down.

This was one of the other pieces of being a soldier, the one people didn't like talking about, the things that happened out of sight, in the dark...because everyone knew being a soldier meant you left parts of yourself behind. After being overseas, stationed for months in a stress-filled environment, men sloughed off the trappings of civilization in so many ways. Innocence, belief in humanity, trust—those were things cast aside during deployment in a hostile land.

What most people did not realize was when you came home, when you left the battlefield behind, sometimes you brought things back with you, too. Tipping his head to one side, out of the corner of his eye he looked at the chair beside the bed, relieved when it was empty today.

***

Lane pulled up in front of the house, heeling down the kickstand and sitting astride the bike for a minute. Looking through the large windows into the living room, he saw Winger sitting in his recliner, his wife DeeDee perched on his lap, her hand affectionately resting on his chest. Winger had a tolerant smile on his face as he looked towards the door, and Lane suspected it was because his daughter stood just on the other side. At an unexpected noise behind him, he twisted from the house, fluidly swinging off the bike and moving into a crouch, yanking a knife from its holster in his boot. "Lane," he heard his name, and recognizing the voice, closed his eyes, trying to moderate his breathing and heartrate. "I'm sorry," she whispered, taking a step backwards, instinctively trying to give him room to recover.

"Little sister," he said, his voice gruff as he shoved the knife back into place before unfolding and standing upright. "No worries, honey. I just didn't hear you coming up behind me." The easy feeling he had from watching the small family, comfortable in their home, was gone, leaving behind the shaky quiver in his gut that the fight response typically brought. He looked down at the woman, struggling to bring a smile to his face for her. Melanie was Winger's daughter's best friend, and frequently around the club. Her parents were useless as tits on a boar hog, and she got all her mothering from DeeDee, making them both happy for a variety of reasons, secure in their knowledge that family wasn't always restricted to relatives.

The front door opened behind him, spilling light across the yard and walk and he saw a wet glint in Melanie's eyes. "Everything okay, little sister?"

With a laugh, she shook her head. "I just love you, ya know?" Her statement surprised him, made his throat tighten with an unfamiliar emotion. Unable to respond, he nodded, watching as she lifted a hand to wipe at her cheek.

He never had siblings; Kincade was as close as he came to family once he left Louisiana behind, but with Lockee, Winger's daughter, and Melanie, he had found an easy comradery that he believed simulated the experience and feeling of having sisters. The two were thick as thieves; you seldom saw one without the other, with Lockee most often leading the charge towards some outrageous adventure. To prove this point he heard another bike coming up the street, and looked up without surprise to see PBJ rolling up alongside where his scoot was parked. When one rode, both rode.

Loud laughter preceding her, Lockee skipped down the steps of the house, headed for their little group. She had decided earlier today that she wanted to take a run, and Winger, never able to tell her no for long, had indulgently arranged to have two Rebels come pick up the girls. Swinging a leg over his ride, he reached back to give Melanie a hand onto the back of his bike. "Ready?" Lockee's bright voice sounded over the rack and ring of the bikes' exhaust pipes and he nodded at PBJ. She kept talking as she climbed onto the back of PBJ's bike. "Did you see Daddy's new bike, Lane? He got it from that shop on the east coast, it's beautiful. We rode back from Chicago last weekend, and I got to ride with Bear."

He had heard all about the trip already, listening to some of the brothers in the clubhouse bitching about how she and Melanie had hung all over the citizen who—he was a little peeved—had somehow already earned a road name. "So I heard," he said, steadying the bike between his legs, fingers holding the front brake tight while Melanie settled on the seat behind him. "We going to ride, or talk?"

Lockee laughed again, "Both." PBJ twisted the throttle on his bike and took off smoothly, leaving peals of Lockee's laughter trailing behind him up the street.

Lane slipped his brake, twisting the throttle and quickly moving from first to second gear, following PBJ out of the neighborhood. Turning his head, he asked Melanie, "Know where we're headed?"

She leaned up, chin on his shoulder as she said, "Nope, I think she just wanted some wind therapy, but Winger wouldn't let her get on her bike after dark." He nodded, shifting to third, and then jolted when she said, "I'm glad he called you, Lane. You look like you needed a run, too. You're doing okay, right?" *Yeah, brother, you doin' okay?* That last was Kincade's voice, and he jolted again at hearing it in his ears.

Seemed Melanie was perceptive tonight, or he wasn't doing a good enough job to tamp down his fears. In response, he nodded, then turned his head and said, "Yeah, little sister. I'm doing just fine. Hold on." With that small warning, he cranked the throttle open, quickly pulling even with, and then passing PBJ and his passenger. Without caring what the original destination was, he drove into the night, threading through streets and traffic, aware of the cargo he bore, both good and bad.

***

She curled into a tight ball on the floor, trying not to shiver at the chill in the air. Cold for Florida, the temperature would dip below forty tonight, but she knew better than to close the bedroom window, open to capture the breeze off the orange groves as it threaded through the metal rods stretching across the opening. Her heart beat faster when the crunching of gravel came from outside, small pieces of rock grinding against each other, fracturing and fragmenting by minute amounts as they were placed under pressure. The deep rumble of a car's engine abruptly shut off, leaving stillness in its wake.

Counting slowly, she measured time as she waited for him to come in from outside. In her mind, she imagined watching as he opened the driver's door, mentally seeing him stand and stretch out his back before turning to pull a bag from the passenger's seat. Rewarded with the quiet crumping concussion of the car door closing, she imagined him walking around the front of the vehicle, approaching the dark house.

When she came to the bedroom at precisely eight o'clock, there were no lights left burning behind her. That quiet clicking of switches plunging the house into darkness had stirred the fresh memory, striped into her back, of a howled, *"You think I'm made of money?"* She heard the clunk of the key in the lock, which opened only from outside, heard the knob twist and turn in the wood, the tongue of the solid latch scraping along the edge of the doorframe.

"Place?" he called the inquiry, and she immediately responded, letting him know she was where she was supposed to be; she was, as so often instructed, waiting. "Dinner?" That was the next question, and in a struggling voice, she indicated where his plate had been stored. She knew she had a fifty-fifty chance of picking wrong. Some nights, selecting the refrigerator over the warm stove was all it took to tip him to violence.

Violence, she thought with a silent laugh. Raised around the controlled violence of hockey, attending her brothers' games, she remembered thinking at the time that slashing and tripping, hooking and boarding were the worst things in the world. They were the wickedest her teenage self could imagine. Now she knew differently, having learned the lesson time and again.

Slowly counting again, she waited for him to say something, anything to give her an idea of how the evening would go. *Seventeen, eighteen, nineteen... Maybe tonight will be one of the sweet ones*, she thought. *Twenty-two, twenty-three, twenty-four... Maybe tonight he'll ask, 'Baby, why are you on the floor?' Twenty-eight, twenty-nine, thirty... Or he'll say, 'I'm so sorry.'*

Precisely at thirty-five, the crash of crockery sounded, and she recognized the sound of a plate dropping to the kitchen floor. Over the sounds of breaking dishes came his voice, barely audible to her ears, but wounding as if it were the lashing of the sound barrier, a clap of thunder, or the tearing sound of metal peeling back from a car's frame. Not her name, not this time, no more than the hated single word uttered in a tone that caused a terror so visceral it manifested physically as all the hair on her body raised in a futile defense. Clasping her hands together at the back of her head, she tucked her bent elbows tightly against her temples, leaving her ears uncovered so she could hear her fate approaching.

3. Appearances aren't reality

"Prez." The word held a lifetime's weight of responsibility and respect wrapped into a single syllable. Mason waited a beat before responding, to see if the caller would continue to speak, and was eventually rewarded for his patience. "It's Deke, man. Bingo was asking about officer candidates and said I needed to call you before nominating Robinson. You had questions about my guy?"

"Fuck. Yeah, I have questions," he said, leaning back in the office chair, looking at the Chicago skyline out the window behind the desk. He let his eyes lose focus, narrowing his attention to the sounds coming from the phone, the ringing ratchet of air-driven power tools in the background, far away chatter from deep, male voices. The noises echoed in what seemed to be a large space, and he knew Deke was most likely at one of the club's bike garages in Fort Wayne. "You hanging out, or wrenching today, brother?"

With laughter in his voice, Deke told him, "Wrenching. Robinson got a couple of sweet buys at a local auction. I picked one of them up off him and I'm working to strip it down. He looked about ready to puke when he saw what I was doing. Chop shop city, man."

"So you get along with him okay? I don't know much about the man, not anything really. That's an odd place for me to find myself, especially when someone's putting a member up for vote as an officer." Mason scrubbed his hand along his jaw and then wrapped it tightly around the back of his neck, using thumb and fingers to rub and massage the tight muscles there. "I need to understand what it is you see in the man no one else seems to be able to dig out."

The noise level dropped and he knew Deke must have gone into the office of the garage; the soft huff of breath was probably him sitting down on the couch in the waiting area. "Mason," the words came softly, but the voice was steady, "I've never seen a man with as much want as Robinson has. From the moment he learned about the club, he pursued it with single-minded determination. He went from hangaround to prospect in about five weeks. Not because he schmoozed members or tried to make people like him, but because he made the club better. Little things, like noticing a toilet was broken, so he called a plumber. Or brothers were always bitching about the coffee pot being empty, so he got a bigger one. Dude's been a member for several years now, and he still sees things like that all the time. Unlike some of the guys, he doesn't take shit for granted, or seem to become blind to things like the rest of us. Knowing what I know about the Fort Wayne chapter, I think he could aim his focus a little higher than if there's a rip in the felt on a pool table, or if one of the boys is too drunk to ride out."

He waited a moment, but it seemed Deke was done talking for now. "You didn't answer my question, brother."

The confusion was clear in his tone when Deke answered, "I thought I did, Mason. What question did I miss?"

"Do you get along with him okay?" Mason repeated himself and waited.

"I do, yeah." Deke blew out a breath, saying, "Not everyone feels the same, which is why Bingo wasn't one-hundred-percent on board, I suspect."

"He look for fights?" Mason's lips pressed together in a tight line. They didn't need a troublemaker in as an officer, no fucking way.

"No," the response was swift and sure. "He's a big motherfucker, but doesn't throw it around. He's too fucking aware of himself to let people goad him, but like he did during his prospect period, he's not gonna go out of his way to make buddies in the club. He's friendly, but more on the acquaintance level, not close friends with most of the men. Me and Winger, I think we're the only two he hangs with outside of runs, meets, and other shit. He's friends with Winger's family too, dotes on the girls."

"So he's friendly, but holds back. He's loyal, and Winger deems him trustworthy with his old lady and baby girl. He watches and notices things, but wouldn't let people sway him from doing what needs doing?" Mason's question held the key considerations for the position they needed to fill, because the role was definitely one that required neutrality, as well as discipline.

"Yeah, good description, man." Deke cleared his throat. "He doesn't fuck around with whores, either, so he doesn't get into arguments about pussy. He don't bat for the home team, you know, but he doesn't get tied up in knots about chicks."

"He's a vet, right?" Mason already knew the answer to this, as well as his next question. "Honorable discharge?"

"Yeah, Marines. He's all oorah about the service and what he did overseas. His discharge was medical. He got shot and was stranded behind lines for weeks, but made his own way out eventually. Had a fuckton of problems, infection and shit, because he'd gone untreated in all the sand and heat over there, but he's physically fit now. He's worked for me for a long while, and always does a good day's work for a good day's pay."

28

"But he's disabled, right?" *Medical discharge?* Why didn't he know about that? The man never seemed to hold back, no matter what they were doing, so maybe it wasn't physical.

"Yeah, goes to the VA regular-like." The hesitation in Deke's voice said he might be skirting something here, so Mason pressed.

"What kind of long-term issues does he have?" He heard the sigh and waited, thinking he might already know the answer to this question, too.

"PTSD, but...he's good. They simply couldn't use him outside of what he'd been doing, and he couldn't keep doing that after...everything." Deke sounded regretful, as if he expected Mason to turn Robinson down out of hand because of this confession.

There was a familiar perfunctory knock at the door, and with the sound of the knob turning, he glanced at the clock and saw it was time for an update on some local issues. "All right, brother. I'll check him out next time I'm in town. I gotta go, man. Ride safe." Without giving the man time to say more than a quick goodbye, Mason hung up, turning to watch Slate and Bones walk into his office.

***

Robinson stood in the hospital parking lot, trying and failing to slow his racing heart. He caught movement out of the corner of his eye and jerked to the side, trying to avoid the body hurtling his way. Once he recognized the slight, redheaded woman crossing the wide-open space at a dead run to get to him, he stood still, waiting, and allowed her to wrap her arms around him once she reached him. It wasn't until her shoulders shuddered under his palms that he actually believed she was there.

Supporting her weight for a moment, he heard her murmured question and responded, setting her firmly away from him. "She's inside, Melanie. Hoss and Bingo are with DeeDee, but she's gonna need you." He reached out a hand and placed two fingers underneath her chin, lifting her tear-stained face so he could see the expression written there. Flinching at the raw pain she wore, he used the pad of one thumb to wipe her cheek. "I know, little sister. Every one of us is going to miss them. All of us."

She lunged forward again and he took the hit, letting her draw strength from resting against him as long as she needed. They had lost a good man and his daughter today, a senseless accident taking both the wisdom of his friend and the bright laughter of hers, stripping them of that shared future. Winger and Lockee, both gone. After long minutes, her sobs began to slow and he stroked one palm down her long, curly red hair. Reaching back, he pulled a bandana from his pocket, bringing it up to offer to her, smiling faintly at her unladylike nose blowing.

His skin was twitching with the need to get away from this place, and once he thought she had her emotions back under control, he loosened his arms, feeling her gradually do the same. "Go on in now," he softly directed, stepping back and releasing her. She stared at him for a moment, her eyes worried. "Lane? Are you..." Her voice trailed off and he answered her unspoken question. "Yeah, I'm good, little sister. Go on in, now." She shook her head then turned, and without looking back, walked with slumped shoulders into the hospital through the ER door.

He straddled his bike, sitting for a moment, and then started the machine, pulling smoothly out of the lot and onto the main thoroughfare. He followed that road to the interstate and merged into traffic, headed in no particular direction, working his way up the gears quickly. Bending low over the tank, he tipped his hips, tucking his toes behind the rear pegs, streamlining to offer minimal resistance as he cracked the throttle hard, feeling the bike leap beneath him. Eyes squinted against wind-whipped tears, he wove the bike between and alongside the speeding trucks and cars. Hiding in plain sight, he rode with tight control, watching the lights flash past in a whirlwind of color and chaos, which failed to soothe his pain.

**

Davis Mason stood near the bar in the Fort Wayne clubhouse, looking out at the gathered Rebel Wayfarers members. They laid a brother to rest today, and the group was subdued, soft conversations around the room filled with memories of Winger, both as a member and a man—their brother. Mason might be the national president of the Rebels, based out of the mother chapter in Chicago, but long before he seized that title, he had been friends with Winger. Known him before there even was a Rebel Wayfarers MC, and his heart hurt with the knowledge that not only was Winger gone, but the man's only daughter, too.

Winger's old lady wasn't at the clubhouse, not tonight. Tonight, this party was about healing the club, not soothing family, so DeeDee was at home. Mason made sure his cousin wasn't alone; the other women associated with the club would be there beside her, helping support her. He already talked to Bingo about how the chapter wanted to handle things. With Winger gone, they all knew she would have to sell their house. He didn't have much insurance, and it would be too expensive to maintain for only her and the gal, Melanie. The club would stand behind her, exactly as they would have Winger, and they intended to move her into a suite here in the clubhouse. It would be a first for the club, having not only DeeDee living inside the clubhouse, but also the girl she had virtually adopted. Mason figured they would all adjust as they had to, and the club agreed it was the right thing to do.

His gaze caught on one of the members of the Fort Wayne chapter standing nearby, Lane Robinson. He snorted, mentally going over his conversation from a week ago with Deke, and shook his head, realizing he still thought of Robinson as a newer member, even though it had been several years since they patched him into the club. The man was an enigma to Mason. He had an engineering degree, but worked as a dump truck driver for the city. Man loved the club, but damned if he didn't seem to dislike most of the members. If there was a fight in the clubhouse here, chances were good he would be one of the first to throw a punch, or the first to break it up, depending on the day.

On top of being standoffish and quiet, the guy also gave off a seriously damaged vibe. But, Deke swore by the man, said he was shaping up into everything they'd want in an officer. And he trusted Deke. He couldn't discount the fact Winger had liked him too, and a conversation with him had gone a long way to settling some of his nerves about placing any kind of reins in the man's hands. Winger trusted him with his girls, not something he did lightly, and that single thing gave Mason more confidence in what he was considering. Even with that, Mason still found himself still reserving judgment, because for the amount of time Robinson had been patched into the club, no one had gotten close enough to the man to even give him a fucking road name. He sighed, thinking, *So, maybe tonight, you could actually fucking talk to the man, find out what's ticking in that head bone of his. Novel idea, you stupid motherfucker.*

Pushing off the bar, he walked across the room, and even without looking into his eyes, Mason knew the moment Robinson clocked his destination. The weight of his stare was tangible, and a sense of unease at being approached clung to the man, anxiety making the muscles under his skin jerk and quiver. *Fuck,* Mason thought with a shiver, remembering Deke's reluctant admission about Robinson's PTSD. *Is he honestly this unstable? Damn, I like patching vets, but this dude...if Robinson's this fucked up, then what the hell is Deke playing at?*

He offered a silent chin lift, settling his shoulders against the wall. After a few moments, he softly asked across the small space separating them, "Did you know Winger well?"

Nodding slowly, Robinson responded thoughtfully, "Well enough. He was a good man, an honest and fair one. Those are attributes hard to come by, so I hold folks like that close. I spent a bit of time with him on runs and around the clubhouse, and he...Winger taught me a lot. His loss is going to be felt for a long time, and a lot of members will be poorer for never meeting him."

Mason's lips tightened. It was an introspective comment, and one he hadn't expected. "Yeah. I met the man when I was a kid. I know how he liked to pass on his knowledge." He laughed. "Even if it wasn't needed or asked for, he was always quick to offer his advice. Copious amounts of knowledge."

A grin slid across and off Robinson's face, sadness chasing the emotion away. "Yeah, he did. He once spent thirty minutes telling me how to lace my boots the right way. 'Right way' being *his* way."

"That's Winger for ya. An opinion on everything." Mason smiled and then looked up at the wall over the bar, where a large picture of Winger hung. He nodded at it, asking, "Who can get me a copy of his picture for Jackson's in Chicago?"

"If you want the same size, I have an extra, actually. I got them blown up from a picture DeeDee has. I asked her to pick out her favorite one of him to put up. Figured since she's going to be in here all the time, it would make her feel better if she could see him. Why do you need one in Chicag—" Mason snorted silently when Robinson abruptly stopped speaking, interrupting himself to nervously rub his palm over his scalp, probably belatedly realizing he was questioning the highest-ranking officer in the club.

"You haven't spent any time up there, but Jackson's, the club's main bar in Chicago, is where we have our wall honoring the fallen. Winger belongs there, precisely as he belongs here. You did good, brother," he reassured the man and watched as a little tension left his stance at the heartfelt praise. "What can you tell me about Robinson? What other things are you good at, man?"

He ran his palm over his scalp again, and Mason heard the rasp of rough stubble against skin. Robinson was clean-shaven, pate and face, and it looked good on him. His face held enough character it didn't look vain, merely comfortable. "You askin' what I'm good at, or what I like to do?" He laughed, the sound hard and awkward in the moment, because he had turned self-conscious.

Mason shrugged, saying, "Whatever you wanna fucking share, man. I'm just trying to get to know you. I don't like having members in my club I don't have an understanding of."

Robinson stilled, the tension seeping back into his shoulders and neck, hardening his muscles. In a deep, level voice, he said, "I see things that need doing, things other people tend to overlook. I'm good at getting things done, picking apart a project to find the pieces that make the whole. I liked going to Virginia and working on the bikes with Bear, seeing his plans and designs come to life. But, do you remember when Deke wanted help restoring his old man's scoot? Bringing that bike back to factory and primping it up with some chrome? That shit made my dick hard. So, there you go, man. You got two answers for one question."

"What kind of things do you see here?" Mason asked the question without emphasis, not wanting to alert the man to the importance of his answer.

"I see Bingo needs help; he's swamped with his sister's kids. I see problems in the strip club; no one's watching out for the girls. I see other clubs are starting to look our way, eyeballing us to see if we can hold what we have here in the Fort. I see we need strong bonds between our brothers in all the chapters, so we don't lose sight of what we wanted in the club in the first place." He shrugged, trying to lighten the mood. "I could also be full of shit, Prez."

So far, every answer Robinson gave him had hit the right tone, and he seemed custom made for the job Mason was about to hand him. "What were you called in the service?" Mason's question clearly came out of left field, and Robinson looked at him, blinking.

"Gunny," he snorted. "It's corny, but true. A gunnery sergeant is always called Gunny."

Mason raised his head, looking across the open space at the groups scattered around the room. He caught Bingo's eye and gave him a chin lift. With a half-smile, Bingo stepped into the office behind the bar, coming back into view with something in his hand. Holding it up, he shot Mason a questioning look and received a single nod in response.

Bingo lifted his head, shouting, "Listen up, motherfuckers. We said goodbye to a good brother today. A man we all fucking loved. Winger's place in this club can never be filled, but we all know life goes on, yeah?" At the answering shouts and nods, he continued, "Keeping our ranks filled with men we trust, brothers we can count on, is hard when we remember those we've lost, but it's something we have to do. The club has to stay strong, and having people to lean on is one of the ways we ensure our strength carries on. Today, those ranks of trusted grow again."

Mason stepped away from the wall, drawing all eyes to him. He met Bingo in the middle of the room, taking the officer patch from him, and turned back to Robinson, who was still leaning against the wall. Mason motioned him to step forward as he said, "Gunny, you're the Fort's new Sargent at Arms. Welcome, brother."

The phrase repeated around the room, the volume growing as Mason stepped close, handing the patch to the man and pulling him into a one-shoulder clench. He sensed tension flood the muscles under his touch and held him tightly for a moment, murmuring quietly before he released him, "We all have your back, Gunny. You're a good man, and Winger would be proud. Welcome, brother."

***

She smiled, lifting her face to the welcome warmth of the sun streaming in through the high window. Not large, she estimated the square of brilliance was about three feet by three feet, and there were no blocking curtains or blinds on the overhead opening, so on uncloudy days, she had the sun for about four hours. Shuffling sideways every few minutes, whether standing or sitting, she crept across the floor by inches, attempting to stay centered in the light as it snuck across the space, surrounded by the deep shadows covering the rest of the room.

Without glancing behind her, she knew his equipment was standing at attention along the back wall, waiting. Mic booms, klieg lights, and monitors shared the space with her, alongside the harder tools of his hobbies, the wheel and the cross, the iron, and leather. Ignoring the memories of pain that thoughts of his sessions brought, she rolled her shoulders, swinging her head side-to-side, still keeping her face to the sunshine, soaking it up while she could. Her slow movements were nearly a dance, these small joys choreographed, composed as the traveling partner for this celestial witness.

***

He reached down and pulled his keffiyeh up over the lower half of his face, hiding as much of his pale, reflective skin as he could. From his crouched position in the dark shadows beside the house, his gaze swept the neighborhood. He had been out here for a couple of hours now, ever since he woke from the dream. He could hunker down here for hours and none would notice, no one would see him standing guard. Waiting and watching. Always watching.

The houses around him were beginning to brighten from inside as the occupants stirred from their restful sleep, waking to an unthreatened morning. They would pack their lunches, pick up their briefcases, and shrug on their coats, slipping soft hands into softer leather gloves and going about their soft American days. Stylishly long hair would curl at their collars, the hipster scruff along their jaws the only concession to the wild lives they once believed were owed them.

At the house directly across the street, he watched as the garage door soundlessly rose, the yawning darkness swept away by the automatic lights as the man who lived there moved towards his shining new car. *Watch*, Kincade said. *Look over there. Don't you see? Can't you see the danger?* He tensed when he realized one shadow in the space didn't disperse, hadn't flickered out of existence when the light came on, and acting instinctively, he glided across the street at a silent sprint. Noiselessly approaching the man from behind, he grasped him, pressing one hard hand over his mouth and uttering a scarcely heard sibilance to silence the cry of surprise he knew the man's lungs were bursting with.

Pushing the man to the ground, he followed up the quiet directive with a finger to his lips, obscured behind the sand camouflage scarf. Giving the man a 'stay down' motion with the palm of his hand, he moved to the front corner of the car in a crouch, settling to one knee. Looking around the corner, he saw the shadow remained in the same position, same place…waiting.

With a powerfully explosive rush, he charged the corner of the garage and grappled with the person he found there, wrapping his hands around their neck and shaking them hard, rocking them viciously back and forth to entirely disorient the enemy. There was a shout from behind him, followed by the thud of rapid footfalls, and he risked the distraction of a quick glance, his gaze barely in time to see scuffed leather soles of shoes and the flutter of the man's coat hem as he ran back into the house. Whispering beside his ear, Kincade told him, *Complete the mission, brother.*

Twisting to look at the enemy in his hands, he was surprised to find the canvas of a duffle bag instead of the expected keffiyeh-covered face, dark eyes peering from between the folds of the fabric. *Fucking shit,* he thought, throwing the bag to the side in confusion. *Bloody Hell,* an accented voice filled his head, sweeping him suddenly back to the pain of the med unit at Camp Chesty, feeling the prodding instruments dragging sickened balls of metal from his skin. Shaking his head to clear it, he scanned the area, dropping flat to the floor to extend his gaze underneath the vehicles, but could find no threats now. Nothing out of place, except him. *Fuck,* he thought. *Fuck, fuck, fuck.*

He stood for a moment and looked contemplatively at the gaping door leading into the man's home. Kincade was, thank fuck, now silent, no longer urging him into another bad move. With an indrawn breath, he tucked the keffiyeh more tightly around his head and decided not to compound his errors of the day by following the man inside. He sighed and lowered his head, but continued to scan the area, his eyes the only thing moving in his face, hidden by his deeply furrowed brow. *Might be time to take a hike*, he thought and then snorted, *maybe in more than one way.*

The scene in the clubhouse weeks ago kept weighing on his mind, and he struggled every day with the feeling he needed to continue to earn his place in the club. Forget that they trusted him enough to slap an officer title on him, he had to prove his worth, time and again, even if for no one else but him. He had not suffered through an episode like this in a long time, and these past minutes were probably an indication of even more stress he hadn't yet realized he was carrying. Seemed he only ever had twenty-twenty hindsight when it came to his PTSD, and could only map out the puzzle leading to the break after he had fixed himself yet again. Gunny lifted his head and straightened his shoulders, walking out of the building and into the street, hearing the sirens approaching, alarm the sounds should have roused felt as if from far away.

4. Working the bikes

"There's an auction coming up, Myron. I need to take a few thousand in draw, man." Gunny leaned back against the wall of the clubhouse and switched the phone to his other ear. He listened for a couple minutes, and then closed his eyes as he cut off the never-ending spew of words from the club's bean counter in Chicago. Treasurer was his official club title, controller was the legal one, but bean counter fit how Gunny felt most of the time. "Six or seven should do me; let me know the particulars so I can get registered for the auction." There was squawking on the phone, Myron's voice rising in anger, but he simply hit the disconnect button. "Fuck," he muttered to himself, leaning his head back against the wall. "I know I'm not in Bear's league, but I make the club enough money."

"Yeah, you do," Deke said from beside him, and Gunny simultaneously jumped and moved sideways. His hands came up and seized Deke's cut in an instinctive hold, preparatory to either throwing him away or pulling him close; even Gunny wasn't sure which.

As quickly as he grabbed it, he released the leather, hissing another quiet, *"Fuck,"* before yelling, "Goddammit, Deke. What the fuck, man? You know better than to slip up on me like that." He rubbed a shaking hand across his jaw, taking an unsteady breath as he tried to bleed off the energy zinging through him. "You don't know what nearly happened."

"What are you doing hiding out in the hallway?" Deke ignored what he had said and done, setting his reactions aside, which helped to settle him somewhat. "You coming in for church? Bingo called a few minutes ago and said he was ready to start as soon as you and I get in there."

"Yeah, I'll be in. I needed to talk to Myron beforehand. Got to get finances lined out for the auction next weekend. The list shows they're going to offer a bunch of nice classics. I heard this was some farmer's barn collection on the block. Who knows what I'll find in the mix if that's true?" He shrugged, settling his muscles on his frame, consciously attempting to release the last of the tension from his shoulders.

"Nice. Let me know if you need any company." Deke never made a big deal about it, but over the years, his friend had learned most of Gunny's quirks, and he knew a popular auction would bring in a lot of bidders. Crowds were still somewhat of a problem for him, but he hoped he could handle a bike sale without bringing Deke along.

"Yeah, if I need my security blanket, I'll give you a call." He shrugged when Deke gave him a wry look. "Time to hear how badly we're doing, man. I saw Slate in the main room a bit ago, and I have a feeling Bingo's about to step down. With the shit going on with Rabid, and over at the gun range, I believe we might be looking at a management change here in the Fort, brother. Let's get in there and get church over with."

***

Standing with his back to the barn wall, Gunny closed his eyes tightly, listening to the movement of the people milling in swirling crowds around him. *Easy, brother,* Kincade muttered. *Easy does it, brother.* His anxiety amplified all sounds, internal and external, noise swelling larger than life and pressing relentlessly in on him. He could hear the pounding, rhythmic beat of his heart echoing in his ears. The loud sound of his uneven breaths whistling in and out of his nose. The ratcheting click of his suddenly dry throat as he swallowed. *Fuck*, he thought. *I can do this, dammit. I can fucking do this. I can beat this shit. Dammit.*

The announcer read the card on the next bike up for auction, and the make name jarred him out of his head. This was a bike he had long been on the lookout for, but never expected to find. He was shocked, because the bike wasn't on the published list. Opening his eyes, he quickly scanned the paper in his hand to confirm, then looked up and experienced an unanticipated pleasure at the familiar profile and outline of the bike on the raised stage. He didn't move a muscle, didn't give any outward indication of his inward excitement. A Vincent Black Shadow, one of the rarest bikes, and unless he was wrong, it was a C-series, handmade in England in 1948. *Jesus.*

The crisp frame, gracefully bent chrome exhaust pipes, and slightly swept-back handlebars hinted at the power and speed the motorcycle had offered riders right off the line, but the condition of the bike was rough. Rough enough, he hoped it would work to his benefit and hide the real value from the rest of the bidders. Looking at it again, in between blinks, he imagined he could see Mason perched on the seat of the fully restored scoot, and anticipated the pleasure he would take in giving Prez something like this. While Slate might be his local president now, Mason would always be his Prez. The man who saved his life.

Mason was a rider to the core, a man who would appreciate the bike for the classic it was. He knew Mason would take that into account, while still loving the experience enough to ride the fucker like it was meant to be ridden, hard and fast. He wasn't someone to park it in a darkened garage and cover it in silk, waiting for its chance to be trailered to a show and trotted out for the masses to ooh and aah over. He turned to look at the lot following the Vincent, still attempting to mask his interest, and found his efforts validated when he saw several local buyers also turn away from the Vincent and towards the chopped café racers, which would soon be hitting the stage. He grinned at those bikes without actually seeing them, thinking to himself this particular snipe hunt was going to be fun.

When the gavel fell for the final time of the day, he made his way to the cashier's table. Waiting for the closing tally, he gave a private snort when the cute brunette told him somewhat apologetically he owed the auction service nearly five thousand dollars for the fifteen bikes he had won. Making a show of being disgruntled, he paid and then accepted the offer of a nearby day laborer to help him load the bikes.

"What kind of bike is this?" The guy pointed at the Vincent they had loaded in the middle of the pack of bikes. He had given Gunny a questioning look when told to cover it with a tarp, but shrugged and helped him pull the covering taut.

"That bike is a one of a kind," Gunny said shortly, handing him a couple bills before turning to climb into the truck. Seated there, he paused for a moment, looking into the rearview mirror with satisfaction, and repeated to himself, "One of a kind."

***

"Negative. No fab if I can find original. Did you not hear me say what kind of bike it is?" Frustratedly rubbing his forehead with the tips of his fingers, he felt a headache gathering on the horizon and frowned, moderating his tone and repeating his words in a slightly different way. "It's a fucking Vincent. Negatory on the fab, man. Check your shelves for me, okay? I can hold." He had been calling junkyards and dealers for four solid weeks and still hadn't found one of the last parts needed. While he could begin the refurbishing project without the part in hand, it wasn't how he liked to work. His preference was to work in distinct phases, beginning with parts acquisition. If he followed his normal process, he would finish the first stage before he moved on to the next.

Glancing across his garage, he looked at the tarp-covered bike leaning against the workbench. There were color-coded bins on top of the bench, each holding bits and pieces for a number of bikes scattered around the garage in a range of restoration stages. The Vincent's assigned color was black, and the open, unfilled mouth of the bin gaped at him accusingly. Every time he looked at the bike, he knew it belonged to Prez, knew that's where he would eventually get it, so now he simply had to get it ready for him.

There was a scratching on his leg, and without looking down, he reached out a hand, gently grabbing his assailant by the scruff of the neck and picking it up. Winger's widow, DeeDee, had talked him into attending a run the club sponsored to raise money for the no-kill shelter in town, and he had seen the tiny puppy there. By the end of the day, he had adopted the dog, bringing him home tucked inside his shirt, curled and sleeping against the heat of his belly.

Moving with an ease born of repetition, he cradled the puppy belly-up in his arms while he shifted the phone to make the position more comfortable. The beagle blinked up at him, mouth open in a doggy grin with its tongue lolling out the side. He muttered to the dog, waiting for the dealer to come back to the phone, "Hey there, Tank. You bein' good, pup?" Tank wiggled his ass, whipping Gunny's side with his tail in support of his agreement that he had indeed been a good dog. Scratching and rubbing the dog's chest and belly, he grinned as the puppy's eyes sank half-closed in delight at the affection. "Yeah, you are, ain't ya? You're a good pup."

"Gunny, you won't believe this." The Wyoming drawl came back on the phone and he sighed, waiting for the delivery of yet another disappointing answer. "My old man remembered a box of parts he got about twenty years ago. Pops went digging, and I am standing here, holding the front fork for a 48 Vincent Black Shadow in my hands right now."

"No shit?" He straightened, placing the puppy carefully on the floor, watching as Tank ran over to a spare pair of boots lined up along the wall. He tackled one of the shoes and began dragging it back towards Gunny with sharp tugs on the loose laces, growling furiously. "What condition?" He paused, rubbing a hand across the top of his head. "You know what? Never mind. Just pack it up and mail it to me. You should still have my card on file; just charge the card, man."

"Don't you even want to know how much Pops wants for it?" The voice on the phone was teasing and Gunny snorted, shaking his head.

"Probably not, but go ahead and hit me. Harddrive is usually pretty fair." He waited for the information stoically. The parts thus far had cost nearly four times what he paid for the bike, but he counted it money well spent, every dollar getting him closer to seeing Mason's face when he gave him the bike. Idly glancing at Tank, he grinned when he saw the pup had nearly made it across the width of the garage with the boot trailing behind, alternately dragging and tugging it, grunting little puppy growls with each sharp yank.

"A picture." The man laughed. "That's it. Pops said he wants a picture of you on the finished bike, wants you to sign it and send it over. He's gonna frame it and put it in the shop, crow a little bit about having a hand in the restoration."

"That I can do," he said. Reaching down, he rescued the boot from the puppy, watching with a smirk as it ran across the garage again to tackle the other one, the animal running wildly into the side of the boot when it couldn't stop in time. "Thanks, man. Tell your old man I owe him big time."

"Will do, man. He said tell my sister hello from him, give her a kiss and a hug next time you see her." His voice had gentled, become soft, love for the woman he was talking about clear in his tone.

"I can do that, too." Disconnecting, he laughed aloud at the dog, who had managed to turn the boot over and was now trying to climb inside it headfirst. Patting his leg encouragingly, he called the puppy back to him. "Tank, I think you need a friend. Let's go talk to our man PBJ. He's got some pups he thought we might find interesting. I got the bikes, man, but you need a buddy."

***

Frantically, she grabbed at his wrist. Attached to the hand wound tightly in her hair, he was dragging her across the studio floor and she twisted, trying to use that grip to pull herself up, hoping to lessen the pain in her scalp. Keeping her mouth clenched tightly, only the barest of whimpers escaped her lips in response to the brutally rough handling. The back of her pants began to slide down her ass, threatening to expose her, sudden fear evoking another cry from her. The heels of his boots impacted her back solidly with every step as he walked, effortlessly striding across the space as if he were not weighed down by her mass at the end of his arm. She was the least of impediments to his advance.

He dropped her in the middle of the floor, walking around her to sit on the wooden chair he had been dragging with his other hand, the legs of the chair scraping noisily across the hard surface. She scrambled to her knees, desperately straightening her clothing as she fought the urge to run with every fiber of her being. Running was what had landed her here; it wouldn't do to compound those errors while in his presence. Facing away from him, towards the camera, she drew her arms in tight against her body protectively, waiting in stillness for what was coming.

When she heard the sibilant sound made by the slow slide of leather through his pants loops, she swallowed, closing her eyes even before the first blow across her back bloomed into pain. Not moving except when the force of the strikes pushed her forward or sideways, she shoved herself into the room she long ago created in her mind and slammed the door, visualizing her hands engaging a lock to keep everything out, a lock only her fingers could turn. She could stay there forever, it seemed, everything happening to her body removed and far away, outside noises receding as the sound of her breathing filled her ears. Even, smooth rasps drawn in, sipping at the air...count to three...lips pursed and slowly breathe out...count to three...

She unwillingly came back to herself, startled when he grabbed her hair, his vicious grip yanking her head backwards, causing her body to arch towards him. He leaned over her, staring down into her face, his eyes scanning her features. She saw a grim smile break the line of his lips as he drank in her open-mouthed expression, her lips parted in a silent scream as awareness of the pain and the panic of her helplessness crashed in on her.

He released his hold with a harsh laugh, and she lowered her head again, desperately trying to keep from looking into his eyes. *If I don't see him, he can't see me,* she thought nonsensically, waiting for...things to continue. She knew he would keep going until he was exhausted; he always did. He wouldn't be happy until he broke her, stopping only after he saw what he wanted, what he looked for in the surrender of her spirit.

The bowed and repentant angle of her neck telling everyone he had taught her the error of her ways.

The sway of her spine as she buckled, rounding down, drawing herself in small, accepting her insignificance.

The open gape of her mouth as she begged forgiveness, traitorous tongue speaking the words he so desired. Required.

The clasp of her fingers twined together, threading into prayer shapes of blasphemy, apparitions of his disappointment still searing her skin.

He would stop only when she evidenced belief it was futile to try and escape, to try to leave him. Not until then. After all, she belonged to him. "Fucking *look* at me, bitch," he gritted out, his breath coming hard with the exertion he was exercising on her behalf.

In response to his demand, her gaze involuntarily darted upwards, and she was barely in time to see the clenched fist flying towards her face, then everything went blessedly black.

5. No girls, no way

"Fuck that," he told Deke. "You know how I feel about club pussy. Just ain't going to touch it, man." He made a circle with the thumb and finger of one hand, plunging the first finger of his other hand through the hole several times. Laughing, he said, "You wanna hit that loose shit, you go right at it, brother. Be like a hotdog skating side-to-side in a wide hallway, but you go right at it."

"Bastard. I could have done without the visual." Deke laughed then gripped his crotch, shaking the half-hard cock tenting his pants. "Plus, my dick ain't no hotdog; it's a bratwurst, a fucking fat sausage."

Laughing, they clinked the bottoms of their beer bottles together, sitting at the end of the bar in Checkerz. Dixie, the manager, looked up from where she was stocking the cooler and smiled at their laughter, then turned back to her task. Deke tipped the top of his bottle towards the dark-haired woman. "Dix is pretty. Funny, too. Check it out, Gunny. You could go for that."

"Have you seen her old man? He'd fucking kill me." Gunny choked on his beer. "Damn, man. I thought we were friends. You hatin' on me these days?"

"Yeah, he'd roll your big ass, for sure." Deke's voice was heavy with sarcasm and they both laughed. Her old man was big and tough, but he was also firmly secure in what he had with Dixie, putting up with all kinds of shit from the bar's patrons with hardly a blink. The man knew he had a good thing going for him, and trusted her not to stray. Gunny flipped a bill on the bar and waved goodbye to Dixie, laughing at the complaint she called after them, "Quitters!"

As he climbed on his bike, his mind turned back to what Deke had been talking about, finding someone he wanted to spend time with. Not just fuck, which was how he played it off, but someone he could talk to, someone to look forward to seeing, someone who would be waiting for him at home. "Home," he muttered as he rode south and then west, turning into his sparsely populated neighborhood. The last time he moved houses, one of the criteria he set for Myron was a lack of neighbors, and as always, the man had come through for him.

Pulling into his garage, the happy barks and excited growls rang from inside the house and he laughed aloud. Tank and Rocky were always pleased to see him, regardless if he was gone five minutes or five hours. The inside of his house wasn't as empty as it used to be, and it seems he did have someone waiting at home. Maybe not quite what Deke had in mind, but at least his pups wouldn't *betray* him.

With that single thought...single word...he tensed, gaze sweeping the area, nervously watching along the bottom edge of the garage door as it closed, making sure nothing snuck in under the lowering barrier. No people, no sand-covered bodies, no spreading puddle of crimson, nothing. Gunny spoke aloud, "There's nothing there. Fuck, fuck, fuck. Nothing. You know there's fucking nothing there." *You're right; there's nothing to see*, Kincade said.

Teeth clenched, he drew deep breaths in through his nose, neck muscles tensed until he shook with the strain. "Goddammit, you're not fucking here...not fucking here." He took a harsh breath, repeating his words. "Not fucking here." In these moments, it felt as if he were drowning, sucked under the surface of his memories with hardly a ripple to mark his passage, fighting to get back to the air. He had to break the cycle, but he could already feel the tight band of alarm strangling his chest, hands fisting, drawn up into a defensive guard. He was drowning, with no one to save him.

Slinging his leg off the bike, he backed up to the workbench, hand going out instinctively to the stereo and hitting the power button. In moments, the slow strains of Chet Faker poured through the space around him, soothing saxophones introducing the encouraging lyrics of *Talk Is Cheap*, and Gunny took a deliberate breath, held it for five counts, and then released it, repeating this process while the song played on repeat. By the time Faker was done singing for the third time, the overwhelming panic had begun to bleed off, leaving him to deal with the dry mouth and shakes he found typical following a panic attack, the effects of adrenaline overload.

Through the years, he worked hard to develop coping mechanisms to help deal with the fight-or-flight urges that made life so difficult since he came home from overseas. He tried so many different things, compliantly taken the prescribed drugs, treating unwanted side effects with more meds. He had talked to the doctors, talked until he was hoarse and his voice was raw from explaining what he saw, what he perceived. He had even at times exiled himself in an effort to keep everyone safe…keep himself safe from him.

Walking up the last incline before one of his favorite campsites, Gunny's face twisted in disappointment at the sight of a hammock already strung between the trees. It was full dark, and he'd been hiking by headlamp for the past two hours, trying to get here so he could set up in a familiar location. All for nothing, because some fucking weekend warrior decided to hit Knobstone early this year.

April should have been too early for most folks, and if he could believe the calendar on his phone, this was the middle of the week, not the weekend. So, maybe this was a real hiker, someone who would respect this rare slice of wilderness found in southern Indiana. Fuck it, *he thought, I'm not going on to the next spot. Dude will simply have to deal with me being here. He shrugged off his pack, setting it on the carpeting of leaves, and used the headlamp to look around the established campsite as he unbuckled the clips and fasteners by feel.*

At least the site is clean, he thought. He could see where the guy had cooked, a good hundred feet off the trail in the opposite direction from where the hammock was. Then he spotted the bag of food suspended from a sturdy tree branch a hundred feet in yet another direction. Okay, *he thought grudgingly,* dude seems to know his shit.

Setting up camp in the dark wasn't a novelty to him. Even in the dark, he moved quietly, with competence, carefully securing the tent to the poles, laying out his pad and sleeping bag, and readying his morning coffee before crawling into his tent to sleep. Just lay the fuck down already, *Kincade said, and he snorted a quiet laugh in response. Throughout the night, soft groans from the hammock disturbed his sleep several times, and each time, he grinned in sympathy. Knobstone was a tough trail, and if the sounds were any indication of his exhaustion and soreness, the dude had seriously overestimated his ability.*

Waking early, he opened the tent to see only the slimmest glint of sky through the bare tree branches, and estimated the time at nearly six o'clock. Working again by headlamp, he heated water and made his breakfast of oatmeal then set another batch of water to boil on the lightweight stove he carried, arranging two cups and a baggie of coffee nearby.

He heard shifting in the hammock and watched the cocoon of silk fabric as it slipped and slid in response to the hiker's movements. The guy stretched luxuriously, feet pushing at and making temporary impressions on the material. Fingers appeared, spreading the edges of the hammock apart, and then rising into the air, the hands and long-sleeve covered arms stretching and rotating before disappearing back into the warmth the cocoon offered. Gunny frowned as he made his coffee, thinking, Dude's hands looked small...

The hands came into sight again, and elbows pressed the edges of the hammock down as the guy levered himself semi-upright, a knit beanie hat pulled down low over dark hair drawn back into a ponytail. A face popped into view, and he immediately had to revise his thoughts about the hiker. This middle-aged woman was either stupid or brave to be way out here all by herself.

She eyed him uneasily, and he realized for the first time, he had effectively set his camp up inside hers, his tent a bare three feet away from where her hammock hung. Conscious of how this must look, he smiled in what he hoped was a disarming fashion and held up his untasted cup of coffee in a peace offering. "Coffee?" he asked, and was pleased when she mutely reached out and accepted the mug, lifting it to her face and smelling it before giving him a tight smile.

"I'm Lane," he said, "Lost Lane."

She nodded, still not saying anything and he poured himself a cup of coffee, making a production of taking a sip, wordlessly trying to reassure her the drink was safe. "You headed north or south?"

"South," she said, her voice low and melodic, sleep-roughened. She lifted her hand, slowly sipping from the cup. "Peepers."

Accepting the trail name, he nodded. "I'm going south too. You got water?" Simply by looking at her, he already knew whatever water she had wasn't enough. She had dark circles of dehydration under her eyes, indicating to him she had missed matching exertion to intake, and knowing the trail as he did, he suspected she probably had gotten lost in the blown-down section of the trail yesterday. If she was stuck out in the open with no easy access to fresh water, carrying two or three liters simply wasn't adequate, and the evidence showed on her face. He focused on her hands, seeing the cuts and bruises there, knowing they were most likely from climbing over the deadfalls caused by a tornado *plowing through this area a couple of years ago. She was beat-up, but had kept on, and that perseverance earned her his grudging admiration.*

She nodded in response to his question about water and he stifled a laugh. "Did you cache?" He had. Had paid a local to drive him to all the places the trail crossed the road system and hid a gallon of water at every likely site. Most people expected the early spring to be wetter, but he had been walking this trail off and on for most of a year and knew better.

"Couple of places," she said, her voice still hoarse, and he knew his earlier suspicion of dehydration was correct. "I filter before stepping over water, too." As long as she had a decent filter for cleaning the water, it was a good hiking habit. Not passing up a water source was a lesson most casual hikers never learned. "Trying out a new Sawyer this trip." He nodded; that was a good system, easy to work and did an excellent job. "I got stuck out in the deadfalls for a bit yesterday." Bingo, he thought.

Storms were a hiker's enemy. They could destroy trails in moments, and then the task of organizing volunteers to restore the conditions and usability could take years or decades to complete. George Carlin had it right when he termed it NIMBY, 'Not In My Back Yard.' People didn't fucking care much about what happened where they didn't live. Like the war overseas, people didn't understand how critical it was to eradicate the enemy, support the friendlies, make the world safer. That was a fucking shitstorm in progress right there. Stupid fucking politicians sitting in their safe, little offices, playing chess with good men's lives. He gritted his teeth. "Tornado tore shit up." Her eyes widened at the unexpected anger in his voice and she nodded slowly. Knowing she couldn't hear his internal dialog, he attempted to moderate his tone when he continued, trying to soothe her, "Hot as hell in that valley, too." She nodded again, shifting in the hammock. "You got breakfast?"

She pointed towards the food bag he had noticed the night before. "I usually eat my dinner leftovers." He nodded again. That was smart of her; one of the most fundamental rules of backpacking was zero waste. If it was worth packing in, worth its weight in the bag, then it needed to be worth using or eating. She finished the coffee, using a corner of her bandana to wipe the mug clean before wordlessly handing it back.

Stretching, she rolled to the center of the hammock and flipped her feet and legs over the side, sitting in it like a swing for a moment before digging her toes into the ground and standing with a soft groan. Pushing glasses to the top of her head, she rubbed her face with the palms of both hands, trustingly blinding herself for a moment. She needs to break that habit, *he thought, looking down at her feet. He could see tape residue on her toes and across the arch of her feet, saw where the angry, red flesh surrounding the broken blisters bore witness to her efforts of the previous couple of days.*

"Thanks for the coffee, Lost Lane," she said softly as she began the process of breaking her camp. He saw her sway a couple of times, then watched with surprise when she pulled out a blood sugar test kit.

"You diabetic?" he asked incredulously, pulling on his pants while still in the tent. He didn't think she would appreciate the appearance of his dick right after he finally made her comfortable, so figured he should cover up before making his way out.

She nodded and scrunched up her nose at the results on the meter before packing it away with the rest of her things. The only items still left to pack were the hammock and her food bag. He watched as she slipped on lightweight flip-flops, retrieved her food bag, and carried it to where her cook spot was. As he settled and stowed his own gear, he watched her out of the corner of his eye. She doggedly ate the cold remains of her dinner from the night before, then poured hot water directly into a waxed envelope of oatmeal and ate from the package. Her filter bottle was sitting beside her feet, and he noted she hadn't picked it up once to drink, only pouring a metered amount into her cook pot to heat.

Her being diabetic changed her water needs, he knew. His granny had sugar problems, and he remembered her talking one long, hot Louisiana summer evening about how her sugar made her thirsty, and blurred her vision. Bored one day, he had looked up information and found the physical symptoms Granny described were actually damage being done to her body by high glucose levels.

If Peepers was diabetic, then going without adequate water might have long-term impact. He could give her some of his water, keeping back enough to get to the next highway crossing and be okay. But with the independent spirit she evidenced just by being out here on her own, he wondered how he could talk her into accepting his help. "There's water about a mile south," he offered, hesitating. He silently sighed, then said, "Finish packing up and we'll head that way."

Her head snapped up and she glared at him, defiance and a desire for self-reliance evident on her face. "Thanks, I got this."

He stared at her, trying to decide what he was doing. This wasn't what he did. He just walked the trail, bought supplies, checked into the VA in Louisville when he felt too crazy, then walked the trail some more. He hadn't found a place to settle since getting out of the Marines, and he wasn't good around people. In fact, as he told the doc more than once, he didn't do people. "I could use the company," he said quietly.

She pointedly looked at his belt, where he had two handguns in holsters. He knew she had seen the third he put into the holster at the small of his back, too. "I don't think you really mean that," she said softly, looking back down at her nearly empty packet of oatmeal.

"I have PTSD," he said bluntly. It was the first time he admitted it to anyone outside of the VA, and he wondered what her reaction would be. Simply saying the words fractured something in his chest and he growled when he told her, "Believe me; when I say I could use the company, I mean I could use the company."

"Iraq?" she asked, and he nodded. She looked at him for a long moment and he saw a shudder make its way up her frame, then she tilted one shoulder up, attempting nonchalance. "Okay, let me get my stuff stored away." She stood and organized her food, putting on her boots and then efficiently packed the hammock and accruements into a small bag she strapped to the outside of her pack. Slinging the loaded backpack to her shoulder and shrugging into the straps, she settled the weight evenly onto her shoulders with a sigh. She put a cap on her head, and he grinned when he saw it was an Edmonton Oilers hat. Evidently, she had a soft spot for underdogs. Peepers rolled her shoulders again and tilted her head back to look up at him, saying, "Let's go."

"Two things," he said, handing her a bottle of water, pressing it into her hand when she would have waved it off. "You drink when I say so, and we move when I tell you. I never know what will trip me up, so if I act...strange, just go with it." She nodded and opened the bottle, pausing to look a question at him. He grinned and then laughed aloud at her implied compliance, following it with a softly spoken, "Drink."

Shaking himself out of the memory, he looked around the garage. That had been a remarkable trip. He spent three comfortable days in her company, no demands for conversation, and no complaints about being tired or sore. Peepers hadn't complained about anything, no matter how hard he pushed her. An excellent traveling companion, she had been using her time in the woods to prepare for a section hike of the Appalachian Trail. He sometimes wondered how things had gone for her, and knew he had her to thank for where he was in his life. His trail angel, a private version of the trail magic hikers talked about. She jarred him out of the rut he had gotten into, and he had headed into new territory, making his way up to Fort Wayne, eventually meeting up with Deke and, as Deke would say, the rest was history.

The pups were scratching at the door, so he stretched out his hand to turn off the music, settled in his own skin again. *Fuck Deke*, he thought. *No girls, no way.*

***

Crouching in the half-flooded ditch, she eased her aching body down, submerging it below the level of the water, leaving only the top of her head and face in the open air. Exposed skin smeared with mud from her frantic flight, she felt invisible even when the lights from the approaching car flashed across her features. Digging her toes into the mud on the bottom of the waterway, she anchored herself against the slow flow of water here along the edges of the canal, ignoring the touches and brush of trash and branches as they trailed across her skin. It didn't matter if it was more than plastic bags and vegetation sharing the space. Even if it were snakes or alligators, what waited for her if she allowed herself to be caught again would be so much worse than any injury or pain they could inflict.

His car roared past and she carefully followed its progress up the highway from the corner of her eye, watching for any sign of recognition. No brake lights, no interior lights, there was no indication it was slowing down or that he had spotted her. She thought, *Only four more miles and I'll be safe*. Four miles up the road, there was a store that still had a working pay phone, and she could call...someone. She would make it this time; she knew she had to. He would kill her when he caught her again. *If*, she thought grimly, *if*.

"Honey, are you okay?" The words came from the opposite side of the road, rising from the darkness to wrap around her and freeze her body in place, her eyes closing in terror. "Oh, sweetheart, what are you doing? You're all wet. Come outta there 'fore a gator decides to snack on you." *No, no, no, no*, she thought, her muscles tensing to push off the side of the ditch into the faster flowing water behind her, in the center of the canal. Then, the gender of the voice registered. "Come out of there, sweetheart. Let me help you." It was a woman, not him, but in her initial panic, the voice had turned into *his*.

Eyes flying open wide, she looked up into a face that could harbor no evil; no monsters lived within this woman. Green eyes set in a round face, dark hair framing the features split with a nervous smile. "Sweetheart, are you hurt?" There was a strong, generous hand reaching out to lift her up, fingers invitingly curling into the clean, soft-looking palm. All she had to do was take it, grab hold...place herself into it, accepting the help.

Shaking her head, she turned to look up the road, seeing the taillights of the car still receding into the distance, becoming smaller and dimmer with each passing second, with every breath losing their ability to control her, to keep her...to imprison her. "Come out of the canal, hon. Nobody's going to hurt you." At the declaration, her gaze slammed back to the woman's face, taking in the sincerity and honesty there. "What's your name, sweetheart?"

She didn't know when her teeth had begun chattering, when her body began to respond to the environment surrounding her, stealing her heat even as it fed her freedom. She again looked at the outstretched hand, suddenly terrified it would be withdrawn and frantically she stretched one arm up, desperation accompanying the mud-slickened slap of her palm against the clean one. She gasped, feeling the smallest of slips before the hand closed over hers, the grip firm, holding on tightly and beginning to draw her up and out of the muck. She managed to quell her shuddering muscles long enough to whisper, "Shar. My name is Sharon."

6. Moving forward

She smiled, dipped her hands back into the steaming heat, and searched around, exploring with her fingertips for the last piece of silverware lurking in the wash water. Looking out the window set in the wall over the sink, she let her gaze dance across the backyard, taking in the unrelenting ordinariness of the view. The blessed, treasured normality of the child's swingset tucked into a back corner of the yard, the averageness of an asphalt-shingled doghouse roof, the mundane back gate, which led to an unremarkable empty field lying alongside an extremely unnoteworthy section of woods. Normal, ordinary, sane. Safe.

There was a noise behind her and she twisted her head to see Savannah walk into the room, followed by a boy of about fourteen. She was looking up at Shar, and he was looking down at the game in his hand, their postures indicative of their very different personalities. Vanna was always looking outward, seeking interaction, eagerly in search of the next stray she could collect and care for. There were few days that passed where she didn't set an extra place at the table for one or more meals, or bring home a crated animal for care.

Kitt, on the other hand, was painfully withdrawn, hardly bearing the touch of even the friendliest of hands some days. Vanna was religious about exposing him to experiences though, creating opportunities for him to explore. It wasn't uncommon for them to spend a day by the creek, Kitt waiting eagerly on the bank for the waterlogged treasures his mother brought him. Him on the bank, because while he loved the crawdads and smooth stones she found, he was powerless to look for himself, unable to stand the sensation of running water against his skin. It wasn't that she ignored or denied his diagnosis of autism, but more she didn't see it as a defining aspect of her son. She often said he would never be able to find his niche in life if he didn't have a chance to discover things, so she made certain he at least had the chance.

In the time since she literally pulled Shar up out of the mess and mire that was her previous life, the two women, who couldn't have been more different, had become close friends.

Vanna was originally from Texas, but had settled in the panhandle of Florida years ago, following her job when it relocated. She had been divorced for a long time, Kitt's father unable to handle the reality of their son's disorder. He cheated, and when Vanna discovered his unfaithfulness, she hadn't hesitated to kick his ass to the curb, confident in her ability to care for herself and her son.

Shar smiled at the pair, and with a glance towards the window, said, "Looks like a hiking day to me," earning a broad smile from Vanna and a twitching shrug from the boy. "I'm done here," she said, pulling the stopper to drain the water, using the spray nozzle to rinse the remaining bubbles from the sink. "Y'all want fanny packs or daypacks?"

"God, don't do that again." Vanna laughed. "A Canadian saying y'all is completely wrong, eh?" Kitt snorted a laugh, and without looking up, wordlessly reached out for the daypack his mother held out to him.

"Okay, eh?" Now Shar was laughing along with them, thinking, *This is normal, too.* "Hand hug," she told Kitt brightly and held out her arm, fingers spread in a 'stop' motion as she waited patiently. He glanced up at her then looked down before placing his palm against hers, their thumbs and little fingers curving around the other's hand in a loose grip he could break as soon as he needed. "Thanks, buddy," she said. "I needed that." She pulled open the door, making a 'go ahead' gesture with her hand.

Walking along the worn path on the way to the woods, she found herself looking around cautiously. The house might have become a place of safety and calmness for her, but open areas still held fear, and even if she knew *he* wasn't here, alertness had become an ingrained habit. In the time since her escape, she never attempted to find out where he had gone, what he had done when he found her missing. She had been too afraid of somehow bringing his attention down on them, and even knowing it was a dangerous blind spot, she had left it alone. That ignorance meant he could be anywhere and she would never know, so for more than a year she had tried every day for invisibility. Until this week, when she tentatively approached a lawyer. He said it would take time, but after hearing her story, promised to do everything in his power to keep her safe while severing ties with *him* legally. "He could be anywhere," she muttered without thinking, and the verbal affirmation of her vulnerability sent the beginnings of panic to place a hitch in her breathing.

"Or nowhere." Vanna spoke quietly, reassuringly, letting her know she had caught the slip.

"I know," she said quickly, clamping her lips closed on a sigh. They hiked in silence for a while, the noise of the insects and birdsong gradually increasing in volume, their movement through the woods slowly accepted by the forest's real inhabitants.

"You sure you're going to be okay with Kitt while I'm gone?" Vanna had been planning and preparing for a hike in Virginia for weeks. Now the days were ticking down and she was fretting over every detail, especially the wellbeing of her son while she was out of state on-trail.

Shaking her head, Shar stepped over a fallen branch and smiled at the woman walking in front of her. "You know I will be. He's my best buddy, and we get on passably well. He's gonna be fine, Maum. Stop worrying." Vanna had been working on sectioning the long trail stretching from Georgia to Maine along the eastern states, doing forty or fifty miles for each of the past several years. Last year, Shar accompanied her on a small hike up in Tennessee, marveling at the confidence of her friend. Vanna was in her element no matter where she was, whether working in a soup kitchen, digging a drainage ditch in the garden, or hiking up a four-thousand-foot mountain. "I worry more about you," she lied, knowing her friend would laugh.

"How are the classes going?" Vanna asked, changing the subject and then muffled a curse as Kitt released a branch exactly in time for it to whip his mother in the face.

Ducking her head safely under the offending branch, Shar said, "Hmm. Is there a word for better than good? Great? Wonderful? Excellent? Yeah, excellent. Classes are *excellent*." Her gaze tracked up the trail and she experienced a strange sense of unease as she watched the heels of Vanna's boots moving relentlessly forward, leading the way up the path. *Deja vu.* She shook off the feeling and said, "The instructor is so good. He's using a pole, but doesn't call it pole dancing, says it's more like vertical gymnastics." She heard another muffled curse, ducked under the still swaying branch, and grinned. "I love it. Feels like flying."

✳✳✳

He sat on the edge of the couch cushion, staring at his friend. "Deke, man, don't do it." His breath came hard and fast and he hated the pleading tone in his voice. "Mason already knows how fucked I am, man. He doesn't need no reminders."

Deke sat on the coffee table, his knees touching Gunny's, the firm warmth of that contact the only thing keeping him grounded. He felt as if he was about to explode, and at the same time wanted to slink back into the darkness within the house, the obscurity of anonymity that had been his refuge for so long. He needed to make his friend understand he would be okay; this was simply another rough patch to traverse. He would make it through; he always did.

"You call Mason and tell him what you found when you walked into my house uninvited, he's going to ask for my patch, man. I can't...you can't take the club from me. I need...*fuck,* this is hard." He shook his head, driving the demons clamoring for attention from the front of his thoughts. "The club is the only thing that keeps me going, man. For so many years now, it's been the club, pups, and bikes. You take one of those things from me, and unbalanced doesn't come close to being the right word." He stared at Deke, trying to determine if his words had the expected effect.

"Lane," Deke shook his head, "I can't keep something like this from Prez, man. You know it. He's not going to ask for your patch—no how, no way. Man loves you like a brother. I think he's as close to you as he is Slate." He glanced down at the object held loosely in his hands, watching as he absently turned it over and over with his fingers. "You say you weren't going to do anything. Well then, why the fuck did I walk in to find you spinning this on the wood where my ass is now sitting?"

Deke held out his hand, the small pistol balanced on one broad palm.

"It's just something I do." He shrugged, not believing his own words. "Like that motherfucker Tug always grooming his face with his fingers, or Myron counting ceiling tiles. It's only a habit."

"Not buying it, brother." Deke spoke softly, but his words hit hard, like the concussive wave of an IED exploding next to the truck ahead of you in a convoy. Gunny rolled his neck, listening to the tendons creak and crack, pushing back the tension along with the memories. Deke said, his voice shaking with intensity, "You need to talk to someone, Lane."

He stood in a rush of movement, rubbing his palm across the top of his head, feeling the drag of rough stubble on his skin. He was afraid to look down at Deke for a minute, afraid he would see pity in place of the compassion his friend had shown so far. "You fucking think I haven't done that? Haven't talked my throat dry? I've been dealing with this for ten years, man. Ten goddamned long years. I know what trips me up. I know, and I. Fucking. Deal." His voice dropped to a whisper, "I just fucking deal." *Yes, you do, brother*, he heard the murmur in his mind, stealing his strength. *You fucking deal. Let the man help you deal. Deal with getting real.* Shaking his head, Deke opened his mouth, but stopped when Gunny's legs folded, dropping his ass back on the couch, disturbing the sleep of the beagle and rat terrier curled up on the cushions beside him. He reached over and dragged his fingertips along their sides, soothing them. His voice so hoarse with emotion he could barely recognize it, he said, "You take the club, you might as well pull the fucking trigger for me."

Deke said, "Then let me help you. Give what I came over here to tell you a chance. I talked to Slate, explained the gun range isn't a fit. Fuck, man, you should have told him that yourself." He gestured between the two of them, his movements impatient. "You and I both know that's probably what triggered you."

Be real, brother, Kincade murmured again.

He nodded, exhaling in a rush. "I know, but the club needed someone to work that cop party. Only people available were prospects or me, so I raised my fucking hand. It's what we do, man. We just take care of our own shit. No excuses."

Deke laughed humorlessly. "My fucking brother's shoot 'em up? Hell, he coulda worked the thing himself. But, here's the thing, Lane; you fucking knew it'd trigger you, and you did it anyway. Without even saying a word, you put yourself into a place that was gonna fuck you up. Prez and I, we sorted it out, which is what I was coming here to tell you. We're going to shift you to Slinky's."

"The strip joint? Watching skanks and hos shake their tired pussies for quarter tips? Jesus, man, you do hate me." He wouldn't admit it, but Deke's solution made sense. Working with DeeDee would be good, they had found their way to an easy friendship years ago, and it only deepened after Winger passed. Being around her wouldn't be a hardship at all, so this sounded good. Sounded nearly too good to be true. "What's the catch?"

"No catch, brother. Just…"—he looked down at the gun still in his hand—"you gotta promise to fucking talk to me."

7. Duty calls

Gunny tensed and shifted, rolling his shoulders as he stood along the inside wall of the club, watching the men who were there watching the dancers. He had been working at Slinky's off and on for a while now, and out of all the jobs Slate had offered him, this one as bouncer of the strip club still seemed like the best fit. Recently, he was up in Chicago helping Bear with some bikes, but then the motherfucker had to go and nearly get himself killed in Iowa. Gunny worked on all the bikes they had in the queue as best he could, but knew his talents didn't lie in overstroking engines or creating café racers out of reclaimed frames. No crotch rockets for him, his thing was still restoring back to stock. He had a full cadre of bikes in garage rot-mode at the moment, because, except for his lone long-term one, he lacked inspiration for his next project.

His gaze swept across the crowd again. Tonight, it was nearly all citizens; only a few of the patrons were bikers, and most of those were members of a different club here in town, the River Riders. That sector of the audience understood it was worth their blood to start trouble in a Rebel business, so he mentally dismissed them and scanned the room again, impassively skimming over the girls dancing, turning back to them only when a note of discord registered. *Something ain't right*, he thought, noting with growing disgust the jerky movements of the girl on the stage closest to where he stood.

Since she took over management of the strip club, DeeDee had been working hard to keep the girls with habits off the stage, but it looked like she misjudged this one for sure. He pulled out his phone, flipping it open and dialing without taking his eyes off the girl. Her movements were fast becoming less coordinated, and with her rapid deterioration, he suspected they would be dealing with an overdose soon. "Slate. Hey, Prez, it's Gunny. I'm at Slinky's. Got a girl needs Goose, looks like she's using." He had a lot of respect for Slate and hated to say what he thought was going on, since the man's little brother Ben had barely left rehab from his recent issues, but he needed Prez to know how serious it was. "I think we need Goose fast, Prez. It won't surprise me if she's in the early stages of an OD."

"Fuck me." Slate's harsh mutter came through the phone, followed by a question. "She passed the screens?"

"Dunno about that, Prez. I'm just sayin' what I'm seein' right here, right now." He shook his head as she stumbled, barely catching herself from toppling off the stage. Glancing around the room again, he confirmed his previous assessment of the patrons. "I need to get her to the back, but there's no one here to cover the door. I got some Riders, but no Rebels."

The outside door opened and he saw Hoss, the Fort Wayne vice-president, walk in, his arm wrapped around Mercy, one of the club whores who occasionally danced. "Scratch that, I got Hoss. Can you call Goose for me?"

"Yeah, I'll call Goose. Get the girl in the back before she pukes on somebody," Slate said, and the call ended.

Hoss looked his way, giving the girl a swat on her ass and directing her towards the bar as he walked over to Gunny. With a chin lift, Gunny asked, "You mind watching the door for a bit?"

"Naw, don't mind it. What's up?" Hoss tilted his head inquisitively.

Tipping his head towards the girl on stage, Gunny said, "Need to take care of something."

Hoss looked at her and frowned, looking back at Gunny with hard eyes, asking with surprise in his voice, "What the fuck, Gunny?"

"She's not my gash, man. I'm only taking her in the back until Goose can get here. Prez was my first call when I saw the score, and he's calling the cavalry." Shaking his head, he sneered at the man in front of him regardless of his rank in the club, pulling himself up to his full height, towering over the other man. "Fuck you. You don't know me. I got years in the club, and you do not fucking know me."

Without another word, he turned and strode to the stage, reaching up a hand and clasping the girl's wrist loosely in his palm. Quietly, he told her, "Come with me, now," then sighed at the blank stare she gave him. Wrapping one arm around her waist, he scooped her off the stage and set her feet on the floor, ignoring the looks and questions from the men nearby. She wobbled on her heels, hands clutching at his arm for balance.

This bitch is a fucking piece of work, he thought as he steered her stumbling steps towards the door leading into the back of the building. *No goddamn respect for herself. I sure ain't gonna waste my fucking time on her, or any other woman like this.*

***

She lowered her head, staring at the dingy three-inch by three-inch tile directly in front of her toes, her gaze tracking first along one edge, then another, trying to slow down the pounding of her heart. *In through the nose, and out through the mouth,* she thought, taking measured breaths as her eyelids flickered closed. She felt her sense of hearing expanding, rolling outward from where she stood on the edge of the raised platform.

From over by the bar came the clink of highball glasses, the delicate rims kissing the sides of the glass beneath it as the bartender placed stacks of the clean tumblers on the shelf. She made out the buzz from the speaker system and the hum of the air conditioner, feeling a steady draft of cold air dropping down from the overhead vent. Cars drove down Lima Road, past the club; there was a melodic bell sounding somewhere in the distance, signaling the end of the school day.

"Elkins, get ready. Your music starts in one," the manager's voice called from the enclosed DJ area, and she responded with a small flick of her fingers. This was her second audition, and she wanted to nail it, hoping to have a verdict about the job afterward.

She loved this routine, loved this music. The emotion Meg Myers poured into her songs always made her feel as if she could fly from the energy alone, and *Desire* was a dramatic piece, perfect for her dance. After two years of classes, she loved to dance and was confident in her abilities, but auditioning was proving to be nerve-wracking even with no real audience to judge her. Just the manager and the bouncer. *I can do this*, she thought, pushing past the fear.

As the music rose, she brought her head up, unable to keep the smile from curling the corners of her lips upward as she whispered, "Five, six, seven, eight..."

Arching her back, she lifted one leg behind her, curling her knee around the upright metal shaft as she bowed farther, tapping at the back of her head with her toes. Holding for a moment like that, she pretended her head was a balloon, batting it back and forth with her foot before turning to glower at her appendage, then, with a shy smile, playing back to where the crowd would be sitting.

Gripping the pole with her hands, she pushed off with both feet, moving smoothly through a shoulder roll up and back into a modified angel, and then transitioned to a quick layback spin, followed by the dramatic flair of a showgirl spin. Feeling more than listening to the music, she was counting in her head...*four, two, three, four, five, six, seven, eight...five, two, three...*

Maintaining her balance and speed was important, and she made sure to spot to the back of the room on the spins, keeping her posture wide-open and confident. She knew there was a broad smile on her face, letting all the joy she found in dancing shine through. *Eight, two, three, four, five...*

The only fumble came when she moved through a dismount with a downward spin to a seated position on the stage. She spread her legs wide and reached up over her head for the chilly metal, needing to use her upper-body strength to draw herself halfway back up the pole in a pike. *Two, two, three, four, five...*

It was when she was transitioning back onto the pole from the seated position when what sounded like a growl came from the back of the room. The sound so startled her she froze for a half-second, barely anything, but enough to have the final section of her routine be a hairs-breadth off time. She frowned, hoping the manager hadn't noticed, or that the rest of her dance was good enough to overlook the small mistake.

"You're hired," said the manager's voice, and Shar lifted her head with a grin as, just like that, she was gainfully employed.

***

He stood there, grateful for the supporting wall behind him. When DeeDee called him this morning and asked if he would mind evaluating the auditions today, he never expected anything like what he saw a moment ago. The club had hosted an open call a few days ago, with about twenty girls showing up to dance, trying to get a foot in the door of the club. He hadn't watched the dancers that day, trucking in and out of the back helping stock the bar, but he knew some of them he had seen before, either here dancing on amateur night...or at the clubhouse, doing auditions of a different sort.

This round of tryouts was only five girls, the few who had made it through from the other day, each offering something slightly different DeeDee was looking for in her dancers. The club had two openings right now, but given the transient nature of the business, he knew she would keep even the unsuccessful names from today on file for future reference.

Their music swelled and filled the space, and as they danced, he had quietly appraised the first four girls. They were okay, moving well enough, and pleasant to watch. But to him, like the rest of the staff at the strip club, they were bodies to guard, personalities to tolerate, and associations to evaluate.

Until it was time for the last girl. The final dancer in the auditions. She...was different.

From the moment she stepped onto the stage, he had been completely aware of her.

The swing of her hips as her feet set into place.

The allure of her features...the way her lithe body swayed and twisted, appearing to dance in place even as she waited for the music to start. Something about the way she moved called to him, and instinctively, he was already two steps away from his position at the wall before catching himself.

She looked small and vulnerable, and he found himself wanting...needing to protect her.

His eyes focused on her, noting the tightly controlled breathing, the tense frame created by her shoulders, the lines of her muscles screaming fear to him...then he heard DeeDee's voice speak a name, "Elkins."

The music played and he recognized the melody, a frantic-sounding song with a slower, deeper subtext, filled with fraught pauses and sensuous language, which made every nerve in his body leap. For the first time in more than a decade, he was awake.

Then she danced...and he was lost.

**

"What'd you think about the girls I hired?" DeeDee handed him a beer. It was about an hour before opening time, and with all the prep work finally complete, they were taking a break, seated at the bar.

He shrugged, still struggling with his reaction to the last girl, Elkins. "They were good enough, I guess."

"You don't like any of my girls." She laughed at the face he made and wrapped a napkin around her bottle of water.

Shaking his head, he said, "Not true. I like most of them. I absolutely do not want to fuck them. Big difference."

She snorted, tipping her bottle up and taking a long drink. "You're an odd duck, Gunny. But, I kinda like you."

It was his turn to laugh and he reached out, tucking a strand of hair behind her ear from where it had escaped her ponytail. "I kinda like you too, DeeDee. Love you; love little sister. Glad she found her way with Slate. It's been fun watching her turn into Ruby. Been fun watching a lot of things." He tilted his head, cupping her jaw for a moment before he grinned and said, "Still don't want to fuck you, though, so don't go getting any ideas."

"Wouldn't think of it, my friend." She leaned back, grinning around the mouth of the bottle at him, taking another drink. "Seriously, what did you think about the two girls?"

He barely suppressed a shudder of desire, feeling the muscles in his belly and groin grow tense, his balls tightening and pulling up against his body as his cock filled with blood, fattening and straining against the fabric of his jeans. "Good enough," he repeated laconically, taking another slow drink.

"I think the last girl is going to do well. I hope she does, at least. I really liked her, but did you hear her one stipulation?" He shook his head and then jerked in reaction when she continued with a laugh, "No nudity."

"Seriously? She knows what kind of club this is, right?" Gunny was astonished at the mix of emotions flooding him—relief he wouldn't have to watch as she bared herself to the patrons, but also an acute disappointment he wouldn't get to see that body. At the thought of her body, and her dance today, his cock twitched, pressing harder against his jeans. *God, that body*, he thought.

Nodding, DeeDee stood and stretched. "I guess Shar has some nude-colored costumes she'll wear. I told her we'd give it a try, see where it goes." She yawned, and then said, "I'm exhausted. Slate and Ruby's wedding is beginning to wear me out. I think I'll try to catch a quick nap on the couch in the office. Call me if you need me, okay?"

Shar, her name is Shar Elkins. He nodded, flipping his fingers at her in a 'go ahead' gesture. "I got this, DeeDee," he said, and she laughed.

"Now you sound like Slate," she said, turning to walk away.

"Been called worse things," he yelled after her, picking up his beer and taking a long pull of the cold liquid. "Far worse things," he muttered, glancing around the room, cataloging the shadows and staff, identifying threats with the ease allowed from extended experience.

***

He stood, watching. This was the fourth night this week he had seen her dance, and while each routine was good, none of them held the same hypnotic power over him as her audition had. It had taken him several days, but he thought he could finally put his finger on the difference. She was tight, tense, the fear he had sensed that first day sometimes flowing out so strongly from her that he could feel it, even from his post against the back wall.

The more crowded the venue, the more fear she had to fight through to work her sets. Tonight for example, her dancing was fluid and free, but there were just a double-handful of men spread out across the room, all watching her avidly, with only a couple right up against the stage. Why she would choose to dance when it filled her with fear was a mystery, a puzzle, one he wanted to solve. So he watched, fighting his own battle against his desires.

His obsession wasn't easing, and even as he tried to keep a tight hold on it, he found his fingers clenching into hard fists each time she worked the edges of the stage to pick up her tips. Seeing the smiles she presented the men who reached for her, watching the brush of her fingers against theirs as she accepted the money they offered in return—those interactions, harmless as they were, made him feel wild—he wanted to yank her back, put her behind him, protect her from something that wasn't a threat. In fact, anytime she was in the room, he found himself responding in protective and possessive ways. He had never touched her, but somehow she was under his skin.

8. Ace and Gunny

"I'm telling you, DeeDee, this chick doesn't fit. We need to do a deeper dive into her background," Hoss said, staring at her and ignoring Gunny. Over the years, they had come to the conclusion this was the safest avenue to follow when they were in the same room. Today, they were seated in the office at Slinky's, DeeDee ensconced behind the desk, stiffly upright in her office chair, Hoss lounging on the couch against the opposite wall from where Gunny leaned.

Hoss continued, "She's staying at the local efficiency motel with a rental car, which is not in her name. I don't know who Savannah Reicht is, and don't fucking care. I don't care if you like her or not. In fact, I don't care if this girl is the best dancer in the place. Shar Elkins has got shit behind her somewhere, and I ain't gonna have her shit leaking here." Gunny still hadn't been able to shake his feelings about her and now listened eagerly, soaking up any available information about the girl he had been so carefully watching.

"Lots of girls cut ties with the past before they come to us. This isn't anything we haven't seen before." DeeDee wasn't arguing with him, but was carefully keeping her tone even and Gunny winced, knowing the anxiety this masked. "I'm okay doing a deep check on her. In fact, I was going to recommend it, since our first run didn't turn up much, good or bad. She's Canadian, but has dual citizenship since she married an American. For what I need, she's perfect, because she's not jaded...she can both dance and connect with the audience, which means the men like watching her. I think she does fit, but my gut matches yours on the thought there's something there to find. I'll kick it off, okay?"

Hoss gave her a chin lift then levered himself off the couch and approached the door to leave. Pausing with his hand on the knob, he glanced back at her with an expression on his face Gunny couldn't decipher. *A puzzle.* Hesitating for a few seconds, he dropped his hand, turning to place his back against the door and facing the room.

She looked at him, waiting good-naturedly. Gunny knew from being around her husband, and exposure to the club, she had long ago figured out with men like Hoss, rushing them would never work. If the man had something to say to her, he would work it out in his head first, and then spit it out when he was ready, not a moment before. They both ignored Gunny, and he held himself in check, patiently giving them time to sort things.

"Was a good weekend," he said, and she nodded, but Gunny knew this wasn't what had him hesitating. It was a good weekend, with a monster party for Slate and Ruby's wedding. They had ridden out on Saturday, headed to the coast for a well-deserved honeymoon. But for Hoss, something more had happened, putting an edge on his mood.

"Jase move in?" Tilting his head to the side, Hoss waited for her response. *Huh, there it is. Something's there.*

She looked surprised as she answered, "In progress, but yeah. He's got someone to take over the lease on his condo." They were talking about the man she had fallen in love with, long after giving up on the possibility again. Gunny remembered how broken she had been when Winger and Lockee died, how the grief whittled away at her until there was little of the old DeeDee left.

Jase Spencer was a professional hockey player who met DeeDee when she was covering shifts at one of the Rebel bars in Chicago. He had fallen hard for her, and over the past year, turned his entire life upside down pursuing her. Over the weekend, Gunny heard she finally quit running. But, he wasn't certain why Hoss was asking these questions. The news Jase would be moving in with her had made the rounds of the club within minutes of her telling Ruby, and Gunny had received one of the first calls. Hoss was Slate's second, so he probably had knowledge about it from the club side, too.

"You okay with that?" Hoss watched her carefully, and Gunny stared at him, recognizing for the first time there might have been something more than affection there. *There is a touch of something there, more than fondness, less than desire.*

Her lips tipping up in a contented smile, she nodded and responded, "Yeah, I'm okay with that. We've been coming to this point for a while now, Hoss. It's all good." Gunny knew this was true, because along with watching Slate and Ruby's courtship, he had enjoyed seeing Jase woo DeeDee. Through all of her futile escape efforts, he had kept reeling her in, until the hockey player finally landed her. The fishing metaphor made his mouth twitch with amusement, then the thought *an airless dock* and Eklund's face flashed in front of him, the taste of blood in his mouth jolting him out of the moment.

After a moment, Hoss smiled back at her, his face softening as he said, "Comes a time you aren't okay, you tell me." He cut his eyes over to Gunny, tipping his head. "Me and Gunny, we'll sort that man's shit. I got you, pretty lady, and you know that's the truth." With another chin lift, he turned and opened the door, walking through and pulling it closed behind him, not waiting for her response.

Still smiling, she glanced back at Gunny as she picked up her phone, and he listened while she talked to Myron in Chicago, giving her approval to initiate a more in-depth investigation of Shar Elkins. Since the Rebels owned Slinky's, they were always careful who they hired to work the bar and the poles, not needing attention or scrutiny brought to them by an employee's behavior or messy history.

"I'm going to step out, DeeDee. You need me, just call." She knew the office was wired into the system routed through his earpiece, so she nodded.

He closed the office door behind him, scanning the bar and floor near the stage. There were a few Rebel members scattered around the room, mostly seated together, but some were sharing tables with rival clubs, and he noted both the members and clubs involved in those conversations. You never knew what information might be valuable later.

He had been settled in his place along the back wall for a while, when he saw the door open and caught sight of Shar stepping inside. As the door slipped closed, the light from outside flashed across her face, reflected from one of the many mirrors in the bar, and he sucked in a breath. She had a bruise covering nearly her entire temple. She had pulled her hair forward trying to conceal it, but his stomach twisted as the brilliance revealed what she would have preferred to keep private. Someone had hit her. Someone she knew...maybe trusted, if the shame he read on her features was any indication.

He stepped away from the wall and into her path when she would have walked past him, asking, "What are you doing here, gal?"

Ducking her head, she quietly said, "I need to see missus Moser."

He frowned, because nobody called DeeDee by her last name; this was almost a schoolgirl's response, asking to see a favored teacher or a trusted counselor. Why would she be acting like that? Shaking his head, he reached out to hold her in place, but his hand froze inches away from her arm when she flinched away from him. She said, "Please. I don't care if she's busy. I can wait. I really need to talk to her, but if she's not in her office, I can wait. Please."

Shaking his head, he urged, "Talk to me, Shar. You don't need to bother her with this."

Moving sideways, trying to step around him, on an indrawn breath she said, "No, please. Can you just tell her Sharon Spencer needs to talk to her? I'm sorry, eh?"

He shifted and put out a hand again, pausing when she cringed, then saw her face lighten as he shoved at the office door, pushing it open wide and letting her step inside. He followed her, his hand finally closing on her arm, and looked up to see DeeDee's attention was already focused on the girl, knowing she saw the same damage he had.

"I need to talk to you, missus Moser," Shar said, wincing and pointedly scowling down where Gunny's hand gripped her bicep. A sense of calmness had settled over him at the feel of her soft skin under his rough palm, and he took in what seemed like the easiest breath in a decade, holding her arm. It seemed like...everything that had ever troubled him just...receded, pulled back for this moment, gave him peace.

He could feel the fast thud of her heart through that connection, understood she had fear running wild through her right now, but somehow knew it wasn't of him. In fact, her heartrate was beginning to slow, to calm, as if this feeling of comfort and ease went both ways. He knew his grip over the bruise had to hurt from the look on her face, but he didn't think he could let her go now that he had his hands on her. He took another breath, feeling his ribs expand and his chest rise with the inhalation, watching as Shar exhaled along with him, slowly and evenly.

From far away, he heard DeeDee say, "It's okay, Gunny. I'm good. You can be in or out, but let's close the door. Sounds like we'll need a little privacy for this chat." DeeDee gave him a calm look over the girl's shoulder, not trying to direct him, but openly asking for his patience.

He frowned at Shar, noting, not for the first time, the beauty, dignity, and poise she exuded. Even standing in the office of a strip club with a black-leather clad biker at her back and a growing bruise on her face, she looked calm and collected, her bargain-bin clothes draping her frame as if they were designer label. So different from the rest of the dancers here, she moved like class and looked like class, like the pretty girls from Baton Rouge, and he wanted...

Keeping his one hand on her bicep, he put his other on her back and gently moved her farther into the room, pushing the door closed with his foot. Having both his hands on her amplified the feeling of being...centered...whole. He inhaled again, saw her shoulders relax slightly as she breathed along with him. Reluctantly removing his hands, he folded his arms across his chest to keep from touching her again, scowling down at the back of her head. *What is it about this chick that makes me...what? Want? Feel?*

Making a good effort at ignoring the wall of muscles and leather looming behind her, Shar raised her eyes to meet DeeDee's in what looked like a definite plea, but Gunny didn't have the first clue about what. He hoped DeeDee had been paying attention, because he had questions of his own since the girl had used a name they hadn't known about.

"So, tell me. Shar Elkins becomes Sharon Spencer, how?" DeeDee's opening gambit made the girl recoil, even as it reinforced his faith in her. DeeDee was a smart cookie, and given her and Hoss' distrust of what they knew about Shar, he knew she was intuitive enough to press on this tidbit.

"Elkins is my married name." The girl tossed her hair over her shoulder, wincing with the movement. The shift in stance exposed the side of her face, and he could better see the large, dark bruise covering her temple and spreading across her cheek. *It would take a hell of a hit to leave that mark*, he thought, feeling his arms tensing with building anger.

"Is Spencer your maiden name then? Or from a different marriage?" DeeDee's question was quietly stated, and Gunny nearly shouted with frustration because he didn't give a fuck about names after all. He was struggling to stay silent, knowing he should let the women keep talking, give Shar a chance to say what she had come in to say, to explain what she needed to communicate. But, on top of the pain in her stance and on her face, there was a frightened undercurrent of emotions flooding the room, and he needed to understand what was going on right the fuck now. Someone had put their hands on her, and now she was trying to leave a place she should know was safe. *Why? She dances through her fear, is this what she dreaded seeing in the crowd? Is this what she's been running from? What waited in the shadows for her?*

"It's my maiden name. Missus Moser, I wanted...I'm sorry. I thought I needed to tell you face-to-face I can't work here after all." As she spoke, some of the composure bled out of Sharon's face, a miserable, defeated look settling there in its place. She was giving up something she wanted a fuck of a lot, because of whoever had hurt her. *Fuck if I'll let her do that*, he thought. *She deserves more.*

Because DeeDee was watching the girl so closely, he knew she almost overlooked the instant he realized what he was seeing through Shar's clothing was bruising—not a tattoo and not shadows. As if he would have missed seeing and noting the location of a tattoo given his scrutiny of her at every opportunity. This was brutal bruising, she was marked all to fuck and back. And, when he looked closer at her back, he recognized the whirls of dark color across the top of her shirt was not ink in the material. Dark, saturated sweeps of fabric, it was wet with the blood trickling down from her hairline.

DeeDee nearly missed the moment he grasped the extent of the damage...the nature of the injuries on Sharon's body. But, she didn't, and her study of his reactions was intense but discrete. Without knowing exactly what it was, she still knew something disastrous was happening. He could read the concern in her gaze and felt the already deep frown on his face deepening even more. The muscles across his shoulders tightened again, and the leather of his cut creaked audibly in the room.

"Shar, you came to me for the job; it was not something I pressured you into. You auditioned and then pestered me for days to make a decision. Sure made it seem like something you wanted. It's all on you, and I certainly won't try to force you to stay. If you want to quit, then you are free to leave, but with no reference. I'd like to think you owe me an explanation, though. I want to understand why you're leaving, after all the energy you poured into getting this job." Sitting quietly, she waited for the girl to talk to her.

"I just…I just can't work here is all—" Tears choked her voice as she began, and then Gunny spoke, interrupting her. *Enough with the pussyfooting around*, he thought, the fury inside him demanding to know who had laid hands on his girl.

"Who hit you, girl?" His voice came out in a rumbling growl he didn't remember ever using before, but the bruises and blood he saw, paired with the fear in her face and posture, was torturing him. "Who fucking *hit* you?"

Shar recoiled at his first words, turning her face away to avoid a blow which would never land, not in this office, and under no circumstances from him. "What? No! No one hit me." Ducking her head to avoid their eyes, the look on her face told them she knew her actions didn't support her words. Gunny took a step forward, crowding up behind the girl without touching her. He topped her height by nearly a foot, her head barely reaching as high as his chin.

"I felt you flinch, both at my hand on your arm and on your back. Your hair don't hide shit. You took a hell of a hit to the face, and from where I'm standing, I can see the bruising on your back through your goddamned, fucking shirt, girl. You also got blood in your hair, making itself known. So, don't you try to tell me nothing's happened to you. Don't you fucking *lie* to me." He leaned in, standing so close to her, still without daring to touch her again. "Who. Hit. You? A customer?" *I'll kill the motherfucker*, he thought, impatiently waiting for her response.

"No! No, not a customer. They're...nice. Not a customer. But he...I can't...he won't let me work here." Her chin quivered, and then he watched as Shar set her teeth into her bottom lip, eyes closed, holding onto her composure with the most tenuous of grips.

DeeDee lifted her gaze, clearing her throat to pull his attention to her, meeting his stare over Shar's shoulder, and he nodded, correctly reading that she wanted a few minutes alone with the girl. It was fine with him, but he needed to remind DeeDee they wouldn't have privacy, not really, because he would hear every word. *Thank God for Myron and his toys*, he thought.

"DeeDee, I'm going to step outside, but I ain't going anywhere. I want to *hear* the truth." He saw her nod, and without another word, turned on his heel and left the room, but settled his bulk against the door, effectively blocking the entrance. Doing so made the unspoken statement to them both that no one would enter or leave the room without going through him first.

Through his earpiece came the scrape of a chair, and he knew DeeDee had stood and was probably walking towards Shar...Sharon.

He remembered nights lying on a corn shuck mattress stretched across a woven rope bed, hearing the groan of the floorboards as his granny walked, pacing back and forth through the darkness inside their small shotgun house. Her Bible in one hand, and a closely shuttered hurricane lantern in the other, she would read for hours, carefully flipping pages with one thumb, mouth moving almost soundlessly as she recited verses. Her favorites were in the book of Solomon. Solomon's love songs, she called them, written about a bride and groom. Rose of Sharon, the Lily of the Valley.

Rose of Sharon.

The couch cushions creaked and he closed his eyes, using the darkness to picture them seated side-by-side. In his mind, he saw DeeDee settling the two of them on it, leaning back and snuggling the girl into her side, head on her shoulder. Without speaking, she would gently stroke Sharon's hair, maybe sigh when the tension began to leave the girl's muscles bit-by-bit as she relaxed into the comforting embrace. He was anxious, because it seemed to take a long fucking time, but he finally heard DeeDee's voice, asking in a quiet tone, "Boyfriend or husband?"

She let the question hang in the air for long minutes without any accompanying words, seemingly content to wait and carefully not pressure the girl. Sharon's voice broke the silence, saying, "Husband. Ex-husband, actually." She gasped with pain, and he imagined she had moved, and winced at the thought of the injuries needed to pull that sound from her mouth. Her voice quavered when she said, "I thought I'd gotten clear."

Behold thou art fair, my love: behold, thou art fair; thou hast doves' eyes.

"How did he find you?" DeeDee's voice was still calm, but he heard the steel threading through it and knew she was as pissed as he was.

"I don't know. I've been flying under the radar, using cash for motels and a friend's card for the rental. I ditched...everything. Years ago, I cut ties with everything." Her voice dropped to a whisper. "But there he was, standing outside my room at the motel, ready to express his intense displeasure at having to locate me, his unhappiness at having to endure years of my absence, as well as his disappointment in my current career choices." His hands clenched and released when she choked back a sob, repeating, "I thought I'd gotten clear."

I sleep, but my heart waketh: it is the voice of my beloved that knocketh, saying Open to me.

"Where is he now?" This was a good question, and he clenched his fists again, waiting for the answer, hoping the motherfucker was near so he could explain how you never, ever raise your hand to a fucking woman.

"In a truck outside. He has all my stuff in his camper, cleaned out my motel room of everything. He found all my money too, eh?" Her voice hitched. Motherfucker was outside the building right now, waiting for a woman who was never going to make her way back to his side. It made Gunny sick to think how closely this had skirted the edges of disaster. Sick to think that if he hadn't said something, if DeeDee hadn't been paying attention, the bastard's self-confidence would have played out, the night ending with Sharon climbing back into the seat beside the fucker who had done this to her, because she didn't think she had any other choice.

Rose of Sharon.

"Let's take a look at you, see what we've got here, okay?" He heard movement, shifting on the couch, and then the quick draw of a pained breath. DeeDee's voice was soft and filled with dismay when she said, "Oh, baby. I'm so sorry. This has to hurt you like crazy. Let me call Goose; he can help us out." He shook his head at the immediate and negative noise from the girl, but before he could move, DeeDee was telling her, "He's safe. He's the club's EMT, okay? Totally safe, sweetheart. Now, I'm going to step outside and call Goose, and then I'm going to talk to Gunny for a minute. You trust Gunny, right?"

He held his breath until Sharon softly responded, "Yeah. I trust him. He's...yeah."

My beloved.

DeeDee said, "There you go. Between Gunny and me, we'll sort this all out. That's our job. Your job is to stay right here, okay? You're safe here, baby. Safe as toads." She repeated even more softly, reassuring the girl, emphasizing each word as she said, "You are safe here."

There was more movement, and then DeeDee said, "I'll be right back, honey." She repeated Hoss' words from earlier, and they were as true now as then, "We've got you. You're one of us, part of our family. No worries, sweetheart, we've got you."

My heart waketh.

Tapping on the door, she waited for him to open it from outside, catching his gaze and shaking her head, holding a finger to her lips for silence. He tried to look around her, but couldn't see Sharon...his Rose of Sharon. He reluctantly trailed her when she stepped out and closed the door then motioned for him to follow her over to the bar. Her gaze swept the room and she crooked a finger at a couple of members who had looked up, noticing the activity. She waited for the three men to cluster around her before speaking.

She reiterated what he had already heard, but the look on her face gave her words greater gravity. "Shar's been beaten. Badly. The man's name is Elkins, and he's in the parking lot in a truck with a camper. I'm not sure if it's a pull-behind or a topper, but he's got her property and money. He's an ex, and I'm thinking he didn't like the ex part of being ex. She is fucked up bad." She paused, taking a moment to breathe. "Really bad. I'm going to call Goose. Right now, she's running on adrenaline alone, and is about to crash hard."

As she spoke, Gunny's focus narrowed until only one thing mattered, finding this motherfucker and dealing with him in a way that would make it clear Sharon wasn't his concern any longer. Muscles jerking, he was enraged and as near to out of control as he had ever been from anger. Breaking from her when a soft sob sounded through the earpiece, he swung fast to look at the office door, feeling a smothering of his senses simply knowing there was a barrier between him and Sharon. Without looking away from the door, he spoke to DeeDee, needing clarification before he went hunting outside, asking her in a hard tone, "Exactly how fucked up?"

85

Guardedly, she said, "I...I think he worked her over with a club, as well as his hands. Every inch of that girl's skin has been used hard. There is nowhere on her back I could find that isn't tore up. That's as far as I got, Gunny. But, by the way she's moving," she paused and took a breath, "I suspect we'll find more...and worse. Plus, she didn't say it, but you can tell it's been going on a while. She's scarred all to hell and back. It's been going on a fucking long while. I get the whole 'no nudity' thing now." She paused again when he ground out a savage noise, which even to his ears sounded suspiciously feral.

"Gunny, do you think you can get her stuff from him? I'm going to take her home with me; she and I can meet Goose there. When she's better, it will be good for her to have her own stuff, if we can." She was always respectful, and never presumed to tell the members what their roles were, but seemed on board with his expectation that the club would deal with Elkins. Right now. Today.

He nodded and said, "Go ahead and call Goose, but don't move her until I come back inside. I don't want you coming out in mid-conversation." He looked around the bar and whistled, calling additional members to his side. Looking down at DeeDee, he wordlessly tipped his head, directing her back towards the office, and she nodded, turning to walk back in and wait.

***

Sharon rested on the couch, absorbing a feeling of safety, along with warmth and comfort from the blanket DeeDee used to cover her. She scoffed at herself, because she hadn't been this safe and cared for since...forever, and wasn't it ironic it only came after yet another horrific beating?

DeeDee had come back to the office and now sat beside her, hand softly stroking from hip to thigh and back again. The calmness emanating from her helped smother the fear that had driven Sharon all day, snuffing the panic out like fire deprived of oxygen. She had called the EMT, and then left a message for her boyfriend, making it clear Sharon would be staying with them. Now, together, they waited in silence for Gunny's return. Sharon found herself dozing, shivering and jerking herself awake dozens of times, gaze darting around the room in renewed fear each time, slowly calming when she recognized DeeDee sitting nearby.

Finally, there was a tap at the door and Gunny stuck his head in, nodding at DeeDee as Sharon picked up her head slightly, feeling woozy at the motion. DeeDee stood, reaching out to help her off the couch. "Let's go, Shar. You're going to stay with me for a few days. Here we go, sweetheart. Come on, baby, let me help you up."

Her muscles had stiffened from inactivity and were now trying to hold onto that stillness with a throbbing grip, so, gritting her teeth, she brought her arms up to lever her torso off the couch. She groaned softly as pain washed over her, and at her involuntary noise, the door swung open wide. Startled, she looked up as Gunny paused in the doorway for a moment before taking the two strides to the couch. Wrapping her in the blanket, he gently picked her up, freezing when she hissed at the movement. "Relax into me, girl," he muttered, the words rumbling in his chest. "I got you."

When he approached her now, as it had earlier, the fear lodged inside her swelled as it always did just because he was male, but far stronger than alarm was a sense of coming home. Held in his arms, she was peaceful, because she would never have to fear, not while in his presence. He would protect her, would never hurt her. She felt no panic, because with him, she was safe.

He carried her out to a van parked behind the bar and then folded into the back, settling down onto the seat with her still cradled in his arms. The supportive pressure from his arms wrapped around her was comforting, and against his bulk, she felt nearly childlike, as if she were a youth who had fallen asleep riding home in the car and now would need to be carried to bed. She watched his face as he flicked a glance at

DeeDee, who had followed them outside, and listened as he grunted instructions to her. "Keys are over the visor; the boys will bring your scoot and her shit. Let's take our girl home, yeah?"

Safe, she thought. Then his words struck her and she wondered aloud, "Our girl?" Leaning her head against his shoulder, she took a deep breath and began relaxing, even as she sensed him stiffen in response.

***

Even though DeeDee drove slowly and carefully, the ride in the van was still painful, and Shar was glad when she saw the EMT waiting for them at the condo. Still carrying her, Gunny followed him down the hallway to a bedroom, with only a curt word of greeting. He put a knee to the mattress, turning on the bed before leaning his back against the headboard, cradling her in his arms and on his lap. Goose looked a challenge at him, and she felt him shake his head, responding in that vibrating rumble from between gritted teeth, "Can't set her down yet, man. Don't fucking ask me to try." She didn't understand what he meant, but in her exhaustion was glad he was willing to hold her a while yet.

Frowning, Goose shook his head, but settled one hip onto the edge of the bed, stilling as he looked at her, obviously running a visual assessment. He introduced himself, gently asking her name and some basic information before querying her directly, "Honey, you want this man gone while I look after you?"

She nearly panicked, fear tightening her muscles painfully as she thought, *Oh, God. What if he won't stay? If he wants to leave me alone?* Then she experienced the reassuring rumble from his chest as Gunny growled at the man who had dared suggest he go away. He quieted when she shook her head, slowly relaxing, and she didn't care they could all see the way her hands were curling into the shirt underneath his leather vest. How she was molding herself into him. He felt like her lifeline.

*   *   *

With every additional inch of abused flesh exposed, he knew the strength of the enraged vibe from him intensified until the air was thick with the promise of violence. Sharon shuddered constantly, unending waves of spasms rolling down the muscles of her body. Goose lifted his head, surveying Gunny's face. They all heard the concern in his voice as he spoke soothingly to the girl while locking eyes over her head with his brother, telling him quietly, "Reel it in, Gun. Come on, man, shut it down. Sit on your shit. I don't know what's going on here, but you are not helping her like this."

Gunny didn't know why he was reacting the way he was either, but he nodded, trying to tamp down the fury threatening to swamp him as he looked at the damage done to Sharon's body. Elkins had done a number on her. There were few places on her torso that weren't bruised or bruising, the range in color giving their private audience of three a glimpse of her horror, knowing her ex must have kept after her for hours.

There was a concentration of marks over her flanks, and she nodded when Goose asked her about blood in her urine. About halfway through the exam, he finally gave her a shot of something for pain, and Gunny sensed her muscles easing, loosening as she fell asleep, her head resting on his chest, having somehow snuggled her way underneath his leather vest.

He watched as smears of red stained the gauze Goose used to clean her, the feelings of helplessness and sickness validated when he caught Goose's eyes and saw shock had taken up residence there. Finally—*thank God*—Goose was done, and DeeDee wrapped a clean sheet around the girl as best she could with Gunny's arms and body in the way, but he still couldn't put her down. Not yet.

DeeDee was staring into Gunny's face as she leaned close, and he bore the weight of her appraisal as his eyelids slid closed. He drew a deep breath, relaxing a little now that the ordeal was over and Goose had moved away. But, he knew she had seen the tension every time the EMT's hands touched Shar's skin, how he helplessly ground his teeth when Goose delved between her legs to catalog and repair the damage there.

For the first time in a long time, he was afraid she looked at him as an outsider would, seeing not the man she had grown to know and love, the man who had been friends with her husband...with her, but the man the rest of the world saw, and judged. He was afraid now, after today, that she couldn't help but see only the outer wrapping, his visible persona. Tall, he was nearly six-foot-five, and held himself so rigidly he appeared nearly as wide. Not soft, he was all hard bones wrapped in strong muscle, and he was big, imposing...frightening, maybe. He knew his face was broad and craggy; his nose broken more than once, each fracture leaving footprints behind in bumps and twists. No stranger to fights, he bore more than one scar, his shaved head hiding nothing from view.

Gently placing her hand on his thigh, she whispered, "Why don't you lay her down, son? Rest beside her if you need to, but let her stretch out a little."

He tensed under her hand, and without opening his eyes, he first nodded, but then sighed and slowly shook his head, admitting the truth. "Don't think I can, DeeDee. Don't want to wake her, and I can't let her go."

Goose spoke from the other side of the bed, the hardness in his voice pulling Gunny's eyes open. "She won't wake up, man. I dosed her good. She needs rest—real rest. There're no bones broken; the bastard saw to that, at least, but she's dealing with a lot of trauma over large areas of her body. I've stitched everything that needed it, but I'm pretty sure she's got renal contusions on both sides, especially since she saw blood in her piss, and that ain't anything I can treat, man.

"I'm not entirely convinced she doesn't have a concussion, but at least it looks like his surprise attack was the only one to her head. Line all that up with the banded bruising, vicious bite marks, vaginal and anal tearing and scarring, and...*Jesus, God,* he fucked her up. We both know what she really needs is a fucking hospital, but barring that as an option, she at least needs a fuckton of rest to heal. You stay with her if you want, as long as she'll have you...but, brother, she asks you to leave, you'll fucking leave, man. No argument, okay? This woman's been through plenty as it is, and doesn't need to worry about, or fear, pissing you off, too. Gunny, you have to know this isn't the first time someone's been at her, so this shit's going to be hard enough for her to deal with. Let her rest, man. Lay her down for a bit."

Recognizing the reason in their arguments, moving slowly, Gunny lifted her off his lap and swung his arms, settling her onto the mattress by his side. She groaned in her sleep, and he froze until she quieted, then sat up on the edge of the bed, toeing off his boots. He stood and took off his cut, draping it over the back of a chair, and then reached to unfasten his belt, eyes flicking to DeeDee when she made an involuntary noise. Seeing the look of disbelief on her face cut through him like a knife and he felt a desolate pain run through his chest. Now certain he had lost her hard-earned trust, he answered the unspoken question with a flash of anger as he ripped the belt from his waist and threw it on the floor. "Not gonna fuck her, goddammit. I just don't want the buckle to hurt her. My honor, woman. *Goddamn.* What kind of fucking animal you think I am, DeeDee?"

Without waiting for her answer, pulling his shirt over his head he turned to Goose, the two men motionless as they exchanged a look. What had gone down in the parking lot earlier wasn't nearly enough payment for what the man had done to Sharon. *My Rose of Sharon.* Elkins needed to be put to ground, and he wanted to make sure Goose was on board. Coldly, he said, "You call Deke for me. Tell him find this ass again. Blood for blood, it's the right thing, man. She's ours—*mine.* Tell him I want…need him to pick up that trash and hold it for me, yeah?" Goose nodded and they shared another look, which said they were on the same page with this decision.

Goose turned to leave the room, and DeeDee hovered close by as he carefully settled in next to the girl while still wearing his jeans. "Get the fuck out," he said without looking up, and after a moment, the door closed quietly. He took a breath, and then another, knowing they were finally alone. He pulled the comforter over them both as he rolled her to his side, wondering, *What the fuck am I supposed to do now?*

***

Less than an hour later, the door opened and DeeDee stepped back inside, a stiff piece of paper in her hands. She held it in front of her, and he watched as her eyes moved from the paper to the face of the woman in his arms then back again. He waited her out, knowing she would have a good reason to be back in here so soon after he kicked her out. She did the same comparing thing several times, looking back and forth until he finally heard her sigh. "Sharon Spencer," she said, moving towards the bed and sitting on the edge. She reached out a hand to push the hair back from Sharon's face, and he made a noise, feeling his face twist as she paused.

"I know you're not going to hurt her, Lane, and neither am I." Using his given name intentionally, she made the statement soft and sure and waited; finally, he nodded, giving permission of a sort. Weaving her fingers through Sharon's hair, she frowned as they snagged in the blood matted there. "Jase Spencer," she said and cut her gaze up at him as she handed over the paper. A jolt of emotion and denial flashed through him as he caught her meaning, inferring the relationship as gently as she could. *No, she isn't Jase's; she's mine,* he thought, and then caught himself again. She wasn't his; she was one of the dancers from Slinky's. She belonged to the club. Regardless of where his thoughts ran, he was only helping her. That's all. All it could be.

He saw a flash of tawny desert, noted the give of sand gritting under the soles of his combat boots, saw Kincade falling forward, surprise and pain on his face. He heard him say, "Let it go, brother. You can't help everyone, but you can save her. You couldn't help me, but you can help her, your Rose."

That was all this was; all it could be. Him helping her.

Holding up the picture where he could see it, his eyes glanced across the image, cataloging the similarities between the girl captured in an awkward high school moment and the woman he held. Without question, they were the same person, and he flicked his gaze at DeeDee. He tossed the picture towards her, snarling, "What the fuck you want me to do, woman?" Sharon groaned softly and he relaxed his arm, realizing he had tightened it around her.

"Jase wants to see her." She was looking down at her fingers, still working through the matted hair, separating strands gently, working through to the scalp. "He hasn't seen her since she was a teenager, when he left to play hockey overseas."

"Brother?" He didn't know why he felt the need to clarify the relationship between his woman and DeeDee's man, but he wanted it spelled out. Then he realized where his thoughts had gone again and he shook himself mentally, reminding himself, *She is not mine.*

"Yeah, she's his baby sister, youngest of the family." He watched as she trailed the backs of her fingers across Sharon's cheek, gently caressing her, fingertips tracing the arcs and curves of the bruising visible on the girl's skin. "He's only talked about her a little. I always got the impression it was a painful topic."

"Send the motherfucker in," he said, shifting Sharon slightly, moving her away and out from underneath DeeDee's fingers, settling her against him, even as he stared a challenge at the woman who had become like a mother to him. *I am so fucked up*, he thought, watching the door close before his gaze dropped back to Sharon's face, dipping his lips to trail across her cheek, wiping away DeeDee's touches with his own.

***

It was with mixed emotions that Gunny watched Jase crawl up into the bed with him and Sharon. He moved cautiously, seemingly as afraid of the biker as he was of disturbing his sister's sleep. He had muttered a pet name from across the room, but hadn't spoken since. He was staring at her as if she was the most precious thing he had ever seen, and the tightness in Gunny's chest eased a notch. A sick look flashed across Jase's features when he took in the vivid bruising on the side of her face, and Gunny said, "If that shit turns your stomach, you sure don't want to look at the rest of her, man."

Jase shook his head, settling a little deeper into the mattress, his focus on his sister, so he missed the scowl Gunny shot his way. "How bad is it?" he asked quietly.

He looked at Jase for a minute, and then decided to lay it all out there. He had some hard questions for him later, and if he could shake him up a little now, he might get honest responses a bit easier. "Bad. Real bad." He took a breath. "Bad enough Goose doped her like a fucking racehorse so she would pass right the fuck out."

Watching closely, he saw the dismay on Jase's features, an emotion real enough it would have been hard to fake. Jase asked, "DeeDee tell you she's my sis?"

This was the opening he had been hoping for, hoping the man would bring up their relationship so he could figure out what had happened to this woman he was holding. He needed Jase to understand there was something here between… He halted his thoughts, scowling at himself. What was wrong with him? *Fuck*, he thought, *focus on the woman.* "You and I are going to have words about that, man. What kind of man doesn't protect his fucking sister from shit like this?"

Jase looked at him for the first time, and slowly nodded as he explained. "It's hard to protect her when I can't find her." As Gunny relaxed, he reached out to touch Sharon for the first time. He knew he was glowering as his gaze chased the progress of Jase's fingers on her skin. The man had continued speaking, but Gunny didn't hear anything, could only track the movement his fingers made, memorizing the paths for later, until Jase said something about hiring investigators to find her.

"You hired folks?" he interrupted the flow of Jase's words, taking the opportunity to move her towards him in the bed. They were plastered, one against the other, his chest tight against her side, but as long as the other man could get his hands on her, they wouldn't be close enough. Gunny frowned, his brain going a dozen different directions, but they all seemed arrow-straight right to her being with him. He felt her breath against his skin, the brush of the air teasingly warm and soft.

The doorknob rattled in the frame and he jerked his eyes open, hadn't even realized he closed them, trying to feel every nuance that was Sharon. Movement caught his attention nearby, and he saw with dismay that Jase was openly touching her face now, cupping the side of her head in his hand, stroking across the bruise on her forehead with his thumb.

Fuck, he thought again, bringing his eyes back up to DeeDee. *There are too many people in the goddamn fucking room.* No fucking way he could keep her safe with so many bodies crowding around. He felt his nostrils flare, heard the bones in his jaw creak as he clenched his teeth. She fucking asked about food, and all he could do was nod. There was no way he could squeeze words past his lips with so many damn people in the room.

DeeDee left, and at least he could breathe again, anxiously shifting about in the bed. He asked, "How much do you know about what she's been doing?" Maybe Jase would have some insight into her recent history, give them something they could use to sweep her fucking ex back to the clubhouse to have a 'come to Jesus' conversation, but he disclosed their family hadn't heard from her regularly for years.

Gunny tensed when Jase referred to the ex as the 'love of her life,' because any motherfucker who could do this to a woman didn't deserve to keep breathing, much less hold a title like that. When her brother moved closer, placing his head on the pillow inches from Sharon's face, his muscles bunched and twisted in unspoken protest. The only thing holding him still was the love the man had for his sister. It was there, plain as day. You could see all the pain he had been through, wondering for years if she was alive or dead, and now his cautious joy at her being here...finally within reach. He also recognized the tightly controlled anger about the condition she was in now. Like himself, it seemed Jase wouldn't be taking the abuse of his sister quietly, not if what he saw on the man's face was truth. Knowing there was deep love and loyalty for the woman somehow made it easier for him to talk.

It seemed almost like a confession as he opened his mouth and said, "Elkins was the name of the man who fucked her up, yeah. We had a discussion with the man, but that was before I saw how bad shit was for her. Boys are picking him back up; they'll hold him for me to deal with." He sighed and shifted again, tightening his arm around her. "He fucking beat her everywhere it would be hidden by clothes. Not the first time she's endured this level of abuse, either. She's got fucking scars all over her goddamned body.

"She walked into Slinky's to talk to DeeDee with her head high though, and didn't want to cop to the shit either. Had to convince her to unload. She's one tough fucking bitch, man." Jase turned to look up at him, the awkwardness of their positions having faded somewhat. Gunny kept his focus on Sharon as he collected himself and drew a shaky breath then looked up at Jase.

"Took care of that piece of shit and got her stuff back. Got her money back. Went inside to tell 'em we could leave, and she's hurt so fucking bad she can't even sit up, man. I picked her up and she latched onto me. Grabbed ahold of me as if I was a fucking life jacket, like I was saving her. Wrapped her fingers around my shirt and wouldn't let go." He took a deep breath, "Latched on like I was the last knot in her rope." He experienced a renewed sense of awe at the memory. Her trust in him was still overwhelming, because for a woman...for her to have been so hard-used, and then turn around and find comfort in a man's arms...in his arms, was incredible.

He looked up at Jase, seeing his gaze stuck on Sharon's face. "I held her in the van and she cried with every bump, but she wouldn't let go. Got here, she still wouldn't let go, and you know what? I didn't want her to. By the time we got in here, I was the one holding on, the one that couldn't let go. Couldn't put her down. Made Goose triage her in my lap, man. Couldn't let go. Been holding her for hours, and still can't let go.

"I don't know what the fuck's wrong with me. I laid her down like I knew she needed to be, and I couldn't breathe. Couldn't fucking breathe until I was touching her again. He fucked her up, Jase. Seeing her laid out like that for Goose to do his thing about made me sick. All I can think of is watching her walk into the club with her chin in the air, trying to convince us that everything was o-fucking-kay, when she's beat to shit and back. So fucking strong." His throat tightened, choking off his words, and he tipped his head down, resting his forehead against hers until she moved restlessly. He watched as she fought her eyelids open, knew the moment when she saw Jase for the first time, felt the drawing anger of jealousy when she spoke to Jase, love evident in her tone.

Then, she blew him away when she angled her neck, looking up at him with the same love he heard in her voice. She looked at him, her face soft, expression open and trusting, and he felt his lips move, curving up into a smile when she told him how she felt. "Safe."

Her hand tangled in the covers as she was trying to bring it out from underneath, her movements made difficult by the sedative Goose had given her. When he got her free, she reached up trustingly, lovingly, touching his face, and he held his breath as she pressed her palm against his cheek, saying simply, "Thank you." Closing her eyes again, she snuggled against his chest, pulling her hand down to tuck it beneath her head. Barely audible, she murmured, "Ace and Gunny. Safe."

9. Sleep, baby

Gunny laid on his back next to Sharon, still in the guest bedroom of DeeDee's condo. He had only turned loose of her twice through the night, once to relieve himself in the adjoining bathroom, and once to get the pain pills Goose had left for her. Even though he told Jase he needed to sleep, it was just to get the asshat out of the room. He knew the fucker was his girl's brother, but it chapped his ass to see him touching her, even as gentle as he was. He nearly growled at the man a couple of times, and then decided running him out was the best thing for both of them. With as out of control as he was feeling, it was the safest thing, for Jase.

Sharon twisted in his arms several times through the night, trying to wake from dreams that threatened to pull her into darkness. Each time, he put his lips next to her ear and sang her back to sweet, drawing her out of the nightmares and back with him, easing her down into calm, restful sleep with his voice. Something he had wished for himself many times through his life.

From what she said in the office at the club, he knew she had been running for a while, the constant fear of exposure and discovery weighing her down every day. Looking over her shoulder no matter how safe the refuge, watching for her demons to appear in the flesh. So even without the injuries sustained from the beating, he knew she had to be exhausted to the bone, needing the solace of a deep, sound sleep. Naked, having discarded his jeans for comfort sometime during the night, he twisted in the bed, rolling up onto one hip, maintaining the full-body contact he had with the girl. Stroking a hand up her arm, gently touching her, fingertips barely brushing her skin, he watched as they raised a wave of goose bumps in their wake, and then soothed them with a pass of his palm.

She shuddered and jerked in fear again, tilting her head to look up at him, eyes slowly focusing on his face, and her body gradually relaxed. Through the hours, each time she had done this, she recognized him as someone safe—sometimes remembering his name right away, and sometimes not—but always knowing she was safe with him. Even with his battered face, she hadn't been afraid of him, not even once. This time, she knew him, saying his name with something like surprise in her tone, "Gunny."

He nodded, taking a deep breath to push down the lust and heat caused by hearing his name roll off her tongue. "Sleep, babe. I got you." He shifted, sliding his arm out from under her head, but he froze when she jerked, her eyes going wide with terror, fingers clutching at the sheet.

"Don't leave me. Don't leave," she panted in quick, tiny bursts of sound, panicked. "Don't leave me. You'll leave me. Don't. Need you. He'll get me. Don't. Don't leave. Don't go—"

"Shhhh," he interrupted, speaking over the top of her words, halting the pain-filled flow. "No, babe. I'm not leaving, merely trying to make you more comfortable. Shhhh. But, now that you're up, we need to hit the head. Time to check how things are," he spoke calmly, and she seemed to take comfort in his low, rumbling tone, her hand lifting uncertainly to touch his face.

"Not leaving?" she asked in a small voice, and he shook his head, hating having been the cause of her fear. He shivered when she touched him, surprised once again at the strength of the connection between them.

"Not leaving," he tried to reassure her, and then said, "Come here, babe." He reached to turn her over slowly, pausing for a moment when she scrunched up her face in pain. "Keep going, baby. Just a little more. On your back, all the way over," he urged, sliding his arms under her knees and shoulders, leaving the twisted sheet behind to rise from the bed with her naked in his arms.

Walking to the bathroom, he toed the door open and carried her in, seating her on the toilet. Kneeling next to her, he wrapped his arms around her and waited, steadying and letting her lean into him while she cleaned up. "It hurts, Gunny," she whimpered, whispering.

"I know, baby," he whispered back, "but there's less blood every time you piss, which is good. We'll get you healed up in no time, back on your feet. In the meantime, I got you, babe. Won't let you go." His voice deepened, "Not leaving you."

She draped one arm around his neck as he carried her back to bed. Propping her in his lap, he shook a pill from the envelope and put it in her mouth, lifting a bottle of water to her lips, murmuring encouragement and praise in an unceasing stream of words and endearments. Tucking her into bed, he leaned down and kissed her forehead. "I'm stepping out for a minute, baby, but you aren't alone. Never be alone again. I'm right here, all right?"

Her gaze warily tracked him as he walked across the room, so he left the bathroom door open, letting her keep him in view. "I'm right here," he called, hearing her noise of assent.

Walking back towards the bed, he saw she had struggled up onto one elbow, straining to hold her head upright so she could see him. "Babe," he scolded, sliding into bed behind her. There was no missing the sigh, the tension released when he slipped his arms around her and pulled her to his chest. "I got you," he murmured into her ear.

Laying his head on the pillow behind hers, he pressed his lips to the skin right behind her ear, picking up where he left off earlier, choosing a low-pitched Chet Faker song, *I'm Into You*. Seamlessly shifting between humming and singing the lyrics softly, he held her as she dropped back into a healing sleep.

Hearing the doorknob move a few hours later, he opened his eyes to see DeeDee looking around the doorframe. *Go the fuck away*, he thought. She clearly didn't have mindreading talents, because instead of going away, she walked into the room, seating herself on a corner of the bed.

Whispering, she asked, "How's she doing?"

He stared at her, scowling but not answering. *Go away.*

"Gunny, you don't scare me," she scoffed, rolling her eyes at him. *Goddammit, she rolled her eyes. No fucking respect. Trust, but no respect.* He snorted. *I'll take it, I guess. Woman matters to me more than she knows. Guess I'll have to overlook the eye roll.*

"Better hope you don't fucking wake her up," he gritted out in a barely audible voice, and bugged his eyes at DeeDee when Sharon shifted against him, her breath becoming uneven.

"You want food, Mr. Big Time Bad Guy?" She whisper-laughed, grinning and looking over at the supplies stacked on the nightstand. "I'll bring in another couple bottles of water. You want me to make you something to eat?"

He gave her a single shake of his head, watching until she left the room, shutting the door behind her. Closing his eyes, he nestled his cheek against the top of Sharon's head, shifting his legs and feeling her ass push back against him. Lips to her ear again, he sang Faker's haunting melody, voicing the hypnotic words to the song, her sleep deepening as she relaxed trustingly into him. He laughed silently. *If she only knew how hard it was for me to be still, only using my voice to caress her.*

The next few days passed in much the same fashion. Her brother and DeeDee wandered in and out, and Goose stopped by and pronounced himself pleased with her progress. Word finally came from Deke that Elkins was enjoying club hospitality, awaiting the pleasure of Gunny's presence in one of the holding rooms at the clubhouse. He knew he would have to deal with the fucking scumbag eventually, but fuck him if he would worry about Elkins yet. Motherfucker could drink his own piss and starve in that small, cold room, as far as he was concerned.

Sharon's alertness increased, but he was thankful her level of comfort with him remained much as it had been from the beginning. He had watched her since she started working for DeeDee, but the first time he let himself touch her was escorting her into that office, hand on her arm, then her back, and finally having her in his arms. Now, he couldn't let her go.

***

Safe. As she drifted in and out of consciousness, that was the one word that continued to resonate in her mind. Rising from the muddled confusion caused by the pain pills, she gradually became aware of her surroundings, but without fear, because *safe* was the first thought that filled her awareness.

Even before the strong arms registered, before she felt the hand palming her breast or the hard planes of a man's muscular chest at her back, she thought *safe*. She believed *safe*. Then the memories crashed in—*opening her door to find Derek standing there, the feel of his hand crushing her throat as he choked her, seeing his other hand fly up into view with a short baton clenched in his fist.*

She jerked, and then came a man's deep voice, tenderly saying, "Shhhh, babe. I got you."

Safe. That was not Derek's voice whispering to her. Not Derek's lips so near her ear she could feel the puffs of air as he spoke. *Red Rover, Red Rover, let Sharon come over*, she thought childishly, then wanted to laugh at the ridiculousness of her idea of safety. She thought she had gotten clear of Derek and his insanity, thought she was safe from his need to control every aspect of her and her life. *Against all odds, there he had been, his punishing hands reaching out to shove her, forcing her to stumble backwards into the room she had rented for two weeks with the bright hope that her new job would work out.*

More memories flooded her, snapshotted moments of the hours he trapped her in that room. *With his favorite toys. With his fists. With him. She knew from experience if she didn't provoke him, he would leave her face unmarked. He didn't like the questioning looks they received when he forgot himself and left visible evidence of his brutality.*

"I got you," the man's voice spoke again, and she jolted, startled, because she had become so lost in her memories she misplaced the knowledge she wasn't alone, even with his heat wrapped around her.

She felt a naked thigh between her legs, bristly hair scratching and rubbing at her skin. There was what seemed like an enormous erection pressing against her ass, and as soon as that presence registered, all thoughts of safety fled and she moved, fighting and twisting in an effort to get away. Her movements woke the pain which had tricked her, because it had been waiting oh-so patiently on the fringes of her consciousness, playing possum, as she herself had done so many times. Tensing and trying to use her muscles allowed it to roar in, freezing her in place and releasing a deep groan from her throat. The arms wrapped around her tightened, cradling her into his torso, holding her against him.

She could feel individual areas of agony now, the last numbing vestiges of pain medication receding in the face of the misery flooding in, laying claim to her nerve endings. She wanted the numbness back, tried to hold onto it, but it was slippery, and shifted away, hiding from her.

Olly olly oxen free!

All across her chest and between her breasts hurt, as did her back. The back was easy to figure; her kidneys had frequently been the focused targets of his attention, because the reminders of discipline lasted so much longer there. For every day she pissed blood, she would remember the lesson an extra week or more. *Mother may I?* she thought, and a manic giggle escaped her lips, along with another moan of pain.

"Baby, be still. I got you," the voice said again, lips placing an open-mouthed kiss on the side of her head.

Her sternum was not commonly an object of attention, but he had tortured her this way before, so she knew at some point during those terrible hours, Derek must have knelt on her upper body, using his weight to starve her of oxygen. When things first went bad, the early days of their deteriorating relationship, sometimes he would choke her until she passed out, but as things progressed, that could leave bruises on her neck and people wouldn't pay as much for access to his...content. It was never about sex for Derek, power was his currency of choice and in the end, he had ruled over much of her existence. It had crept up on her, his need to control things, and she remembered wondering one day how it had become her life. They had gone from her thinking it was sweet that he ordered food for her, to her sitting shackled to the floor of a studio so fast it made her head spin to think of it even now.

Nauseous, she remembered him chatting with his sick, online fuck-buddies during one session, and chortling with glee when he found a better solution for air deprivation. By kneeling on her, pressing her into the floor, he could transfer more and more of his mass to her torso, compressing her ribcage until she could no longer take in enough air to support consciousness...or life.

But, I am alive. How? Part of her simply wanted to float, forgetting everything, but her traitorous thoughts kept trying to drag her mind into awareness. *Just keep forgetting.* Her body was shaking, vibrating. When she concentrated on the noises in the room, she realized it wasn't her body trembling, but the one wrapped around her. The man was humming a song. She lay on her left side, with him curved around her, his left bicep under her head, elbow bent to bring his arm across her front, hand cupping her right shoulder, pinning her against his chest. His right arm crossed her waist, wrist curling up between her breasts, his hand covering one soft mound, his thumb idly caressing her nipple.

He was a furnace, the welcome heat of his body pressing against her back working better than a heating pad to ease the pain behind her kidneys. His belly was tight against her lower back and ass, and his muscles clenched when she tipped her hips experimentally, testing the soreness of her muscles. The presence of his erection registered again, the humming abruptly cutting off as he thrust his cock up between the globes of her ass and held, his coarse pubic hair grinding into her skin, along with his pelvis, fingers stiffening around her breast, molding it to his palm. Her nipples tightened and peaked, and she shivered as, even with the pain threatening to swallow her whole, she discerned a clenching low in her body, the stirring of a craving she thought long lost.

"Sharon, babe. I've been holding you for four goddamn days. Need you to keep your sweet fucking ass still." This was a growled command, his chin pressing into her shoulder, the side of his face against her neck. "Baby, I've got you."

"Safe," she whispered into the stillness following his words, amazed at the security she found in his arms, even with their positions.

Sanctuary while vulnerable, naked, with proof of his arousal pressing against her. *Safe.*

"Yeah, babe. You're safe. I'm right here. Not going anywhere." He shifted on the bed, hands releasing their hold on her body, and he slid his arm from underneath her head, pulling it back so she rested on his forearm. Eyes still closed, she reached a hand up, cupping her fingers around his wrist, sliding until she could twine her fingers with his. Licking her lips, she twisted her head slightly, softly kissing the inside of his arm, exploring that almost-foreign feeling.

"Fucking hell, baby. Hold the fuck still." He was growling again, and she smiled, her lips moving against his skin as he tightened his arms around her once more. *Safe.*

She dozed, and more memories inundated her.

Derek pulling her purse out of her hands, taking the car keys and stripping money from her wallet. Questioning her, using his baton on her thighs, the crack of wood on flesh echoing loudly. He threw clothes at her, shouting at her to get dressed as he swept around the motel room, gathering her things, shoving them into bags and boxes. She shuddered with remembered pain when, with her mind's eye, she watched his hands rising and falling on her body again, because she moved too slowly. Then he was pushing her into the camper on the back of his truck, the lock snapping noisily into place on the outside of the door.

Wincing at a light blooming in front of her closed lids, she turned her face into the warm arm, for a moment able to relish the feel of a gentle hand slowly stroking up and down her side, hip to shoulder, again and again, before the vortex of memories pulled her back down.

Derek dragging her from the camper with a hand in her hair, feeling the sharp pain as her scalp tore, blood trailing lazily across her skin, watching as he flicked a thick hank of hair to the pavement, seeing the gobbet of flesh still attached to the roots. "You said you have money in your locker, so get the fuck in there and get it, bitch." That voice was wholly Derek and she pulled in a harsh breath, holding it against the anticipation of pain as remembered blows landed on her back.

Stepping into the club, she immediately saw Gunny standing against the wall, knew his eyes were on her. She always knew when he was in the room; it seemed as if the air were electrically charged whenever he was near her. Since she first walked into the place, he watched her, stared at her like he was the big bad wolf and he was ready to eat her right up. His grins were a little too toothy to be comfortably viewed, but his voice stroked her like a caress, always...a fierce desire for him lodging deep in her belly with every word he spoke. She knew she had to stay away from him, push down her interest...longing. Leaving the refuge of Vanna's, striking out, this whole trip was about proving to herself she could make it on her own, not scratching an itch with a convenient and oh-so-attractive man.

Turning her back on him, she was nearly to DeeDee's office, nearly safe, when she sensed Derek's presence at her back. She knew his hard hand was reaching out to grab her and she swung around quickly, terror bubbling in her already raw throat, ready to scream for help until she saw it wasn't the monster at all, the outstretched arm belonging to Gunny. She saw a flash of pity cross his face as he looked at her, and couldn't imagine what he was seeing, what she had to look like in her instant of panic. She schooled herself from crying years ago, knowing that particular response only served to enrage Derek further, but the look of disappointment on Gunny's face effortlessly drew her tears to the surface now. Then he touched her, and the gentle way he held her made her feel...safe.

Arguing her way into DeeDee's office, she knew she wouldn't be able to stand talking about Derek with Gunny in the room, but he wouldn't leave. He wouldn't go away, and in despair, she was already resigning herself to the inevitable when he spoke up, demanding answers for the evidence he could see written on her skin. Not exactly certain how it happened, a few minutes later, she found herself lying on the couch, covered with a blanket. Then he burst back into the room, his long legs effortlessly eating the distance between them. He lifted her, holding her still and steady, the pain caused by his grip offset by the knowledge that he had her. She was safe.

Someone examined her. The competent, emotionless hands working around where Gunny's arms still had her wrapped up, bands of steel holding her against him. Safe.

She realized his arms still held her even now and she cracked her eyelids open, tilting her head upwards slightly, blinking as she looked into his eyes. "Gunny," she whispered, hoping she wasn't dreaming.

"Yeah, babe. I'm here." She experienced his words as much as heard them, the rumble of his voice transferring through his chest to her body.

Eyes easing closed, she struggled to hold onto the fraying filaments of memory that would lead her to today, the point where she currently was, naked, lying in a bed, held tightly in the arms of an also naked man who she desired. Taking in a startled breath, she licked her lips, following the tattered string of a memory to a familiar voice, eyes much like her own. "Ace," she whispered.

"Why do you call him that, baby?" Another rumble, followed by a laugh. "Smiling sure looks good on you." She hadn't even realized her lips had moved, but she *was* smiling at the memories evoked by his question, couldn't deny it.

"I'm younger, by several years." Her voice sounded unused, rasping and scratchy. She swallowed painfully then continued, "Apparently, he's been Jase to the folks since before he was born, but then I came along and couldn't make the 'jay' sound, so for me, he's always been Ace." Something brushed her mouth and she opened her eyes again, squinting against the light. He was holding a straw to her lips and she drew it in, sucking thirstily, sputtering and swallowing when cool water hit her mouth. She paused for a minute to croak out, "He's really here?"

"Yeah, baby. This is his and DeeDee's guest bedroom." He must have felt her stiffen, because he made a soothing noise, rubbing his cheek against her shoulder, the stubble rasping gently. "You're safe, baby. Shhhh."

Jase and DeeDee. That was a shock, because while she hadn't been home to see who he brought around, every chance she could, she followed his career. This included saving pictures of him in his suit or tuxedo at award ceremonies and events, seeing him on the red carpet with beautiful women on his arm. Never the same woman, but they were definitely a type. Tall, pretty...and young. DeeDee was tall enough, and beautiful, with her red hair down to her butt, but one thing she wasn't was young. If Sharon had to guess, she would put the age difference between them at maybe twenty years or so. Examining her thoughts and feelings, she decided she didn't care one whit about something as trivial as age difference. She liked DeeDee for her brother; the woman was smart, cute, and confident, much like her friend Savannah. *Savannah.*

"Vanna," she gasped, jerking and groaning. "I need to call her, warn her. He saw the papers on the car. He'll find her. Know she helped me. I have to call."

"Covered, babe," he whispered. "Shhhh. We got it all covered. Contacted her, and she's covered... protected by a club out of Atlanta. But, I need you to know that motherfucker is contained, baby. He's waiting for me to unwrap myself from around you so I can go deal with him. Ain't gonna be now, but he'll be mine eventually. Your gal Vanna is safe. Shhhh."

Closing her eyes, she let her head slip sideways, resting the side of her face against Gunny's muscular forearm. Sighing, she evaluated the pain in her body, feeling mostly aches, but few sharp pains now. "How long?" She shifted, twisting her torso to take painful pressure off her breastbone. He turned with her, pulling her onto her back, and her eyes flew wide open as he got to his knees and effortlessly scooped her into his arms. "Wait," she squawked and felt the rumble of his laughter.

"Hittin' the head, baby," he said as she looked down at her body suspended against his chest. Dark bruises scattered across her chest and upper arms, with even deeper colors on her hips and thighs, showing the heavier damage that tissue had taken from Derek's focused attention. "Just four days, Sharon. A ways to go before you're healed up, baby."

"Is he happy?" God, she was tired. Her head leaned on his shoulder of its own accord, but her nose nuzzling into his neck was entirely voluntary. *He smells good,* she thought, and wondering, darted her tongue out, licking a wet trail across his collarbone, and he stopped moving, taking in a deep breath.

His tone was stern, brooking no argument when he said, "Babe. No."

Chastened, she bowed her head against his chest, her hair falling around her face in curtains, hiding her flaming cheeks from his gaze. "Sorry," she whispered as he resumed his stalk across the room. "I can walk, Gunny." She twisted in his arms. "Put me down." More twisting, futile it seemed, because he didn't put her down.

"Not a fucking chance, woman," he growled, pushing the bathroom door open with one hip. As he settled her on the toilet, she knew from the casual way he steadied her this wasn't the first time he performed this duty, and her face flamed again. "Stop it, Sharon." His voice was gruff when he said, "I got you. Nothing to it, baby." He went to one knee beside her, allowing her to rest against his side as he wrapped an arm over her chest, curving it underneath her arm and around her back. Naked and confident, he was unconcernedly comfortable in his own skin, and she risked a glance to find her estimation of his...size...had been somewhat conservative. The heat of his skin pressed against her felt good, and she was surprised to find his nudity wasn't intimidating. He just...was.

God, so tender down there...I'm so sore, she thought as she carefully cleaned up. Averting her face, she nodded when he asked if she was ready. As they had before, memories rose, threatening to swamp her with emotions, and she wasn't even aware she was crying as he carried her back to the bed. He laid her down, pulling the covers up before he cupped her face in his big palm, his gaze sweeping her face searchingly for a minute before he shook his head slowly, hand falling to his side as he walked away. She covered her face with her hands to keep from watching the play of muscles across his back and ass as he moved across the room. If he didn't want her mouth on him, she needed to shut this feeling down, and watching him wasn't going to help in those efforts.

She jolted awake, feeling the bed shift and sway, and she whimpered in alarm and pain as she moved to escape, clambering ineffectually across the mattress until an arm circled her waist, holding her in place. "Babe, it's only me. I got you."

She sighed as she recognized Gunny's voice, relaxing into his hold once again. A few breaths later, she tensed, remembering her unanswered question. "Is he happy?"

"Who, Jase? Yeah, he and DeeDee are a good match. They had it rocky for a while, but he talked her around to his way of thinking." His voice was still rumbling in his chest and the vibration triggered another memory, this one much nicer than the others she had been suffering through since waking.

"You were singing to me." She shifted, twisting her head to look up at his face, hearing the wonder in her own voice. "I don't know the song, but it was nice."

"Kept you from twitching around, hurting yourself worse. And there's that damn smile again, Sharon. Rose of Sharon. You look good wearing that." There was amusement in his voice and she closed her eyes, rocking her head to lay her cheek against his chest with a sigh. "Woman, are you tryin' to kill me?" He moved and his hand left her belly, going to his crotch, and she realized she once again had been feeling an erection poking her hip.

"I'm sorry," she whispered, pressing her lips into a tight line, hating the feeling of rejection threatening to push away the safe.

"Don't be sorry, baby. I'm not one to hurt women in bed, unless it's pleasurable pain. My cock has other ideas, but the little bastard can just deflate on his own." His hand came back to her belly, fingertips trailing across her skin, caressing hipbone to hipbone, back and forth slowly, and the tightening in her core flared again. *Surely he wouldn't touch me like this if he didn't want me*, she thought.

He continued talking, and the import of his words hit her like a blow. "Elkins had at you with something, baby. No fucking way will anyone touch you again until you want it, until you ask for it. My honor, Sharon. Goose said you didn't need stitches there, but it was a near thing, 'cause the motherfucker tore you up, baby, pussy and asshole. That's why you can't put your mouth on me, because I want to fuck you and can't. And that's why your sighs and touches are torture, because I'm going to have you. I will have you...just not right now."

His words reassured, even as they bit deep into the wall holding back her memories, and she jerked, her mind showing Derek's face hovering over her.

Features twisted in fury and sadistic craving, she could see his shoulder moving, shaking as his arm swung again and again. Lying on the floor, her body lurched against the drag of the carpet with each shift of his limb. Her eyes fluttered closed and she felt a hard blow to her face, jarring her alert. "Fucking feel this, bitch," he snarled into her face, spittle flying from his lips. He brought up his hand again, showing her the blood covering it before he wiped it across her breasts.

"His baton," she breathed, twisting her neck to bury her face in the pillow in shame. Voice muffled, she wasn't sure he'd hear her words.

"He always used the baton...never anything else. It's not the first time. I'll heal."

The rumble didn't scare her this time when it came against her back. "Yeah, baby. You'll heal." He sounded angry, but she knew it wasn't directed at her. "Last time you'll ever feel his goddamned touch, Sharon. He's never going to hurt you again. You have my promise, babe. On my honor."

"Safe," she agreed, lifting her hands to cup around his wrist where it crossed her belly. "Gunny."

"Yeah, babe. You're safe with me. Never have to worry about that shit-heel again." She was drifting back to sleep when his breath stirred the hair on the side of her head, his mouth so close to her ear she heard the rasp of his tongue against his lips. "I got you."

***

A roar split the air, ripping her from sleep, and Sharon moved instinctively, frantically rolling off the bed to wedge herself between the frame and the wall, cowering and hiding there in terror. Loud words followed, but they were muffled by the walls, and she could only hear fragments of the conversation. She couldn't be sure, but thought the identity of the person shouting was Gunny. Not certain enough to risk exposing herself, she remained where she was, scarcely breathing, making no sound. The uproar and noise were approaching the room she was in, and gradually, she could begin to make out what was being said.

"...fuck do you mean..." There was a pause, then she caught, "...fucking kidding..." The doorknob rattled as it turned. "...excuse for a prospect..." The door opened, and *his* voice filled the room, "...no fucking way am I going to let this go, Sla—" The words cut off mid-syllable, and the energy in the room became dense and tense, the air thick with menace. "*Fuck.* She's gone, man. Hang on."

She only realized it was Gunny, wasn't *him*, when he called her name, "Sharon?" Panic still had her frozen in place, and she couldn't seem to make her body obey to respond. He moved away, probably headed to the bathroom. "Baby, where are you?" There was a tension in his soft voice she hadn't heard before, and the sound of his distress broke the hold the fear had on her. She shifted, sliding her torso painfully along the wall, working her way into a sitting position. He strode out of the bathroom, phone pressed to the side of his face, and stopped when he saw her. "Got her," he said brusquely, bringing his hand down and tossing the phone onto the dresser.

She watched the big man standing in the middle of the room. He was motionless except for restless hands clenching into fists, and even from her position, she could see the tight coiling of his every muscle. Danger radiated off him like a miasma, but his voice was intentionally gentle when he spoke to her. "Baby, whatcha doin' on the floor? It's okay. Let me make it okay, yeah? I got you."

She nodded at him, breath coming painfully fast as he slowly walked across the room towards her. "Come on, baby. I got you." He had said the phrase so frequently over the past few days that when uttered in his voice, the words had become synonymous with safety, and the now familiar sounds reassured her, as was his intent. As she slowly relaxed, she saw that with every moment, every step towards her, his tension lessened too. She reached up a hand, but instead of taking it, he gripped her underneath her arms, smoothly lifting her out of the small space and back onto the bed as she groaned.

"Did you fall off the bed, baby?" He settled onto the edge of the mattress next to her legs, leaning forward with his arms propped on either side of her waist.

She shook her head, trying to control her breathing, his hazel eyes piercing her and holding her still. "Got scared," she offered, and he flinched.

"Of me?" he asked, teeth clenched tightly, lips twisted in pain, and she shook her head again, but could see he didn't believe her.

"I was just startled when I woke up." She closed her eyes, biting the inside of her cheek, wanting to make this right. *I'm not afraid of him.* "Sorry I scared you, big guy. I didn't mean to hide from you."

He lifted a hand and she eagerly pressed her cheek into his palm, drawing a ghost of a smile to his lips as she felt him begin to relax. "I know, baby. I was loud, yeah?"

She nodded, making a face, asking, "Is everything okay?"

"Nope, not even close. But, it will be. We got brothers on the problem. Elkins clocked a prospect on the head and pulled a ghost. He's in the wind right now, but he sticks his head out of his rat hole and we will have his ass. I got you, Sharon. You are safe with me, okay?" His unflinchingly matter-of-fact tone as he gave her the update was more reassuring than if he tried to sugarcoat it, and she nodded. *Safe with him*, she thought in agreement.

"All right, then," he said, shifting to lie on the bed beside her. The fabric of his jeans was soft against her skin, but she found herself begrudging even that small separation from him. Then, his arm circled her waist, turning her onto her side and tugging her back into his chest, his hand casually cupping her breast, scorching heat from his touch causing a hitch in her breathing. "I got you. Sleep, baby."

***

She sat on the edge of the bed, slowly raising and lowering her legs, mentally counting off the repeats of the motion. Goose wanted her to take it easy for another few days, but Sharon was ready to get off her butt and work her way back to being healthy. Eyes closed, she was focused on completing each phase of the controlled movement smoothly, and missed the noise that generally accompanied a visitor to Jase and DeeDee's home. So, when a discreet cough came from the doorway, it startled her and she jerked her head up, feeling her eyes open wide and barely stopping herself from rolling backwards across the bed.

"Sorry, gal." This gruff declaration came from a tall biker standing in the doorway. With a shiver, she remembered a recent incident in Kentucky, but then pushed down her fear. If this man was here, this close to her, it meant Gunny had allowed it, and so, by process of deduction, she was in no danger from—she squinted, reading the name patch on the front of his leather vest—Deke. "Didn't mean to scare you." He continued speaking, but hadn't moved, and was still taking up the entire width of the doorway.

She nodded and waited. If he was here to see her, he would let her know why, she was sure. "I'm Deke," he said, and she nodded again. "Friend of Gunny's."

That was interesting, because up to this point, no one had claimed friendship with the big man. Goose and Jase both seemed to respect him, but neither had seemed close to him. DeeDee was different, because she mothered everyone around her, so her patient and caring attitude didn't count.

"I'm only here to see how you're doing," he said and moved slightly. She wasn't even aware she had reacted, rising to her feet, until he put out both hands, palms down. "I'm not going to hurt you," he said in a low, calming tone, and she nodded at him again.

Stepping backwards, she found the chair at the back of her knees and lifted a foot to the seat, wedging herself into the corner, bending her knees and bringing her feet to the cushion. She wrapped her arms around her knees, cupping her palms around her elbows, keeping her eyes on Deke. When she heard Gunny's rumbling voice from out in the condo, she relaxed minutely, and Deke smiled at her. "Yeah, he ain't too far, gal. But, I wanted to talk to you for a minute."

Time to enter the conversation, she thought and took a breath. "I'm Sharon," she said, and he nodded. "Are you in the motorcycle club with Gunny?" He nodded again, taking a measured step into the room, and she motioned to the bed with a tilt of her head. Moving slowly, as if he were afraid she would bolt if he startled her again, he moved to the bed and sat on the edge, nearly in the exact place she had been a few seconds ago.

"Yeah," he said. "I'm the one who recruited him. Been his boss for more years than I care to count at this point, too." He trained his gaze on her and she suddenly felt exposed, as if this man could see far more than she wanted him to, just by looking at her. Pinned in place, she shrugged and he laughed. "You don't talk much, do you?"

"Depends," she said, and when he looked down at the tips of his boots, she took a deep breath. "You're his friend?"

"Yeah," he said quickly, his gaze rising to her face again, but less intense this time. "He's a good man."

She felt the corners of her mouth curl up, and he accepted the smile as a natural expression, returning it with one of his own as she replied, "Yeah, he really is."

"Don't mean he doesn't have his fair share of issues." He shook his head, looking back down. "But you're doing okay, right?"

She nodded, feeling the subtext of the conversation was narrowly out of reach. There was something he was trying to say without speaking the words, but she couldn't hold onto the edges of the feeling long enough to figure out what it was, so she waited. He continued, "I mean, you're okay with Gunny, right?"

Puzzled, because this entire conversation seemed odd, she nodded again, and then said, "Yes, I'm okay with Gunny. He's been patient with me, good to me."

Deke wrinkled up his nose and huffed out a breath, apparently as frustrated at her answers as she was with his questions. "You going with him tomorrow?"

She tightened her arms around her legs and shivered, because he was talking about the non-conversation she had with Gunny yesterday.

"Getting a cage tomorrow, taking you home," he said, stepping *between her knees where she sat on the bathroom countertop.*

Startled, she looked up into his face, a sudden fear spearing her chest, precursor to panic. "A cage?" *Wincing when her voice squeaked, she frowned when he laughed at her.*

"A van. Not a cage, baby. I'd never" —his voice dropped in tone, *becoming husky and tight—* "you never have to think I'd try and control you like that." *He stared intently at her.* "But taking you home, that part is truth spoken."

"Taking me back to the motel?" She ducked her head, suddenly remembering that Derek took her money, so she knew she wouldn't have enough to rent the room again. Plus, she hadn't been able to work for days, so she didn't have any money coming in, either. She didn't know where the rental car or any of her stuff was. Even the tee she was wearing right now wasn't hers, it belonged to Gunny. Her things. None of it had even crossed her mind, because she felt—

There was a tight feeling in her throat, the panic building, it was as if she couldn't breathe deeply enough. Time to wake up, chickie. He's bored with the nursemaid routine, *she thought, feeling a shiver shake her body.*

His hands rested on her thighs, and he slipped them up and over her hips, splaying his big palms across her back under the shirt, one low and one high, pressing her body into his. "Baby," *he scolded gently, and she shivered again.* "Taking you* home." *He placed subtle emphasis on the last word, and she shook her head.*

"I don't understand," she whispered.

He rested his cheek on top of her head. "What's to understand?"

"I don't know where you're...the motel... Why can't I stay here?" She knew the sob was coming and cut it off, ruthlessly forcing it down, taking small sips of air as she waited for his response.

"Because I want you in my home, baby. I can't keep having folks take care of my pups, so I need to go home. But I want you with me." He said this simply, as if it made all the sense in the world, when she was still scrambling to understand.

"You want me to stay at your house?" 'Move in with you' had been on the tip of her tongue, but, still panicky, she had stalled that part of the question at least, replacing it with the less needy words.

"Want you to move in with me, yeah." He kissed the side of her head, chuckling at her gasp. "What's so hard, baby?" He moved, leaning backwards and looking down at her. Upon seeing her expression, the one on his face changed, hardening and growing distant, impassive. "Unless I've read things wrong, Sharon. Motherfucker twisted every good thing, I know from what you've told me. This thing between us is fast, and I know that, too. So, baby, it would kill me, but you need space, you got it; all I can give you...anything. Every choice is yours, baby."

She smiled now, thinking of the look he wore when she stretched up to brush his lips with her own. Like a kid in a candy store, his grin had been immediate, broad and joyous. Now, sitting in the room she had shared with him for days, she answered Deke's question in a clear voice, not wanting any misunderstanding, because she thought she knew why he was here. "Yes. I'm going with him tomorrow. He asked, and it's what I want. But, I promise you; I'm not going to take advantage of your friend, Deke. I'll only be there as long as he wants me. When he's done with me, I'll...I'll go away, won't bother him."

Standing, Deke stretched his back and looked down at her. "Got that bit wrong, little one. It ain't Gunny I'm worried about getting tired of the arrangement. He gets pretty…intense." Reaching into an inside pocket on his vest, he pulled out a card and handed it to her. She flipped it over between her fingers, reading the name Grant Williamson. There was a phone number, and when she looked up at him, he nodded. "Yeap, that's me. If you need me, Sharon, I want you to call me. Day or night, if you or Gunny need me, you pick up the phone and call. He's my friend, and my brother, which means if you are his, then you're mine, too. I got you, little one. You need me, I got you."

Amazing how reassuring the phrase had become to her. When Gunny spoke it, she believed down to the tips of her toes it was true. Now, hearing the same words from his self-proclaimed friend, her belief morphed into trust. Deke was a man she could trust.

He turned and walked out as she sat there looking down at the card. In a moment, she sensed the presence in the room that she had come to depend on, and looked up to find Gunny leaning in the doorway. If she thought Deke had taken up most of the room in the opening, she was wrong, because Gunny took up all of it, his shoulders stretching nearly from edge to edge.

"He get his words out finally?" He asked this with a grin, and she knew he had been waiting impatiently for Deke to leave.

She nodded and flashed the card at him, frowning when the smile fell from his face. He nodded and sighed, then said, "Keep the card, baby. Use it if you need to." Walking across the room, he leaned down and scooped her up out of the chair, turning and settling them onto the bed. "Napping is the order of business right now. Goose said you need rest." Kissing the top of her head, he told her, "Sleep."

***

Safe. Four letters, but a depth of meaning beyond those vowels and consonants that was hard to describe, she thought, then shook her head. Standing in the doorway to his bedroom, she glanced down the stairs to the rest of the house, trying to put her finger on what made this feel more comfortable than the bedroom she had been sleeping in for the past few days, and couldn't. *My head hurts*, she thought, lifting one hand to rub her fingertips across her forehead. Even though she hadn't had to lift a finger today, she was still exhausted from the move.

Snorting at her oh-whine-is-me attitude, she twisted to look at the sum of her possessions—a pleasant surprise Gunny presented her with today—her purse with the money retrieved from Derek, and three not-large boxes lining the bedroom floor beside Gunny's closet door. He hadn't made a big deal out of it, but when she asked about the guest bedroom on the main floor, he simply shook his head and said, "No, baby, you're in mine."

As he had the last time they traveled in a vehicle together, Gunny held her in his lap the whole way here, in a van driven by one of the Rebel Wayfarers members. He had cradled her to his chest while he talked about Slinky's with the driver, his hands ceaselessly stroking and soothing her. Being out in the open after being closed up in the condo for so long made her nervous, and she had found herself looking anxiously around the neighborhood. Logically...intellectually, she knew looking for Derek wasn't reasonable, but since he hadn't yet been found, she couldn't help herself.

She wandered back down the stairs and out to the living room, listening closely and pulling to a stop when she realized she couldn't hear Gunny, but she did hear birds. Turning her head, she isolated the direction and walked across the room, pulling back a section of floor-to-ceiling curtains to see a large, groomed backyard complete with a grill and patio. With a smile, she worked the latch on the sliding door and walked outside.

She took a breath, and then another, realizing she wasn't nearly as nervous here as she had been standing in the driveway outside Jase's condo, because this area was surrounded and protected by a tall fence.

And, because this place, everything she could see, all of it normal, ordinary, and sane...was Gunny's. Tilting her head up, she closed her eyes and let the sun bathe her features, the warmth sinking into her and allowing her to relax a little bit more. *Safe.*

***

He hung up the phone with Goose and stood in the kitchen, looking out the opened door into his backyard, staring at Sharon. So fucking beautiful, she was standing in the middle of the patio, hands cupping her elbows protectively. But her face was lifted to the sun, and even from here, he could see a small smile stretching her lips. As he watched, he could swear he saw her shoulders inch lower, see the muscles in her back uncoiling and relaxing.

In the van, she had been tight and tense, holding herself stiff as a board. She hadn't given anything of herself. Even when he kissed her temple, she hadn't leaned into him, hadn't sought any comfort. He tried to keep the focus off her, but he had seen PBJ carefully watching her in the rearview mirror.

He knew some of his brothers were worried because of his behavior, worried and comparing it to his past episodes, but this wasn't like anything he ever experienced before. He simply had to know...needed to know she was okay, needed that to breathe. And sometimes, when he thought he saw pieces of his own fear and terror in her eyes, he wanted her to know she wasn't alone, would never be alone again.

He had tried to be okay with Deke talking to her yesterday, giving them all the privacy he could manage, barely able to stay in the kitchen until Deke walked out. He was obsessed, sure. He would admit that in a heartbeat, but this was different. What he had in his heart for Sharon was so much more than anything he had before...even Wardah looking bland in comparison. *Wardah,* he thought, and the scene before his eyes changed.

Sand underfoot, coating everything in a fine layer of grit, his keffiyeh covering his mouth and nose to try to filter out the powder drifting in the air. The first time he saw her was when he walked with his team to the house their interpreter shared with two other families, she had been seated in the corner of the main room with the rest of the women. Dressed conservatively, the colored veil covering her hair made her dark skin look even more exotic.

Eklund had finished his conversation with their contact, and Robinson walked out of the building alongside his team, never expecting to see the woman again. But, she had been there the next time they visited, and then again the time after that.

At the time, it had seemed nearly too good to be true to find her waiting for him one night, standing at the checkpoint by the gate, and now he knew it had been. Night after night, until he was entirely wrapped up in her. In her eyes, she had sacrificed her body to gain information on her enemy. He knew, as infatuated as he was with her mysterious beauty, he had been too easy to give it up, indulgently answering her questions while lying beside her, thinking she was only trying to get to know him better.

"Stupid," he hissed, and saw Sharon move. *Oh, fuck. Did she hear me? Did she think—* His thoughts stuttered to a halt and he smiled, because his pups had found her. He frowned, watching her move slowly and painfully, squatting down to pet them, and he hated the hurt she still suffered, the discomfort revealed in her movements. Her hands stroked over the dogs, rubbing and patting them, effortlessly calming Tank, who was easily excited, and soothing Rocky, the nervous one.

She turned and caught sight of him, and he smiled back at her, because the joy on her face was completely pure. "These are your pups, huh?" She called the question and the dogs looked up at her, tails slowing as they recognized they had momentarily lost her attention. "What are their names?"

Walking to the doorway, he looked out at her, seeing her hands still moving over the dogs, giving each equal attention. "Short stuff is Rocky; he's a rat terrier." The dogs laughed up at him, mouths open with good humor. "The whirlwind there is Tank; he's my beagle."

Sharon laughed, and the dogs' heads swung back to her, apparently as taken by her as he was. "He's your bagel? That's hilarious." Pursing her lips, she glanced down at the dogs, cooing, "Who's a good bagel? Hmmm?"

Gunny squatted next to her, and then settled onto the patio, feeling the heat of the cement under his ass and legs. "Beagle, not bagel."

"I like your accent. It's cute...you're cute. But, my way is more fun," she teased, head down, looking at the dogs.

"Yeah," he said, reaching out a hand to stroke her back from the nape of her neck to her waist, and then back up. "It sure is." Her finding humor in anything, even his southern accent, made him want to give her more of whatever it was that made her laugh. Even if her thinking him cute were absurd, he would give her that, any day.

"They are adorable," she said softly, rounding her shoulders and leaning into the pressure from his hand. "Mmmmm," she hummed, fingers slowing but still touching the dogs. "That feels amazing."

"You need a massage, baby?" He twisted, putting himself behind her and resting his other hand on her shoulder.

"God, that would feel so good," she murmured, and he could tell her eyes were closed because of the tilt of her head. She was taking in the sun's rays on her face again, and he smiled.

"Come on, then." He climbed to his feet then reached down and plucked her from the awkward squat she was maintaining. Carrying her up to the bedroom, he laid her face down on the bed, climbing up beside her and then straddling her ass, placing one thigh on either side of her.

He read the anxiety in her body as she twisted her neck to look back at him, so he was ready for her questioning tone when she started talking. "Um. Gunny? Goose said...um, still..."

"Sharon," he scolded, "I know, baby. I just got off the phone with him. This ain't me demanding anything from you. I ain't fucking you. We've done had this conversation. You don't have to worry about me pushing you. We ain't going there, not until he clears you, and even then not until you're ready. And if you ain't ever ready, baby...I'll still count myself lucky to have this much of you." He pushed her shirt up and winced in sympathy when she reached over her head to gather the fabric up, hearing her groan as she tugged it off with his assistance. Stroking slowly up her back, he gently used the heels of his hands and his thumbs to find the knots and sore spots, cataloging the colors still marring her skin. "Count myself lucky," he repeated under his breath, feeling her relaxing under his ministrations. "Goddamned lucky."

10. Under my skin

Standing at his post inside the front door, opposite the bar, Gunny surveyed the patrons of the strip club. His face impassive, he looked around and realized he counted no person in the room a friend. Some were his brothers, men he would gladly die for, but they were not friends. Not a one of them. He was fucking pissed off to be here and not in California, where he was needed, where his damn friends were. Leaning his shoulders and ass against the wall, he forced himself to present a calm, relaxed self-possession and casually crossed his legs at the ankle.

He knew why he had been left behind, but knowing he was trusted to keep things under control *here* did not ease the rub of not being *there* much. The office door to his right clicked and opened, and he shifted his gaze that way, seeing DeeDee standing in the doorway. "Did you hear anything yet?" she asked, and he shook his head, watching as she scrunched her face in response. "Do we know anything more than we did two hours ago?" He shook his head at this too, and she nodded, closing the door behind her as she went back into the office.

Pulling out his phone, he sent a quick text to Slate and waited on a response, sighing when he received a curt two-letter reply. Slate had also been prohibited from this trip, due to an entirely different reason, and for both of the men, knowing their friends were engaging enemies without being there to back them up was hard. Onstage, the acts were changing out, the two girls on the side stages sauntering backstage carrying their costumes in their hands. Slinky's didn't have a DJ or announcer during the day, but the next shift of dancers usually warranted the expense, and sure enough, Gunny heard the buzz and hum as the PA system clicked on.

The speakers popped loudly and then a smooth voice slipped through the room. "Good evening, gentlemen. We would like to welcome you to Slinky's, where your every desire is ours, too. We are very pleased to invite a beautiful lady back to our stages. Too long gone from view, she's here tonight for your yearning pleasure. I give you the stunning Sharmane." Loud pop music blared as Gunny went rigid at Sharon's stage name, jerking upright, his eyes locking on the center stage in disbelief. *What the fuck...*

He watched as Sharon strutted into view, her full lips curved into a smile, her gaze sweeping the area around the raised platform. *That's my woman. What the hell is she playing at?* The click of her stiletto fuck-me heels might be inaudible over the music, but there was no missing the seduction implied in the sway and pop of her hips as she worked the edges of the stage. His gaze traced her form down and then up, making that circuit twice in the time it took her to circle the stage once, her carriage and the way she moved resonating with pure class. Slipping her shoes off, she lined them up near the edge of the platform, placing them neatly side-by-side before turning her back to the audience.

Most of the bruising from the beating had faded, and in the areas where he knew she still carried marks, it looked as if body makeup evened out the flaws. Tonight, her movements were fluid, the smoothness at odds with the jerking, flinching woman he had held such a short time ago. Lying in bed last night, his hands had moved over her shoulders and back, gently tracing the outline of the remaining bruises. He hated she still carried marks from Elkins on her skin, and resting there beside her, he had to work hard to make certain the tension of knowing the motherfucker was still breathing her air never made it through his fingers and onto her. He shuddered now, thinking, *She doesn't need that. Not last night, not ever.*

The sheer dress she wore floated around her as she twirled in the space between the end of the stage and the pole. Her face lifted to the ceiling, and his mind went back to the first time he saw her in his backyard, recognizing the pose. He saw she was looking up at the stained tiles above her head as if they held the sun, with its warmth drawing her onto her tiptoes, arms spread wide. Spinning slowly to a stop, she dipped sideways and rested one hand on the pole, eyes closed, touching it tenderly with the backs of her fingers and hand, as if she were reintroducing herself to the feel of a lover. *God, I fucking love it when she touches* me *like that.* Swaying in harmony with the music, her face broke into a smile when she leaned close, nuzzling one cheek against the pole, saying hello to a favored friend. *That is* my *smile.*

Arms out, as if playing airplanes with a child, she ran swooping and twirling around the pole, spiraling closer and closer with each circuit until she was standing tall, face-to-face with it. Whirling to place her back to the pole, her head tipped back, her cheek again stroking along the metal.

His mouth drew tight on a silent groan, watching as her eyes snapped open, looking at *him*. His breath caught in his chest as he took in her eyes, the look on her face. *She's dancing for me.* A sultry smile crossed her face while her chin tilted down, eyes inviting all viewers in on a secret, making each person a participant in her performance. *Dancing only for me.* Elegantly stretching one hand over her head, she used the other to grasp the hem of her dress, pulling it up and off in one movement, abandoning it near her shoes, and his shout of panic stopped in his throat. Undressed, but still covered in nearly nude shorts and a sports bra, she looked completely accessible, but was fully shielded from the men's eyes. *That is* my *body, goddammit.*

One hand on the pole, she danced in a curving arc around it, winding around and gaining momentum until she reached up, her hand clasping and lifting herself off the floor, her upper body strength allowing her to pull up the bar, hand over hand. Still twirling around the pole, she flipped sideways, pushing her leg around the pole and locked it into place with her arm, spinning slowly towards the floor. It looked as if she were drifting downward, nothing holding her up but the air beneath her.

Pausing the descent mid-pole, she continued her spin, moving slowly and gracefully from position to position, legs twisting around the pole, and then spread wide as she whirled. Hands and feet vied for position; she angled her body to gain or lose speed on her spin, maintaining the impression of effortlessness. *Fuck me, she's become my obsession. I can't wait to be buried deep inside her.*

With a start, he shifted his gaze around the room, realizing he had been staring at Sharon since she came on stage. Looking around at the other men in the room, he understood every man who was the same way, fucking mesmerized. He felt his cut shift and realized he had tightened his shoulders, was clenching his fists. Every one of those motherfuckers was looking at his woman, wanting to fuck her, and he was ready to take them all on. She was seducing the entire fucking audience, and still had her goddamn panties on. *That's my goddamn pussy.*

Gunny realized that damn smile had never left her face. *My fucking smile.*

She dismounted twice during the set, the first time climbing back up the pole upright, hand over hand. Her body swayed alongside the bar, as if it were a mast and she the sail in a high wind, flipping and fluttering as she willed. He watched without breathing as she set her arms wide on the bar, effortlessly looking like she was flying free as she whirled in space.

The second time she mounted the pole upside down, her bare soles looking somehow more intimate than any other part of her body as she flexed and pointed her feet, trapping the bar between them and then releasing it in natural, relaxed movements. He had never been possessive about a woman like he was with Sharon, and it had him feeling out of control, greedy, and mean. If any one of these motherfuckers tried to put a hand on her, he would lose his mind. *She's mine.*

From the way her head whipped around, turning back to him again and again, he knew she kept her eyes where she *believed* he would be, even if there was no way she could see him through the spotlights. His smile on her face. Dancing for him. *My woman.*

She spun faster then shifted to an upright position and pulled herself back up the pole, where she froze in a pose that looked as natural as breathing, simple to hold. He watched her slide slowly down, dismounting a final time to collapse gracefully into a pale puddle on the floor of the stage.

When the men in the room stood and applauded, he realized not one of them had thrown money on the stage during her performance, which was the highest compliment they could pay. So wrapped up were they in the illusion she wove on the pole, they forgot she was an erotic dancer for their pleasure, appreciating the beauty of her movement for what it was.

That didn't stop them from plying her with money now, however, and he felt a heavy scowl fix on his face as he watched her waltz around the stage, cocking a hip out for those motherfuckers to tuck money into the edge of her costume. He heard a desperate groaning sound and realized it came from him as he watched their goddamn fingers plucking at the elastic sides of her shorts. *So close to my pussy.* He could only watch as their dirty fucking hands glanced across her skin, saw her execute a twisting dance, moving away from men who wanted more than a sidelong touch. *Touching what is mine.*

Why the fuck had she done this? Without saying a goddamn thing to him, why had she gotten back on the stage right in front of him? Was it a statement, a question? *Does she think I can't take care of her? Think I won't want to take care of her? Is she getting off on letting men touch her for money when she is mine?*

Distracted, he nearly missed the buzz of a text. Pulling out his phone, he breathed a sigh of relief, some of the tension rolling off and away as he read the message from Mason: **Got them. Bringing everyone home alive.**

He had reached out a hand to knock on the office door when it flew open, DeeDee coming around the doorframe to meet him halfway, her phone in her hand. "They're alive," she breathed, and wrapped her arms around him tightly.

"Did you ever doubt Mason?" he joked, lifting his eyes to see Sharon frowning at him from the stage.

* * *

"So tell me again why you didn't go?" Sharon reached out and took a forkful of his potatoes, dipping them into the puddle of steak sauce on her plate before putting them in her mouth. Seated across from him in a booth at the Greek restaurant next to Slinky's, she watched him carefully as she chewed and then swallowed the bite of food. He shook his head, content to watch her until he saw a flash of uncertainty cross her face. She tried to strike a teasing tone, but failed, a hitch in her voice as she said, "Not gonna answer me tonight? Are you really that mad because I didn't tell you I was going to start back to work?"

Shit. I didn't mean for her to take my silence as punishment. Her working wasn't something they discussed beforehand, but there was no way for him to tell her no to *anything* she wanted to do, not after hearing how Elkins had governed her every action. "Might have been nice to have a fucking heads-up, baby." That was as close to a scolding as she would get from him, and even the gentle tone he used still made her flinch. *Fuck. If she needs me to be soft, I can do soft for her.* "Sharon, I ain't gonna tell you what to do, or not do. I might not like seeing their hands on you, but I can deal, baby. We're cool."

He rolled the tip of his tongue across his bottom lip. "And, to answer your other question, there were only so many people Bear could take with him to bring his woman home. I was needed here."

"But you'd rather have been there, where you could help out." Not a question, he treated it as the statement it was and ignored it, forking a big bite of chicken fried steak into his mouth. Frustrated, she frowned at him, curling her lip comically, and then broke into a smile when he grinned at her. She asked for reassurance, her fingers playing with the edge of her plate nervously, "We're really okay?"

Fucking hell, she's cute. "Yeah, baby. We're okay." He reached out a big hand to cover hers, completely engulfing it in his grasp. He never allowed himself to forget the differences in their size, or his strength against hers, always careful to handle her with care. Using his thumb to stroke the back of her hand, he tugged gently, seeking her attention. When she looked up questioningly, he said softly, "Your dance tonight. I watched you dance before, but this was different, more like your audition. I never have...where did you learn that?"

Grinning, she took a drink from her water then leaned back, retrieving her hand from his grip, and immediately, he missed the heat from her grasp. "I took lessons, eh? Smarty pants biker guy." Sticking her tongue out at him, she picked up her fork again.

"Not from a stripper, you didn't." He shook his head, certain in his response.

"No," she laughed, "from a dance instructor. I started taking lessons after—" She abruptly stopped speaking, and he saw a too-familiar dark cloud cross her face and knew it was a memory of Elkins that stole her voice. Physically shaking her head and forcing brightness into her tone, she swallowed, taking a deep breath and beginning again. *My woman is fucking brave.* "From a dance instructor. He taught it as an art form, as if it were any other interpretive dance that used a prop, like ribbons or a hoop. It was fun, and apparently I've got the form for it, being short and stubby."

"Petite," he corrected her, "and strong," happy to see her grin as he intended. He asked, "Did you dance anywhere before you came to Slinky's?"

Losing her smile to a frown, she used her fork to stir the vegetables on her plate, pushing them back and forth across the white expanse. He didn't like the look on her face and frowned. "Only one, a place down in Kentucky. I...I didn't do well there." She dropped her fork, reaching up to push her hair back away from her face, calmly stating, "I like Slinky's though. DeeDee is more than fair as a boss, and no one makes me take off anything I don't want to."

Pushing down the growl that wanted to escape his lips, he turned the intensity of his stare towards the cashier's station and forced his tone to sound unconcerned as he asked, "And at the place in Kentucky? What did they do?"

"Their customers expected nudity, but I didn't wanna. It was okay until this one night, when several local guys decided to try and enforce their demands, and there was only one bouncer on duty." Her face became impassive as she shut down, what he recognized as her response to remembering something painful. "Taking off my shorts and top was easier than seeing him get beaten up by a bunch of bikers." She ducked her head, the biker comment apparently slipping out. When he didn't react, she shrugged and said, "I didn't go back there to work again. Didn't even go back to gather up my things. It was easier to leave the few belongings in my locker and simply keep moving."

Still feigning casual, he leaned back, keeping his gaze firmly on the cashier, who had begun moving restlessly under his scrutiny. "I hear ya;

sometimes easier is better. What was the name of the place in Kentucky?"

"Most of the customers were actually okay. Some were even funny. The nice bikers kept asking me if I wanted to take a ride, but I knew they weren't just talking about their bikes. I didn't want to make them mad, so I always played the silly card when I said no." Her voice faltered, and then she said, "It was a different group that came in that last night." She shook her head, pushing her food around her plate again. "The club was called Shinedown," she scoffed. "Something to do with moonshine and getting down, I guess. John, the owner, was nice enough, but he was hardly ever there."

Making note of the name for later, he looked back at her. "We about ready to head home, baby? You have to be tired, even if you only danced the one set. How long have you been exercising and working out to get prepared for tonight?"

She nodded. "I am exhausted, no reason to try and deny it. Been working out as best I could for the past few days. Even big cans of vegetables don't provide a lot of resistance when used as weights, but I made do. You should be proud of yourself. It was hard to get in the workouts I wanted. You, my dear mister Gunny, are a hard man to sneak around."

"Not gonna get any argument out of me on that. But now I know what you were up to, I don't think I've been paying close enough attention, or obviously I would have cottoned on to the fact you're so much better." He stood, reaching for his chained wallet, removing bills to set on the table, and then tucking it back into his pocket. He held out his arms. "Are you too well for a ride, baby?"

She laughed and stood on the bench seat, shrugging her small messenger bag over her head, the strap crossing between her breasts highlighting the fact she had gone braless under the loose-fitting cotton shirt, a fact he hadn't realized until now. *Fucking killing me.* Adjusting things to her liking, she reached out to clasp his forearms and he lifted, the tension of their arms supporting her as he swung her around to his back, where she grabbed onto his shoulders. Her legs wouldn't come near to going around his waist, but he supported her ass with one broad palm. He smiled when she said, "Never too well for a ride, Gunny. Home, my dear man. Take me home."

He paused a half step. *That was twice in as many minutes she called me her dear.*

In the parking lot, he backed up to his bike, easing her onto the seat and handing her the helmet, which had quickly become hers. Mounting the bike in front of her, he waited for a signal to start the motor, feeling her snuggle up behind him, her legs spreading wide around his ass, thighs sliding up along the outside of his legs. He smiled broadly when the signal came in the form of her arms slipping underneath his jacket, holding onto the belt loops of his jeans, and her calling out a clear, "Ready."

A half-hour later, he pulled into the driveway of his house, waiting for the garage door to rise completely before backing the bike into the sole empty spot. He settled the bike into place and felt the change as Sharon slid off. Without looking, he reached back for the helmet, taking it from her hands and hanging it from the handlebars. This had become a comfortable routine for them both.

"I can't get used to seeing all these bikes," she said, wonder in her voice. He looked around the space, taking in the pieces and parts of his in-progress bikes lying here and there, but what she was looking at were the completed motorcycles, his successes.

He and Bear worked together on a lot of projects for the club, with Bear doing most of the customization planning, working with machine shops for performance enhancing changes to an engine or suspension. Bear also designed custom paint jobs, which everyone loved; the club couldn't roll the iron off the line fast enough to meet the demand.

Gunny was good at wrenching for someone like him, skilled at working on the bikes Bear needed help on, but his real love remained restoration. He was happiest when he could bring a bike, any bike, back to factory specifications.

This garage was evidence of that love, filled with uncommon motorcycles from a dozen different manufacturers. There were rare bikes sitting alongside classics, road cruisers parked next to full dressers.

He turned his head, looking at the project he had been working on over the last couple of years. Finally nearing completion, he still intended the Vincent as a gift for Mason, and couldn't wait to present it to him. The hand-built series 'C' bike was a one-of-a-kind motorcycle any collector would give their eyeteeth to get their hands on.

Gunny believed the bike fit Mason; it was fast, unusual, striking, and sought after. As he always did when beginning a new project, he had done research on the bikes as well as the people who rode them, and found the Vincent had a more famous than usual enthusiast in the writer, Hunter Thompson. The author had said by simply existing, the Vincent Black Shadow was a challenge to riders, a test of both courage and skill. *Mason certainly had the balls to ride it*, he thought with a grin.

Pulling his attention away from the Vincent, he realized Sharon was already standing across the garage, watching him with a look of amusement on her face. "Let's get inside, baby," he said, dismounting the bike and walking to the interior door. There was a scrabbling noise coming from inside the door and he looked at her with a smile. "Somebody's happy we're home."

In a deep, sonorous voice, she said, "Release the hounds."

He laughed, opening the door, futilely using his foot to try to push back the two dogs struggling to get past him to her. The beagle ducked underneath the sole of his boot with a delighted yip, launching itself at her and stretching up on its hind legs to reach her hands better. Unfazed, the rat terrier next escaped his attempt at control, jumping and knocking the beagle to the floor in an effort to gain her affections also. "They crack me up," she said with joy in her voice, looking up at where he stood in the doorway, her mouth stretched wide in a grin. *That goddamn smile gets me every fucking time.*

"Come on, guys. Let's get back inside. Come on," he chided the dogs, reaching back to clasp her hand and lead her into the house they had been sharing for the past couple of weeks.

The dogs followed her inside, watching intently as she lifted her bag over her head, and he narrowed his eyes, staring at her. She had been spoiling the dogs since she could get out of bed without help. "You didn't bring home leftovers, did you?"

"Just a potato or two," she said, digging in the pack and coming up with a soggy, grease-soaked napkin. "Here we are, boys. My good boys," she crooned then looked up at Gunny, saying brightly, "They love fries." *They get the love, and I get the matter-of-fact voice*, he thought testily.

"Yeah, but people food gives 'em gas." He sighed at the disappointment in her face, looking down at the dogs, so completely focused on her. "Go ahead, but only a couple each, all right?"

"Who's a good boy? Who wants a fry?" She stuck her tongue out at him, and then looked down at the dogs. "Not Daddy, that's for sure. Nope, nope, nope. Just my good boys. Who wants a fry? Can a good boy sit?" Both dogs immediately sat, eyes still boring holes in the fry-filled napkin, tails working overtime, enthusiastically flipping back and forth.

"Oh, what good boys. Good sit. Can a good boy down?" The beagle lay down, and she frowned. She said, "Good boy, Tank. Good down. Rocky, can a good boy down?" Her words prompted the terrier to join its partner in crime prostrated on the floor. "Oh, good down. What good boys you are." She squatted, placing one knee on the floor as she released them from the position and handed each a fry. Running her hands over their heads and muzzles, she leaned down farther to gently kiss between their ears as she continued praising them.

From where he was standing, he could barely see the curve of her ass, the sway of her back. He sucked a deep breath. Looking at her had become one of his favorite pastimes, and it was probably one of the reasons he so enjoyed watching her dance tonight. Wanting to see more, he stalked across the room and stood behind her, admiring the way she filled out her jeans when she was squatted like that. He loved those curves, the crease at the top of her legs where they joined her ass, the dimples exactly below where her waist tapered inward before flaring out into her ribcage.

I can't wait to get my hands back on her. God, to be able to finally drive deep inside her heat. Rolling his neck, he sighed, reaching down to shift his rapidly thickening cock so it settled more comfortably in his jeans. Her backwards glance caught him mid-adjustment and her face stilled, settling into longing lines. She turned back to the dogs, but not before he saw the sadness rolling across her features.

Reaching down, he scooped her into his arms, ignoring her squeal of surprise and laying his head on top of hers when she leaned into his chest. "We'll get there, baby," he said quietly, acknowledging the frustration she felt at not being able to be intimate. In the weeks they had known each other, her complete trust and easy friendship with him had quickly morphed into something more. He had teased her about being slow, telling her he had known within hours of first touching her that she was his, but it seemed to him, her affections now matched what he felt.

"We're really okay? You're not mad I didn't tell you about going back to work?" She whispered the questions against his neck, pressing her face into his shoulder. "I didn't want you to be mad, but I want to work. I want to pull my weight. I'd have never gone against you if you said no, and I still won't, Gunny. You tell me it's not okay, and I'm done at Slinky's."

"Baby," he murmured, walking them into the living room to sit on the couch. "We're okay. And, I get it. I do. I ain't gonna pretend to like their hands on you." He took a breath, nuzzling against the side of her face. "But, Sharon, baby...*goddamn* you are beautiful when you dance, and I can see how much you love it. As long as you always come home with me, we'll be okay. I know what it's like to have that kind of hunger for something, that kind of wanting twist in your belly, and I ain't gonna tell you no, when it's something you want so badly."

He settled her across his lap, keeping his arms around her, holding them both still. Releasing a contented sigh, he relaxed into the cushions, satisfied for the moment simply to hold her. "I want you to understand about me, baby." He refused to tense up, couldn't let her know how important this was. "I can deal with all that, as long as I know you're mine. I don't fucking play games, baby, and I think you get that about me. I suspect you've gotten that from the beginning, yeah?

"Up until a few weeks ago, the only things that mattered in my life were my band of brothers, my bikes, and my pups. I got played once, and it turned me off the entire fucking female species. Not sayin' I haven't fucked, because I've done a fair amount of that, no lyin'. But, the only woman I ever felt for, she played me. I told myself I was done, called it quits...wouldn't touch a woman. Hell, I jacked off for two years, wouldn't go near pussy. Then I found the club and my brothers, and never fucking looked back."

She shifted and he tensed, moving one hand, slowly stroking the length of her spine. "Shhhh, baby. Let me talk, yeah?" She nodded and he relaxed again. "When you started working at Slinky's, I noticed you. Tried to tell myself it was simply paying attention to business because you were new, but I couldn't *stop* seeing you. You have no fucking idea how many times I pulled my hand back from where I stretched it out, wanting to touch you as you walked past. How often I caught myself moving through the crowd to stand behind you. Close enough to smell you, but not touch. Fuck, I had your back before I even recognized it myself. Hell, I felt like a fucking freak, because I wanted to know...had to know how your skin felt underneath my fingers, under my hand, what it would feel like to smooth it like this." He stroked up her arm with his hand, cupping his fingers around her shoulder and then dragging them back down the length of her arm, stopping as they made a bracelet around her wrist. "Touch you. Have the right to touch you.

"Then, baby." He realized he had tensed up again when she made a noise against his chest, and he loosened his arms. "Then that motherfucker put his hands on you. God, that shit tore me up. You got hurt. And I touched you. Finally, after weeks of wondering and wanting, I touched you and I couldn't let go. I still can't let go. That first touch of skin between us? Brought us to where we are right now, because I can't stop myself from touching you. Wanting you. The hell with stopping, because I don't want to. Can't." He sucked in a ragged breath, "Won't go back, baby. Can't. But, it's not just that, because now when I don't hear your laugh, or see your smile, it feels like I've misplaced something important. Like a critical piece of me is missing when my hands aren't on you. When you aren't around.

"Fuck, you're under my skin, baby, and I like you there. I want to keep you safe, keep you from harm. I want to give you everything you want...any desire, just so I can keep seein' your face. I would beggar myself to keep you, baby. So don't dance because you want to pull your fuckin' weight. Simply by breathing, you make my life better, so don't think your money will make a fucking speck of difference to me. I'm keeping you, regardless.

"Don't dance because of money. And, baby, don't dance for those other men because you want to make me jealous. That's another thing you don't have to work to do, because it's as easy as fucking breathing. Tonight, I would have gladly killed every motherfucker who touched you for one second longer than you allowed," he growled, arms tightening around her again. "One. Fucking. Second. And don't try to say there weren't any, because I saw you avoiding the men who wanted to get fucking handsy. I marked every goddamn face, and you give me the word—baby, they don't show again.

"Babe, dance because you love it, and I know you do. Your face tonight was…I don't have the fucking words, baby. Such classic beauty on a sow's ear of a stage. It's been a long time since I had something I wanted like I want you, been a long time since I felt the lightness of beauty in my life like I saw tonight. Dance, because you love it."

He drew in another hard breath, leaning in to kiss her temple. "I don't know what this is between us, but I like it, baby. I like looking at you and knowing you are mine. I know I ain't the most handsome motherfucker in the room. I know I'm rough, not cultured like you deserve. But, baby, you let me see what this is like. I can't go back, Sharon. Can't go back to before you. Now that you've given me *you*, I would die for you."

She was silent and still in his arms while he waited patiently, listening to her soft breathing offset by the occasional whimpers and sighs of the sleeping dogs lying on the floor, dreaming at their feet. Branches brushed against the outside wall, the soft noise somehow soothing. He sat holding her for so long without her moving or speaking that he believed she had gone to sleep resting against his chest, arms folded in front of her, fingers twisted in his shirt as they usually were. Comforted by his words. Holding onto him.

Gradually, he became aware his chest was chilled, it felt like his shirt was…wet. Bending his head to look down, he used his nose to nuzzle the top of her head, nudging it back until she was looking up into his face. Eyes reddened, ringed by swollen lids, once their gazes clashed she let out a sigh, the hiccupping catch in her breathing the only other indication she was crying.

He softly kissed her forehead, her temples, tasting salt as he trailed his lips along her cheekbones. Bringing up one hand to cup her cheek, he used his thumb to brush away the steady stream of tears flowing from the corners of her eyes. "Gonna tell me, baby?" he asked, rubbing his beard-roughened cheek against hers. She pressed her mouth closed and slowly shook her head back and forth, shoulders hitching with another hiccupping sigh. "You sure, baby?" he asked again, nibbling at her lips. She nodded, her hair brushing against his neck as she did.

"Okay," he said easily, granting her the space she needed, for now. "Gonna tote you to our bed, baby." He didn't wait for her assent, simply stood and carefully stepped over the stirring dogs. Moving up the hallway to the stairs, he ascended them two at a time, and then stepped into the first doorway on the left. Using his elbow to turn on the light switch, the room softly illuminated with light from lamps on the nightstands, positioned one on either side of the headboard. Gently setting her on the bench at the foot of the bed, he leaned down and kissed the top of her head, listening as the dogs came into the room, throwing themselves onto their beds with disapproving sighs at having to move.

Sitting beside her, he took off his boots and socks, flexing his toes in the lush carpeting. "I'm gonna take a shower." He cupped her jaw in his hand, looking into her face until he was convinced she was calm, not sad and not afraid. He still didn't know why she had cried, and while it didn't seem to be from negative emotions, he felt the need to reassure her, "Babe. I promise you, we're okay."

Her lips twisted up on one side into what looked like a reluctant smile and she nodded.

He pulled a face. "Now you ain't talking to me?" Her jaw still caged in his hand, he used it to direct her head down, kissing her nose then her forehead, and finally the top of her head. "Back in a few." Standing, he stripped off his shirt, tossing it into the basket in the corner as he walked into the bathroom.

***

In her head, his words sounded again. *Dance, because you love it.* No one had ever given her such candid permission to please herself. Even more than when she danced, the feeling in her chest right now felt like flying. She hadn't felt such acceptance since she was a kid.

A kid, she thought with a broken laugh. Ace had been her rock when she was little, but then he was gone, and she became...unmoored. From the time her favorite brother had left to play hockey in Russia, she drifted. First into parties with boys far too old for her, with easy access to alcohol and drugs found in their parents' medicine cabinets. Then into worse situations, with long-reaching repercussions. Unconsciously, she trailed fingers across her belly. Finally, into the relationship with Derek, who had worked at wooing her with pretty words and flowers, until she settled and they moved, isolating her from family and friends. Lost innocence...lost youth...lost love.

That's why she wept, cradled to Gunny's chest, because of the sheer absence of love in her life for so long. She cried for those vanished years with Elkins, because of innocence stripped away when she was a teen. She thought about all her mistakes and rubbed her forehead, then used the fingers of both hands to wipe her cheeks dry.

When he said they couldn't go back, he was right. For the first time in years, she had someone to hold close to her heart. And he trusted her, all of her. She knew he did. She realized Gunny wouldn't hold anything against her, none of her past, and not even anything here, in her present or future. *He said he would die for me,* she thought and shook her head. *I'd die before I did anything to lose his trust. He brought me here, in his house, where few have been. Trusts me with his pups, his furbabies.* She smiled. *Trusts me in his bed.*

Now I just need to trust me. She remembered her visit with Goose today. *"Yes, you're healed up, girl." He said the words as he used scissors to snip the last stitch from her head. She reached up her hand, fingers tracing the dip she found underneath the scar, and she looked a question at him. "Probably always have an indentation right there, hon. He tore out a big chunk of your scalp." He shook his head. "I'm proud of you, Sharon. Most women would have crumbled in the face of what you've endured."*

Looking down at her knees, she shook her head. "My friend in Florida, the one who saved me? She tried to tell me the same thing." Glancing up, she met his gaze then her eyes skittered away as she said, "I know better. Only a weak person would have let themselves get into that position to begin with."

Warm fingers cupped her chin, lifting her face and forcing her to meet his gaze. "I call bullshit. Bull-fucking-shit. People get into situations all the time. It's what you do when you find yourself there that can set the tone for the rest of your life. You got yourself out of there, took steps to separate yourself from that animal." He shifted his grip, tilting her head back and forth to check for any bruising still on her face. "And now you've got a good man. Someone who will protect you against anything."

She couldn't stop the smile from curling the corners of her lips and he laughed. "From the look on your face, I'd say Gunny's got himself a good woman, too." He released his hold and sat back on the bench, reaching down to straighten the supplies in the toolbox he carried. They were in the back dressing room of Slinky's. Two days ago, she told DeeDee she wanted to go back to work, and when arguing hadn't changed Sharon's mind, DeeDee had agreed that if Goose said she had healed enough, then she could dance. He shook his head and cut his gaze up to her. "I'm not sure you know what you're doing tonight, woman. But if you want to dance, you have my blessing."

Nodding, she looked down as he stood, seeing his boots take a step towards her. Without looking up, she quietly said, "Thank you, Goose. For everything. For taking care of me when it...happened. And for this. Don't tell him, please. This dance is for him." She looked up and instinctively shrank back when she saw him towering over her, a sudden image of Elkins flooding her mind.

He must have recognized the expression of fear, because he took a step backwards, then another one, giving them a good five feet of space *between them, and she took a deep breath. "If he doesn't want me to work here after this, I won't. But tonight, this one dance...it's for him."*

And she had danced. She stretched now, feeling the pull of muscles, which she knew would be sore tomorrow, enjoying the movement and feeling of satisfaction. She danced, and he knew it was for him. She saw it on his face as he watched her, the rest of the room fading away. Nothing in her mind but her feelings for him, her trust in him, her joy at being with him...here...now.

Wiping her cheeks again, she sniffled and laughed. If she didn't get in there, the man would be finished with his shower before she had a chance to join him, and that would be a damn shame.

11. Putting my life in your hands

He knew she saw Goose today and had been given a full release from the few restrictions he kept on her last time, one of which had been the 'no sex' rule. Idly wondering if Goose was aware of her back-to-work scheme, he turned on the shower and adjusted the water, pulling a towel from the cabinet and draping it over the rod. Looking into the mirror, he turned his face side-to-side, rubbing his palms over his jaw and head, feeling the dark stubble.

Reaching into the drawer to his right, he pulled out his straight razor and shaving gel. Turning his head side-to-side again, he filled his palm with the foam and smoothed it across his scalp. Picking up his razor, he made careful sweeps with the blade, traveling from front to back using smooth, familiar movements. He paused after every stroke to rinse and clean the blade in the sink, working cautiously around his neckline and ears. Seeing movement from the corner of his eye, he glanced towards the doorway using the mirror, to see Sharon leaning on the doorframe.

He gave her a chin lift, and after making the final sweep of this first pass, rinsed the blade again, setting the razor aside and filling his palm with gel. Coating his scalp with foam again, he repeated the process, working steadily until he felt her fingers on his hip. Halting for a moment and looking down at her with a questioning crook of his eyebrow, he waited for her to speak.

"Can I help?" she asked.

"Nearly done, baby," he said, making another slow, steady sweep with the razor.

She stepped around him, moving to stand on top of the toilet seat beside him. "I can get the places you can't see."

"Got fingers, babe. I can find where I miss," he said, demonstrating by rubbing his fingertips over his scalp and finding a small strip he missed earlier. "Been shaving my head since I left active duty. Before that, I did my own high and tight in the field."

She twisted sideways, looking at the back of his neck. Standing on the elevated surface as she was, she was still barely eye-level with him and he grinned. "You even seen the back of my head yet, baby?"

She made a face at him. "Yes, you big oaf. I have. I do, every time we ride the bike. Which is all the time, since you turned my rental car in, eh?" She stuck her tongue out at him and he laughed.

"Got your money back, didn't I? You couldn't drive it, baby. No reason to pay for what you can't use. And when you're ready, I got wheels that won't cost you a dime." She continued watching him as he finished shaving his head. He had rinsed his scalp and was beginning to apply the gel foam to his face, when he looked at her in the mirror, his motions slowing.

"You ever shave someone?" He asked the question idly, fiddling with the handle of the razor.

She nodded. "Ace used to have me shave him before every home game. It was part of his ritual." Tilting her head to one side, she said, "Not with a straight razor, though."

"Spencer has a ritual? He doesn't seem like much of a superstitious guy." He stood still, thinking, considering it, because this appeared to matter to her, but willingly putting himself in harm's way went against everything inside him. Still, it mattered to her, and was connected to good memories, the kind of thing he wanted to help her grow until they outstripped all the bad shit in her head. Until they were stronger than the things that made her cry soundlessly. He wanted to wipe out all her bad dreams, giving her good memories.

"Yeah, he used to. I'd shave him, and Mom would make her lemon cookies. He wouldn't eat any of them unless they won, but she had to make them so he could smell the plateful before we left for the rink. He'd slap the top of the doorframe on the way out to the car, and when we got to the rink, he'd tap the door with his stick. One year, they didn't do well, his team lost a lot of games. Dad and I had to eat a ton of cookies." She grinned. "Most guys have some things they do, like crossing themselves or tapping the sides of the gate when they head out onto the ice. Ace had a bunch before he left for juniors." She laughed, reaching out to steady herself with a hand on his shoulder.

"You want to shave me, baby?" he asked, and one side of his mouth curled up when she nodded enthusiastically.

Handing over the razor, he told her, "Putting my life in your hands. I don't do this lightly."

"I accept the responsibility, my liege," she teased, bowing over his hand as she took the razor from him.

For the next twenty minutes, he was halfway between Heaven and Hell as she shaved him, her fingers touching and tugging his face, pulling and stretching his skin as she dragged the edge of the razor across it. Her face was so close to his that the urge to devour her mouth was nearly irresistible, especially when he felt the heat from her breath ghosting across his skin and him unable to move except at her silent request. Such a private act turning sensual, her touch tender and strong at the same time as she guided his head into the next desired position.

The mirror gradually misted over as steam from the running shower filled the room. Without his reflection to distract him, he found himself focusing on her face, having to fight the urge to smile when he caught sight of her, tongue tucked into the corner of her mouth, held tight between white teeth as she concentrated. He closed his eyes, standing motionless as she wet her hands, running them over his face, feeling for any areas that might require additional attention. He felt her hands slowly still, palms cupping his cheeks, and he opened his eyes, finding her poised in front of him, lips only inches from his. Her gaze was intently fixed on his mouth, handle of the razor clenched between her thumb and palm, the metal heating as it pressed against his face.

"Baby," he whispered and saw her inhale sharply when his breath hit her lips.

"Yeah?"

"You done?" He spoke quietly, not wanting to break whatever this spell was.

"Yeah," she said.

"You wanna give me back the razor?" Still speaking quietly, he watched a hectic color rising in her cheeks, knowing it for arousal. *She wants me.*

"Okay," she breathed, and he took the razor from her hand. Without looking away from her face, he folded it closed and laid it on the edge of the sink.

"You wanna kiss me?" he asked, gaze locked on hers, broken only as her eyes slipped closed on a slow blink.

"Yeah," she whispered.

"I'm all yours," he said, reaching up to wrap his hands around both her wrists, slowly sliding that contact up her arms, past her elbows, and around her shoulders. Slipping his hands down her back, he splayed his fingers wide, suppressing a frown as he felt the bumps and impressions of her ribcage under his hands. *Still too fucking skinny*, he thought, making a mental note to ask Goose about that. He tugged gently, pulling her to him, closing the distance separating their mouths. "All yours, baby."

"Yeah," she breathed and leaned in, her lips pressing lightly against his. It wasn't their first kiss, but he knew this was the one that would lead into their future, knew she needed to feel secure, needed to be in control. He let her guide the way, following her example for the speed and passion of the kiss, slanting his head when she did, and then backing off, gently nibbling on her bottom lip as she tugged on his top one. Forearms leaning on his shoulders, she let her fingertips glide across the smooth skin of his scalp. She jerked when her questing tongue first touched his lips, surprising herself, and then groaned as he opened to her, letting her delve into his mouth, stroking back with his tongue when hers caressed his.

When he gauged she would be wet and wanting more, he pulled back, controlling his response ruthlessly, dusting slow kisses across her lips and up to her nose. "Thanks for the shave, baby," he said, taking a step backwards and turning away to unbutton his jeans. "And for the kiss." Letting them drop to the floor, he made no effort to hide his arousal from her, reaching down to stroke his cock root to tip and back again, then gripped himself firmly around the base, squeezing tight as he let out a little huff of air. "My shower time," he explained, moving back towards where she stood still on the toilet seat.

He reached out and gripped her waist, pulling her in for a brief, soft lip touch before lifting her and setting her down on the floor. Not content to allow their contact to break, he followed her down to kiss her again, smiling as she rose on her toes to meet his mouth. His cock jumped, pressing against her stomach, and she groaned into his mouth.

Lifting his head, he looked down at her face, flushed with arousal, her eyes darkening with desire. "Want you, baby."

She took a breath at his words, shivering under his hands clasped loosely around her waist. She nodded and her mouth parted, the tip of her pink tongue sliding across her bottom lip. Hesitantly, she said, "I saw Goose today." He nodded, and after a moment, she drew in a deep breath and continued, "He told me I get a go-pass in recovery. No more stitches anywhere, and he said I'm healed enough if I...if we were ready."

He slowly shook his head back and forth once, watching as her chin came up; a fierce look on her face, lips gripped between her teeth, she looked prepared to argue. *My woman, fucking spitfire.* He said, "Don't do that, Sharon. Don't get mad at me. You have to know I'm ready to have you. But, baby, ain't gonna take you standing the first time. I'm gonna want to go slow, enjoy the ride. I won't get a second first time, and I want it to be good for both of us. Building our memories, yeah?" He stepped back, opening the shower door, moving it out of the way. "Won't say no to some wet and slippery company, but until I fuck you in my bed, we leave things as they've been these past weeks. Your hands anywhere you have an itch to explore, my hands and mouth everywhere except on that pussy of mine."

She nodded and stepped forward, fingers eagerly working at the waistband of her jeans as she unfastened then pushed them down, stepping out of her pants and panties, pulling her peasant blouse over her head, baring her body to him. He reached out and wrapped one hand around the curve of her naked hip, savoring the skin-on-skin as he pulled her into the shower, under the streaming water, watching as she tipped her head back to wet her hair, steadying herself by resting one palm on his forearm.

Leaning back against the tile wall, he cupped his balls with one hand, tugging firmly on his sac, feeling the head of his cock mushroom larger, the ridge growing more pronounced as his arousal intensified from watching her. Eyes closed, unaware of his scrutiny, she leaned backwards into the water. Lifting both hands now, working deft fingers through the length of her hair. The movement caused her titties to arch up and his gaze tracked down, seeing her nipples soft and smooth on the peaks of her breasts, water sluicing down her body, funneling between her legs and over her pussy. *Fuck*, he thought with what had become a constant sense of amazement, *my woman*.

As if she could feel the weight of his gaze, she opened her eyes, stepping out from under the water and grabbing her shampoo from the shelf. Eyes half-hooded, she watched him slowly stroke himself as she raised soap-filled hands to her hair, exposure to the cool air causing her nipples to pucker and harden. His hands moved up and down his shaft, pulling and tugging his foreskin over the end of his cock, drawing his palm back to reveal the dark purple head repeatedly. His pulse pounded in his shaft, balls tightening and drawing up against his body as his cock bounced and throbbed.

He waited until she finished washing her hair to reach out, bringing her towards him, laughing along with her when his cock refused to slide to one side until she twisted, putting her belly against his hip. Leaning down, he slipped his lips across hers, groaning when she opened naturally for him. He felt her hands on his cock and stilled, closing his eyes to focus on the sensation she was drawing from him, her fingernails scoring the soft underside. He muttered, "Goddamn, baby," when she gripped him firmly, water from the shower making his skin slippery.

Her mouth was on him before he realized what she meant to do, and he threw his head back against the wall. Stifling his groans with gritted teeth for a moment, he bent double, drawing her face away from him, cupping her chin in one hand as he reached past her to turn off the water. "Babe," he said hoarsely, picking her up with one arm around her waist, "I want to touch you, baby." He felt her legs wrap around him, and then the tip of his cock was bumping against her ass and pussy as he walked to the bed, reaching down to knock the covers and pillows onto the floor.

He laid her back on the mattress and knelt between her thighs. Propping himself up on one arm, he teased her opening with his fingers, finding her wet and ready as he dipped inside and withdrew, searching her face for any indication of discomfort. Seeing none, he sat back, drawing his hands smoothly down her body, sweeping the beads of water off her skin, leaving only little waves of shivers and goose bumps behind.

"Babe, gonna love on you," he said, watching his hands, fascinated to see his fingers touching her, stroking her skin, and he leaned in to kiss her softly as he settled his length beside her. "Gotta touch you. My first touch. You're gonna have to tell me if it's too much." Nudging her chin with his face, he smiled as she shifted and exposed her neck, reveling in the sighs and moans she gave when he licked the water droplets there, softly kissing her throat, nibbling gently with his teeth. "Gotta have my hands on you. Need you."

He reached out, trailing his fingertips up the inside of her thigh, cupping her mound with his palm, groaning when his fingers again found the wetness between her legs. "Need this, babe. Need you." Dropping kisses down the slope of her chest, he sucked a nipple into his mouth while his fingers slipped and slid between her folds, circling and teasing her clit, aware and focused on her responses. "My fucking pussy," he murmured. When he found a spot or movement that drew a sound from her, he repeated it, as he did by nibbling on her breast and drawing in a sharp breath, pulling air across her wet nipple and feeling it harden against his lips. She seemed to crave sensation, his hands, his teeth, his mouth—the more he touched and kissed and stroked her, the hotter she blazed for him. "Fuck yeah, you like that. Show me, babe."

Her hips slowly moved in small side-to-side circles, and he ground his palm against her, pushing his thick middle finger deep inside, advancing slowly but confidently, feeling coolness from the little spurt of air against the top of his head that matched her quickened breathing. He watched the muscles of her abdomen bunching and tightening, rubbing his face against her to hide his smile as her arousal visibly played out across her entire body. "Love watching you...so fucking beautiful."

She arched up against his hand, and he let her fuck herself on his fingers for a moment, his thumb grazing across her clit with every pump of her hips. Then, suddenly, he knew she was *there*, her pussy tightening on his finger, and she gasped as he pushed a second finger inside, stretching her and thrusting deep, dragging across her front wall with every plunge, and drawing out her orgasm relentlessly. "Oh, baby, come for me. Just like that, babe."

He gently bit down on the side of her breast when he felt her breathing beginning to even out, and worked to pull her back up the wave. Driving her onwards with his hands and mouth, he smiled, lips curving against her skin when she said his name softly, gasping, "Gunny."

He moved up, capturing her mouth with his, kissing her deeply, tongues stroking against each other in a frantic effort to communicate the passion and arousal they shared. "Want to be inside you. Need you, baby." He rolled to his back, reaching to the nightstand and pulling out a condom. Rolling it on quickly, he moved and lay between her thighs. Before she could say anything, he reached between them, using the head of his hard cock to hammer on her clit several times before slipping it down and stilling, poised outside her entrance.

He looked into her face, their gaze locking, and he said, "Need to know you'll be honest, baby. Tell me if I hurt you." She made an impatient noise and arched her hips up, but he moved away. "Ain't fucking around here, Sharon. I know I'm a big motherfucker. I have to believe you'll tell me, or this stops here, even if it kills me."

"Yes," she breathed, "I'll tell you if it's too much."

"Okay. I'm gonna try to go slow, babe. Want this first time. My first with you. God, I wanna fuck you hard, hear my name from your mouth again...but gonna try—need you." With a groan, he slipped inside her by a couple inches, and stilled, teeth clenched and breathing through his nose when she froze underneath him. "Baby?"

The one-word question was scarcely out of his mouth before she was arching up into him, saying, "It's good, okay? Please."

He pressed farther inside, gliding slowly but steadily into her pussy, gritting his teeth, because she was so fucking tight...she felt so fucking good stretching around him it nearly stole his wits. Finally, after what seemed like a lifetime, he felt his pelvic bone press firmly on her clit, thinking he was as deep as he could go, and then she shifted her legs up on his hips. With a rumbling groan, he found the room to drive a little deeper. Seated inside her like that, he stopped in place, his muscles jerking as he fought the urge to take her hard, fuck her like he wanted, pull her onto his cock and feel his balls slapping her ass. Take her slow, drink from her mouth with long kisses...fuck her until they were both sated and exhausted, worn-out from rough sex and sweet loving. He wanted everything.

"Fuck," he ground out, needing to move...to feel her sliding on him, wanting her satin wrapped around his hard-on, and he allowed himself two fast, reckless strokes, then slowly pushed deep, burying himself inside her again. "Babe, stop it," he gritted in response to her pussy tightening and relaxing around him, opening his eyes when she laughed.

"Gunny, you're not going to hurt me. Just love me already," she teased, tilting her head up to look him in the face. His body engulfed hers and he rounded his shoulders, bringing his face down for another hard, hungry kiss. She moaned into his mouth as he moved and lifted her hips, bringing her pussy up to meet every slow, downward thrust of his cock.

"Oh, yeah. Fuck me back, baby. Like it when you move like that." This was muttered against the skin of her shoulder, his teeth dragging back and forth across the taut muscle where her neck joined her body. He buried his face into that crook, feeling sweat breaking out across his back and ass. He shifted his knees a little wider, forcing her legs apart even more, and it felt like he plunged even deeper with every hard thrust. "You feel so good." He kissed her skin, trailing his tongue along her neck. "Taste so fucking good."

Her hands were on his neck and head, holding tightly to him. "Wanna wrap yourself around me, baby? Touch me? Fuck, I want your hands on me," he growled, then roared wordlessly when she gripped his ass tightly and her fingernails dug in, pulling him into her. "Fuck yeah, like that," he gritted, thrusting faster.

"You like ass-play, baby? Little gentle push and pull?" he asked, and when she gasped, "Yes," he adjusted again, sliding one hand down and between them. He pulled his cock out to plunge his fingers inside her, thrusting back in quickly as he moved the hand around her thigh, pulling her leg up and teasing down between her ass cheeks with a brush of his knuckles. With his slippery fingers, he played with the taut pucker there, pressing then circling, retreating several times before finally dipping a fingertip into her anus. He pushed past the ring of muscles and groaned as her pussy clamped down on him in reaction. "Fuck yeah, you like that. Like ass-play," he said, pushing his finger deeper, going to the second knuckle and holding there for a moment, then thrusting in and out in counterpoint with his cock in her pussy. "Little push and pull, fuck yeah.

"Goddamn. You're fucking tight everywhere, baby." He groaned against the side of her head, feeling how the sweat made their bellies slippery as they slapped together. "Baby," he said, "talk to me. Tell me what you want." He could feel his cock moving inside her against his finger in her ass, and suddenly wanted his mouth on her, but goddamn fucking condoms tasted terrible, so he would have to wait for that first time until... *Fuck*, he thought, as she tightened around his cock and finger.

"You coming again, baby? Talk to me," he demanded, plunging into her hard.

"Yeah...coming," she breathed, pressing her ass back against his hand, forcing his finger deeper. "That's good, Gunny. So...good," she said, groaning again, shuddering, pressing her head into the mattress, and he bit down on her neck, pulling his name from her on another deep moan. "Gunny."

Hearing her voice, the sound of his name rolling off her tongue brought him to the brink, and then two more hard, deep thrusts took him over. He roared again, coming for a long time, his head thrown back, cock pressed deep inside her, feeling the heat from their combined orgasms surround him. Gasping, breathing raggedly, he moved against her, slowly and carefully slipping his finger out of her ass, sliding his hand between them and stroking her softly as he withdrew.

Lying on his side, he let his latex-covered cock rest against her belly, telling himself he would get up in a minute and take care of it, get her a cloth. Stirring himself, he dragged a heavy arm up her torso, cupping her breast in his hand. Still breathing deeply, he pressed his lips against the side of her head, bending his knee, resting his thigh across her legs, pinning her into place beside him.

"Babe?" His questioning tone drew a wordless, humming response from her. "You okay?" When she didn't answer, he lifted his head and opened his eyes, searching her face for any indication he had hurt her. Eyes closed, there was a gentle smile curling up the corners of her mouth, and as he watched, she brought her arm up, fingers curling around his wrist, holding his hand against her breast when he would have moved and released her. "Babe?" he repeated the one-word inquiry and was relieved when she moved to snuggle against him as best she could with him wrapped around her like this.

"I'm better than okay, Gunny. I'm great," she said softly, pressing her lips against the dip in his throat. "That was amazing, eh?"

He chuckled, and she must have found the rumbling in his chest amusing, because she laid her ear against him, laughing along with him. "Better than okay?" He simply wanted confirmation, pressing her for an answer. "I didn't hurt you, did I?"

"No, baby. Other than the pleasurable stretching to take all of your enormous cock, there was no pain I didn't welcome." Eyes still closed, she laughed again. "And note my use of the word 'pleasurable,' because it was all of that. I don't think I've ever come quite so hard." She made a noise in her throat, tunneling her face against his chest as she said, "We fit, you know?"

"Yeah, babe. I know. We fit," he said, wrapping his arms around her. "We do fit."

***

Head propped up on her hand, she watched him as he slept. Her gaze traced his features, relishing the calmness she found there. She watched the way his nostrils flared on each intake of breath, how his lips pursed slightly as he breathed out. Lying flat on his back, he didn't move much as long as he had a hand on her, as long as she lay pressed against his side. As from the first night she remembered them sleeping in the same bed, it was only when she tried to move away that he became restless, breath coming faster, his large hands seeking, groping the sheets. She glanced down at where his arm wrapped around her back, possession evident in his hand resting on her hip, fingers curling around to her belly. Once she nestled back into his side, he stilled, peaceful again, his breathing becoming deep and even.

His other hand lay relaxed on his chest, and she reached up to curl her fingers around his wrist, silently laughing at her efforts when she failed to span the thickness by several inches. She remembered she couldn't encircle his cock, either, her pussy tightening at the memory of being filled by him. God, she never felt so cherished, loved. When he said he was going to love on her, he meant every word.

Using one fingertip, she gently traced the veins in the back of his hand, marveling at the size and strength of the muscles and bone bound by soft skin. Stretching out her hand, she laid it on top of his, smiling again at the difference in the size...the length of their fingers, the width of their palms. They were an unlikely pair, so different, but they fit. She knew they did.

It was unbelievable to her that someone so strong could be so gentle, caring for her in a way that left her feeling secure, not frightened. To think, he could crush her with one hand, probably without breaking a sweat, but for all his size, she knew he would never hurt her. In her heart, she knew he would die before hurting her. For days now, she witnessed firsthand his attention to her comfort, his concern for her safety. Even with how aroused he was tonight, how frustrated he had to have been, considering he had an erection pretty much since she woke in bed with him the first time, he had been careful with her. Considerate. Loving.

She frowned, trailing her fingers up his arm to his bicep. He had a tattoo high on his shoulder and, distracted for a moment, she traced the outlines of the ink, her mind wandering. When she had been with Derek, she had been taken without being prepared before, and it hurt...badly. When she ran away from him the last time, when Vanna found her, saved her, she swore she was done with men. Snorting softly, she remembered telling her friend her own fingers had been a better lover than her husband ever thought about being, and the echo of sentiment in what Gunny had told her earlier wasn't lost on her.

Gunny was...different. It was as if her enjoyment mattered more to him than his own. Pulling back in the shower, when she would have been happy to please him with her mouth, he stopped things because he wanted it to be good for her. And, even as hard as he had been, as ready as he had been to make love, he had taken the time to prepare her, made the effort to make sure she was primed. By the time he pushed inside her, she didn't think she had ever wanted anything as badly. In this bed, there was only good, no fright, and no paralyzing pain. *I know he'll never hurt me*, she thought then frowned again. *I trust him. The only way he could hurt me will be when I have to leave, when he gets tired of me.*

That thought startled her, because it hinted at a deeper feeling than she expected. Leaning forward, she pressed her mouth against his chest in a soft kiss, running her nose back and forth across his skin. She liked the way he smelled, loved how his mouth tasted. She reached up, tracing the seam of his lips with a fingertip, grinning when he frowned slightly and his mouth gave the smallest twitch.

Why would it hurt me to leave him? He's just my rescuer, isn't he? Did she think there was more? Was she saying...did she love him? *Silly woman, it's too soon*, she thought, kissing his chest again. Pulling back, she looked into his face, seeing beauty there. She knew he believed he wasn't attractive, which she never would understand. *Would you look at him,* she scoffed in her mind. *Gorgeous. Combine that face with the body, and then throw in the gentleness? My gorgeous, gentle giant. What's not to love?*

Laying her head on his chest, she sighed when his arm tightened around her, his hand slipping down to tightly cup her ass for a moment then moving back up to settle on her hip. Maybe he liked her a little. Even DeeDee thought he had feelings for her; she as much as said so last week.

"You need to take care, sweetheart. He's been hurt," DeeDee said, leaning over and pulling bottles of beer out of the cooler, handing them to her by twos and fours. Since she couldn't dance, she had been helping around the club, and they were rotating stock before opening for the day.

"He's hinted, but never come out and said what happened." She nudged the full bucket out of the way, sliding an empty one into easy reach. "I got the impression he hadn't had a girlfriend for a while, though. Was I wrong?"

"No, not wrong. He hasn't had one for as long as I've known him." That response surprised her, and DeeDee must have seen it, because she laughed and straightened, using the back of one wrist to push her hair from her face. "He doesn't have any girlfriends, and he doesn't take free dances, if you know what I mean. His troubles lie further back in his past, and the little bit I know is ugly."

"When the club put him to work here at Slinky's, I questioned it. I've always liked Lane, but he seemed particularly...unstable, at the time. Talked to Deke, found out he'd been in Iraq. I figured he saw some bad shit there. When he joined the Rebels, some days he would show up at the clubhouse—this was before Winger passed—Gunny would show up at the clubhouse and some days he looked completely lost. In those days, he was Lane, not Gunny. Sometimes he would want to talk, and I'd sit and listen for as long as he had words."

"You know he didn't want to quit the military? Said he was a Marine for life. Planned to die a jarhead, but they kicked him to the curb. Told him he was 'undeployable,' the bastards. Gave him a medal...have you seen his scars? Did he tell you the story?" She paused, and Sharon shook her head, praying she would continue talking. "Those are from the ambush that took his team, took his military family from him. He got shot three times, saw his entire team die in front of him. He said it took him over three weeks to make his way back to safety. Then they took it from him. Everything."

She stared at DeeDee. She had seen the scars, but had only asked him about them once, and when he glossed over her questions, she stopped, giving him the same space he gave her when she didn't want to talk about things.

She moved slightly, hoping DeeDee would keep going. This was the most she had ever heard the woman say, and it was everything she wanted...needed to hear.

"When you were first hurt, did you know he didn't leave the room for four days? Scratch that—he came out and got the pain pills, but other than those few moments, he stayed with you. Stood in the shower and held you while I washed your hair. Growled at me when he thought I was taking too long. Got pissed off at Jase when he wanted to sit with you." DeeDee laughed and leaned back into the cooler, pulling out the last few beer bottles. "I've never seen anyone react like that before. I was worried so I spoke to Deke and Goose about his behavior because I thought maybe it was a PTSD episode. I knew he had some bad ones in the past. They both laughed and told me it ran much deeper than that."

She twisted her head and looked at Sharon. "I know what they were talking about now. He likes you, Sharon. Whenever you're in the room, no matter what else is going on, it's as if you are the only thing he can see. The man likes you a lot. Just...tread softly with him, okay? Don't hurt him. He matters to more people than he knows. He matters to me."

She smiled, pressing another soft kiss to his chest and felt him stir, his sleep roughened voice asking, "Babe?"

She nuzzled into him, sighing again, and repeated the words he had so often given to her, "Sleep, baby." *Yeah, I love him,* she thought. *He just doesn't know it yet.*

12. Rebels ride

From a table along the back wall of the clubhouse, Mason watched members as they moved through the main room into the kitchen or up the stairs to where the bedrooms and suites were located. He had been seated there for about two hours, entering the clubhouse during a slow time of day when only a couple of prospects were present, and he silenced them with a look, wishing to retain anonymity as long as he could, even if it were only for a brief time.

As he sat there relaxing after the long ride, he turned recent events, and their causes and repercussions, over in his mind. Things had begun to fall into place over the past year or so, and every chapter of the club had stable, legit businesses turning a profit, which meant all the members were being taken care of; his brothers were secure. In the twelve official chapters chartered as of last weekend, he had more than two thousand brothers ready to ride at his back with no more than a phone call.

This was what he sought all those years ago, what he wanted when he went against the deep-seated loyalties that had become an essential part of his life. It was what he needed when he wrestled the club out of his president's grasp, when his takeover had stripped Deacon of control, putting the binders on the slow, precarious slide into collapse that the club had been courting for a long time. This is what he prayed for when he put his best friend in the ground to save his brother's life, when he killed Ripper and then had been betrayed by blood. Maybe, after working towards it all this time, he would be able to see his way to everything being worth it, and finally reckon his penance paid for decisions long in the wind.

After the events of several weeks ago, when he took a handful of brothers to California to retrieve one of their own, nearly losing a brother in the process, he wanted that for himself. He wanted to lay it all out there and have people he trusted tell him he'd done good, that—as Ripper had often said—he had found the win. That was his intent with being here tonight, his mea culpa, because in the end, it was all on him. He had done what he had done, and believed they were the right things for the right reasons, but his brothers needed to understand what was still to come.

He watched as a group of several men came in through the hallway leading from the outside door, saw them enjoying an easy, comfortable camaraderie with each other. There was a definite level of confidence present between the members, and he found this rewarding to see. No more looking over their shoulders, and no more eyeballing each other, trying to catch the knife before it found its mark.

Over the years he had learned a lot about how to run a club, first with the Chicago chapter, of course, but then in how to expand into new chapters with St. Louis, then Kansas City, Memphis...Fort Wayne. A couple of the lessons had been more of the 'what not to do' variety, but everything sorted out in the end. The roads before them might not be paved with gold, but they were solid and rideable; the club was stable. He had somehow managed to get the critical things right, making sure the correct people were in place at the precise time needed, for the most part, and was proud of this outcome.

Like any typical Saturday night, the clubhouse was filling up quickly, and he knew he wouldn't be able to remain in the shadows much longer. Frankly, he was surprised no one had noticed him yet. As the thought crossed his mind, there was a startled shout of his name.

Looking up, he saw Tug walking his direction with a beautiful, dark-haired lady at his side, one strong arm slung around her shoulders. Drawing in a deep breath, Mason stood, slipping his beanie into his back pocket and sticking out an arm for their usual warrior's greeting. He pulled his friend close, bumping shoulders with the old man and thumping his back twice, three times with his other fist. Moving back, he inclined his head towards the woman, saying softly, "Maggie, how you doin', hon?"

She stepped forward and wrapped her arms firmly around his waist, hugging him tightly and not even flinching when her hands grazed across the gun holstered at the small of his back. He smiled, because, for someone who had only been introduced to the lifestyle a few months ago, Bear's mother was awfully nonchalant about such things. "Davis Mason, I didn't know you were in town, but it is good to see you. I'm doing fine, son. How about you?"

Mason warmed at her use of the word; it had been a while since a woman had called him that. He told Bear a long time ago to cherish his mom, because not everyone had the kind of sweet she brought into the world, and now he was reminded of this when he looked into Tug's face and found him gazing down at the woman, seeing the expression of deep affection written on his features. Mason thought to himself, *Looks like the old man found something worth keeping.*

Slate had stepped out of his office at the exchange and stood across the room, a pleased smile on his face before it disappeared behind his cupped hands. His shout amplified and rang through all the rooms of the clubhouse, drawing members and their women to the main room. "Mother*fuckers*, our Prez is in our house. Give the man some hospitality, and for fuck's sake, get him a goddamn beer!"

Striding across the room with his hand outstretched, Slate's smile slipped a notch when the wavering tones of a baby's cry rose from an upstairs hallway. Greeting Mason, he ducked his head a little and appeared to be waiting for something. Mason cocked his head, looking at him curiously, and Tug laughed, saying cryptically, "Five, four, three, two—" Before he could finish the countdown, Mason heard a voice he recognized, and at the words yelled from upstairs, he found himself laughing along with Tug and all the brothers.

"Slate...Prez, did you have to shout like that?" A second baby's voice joined the first, and the doubled volume caused Slate's shoulders to rise another inch as the woman's voice rolled down the stairs again. "Oh goodie, now Dani is up too."

"Fuck me," Slate muttered.

Mason reached over, tapping his fist on Slate's shoulder. "Twins, man. That's crazy shit. Y'all going for round two anytime soon?" He paused and laughed, "I guess actually that'd be round three, huh?"

"Fuck you, Prez. Ruby says not yet, but you never know." He laughed in response, and Mason watched him turn to look at his wife walking down the stairs with a child held securely in each arm, pride bright on his face at the sight. "Wanna see my babies again?" his friend asked with a broad smile, kissing Ruby's forehead before taking the blue-swaddled infant from her. "I'm told I make pretty babies, Prez."

Ruby rose on her toes to kiss Mason's cheek. "Hey, Mason," she said quietly, and then turned to Slate, her next words drawing more laughter from the gathered Rebels and their women. "*I* made pretty babies. You provided the fertilizer."

Later in the evening, after the old ladies and babies had gone home, Mason sat behind closed doors in the office with his inner circle of confidants and looked at the faces arrayed around the table. He knew the men had unasked questions, one of which would be about the location for this meeting, because it was one that normally would be held in Chicago, the mother chapter.

He told himself he had called the meeting here tonight, because it was convenient. But, more and more frequently over the past few months, he had found himself making his way to the Fort...because of a woman he first met in the clubhouse of a rival MC. Events set in motion that night had eventually wound up settling in his favor, including his pursuit of the woman. He didn't always seek out Willa Shipman when he was in town, but simply knowing she was within easy reach eased his mind somehow.

Willa, he thought and shook his head. The quick-witted beauty he first saw nearly two years ago was a topic that could wait for another day. This meet was for a different reason, so with difficulty, he put her from his mind.

The club would always be based out of Chicago, having been chartered there in a bar after everything went down the way it did so many years ago. The Monaco had been renamed Jackson's once the blood was all washed away, honoring the memories of everyone left standing. That bar was still the location where the club had their wall of honor, displaying pictures of all their fallen brothers, and Jackson's picture was at the top of that wall, fitting, because the bar was where he died.

Mason smiled fondly, remembering how proud the old man had been to be from Jackson, Mississippi, the town Johnny Cash and June Carter immortalized with their song. Jackson, better known to his family as Phillip Michaels, had been transported back home for burial, with all honor from the club. He had been a loyal member of the Rebel Fiends, and one of Mason's most staunch supporters. Authorizing and organizing his motorcycle escort to Jackson was one of Mason's first acts as the president of the newly renamed Rebel Wayfarers.

Pulling his thoughts back to the present, he looked over at Slate and reached a hand out for the gavel. It was passed over with a frown, and without delay Mason thudded it once on the table. "National meeting, we have enough officers for a consensus. Listen up. I got some shit to lay out, brothers." He reached out to pick up his beer, taking a long drink before setting it carefully down on the table, wrapping his strong fingers loosely around the bottle.

"Judge is still in the wind," he said, referencing a biker patched into the Outriders club of southern California. Two months ago, Bear's old lady, Eddie, had been kidnapped and nearly killed by Judge...her own brother. The Rebels had gotten her back safely, but the insult to the club hit hard. They should have been able to protect their own, and Eddie was theirs, no mistake about it.

"Shooter's doing a nickel, but we all know he'll be out sooner; he knows how to play by the rules and which lines not to cross." Shooter was Eddie and Judge's father, and had been national president of the Outriders since 2000, taking the club over from his old man. That transfer of power happened about the same time as Mason's takeover of the Rebels. They had been brothers, both patched into the previous incarnation of the Chicago club, but Shooter eventually left to head home to Cali, and found comfort in his old club there.

Mason shook his head. It wasn't like him to reminisce so much, and especially not when he had an audience. Everything came down to what he was about to expose to his brothers, a relationship that should probably have been acknowledged long ago, but he had always known there was a fuckton of pain that would come with this, mostly his, so he had avoided it for years.

"You all know the basic history of the Rebels. None of you were around when we formed the club," he said, his gaze slowly scanning the men in the room, pausing on Tug with a nod. "But, some of you were there right after I took over, got to see some of the shit that was still flying around, before and after. Compared to the '90s, our life today is fucking tame, brothers. Remember this before you judge, yeah?"

Fixing his gaze on Tug, the one man in the room with full knowledge of both the club and Mason's history, he began talking. "Most of you won't give a shit about any of this." He glanced at Slate and then Bear. "Some of you will. It's history, but I feel it's relevant, because I want you to understand what my intentions are. In '88, I landed in Chicago, was introduced by Winger to a man named Deacon, president of the Rebel Fiends.

"Within a year, I was patched in. In three years, I became one of his officers, and then eight years later, I cut that same man's rocker, taking the club from him in every way that mattered, a short twelve years after I joined him as a brother." There were questions, murmurings, and several of the men shifted in their chairs, uncomfortable with the idea of a powerful member and officer being brought so low, having the brotherhood of the club taken from him.

"My own hands, I cut a dozen rockers. My own hands, I put six brothers in the ground. My hands are still sticky with my brothers' blood, even though I believed then, and still know now, it was the only way. Our club was dying; Deacon didn't have any discipline, no fucking care for his brothers. He took first from the workings. His was the first skim. My club was dying around me...my brothers going gypsy or nomad nearly every week." He took a breath and then sipped from his beer, placing it back on the ring of condensation on the table.

"Shooter was a Rebel for ten years. I was his prospect when I patched in. He bailed in '98, headed home to Cali and his old man's club. Morgan, his old man, disappeared on a run to Utah in 2000, and Shooter took over that club the same month I bloodied the walls of the Monaco." More noise from the men in the room at this, Tug had probably been the only man who knew Shooter's long-ago association with the Rebels.

Mason ignored the questions thrown at him by the men around the table, continuing with his recounting. "I renamed the club, reworked the charter, rebuilt it in every way with brothers I trust with my life. Carefully recruited members who gave a fuck, who wanted to live their lives free and who weren't afraid to share the burden. Promoted those members, spread our territory, strategically absorbed families who previously wore different colors. Brought you all in, one by one, and now each of you plays a critical part in the club, and I'm here asking for your vote." He paused, looking at each individual in turn.

"We need to set Myron and Gunny to finding Judge, but I know I'm not objective where that boy's concerned. Nor where things touch Shooter. So, I'm here asking for your opinion, your vote...your trust. I won't ever be what Deacon became, so I want to make sure we're going the right direction for all members, not just me." He looked hardest at Duck, sitting along the wall to Mason's right.

Duck's brother had done damage to the club by injuring one of their own, Mica. *Mica*, the woman he had been owned by since the first moment he saw her. Mica, who he had given up for her own good. Duck had endured for years, struggling with the guilt from that blood association, and Mason now understood it more than he was ever able to before. He appreciated the horror felt when you found out your family had done so much evil and there was fucking nothing you could do to change the outcome.

"I'm of two minds for what to do with Shooter, but before we pick a direction, I'd like to have someone reach out to him, take his temperature. See if we can figure out how bound he is on revenge, or if perhaps he's seen the error of his ways." He looked at Slate, then Bear. "Anything other than remorse, we call it. He never leaves lockup." Turning his gaze the other direction around the table, he frowned at the expression on some of the faces, and knew they were struggling on his behalf, because the pull of the club's brotherhood would be strong on either side of the decision.

He had to make it clear the club was his life, that his brothers came first. "Would you deny Eddie is ours? That we have a responsibility to make sure he never gets close enough to touch her again? Shooter's the motherfucker who gave the recall order, handing crazy Judge a blank check on how to execute. We used some important markers to get her back, but it's not a cost I regret. Do it a thousand times over, because she is ours." He shook his head. "We dismantled the Outriders in response to what happened to Eddie. We killed a club that had been around for fifty years. Another thing I'd be willing to do again given the same need. But, we all know there will be blowback for those actions, and it's up to us to see the direction it comes from, so we can track it, and deflect it."

He turned to look at Bear again. "Nearly lost a brother in the mix, because he decided to hero-up on us, but we contained shit and made it motherfucking work. Brought everybody home alive." He shook his head, sighing. "Eddie belongs to us, just like Ruby is ours. Ours. Owned. Like Mica, Maggie, Willa...any of our women or families, if any of them come under threat, then we will put an end to any poison that tries to take them from us with the same goddamn terminal remedy."

"But like I said, I'm not impartial, and this is fucking hard." He felt uncharacteristically troubled and looked down at his hands folded around the bottle on the table, watching as his fingers nervously rubbed the label, twisting the bottle back and forth. Lifting a hand to his face, he scrubbed brusquely across his jaw and neck, feeling the scrape of his short beard across his skin. Setting his jaw, he raised his head, dropping his hand back to the table, and schooling himself to stillness. "I was Shooter's prospect into the club, because he's my brother. My half-brother." He looked at Duck again, seeing the dawning understanding on his face. "Yeah, he's my blood. Judge...that fucking poisonous snake of a rat bastard, is my blood too."

***

Gunny sat at one of the tables in the clubhouse's main room, waiting for the national officers' meeting to end. He knew the gist of what Mason was telling them, had known for a while, because the man had trusted him to keep a watch out for Judge since that motherfucker pulled a ghost out in Cali. Mason had called from the airfield while they waited for clearance to take off coming home, and laid everything out for him, including the blood tie and relationship with Shooter. He had listened silently then asked Mason one question, and after receiving an affirmative response, Gunny had begun to quietly and methodically run through his sources to ensure the little bastard wasn't going to land anywhere near Rebel property or people.

But, he found out more than they counted on when he began digging into the two men and the Outriders. Every stone he turned over held another association between Rebels and the western-based club. More than merely a blood connection, it looked like Shooter had been methodically dragging his spider's web across Mason's path time and time again, but to what gain, no one seemed to know. Beyond the things Mason already knew about, Gunny had found evidence Shooter had been involved or had influenced at least a half-dozen events in the past ten years alone that had resulted in negative consequences for Rebels.

He had been behind their brief but bloody war with the Machos club, feeding the Machos' president misinformation through Monster, a Rebel officer he had known from shared time in the Rebel Fiends, Mason's first club. At the time, Slate had been instrumental to Mason, because he had been part of the crew to stop the initial attack cold. It had been a baptism by fire for the man, because it happened on the same day he patched in as a prospect.

Shooter was also the reason for every shit thing that had happened to Bear in the past several years, at least as far as Gunny could tell. His near-death at the hands of club members in Iowa could be laid directly at Shooter's feet, as well as the beating he suffered in California bringing Eddie home. Last night, Gunny had discovered a well-hidden money trail, and now it looked like Shooter may have even been behind the carjacking resulting in Bear becoming a Rebel in the first place. Shooter and Mason seemed to share a need to manipulate people and events, but unlike Mason, for Shooter, collateral damage simply didn't register. He set situations into motion and designed events without the same kind of care and attention to the individuals that Mason brought to the table.

He felt a vibration in his pocket and reached down, pulling his phone out to look at the email. After reading the first two sentences of the report, he froze, his blood running cold in his veins. John Morgan, aka Shooter, owned four businesses in Kentucky not far from where Mason had grown up. One of those was a strip joint named Shinedown.

He cast his mind back to what Sharon had mentioned about the owner, saying John was a nice guy, but didn't come around the club often. Knowing how Shooter had pulled and pushed his chess pieces across the board, was it too paranoid for him to wonder if Sharon had been intimidated into moving on because of...what? Something. *What am I missing?*

She was sister to Jase, who was a good friend of Mason, and now a solid member of the Rebels. But, that was only one piece, because Jase was also friends with both Daniel and Mica, one of whom Mason was friends with, and one with which he was much more than friends. Indirectly connected with the Rebel president from two different sides, now the problem would be to determine if Sharon's appearance here in the Fort was coincidence, or directed. His gut twisted at the thought she might be working for...no. He trusted her.

Lover or not, if it weren't for the brutality of the beating she suffered, Gunny would probably be questioning her involvement, but he had come to know her well and couldn't believe she could have...but Elkins could. He nodded to himself, quickly tapping out an email response asking for additional information on the local bikers who had shown at the club in Kentucky the last night Sharon worked there, and added a request for info on the bouncer, too. Maybe there was something that drove her concern for the man, which prompted her to submit and then leave. *Fishing*, he thought.

He was just finishing, when the door behind the bar opened and ten men stalked out, led by Mason. He wasn't entirely certain what Prez wanted with him today, but had shown up at the indicated time, expecting to simply provide a report and update.

So, he was surprised as hell when Mason stopped at the bar and leaned into it, giving Gunny his back, but meeting his gaze in the mirror and drawing him over with a tilt of his head. He had taken two long strides headed that way, when a slow clapping started from the national officers who had been meeting with Mason. They had spread throughout the room, and now they were looking at him and putting their hands together in applause. *What the fuck?* He paused in place.

Slate put his fingers to his mouth and whistled shrilly, drawing a halt to the disconcerting noise, and the sound level in the room dropped immediately. Gunny finished walking to where Mason stood, covering the last twenty feet in an unnerving silence, the sharp slap of his boot soles on the bare wood floorboards the only noise. Mason held his gaze in the mirror, waiting until Gunny stood beside him to break the stare, looking down at the bar top and tapping several times with one fingertip.

Glancing down, Gunny saw a patch lying on the bar. Reading it, he figured they must be patching in a new member, but Watchman wasn't anyone he knew. *Maybe he's from one of the other chapters*, he mused, frowning and shrugging at Mason. He motioned for the prospect bartending today to get him a beer, leaning over to toss his empty into the trash behind the bar. Because of his position, he didn't see Mason move, and was unprepared for the touch on his upper arm. The grip seemed to come out of nowhere, startling him and had him lurching backwards, jerking out of Mason's hold.

175

"Hang on, brother," Mason said quietly, keeping his hands in clear view as Gunny struggled to control his physical response, because fuck a goddamned flight response—fight had kicked right the fuck into high gear. He could feel his nostrils flaring as he sucked in air, knew his face was twisted in a combination of terror and fury. "Got something to give you, Gunny." Mason's wary voice was carefully modulated, level and even in tone, deliberately pitched not to carry. "It's all good, man. Not fucking with you, just wasn't thinking." His president was one of the few people who knew all of what happened to him over in the sand wars, the twenty-plus reasons for his self-isolation, and the one reason for his distrustful attitude.

"What is it?" he ground out, drawing up to his full three-inch advantage over the Prez, sweat coating his face.

"Fucking national office," Mason said, tapping the patch again.

"What the fuck is a Watchman?" Gunny asked, not moving, still grimly trying to bring his breathing back under control.

"Someone who watches." Mason shrugged. "Someone who keeps shit in line, because he sees everything that goes on. Someone like you."

"Screw you." Gunny said, offering a one-finger salute and laughing, slowly relaxing now, since he knew this to be a joke.

Shaking his head, Mason said, "Not my type, fucker. But, you are my newest fucking national officer. Welcome, brother." He thrust out a hand, and Gunny gripped it out of reflex, the heat and pressure from the grip working to anchor him and he felt the Pandora's box of his response slip closed.

"Funny shit, Prez." He let Mason pull him into a one-shouldered hold, and then his eyes flicked to a grinning Slate, seeing Jase step out from behind him with a smile on his face. Shuffling backwards, he raised his chin, asking Mason, "You're shitting me, right?"

"Shit-free, motherfucker. Get your gal to sew it on tonight; you know the drill. We can catch up tomorrow to discuss exactly what's expected, but tonight we're gonna fucking party. It ain't every day we create a new office and promote a brother." Mason stepped back, folding his arms across his chest, waiting for Gunny's response.

"National officer? You sure you got the right guy, Prez?" He shook his head, even as he felt the heat of bodies against his back, tensing though he knew it was his brothers circling around. *Every man in here has my six*, he thought, firmly reminding himself this place would always be safe. Every brother trusted.

"Yeap, right fucking brother for the job, man. It's all good, Gunny. You're good." Mason's eyes cut over his shoulder then back to him. Prez gave him a chin lift, a soft tap of knuckles to his breastbone, and a tilt of his head, and Gunny turned to accept the welcome and congratulations of his club.

A couple of hours later, he received a text on his phone and grinned. Standing, he looked around to see Mason sitting at a table across the room, deep in conversation with Slate and Jase. Rocking back on his heels, he called out, "Prez. Got something for you. Somewhat unplanned you're in town precisely when it's ready, but I'll count this as a good thing. A sign." He laughed loudly. "A good fucking omen, man." He tapped a response on the phone and headed for the wide hallway leading to the outside door. "Be back in a few, Mason. Don't go anywhere. Hang tight."

About thirty minutes later, coming up the hallway from outside, he heard the noise and murmurs as the members took in the sight of him pushing a drape-covered bike into the clubhouse. Bringing bikes in wasn't uncommon; at times, it was more typical than not, because no one wanted their ride out in the hail of a summer storm. Bringing them in covered was different though, even for him, and had their tongues wagging.

"Mason...Prez, come over here," he said, pulling the bike to a stop in the middle of the room, nodding to thank the men who had pushed tables out of the way. He toed down the rear kickstand for the bike, tugging back on the handlebars to secure the bike upright, and settled one hip into a comfortable lean on the still-covered seat.

"You are a man well-known for his love of bikes. Unlike our brother Bear here, you don't much appreciate flashy and gaudy, and you sure as shit don't want to ride sparkles and glitter like Hoss." He grinned around the room, noting every eye was on him, and not minding it for a change. This was a once in a lifetime opportunity, and he was going to make as big a production out of it as he could stand. Building memories. "Nope, you are a man after my own heart. Classic and black are two main requirements for a scoot you're willing to plant your ass on. Throw in some chrome, and it's a done fucking deal. I stumbled on this one a couple years ago—" The noise level in the room rose at this admission, and he glared around at the men until they quieted down. It wasn't their place to know the degree of dedication he had for Mason. *Hell*, he thought, *two years ain't nothing. I'd work my whole life to give him something like this.*

"—a couple years ago," he continued. "I found this at an auction. They didn't know what they had, and I sure as fuck didn't tell them." Laughter sounded in the room, but he kept his eyes on Mason's face. "Way I see it, there is no one else this bike could belong to, no one it matches up to like it does you. Because, like our president, like Mason, it is one of a kind, fast and dangerous. Fuck, brothers, my Rose of Sharon tells me Mason is hot as hell. Now, I can't vouch for that shit, 'cause my dick likes pussy, but I know this bike is fucking hot, because I get a hard-on every damn time I look at it." Louder laughter rang out, and Mason tucked his thumbs into his front pockets, frowning.

"This is my gift to you, Prez. Like you have with every man in this room, you've saved my life. This is the smallest of things compared to that." He turned and gathered the silk covering in his hands, dragging it over and off the bike, tossing it to one side, where a prospect caught it.

A deafening silence fell over the room, broken only by a single set of footsteps and a harshly indrawn breath. He hadn't turned from the bike, still admiring the lines and artistry of the powerful-looking machine. "Brother," Mason whispered softly. "This is a Vincent. A Vincent Black Shadow. Nine ninety-eight cc, it came off the line doing a hundred and a quarter, seventy better than anything else in the day. Hunter S. Thompson named it a death machine."

"Yeap," Gunny said proudly, looking from the bike to Mason's awe-struck face. He nodded slowly. "Handmade in 1948 in England, it was hell to find parts at first, but in the end, everything came together like I wanted. We're back to original as much as a sixty-six-year-old bike can be. Bitch can run too, man. Listen to this." He moved to adjust the choke, toggling the kill switch and reached down, flipping out the lever then jumped up, smoothly kicking the bike to life. He looked back at Mason as he rolled the throttle, the powerful rack and ring of the pipes echoing in the closed-in space. At a nod, he killed the engine and stepped around the front wheel, still watching Mason's face as he faced him across the bike.

"I can't, man. This is...it's too much, Gunny. Holy fucking...*Jesus*, it's a beautiful bike, but I know what it's worth, man." Mason's eyes never left the bike, jealously tracing the lines with his gaze, possessive hands reaching out involuntarily to rest on the handlebar and seat.

Gunny frowned at Mason's words, tilting his head as he carefully composed his response. "Brother. Mason, my life ain't worth much, I know, but you saved it, Prez. With the club, giving me all this...you and Deke, but this...this is for you." He shrugged. "I built the bike for you. You don't want it, we'll auction it, and the money can go to the beer fund."

That startled a barking laugh from Mason. "That'd be a fuckton of beer, brother. And your life, the lives of every man in this room, each man wearing my patch...you know you are all worth *everything* to me."

Mason looked away from the bike for the first time, taking in the expression Gunny knew he had on his face. It had to be a combination of hope Mason could understand the worth of the gift he had first given Gunny, paired with disappointment that his friend would consider rejecting the bike. "Every patch is worth my life," Mason said and bowed his head for a moment. When he lifted it, he swallowed, looking at Gunny again with a firm nod. "My thanks, brother. It's a fucking beast. I'm proud to ride it, man." Reaching out a hand, he gripped Gunny's forearm, holding for a moment as their arms stretched across the bike. Tilting his head, he asked, "Quarter mill?"

Gunny waggled the fingers of his other hand, grinning. "Give or take fifty large."

***

Mason scanned the room, looking at the pride on every man's face. His gaze caught on Jase, seeing the moment when his thoughts stuttered at what Gunny and Mason had just said. Jase stood still for a second and then turned to Slate, and Mason heard him quietly ask, "Dollars?"

Laughing, Slate nodded, gaze still on the motorcycle parked in the middle of the clubhouse's main room. "We're a profitable club," he overheard Slate joke, reaching over and picking something up off the bar. "Gunny's a focused dude. When he said the auction didn't know what they had on the lot, he's probably underselling their ignorance. That's an ultra-rare bike; collectors are going to be beating Mason's door down if word gets out what he's got." Looking at the patch in his hand, he glanced over at Jase. "Haven't talked to you much lately, since you're so busy with Myron and shit. How's Sharon? She still dancing?" Shaking his head, he lowered his voice, asking, "You still okay with her being with Gunny, man?"

Mason focused to hear the answer over the growing swirl of noise in the room, because this was a question he had wanted to ask, too. But even before Slate was finished speaking, Jase was nodding. "Hell yeah, I'm okay with it. He's good for her. Man is solid, and she seems...I dunno, she seems to be something he needs, too. It's funny how he is with her, hauling her around and keeping her close." He shrugged. "She's still dancing. DeeDee said the nights she's on the ticket, Slinky's is packed, but she noticed Sharon is careful to keep a distance from the men. Gunny seems okay with it, which honestly surprised me at first. When I asked him about it, he explained he's the only one she goes home with. Shit, Slate, as long as he's okay with it, what the hell am I going to say?"

Slate nodded. "If he says he's good, then he is. It's amazing what finding the right partner can do for a man." Lifting his voice, he yelled, "Bear, come here, brother."

As the dark-haired man walked over, Mason smiled at the good-natured arguing going on between various members about the bike, nuances of its construction, and questions to Gunny regarding provenance of the replacement parts. He walked over to join the little group and, greeting Bear, he listened as Slate first asked a couple of questions about some bike orders in the queue, then about any lingering issues from the injuries Bear took in California. Finally, Slate got down to what Mason felt was probably the whole reason for the conversation. He shook his head as his brother said, "Bear, give Eddie a call and have her let Willa know Mason's here for a couple of nights."

Bear grinned at his friends and pulled his phone from his pocket, pressing a button and putting it to his ear. "Dial home," he said and waited a second. "My heart, do me a favor, would ya? Let Willa know Mason is in town? Yeah, he's at the clubhouse right now. Yeap, I'm looking at him. Uh huh, I think he's here for a couple of nights." He paused. "Sure, I can ask—" He paused again. "Baby, you don't have to do—" He smiled at her interruption, then said, "Okay, sweetheart, I'll see what I can do. Love you, Eddie." His face lit up when she apparently returned the sentiment, and he tucked his phone back into his pocket. "Y'all are all coming to dinner tonight at eight. Bring Ruby and DeeDee.

If you see Tug, tell him and make sure he knows he'll need to bring Mom. Prez, you don't get to tell her no, okay? Eddie's on a mission, it seems."

Mason ran his tongue across the inside of his teeth, then said, "Invite Gunny and Sharon, too."

Bear shrugged and nodded. "Okay, the more, the merrier," he said, pulling his phone out and walking away as he typed a text to Eddie.

He watched as Slate slung an arm around Jase's shoulders, drawing him towards the larger group of Rebels still standing next to the bike. Glancing over his shoulder at Mason, he said, "Prez, let's take that bitch out for a run, man." Lifting his head, Slate shouted, "Rebels ride, motherfuckers."

They watched as Mason carefully maneuvered the bike out of the building. In the parking lot, he straddled the seat and waited for the brothers scrambling to mount their bikes, as he familiarized himself with the feel of the controls and adjusted the mirrors, giving everyone a chance to ready their rides. He glanced over at Jase, where he sat on his bike, and frowned, calling him and Slate forward with a tip of his head. They walked their bikes up on either side of him, and he asked Jase, "Why ain't you riding Winger's scoot, man?" He had bought the motorcycle Bear made Winger, unwilling to see the customized bike go to a stranger in a charity auction, because to him, one of those men unlucky enough to never get to meet the man, it had been DeeDee's bike.

Jase shook his head, patting the tank of the bobber he rode. "Road's bike works for me when I'm solo. I'll grab the Rebel when I pick up DeeDee to go to dinner."

"The Rebel?" Mason asked, and Jase nodded.

"It's patched in, man. Patch is painted right on the tank; that bike is a true Rebel." He grinned and shrugged, settling his cut more comfortably.

Mason nodded and looked around at the more than thirty men sitting astride their bikes, waiting. He gave the prospect manning the gate a chin lift and received an acknowledging nod in return. Once the gate was open, he raised a hand in the air and got chills at the roaring of bike engines in response. Giving an overhead twirl with his finger, he led the group of his brothers out of the lot and onto the street. He rode point on their doubled line of bikes, as was his right, Slate and Gunny side-by-side right behind him.

***

Swallowing hard, she sighed again. "I don't know what I want. One minute, things are so hot between us I can't breathe, and I want to eat you up...want you to make love to me until we're both raw and screaming. Then, in the next minute, I'm scared and I want to run. I've been...I don't know. Lost, maybe? Since I left home in Red Deer, I've been lost. Back then, I was so afraid of being ordinary, forgettable. Ace had done so much with his life even before he hit high school, and I was just me. Our other brothers were all athletes too; you could see the pride on Mom and Dad's faces. And then there was me."

Sharon ducked her head, hair trailing down across her cheek, hiding much of her face from him. Softly, she said, "When I was with Derek, after things...got bad, I tried for so long to be invisible, wanted it, even, but the fear still waits, and it's got big teeth. The fear can still overwhelm me, of being forgettable. But, you? You...oh, Gunny, you ground me, and sometimes it feels as if you're the only thing holding me together. Like I'd fly apart if you weren't here."

She looked up at him from where she was sitting on the floor, a dog curled in her lap. Whispering softly, she said, "There were so many people there tonight. Teachers, educated people, and then...there I was." She shrugged, glanced up at him and back down, and she muttered something, but he couldn't catch the words.

They had barely returned home from the dinner at Eddie and Bear's place, a chaotic gathering of friends and brothers, complete with kids running around. She had insisted on sewing his new patch on before they left, and he glanced down again to see it nestled there over his name. When they got the invite to dinner, she had been excited to meet some of the women. She chattered in his ear all the way over about how nice it would be to have friends in town, and he had frowned, realizing with a start how isolated she had been since moving in with him. Granted, he liked it that way, wanted her all to himself, but not if it made her unhappy. No matter how he preferred to live, above all he wanted her happy, loved to see her smiling.

When they got to Bear's house, she had half-hidden behind him at first, fingers twisting between his, her palm wet with nervous sweat. The greetings from everyone had seemed warm and heartfelt to him, but her tension hadn't lessened, even when he pulled her into his lap. She had stiffened even more when he began openly caressing and touching her as they were sitting around before the meal. He wanted everyone to know she was his, and his hands on her hips and back were an open claim for anyone with eyes to see.

He noticed Eddie wearing a new vest with familiar looking patches sewn to the back. Looking closer, he saw they said 'Property of Bear,' and he looked at the man with a smile.

Not all the women wore vests, but enough of them, and he frowned. He decided he needed to get Sharon a set of rags so she would be publicly claimed in settings like this, or when she was around any of his brothers, with or without him by her side. She was his, and he wanted everyone to know. Bending down, he had nuzzled the side of her head, feeling her tense even more under his hands. "Baby," he whispered, "this is our family." She took a breath and nodded, looking over to where DeeDee sat comfortably on Jase's knee, posture an unconscious mirror of their own.

During dinner, she talked a little at first, but then had gradually grown quiet, listening more as her head turned back and forth at the verbal volleying of the long-time friends present at the table. Insider jokes and childhood stories were related with much laughter, but the only two people nearly as uncomfortable as he and Sharon were Mason and Willa.

Since Sharon clearly wasn't having a good time, he quietly suggested leaving as soon as the meal was done, and she accepted gratefully, silent on the ride home, pressed tightly against his back. Once inside, she sat on the floor, snuggling the pups, their wiggles and licks bringing a small smile back to her face. Where she still sat, taking comfort from their unconditional love.

Gunny still wasn't pleased with what he saw so far, and even less so with what he heard her saying. *How could she ever think she's forgettable?* he wondered. He waited for her to continue, and when she didn't, he stepped over from where he was leaning against the wall and squatted down next to her. Reaching out, he picked Tank up out of her lap, ignoring the complaining sounds from the dog, and sat him on the floor. Then he slid his hands underneath her knees and around her back, standing and lifting her as she wound her arms around his neck.

Walking into the bedroom, he put a knee to the bed, carefully crawling to the headboard and twisting to sit, pulling her into his lap. "Babe, you don't know what you want?" It was a loaded question, and she would know it, because he was a big fan of knowing your own mind, a conversation they had more than once.

She shifted, tucking herself against him, nestling her head beneath his chin. "Well, yeah, I do. Maybe it's more about not being sure I deserve what I want."

"And if I want you?" He asked the question softly, nuzzling the side of her head.

With a quiet sob, she said in a tear-filled voice, "I'm not sure you deserve just me. So much more, baby, you deserve so much more."

"Shhhh, Sharon. My Rose of Sharon, you hush that talk. What if I want *you*, baby? You make me happy. I want you, so can I have you? Do I deserve to have what makes me happy?" He pressed his lips against the side of her head, slowly stroking one hand against the edge of her jaw, cupping his hand around the column of her throat. "Can I?" He traced down her neck with his thumb, dragging it across her collarbone towards the curve of her shoulder. "Baby, can I have you?" He brought his hand across, the backs of his knuckles brushing against her nipples, and he watched as they hardened and pressed against the fabric of her shirt. He closed his hand over her breast, squeezing lightly as he rolled her nipple between finger and thumb.

Her gasp was his only answer and he leaned down, capturing her mouth with his own, lips coaxing hers into responding, opening for him. He pressed his advantage, stroking into her mouth with his tongue, sliding between her lips and tasting her. *Fucking addictive*, he thought. Kissing her recklessly, the excitement and passion in their embrace increased his arousal and he groaned into her mouth, feeling his cock throb and jerk against the buttons of his pants.

"If I want you, can I have you?" he asked again, his voice rough with passion, lips against hers, their foreheads nearly touching. "If I wanted to keep you for myself, could I? All mine?" He traced his nose along the length of her jaw, nuzzling her ear, dusting soft kisses along the way. "Because I want you, babe...wanna keep you," he whispered, his fingers caressing and plumping her breast while he nipped with his teeth at her earlobe. His other hand slid down her back, slipping underneath her jeans to press between her ass cheeks, pulling her hard against him. She sighed at his touch, and he felt her hands moving restlessly up and down his arms, stroking his face, running over his scalp.

"Wanna fuck you." He kissed her. "Wanna keep you," he repeated, nuzzling her cheek and tightening his fingers around her ass. "Wanna have you. Mine." He stroked into her mouth with his tongue, his fingers plucking at her nipple. "Wanna eat you." His arms tightened, hands clenching where they gripped, the kiss deepening and renewing. "Eat you right up, baby. Can I?" he asked, and smiled against her lips at her affirmative response.

"You're *mine*, babe," he said, releasing her and standing, divesting himself of his clothes, tossing them carelessly away from him. He turned back to her, found her still mostly dressed, and reached out, tugging at the button on her pants, sliding his fingers into the waistband and pulling them down, along with her panties. "Need to see you," he whispered, removing her shirt and bra, settling her back onto the bed.

"Have to taste you," he breathed, lips on the inside of her knee as he worked his way between her legs. "You're going to come hard, babe," he said, nipping and gently biting at her pussy lips, tugging them into his mouth before separating them with the tip of his tongue.

Slipping his hands up her legs, he draped them over his shoulders, seeing her toes curl into the sheet in anticipation. "Gunny?" She said his name like a question and he looked up her body, glowing in the limited moonlight cast through the windows.

"Yeah, baby?" he said, twisting and twirling his tongue along her opening, shallowly dipping inside then moving up to circle her clit. He slid his hands along the backs of her thighs, cupping her pussy firmly with one hand. His middle finger slipped up to caress and flick her clit, and he ground the heel of his hand into her, feeling the wetness making her slippery.

"I love you." This was said so softly that for a few moments, he wasn't positive he had heard right, and then he groaned, lunging forward and covering her mound with his mouth, licking and biting, sucking and fucking her with his tongue and fingers, compelled by an urgency that stunned him. Hearing those words from her lips nearly did him in, and he pressed his hips into the mattress, mindlessly trapping his cock between his belly and the sheets, trying to remain focused on her responses to his attention.

Fingers grazed his skin as she touched the side of his face, dragging her fingertips down to his lips, joining his tongue in ravaging her pussy. She slid a finger along each side of her clit, raising and exposing it for his tongue, and he obliged her unspoken need, pressing hard and then flicking it rapidly side-to-side as she gasped. Her other hand found its way to his scalp, fingernails scratching gently across his skin, making him sorry he didn't have hair for her to grip and pull in this moment.

She tensed and he watched ardently as she came, her body shuddering with the force of her orgasm. Her clit was throbbing under his tongue as he licked along where she was touching herself and then down where his fingers still thrust inside her. He continued that movement, pushing and twisting them, retreating and returning again and again. Her shoulders arched up off the bed, her back rounding as she raised to look at him. Her thumb traced his eyebrow before her hand went to the back of her knee, pulling her leg out farther, opening herself to him.

"Told you, babe. You come hard on my mouth every time. Baby," he said, trailing his lips gently across the sensitive flesh of her pussy. "You want my mouth or my cock now?"

"You," she said immediately, her voice raw with having just come so hard. "I want you inside me. Love me. Please, love me."

He stayed where he was for a moment, feeling her pussy still clenching and tightening around his fingers, then he slowly slid them out. Lapping against and between her lips with his tongue, he gathered her wetness into his mouth. Sitting back on his heels, he brought his hand up, watching her face as he licked and sucked his fingers clean, her mouth opening as she gasped, watching his enjoyment of her taste.

Without a word, he leaned over her to open the nightstand drawer and pulled out a condom, pressing against her breasts with his chest as he slid back to his position between her legs. He felt the hard nubs of her nipples dragging along his pectoral muscles, the heat of her body against his, the grasping pull of her mouth placing sucking kisses on his side, up under his arm, across his shoulder.

He opened and slid the condom onto his cock, rolling it down slowly, focusing his attention on her body where it was laid out for him, anticipating the feel of that first slide, knowing how hot and tight she would be around him. His cock twitched, jerking up to slap against his belly, and he shivered, skin breaking into goose bumps.

"Gonna fuck you now, baby," he growled, gripping her thighs in his hands and tugging her towards him, spreading her knees to either side of his hips. He lifted her ass onto his legs, using his thumb against the root of his cock to angle it down so he could slide the tip into the entrance of her pussy. "Gonna fuck you hard, baby," he warned, slipping his cock in a little farther, and then he withdrew and used his hand to swirl the tip around the outside of her pussy, spreading her wetness to ease his way. "You gotta tell me if it's too much," he said through gritted teeth, and lifted her with one hand, the other guiding his cock into her again as he pulled her onto him, thrusting deep inside with a single, slow push and glide.

Raising onto his knees, he held her hips up, forcing her back into an arch, which left only her head and shoulders in contact with the mattress. She was suspended in his grip, and he pushed and pulled her onto him as he drove his hips forward, snapping and plunging deep, looking down to watch as her body took every inch of his cock. She was so tiny; he was always amazed she could take all of him, and he loved to feel her stretch to accommodate his length and girth. He held her hips firmly, and spread his hands wide across her belly, stroking her clit with his thumb pads, alternating left and right as he felt that bundle of nerves swell taut with the stimulation.

"Sharon," he breathed, eyes flicking from where they were joined so perfectly, up to her face, seeing an expression of pleasure on her features. "My Sharon," he repeated, tipping her hips slightly and fucking into her steadily, watching her eyes open in surprise as she gasped. "Is it good, baby?" he asked, already knowing the answer as he increased the pace slightly.

"Yeah," she said on a moan, "Gunny, God. What are you…" Her voice trailed off and he watched as her hands twisted in the sheet underneath her. He changed the angle again and her eyes drifted closed, teeth biting down on her top lip, nostrils flaring with her quickened breath. "Baby, that's so…" Head tipping back, she went silent again, losing her words. He smiled tightly, focusing on skillfully bringing her over the brink again before he gave in to his own orgasm, which was so close he could barely hold it off.

Insistently stroking her clit with his thumbs, he changed the pace again slightly, pulling her against him more forcefully. Grunting as he plunged deep inside her with every thrust, the sound of their flesh slapping together echoed in the room along with her groans. Pressing hard on her clit with one thumb, he slipped the other down and inside her ass, pushing in alongside his cock, filling her even more. The pressure pushed her over that brittle edge, lifting her on the wave of pleasure as it crested around her, leaving her shaking in its wake.

Gunny bowed his head, feeling sweat running down his back, creating tracks across his scalp as he watched her slow glide down from pleasure while he continued to stroke into her. His movements were more frantic now, less paced and measured. Desperately chasing his own pleasure, he suddenly dropped her hips, following her down and tunneling into her as he pressed her against the mattress.

Arching over her body, he curved his arms around her shoulders and back, crushing her into his torso while he fucked her furiously, hips jackhammering his cock into her. He needed it hard, needed the contact, needed to fuck her, mark her. *Mine. My woman. Loves me.*

Only mine. He felt her legs wrap around him and she pushed up against his thrusts, meeting every plunge of his cock, fucking him back, her hands sliding up and down his arms.

He gripped her shoulder in his teeth, biting down, for once careless of the pain he caused, and was surprised when her pussy clenched tightly around him again, her aroused voice softly saying, "Oh," the tone indicative of her own surprise at her sudden climax. That pushed him up to the wall and over it, and he tumbled down the other side, holding onto her desperately as he thrust deep. *Loves me. Mine*. Groaning and calling her name in a gravel-filled voice he didn't recognize, he felt his cock pulse and throb inside her, suddenly wishing he was bare, painting the inside of her pussy with his semen, marking her in a way he never wanted with other women. *Mine*. "Fuck," he ground out when she tightened around him again, pulling another series of thrusts from him, feeling the silken slide of her walls around his still-hard cock.

He rested his forehead on the pillow beside her head, reluctantly dragging his arms from around her, but careful to support his weight on his elbows, listening to her ragged breathing that matched his own. "Baby," he said, shifting his head to press his lips against her cheek, "I think you might have killed me."

"Oh, but it'd be a hell of a way to die, eh?" She laughed and turned her head, grazing her lips across his, flicking out her tongue to trace his bottom lip and smiling. "I taste myself on your lips," she whispered.

"You like that?" he asked, returning her kiss and trailing his tongue across the inside of her lips slowly, pulling back to place a firm kiss on her mouth, and a softer one on the tip of her nose.

"Yeah, I do," she said with a soft smile, running her hands up his arms to his back. She swept up and down slowly with one, while the other went to caress the back of his head, fingertips trailing across his scalp.

He stared at her, gaze running the length of her face and back to her eyes. Suddenly nervous, he licked his lips and asked, "You love me?"

Her smile widened and she caught her bottom lip between her teeth, letting it slip out slowly. "Yeah, Gunny, I do. Lane Robinson, I love you." Her finger traced his cheek and he watched as her eyes followed that fingertip, seeing the small frown that crossed her face when he knew her finger touched the scar in front of his ear. "I love you."

"God, baby, I don't think I would ever get tired of hearing those words from you. Love you're here with me. Loved you since I saw you, since I touched you. Every day brings it to me even more, you give me more. Mine. Love you, babe," he whispered, tracing his nose along her cheek. "I love you." He kissed her slowly and thoroughly, mouth working against hers for long minutes, his cock twitching in response to her slow, rolling, tightening around him, again and again. Finally pulling back, he laughed and said, "Need to take care of the condom, baby." Reaching down between them, he held it in place as he pulled out, grinning silently at the sounds of disappointment she made. Rolling off her to the edge of the bed, he stood, walking towards the bathroom as he pulled the covering off his softening cock.

She joined him a moment later, reaching past him wordlessly to start the shower. Looking over her shoulder at him as she stepped inside, she slowly closed the door, cutting off his view of her.

13. My oath to you

Motionless except for his rising and falling chest, he lay still for a moment, listening to...nothing. Slowly and carefully lifting his head, he blinked bleary eyes and scanned the room. The house was silent, and he wasn't sure what had woken him, but now every nerve was alert, hair on his arms standing on end. He had learned a long time ago to pay attention to these feelings, the unspoken tension silently screaming, *Danger!*

He felt Sharon warming the bed beside him; he was half-curled around her, their legs twined together beneath the sheet, she was pressed into him. Sleeping deeply, her breathing was undisturbed, and he had begun to settle back into bed when there was a faint noise from outside. Likely what had woken him, it was an indistinct scratching of branches brushing up against the siding of the house on the first floor. Muttering a soft, relieved, "Fuck," he eased back down, slowly relaxing and curling his arm around her waist. Pushing his hand down between her legs, he cupped her pussy possessively, and softly kissed the back of her neck, needing to touch her, to reassure himself she was there, was his. *Mine.*

Then his eyes flew open again, straining against the darkness in the room. There had been a different noise. It sounded like one of the pups was having a bad dream, making soft, muffled, woofing noises, but not in the room...from far away. *Something ain't right*, he thought as the bedroom door creaked open a few inches and something landed with a thud on the floor at the foot of the bed. There was barely enough time to react, but he slid his hand underneath the pillow to find the grip of his pistol with his palm a bare second before the flashbang went off, ripping Sharon from sleep as she gave voice to a brief, disoriented scream.

In the moments before he was tackled and driven from the bed, Gunny saw figures moving into the room, the overexposed, bright images on his retinas making it difficult to focus clearly. Then the hit came and, mind clear, he moved with it, using his forearms to brace on either side of Sharon as he took the attacker with him off the bed. Retaining his hold on the gun, running off muscle memory and instincts, he rolled as he landed and pushing up to one knee, took careful aim, firing at the first two targets identified, barely noticing as they dropped while he looked for the next.

Over the ringing in his ears, he could hear Sharon again screaming to his left, so he shifted stance and removed two additional targets. No time for conscious thought, he was trying to ensure she wasn't caught in his line of fire. Blinking furiously to clear his vision, he saw a man looming above him and they locked eyes. *Woolfe.* Despite the shock of recognition that jarred him, Gunny pulled his trigger repeatedly, seeing the strobe effect from the muzzle flash multiple times before he felt the distinctive recoil action of the slide locking open, indicating he was out of ammunition.

The figure had staggered backwards but hadn't gone down. Sinking slowly to one knee, the man knelt in front of Gunny, a hand to his bloodless chest. "Fuck, that hurts, brother," he wheezed out before settling back on his heels. *What the fuck?*

Sharon's screams cut off suddenly, but not in a way that indicated she'd been hurt, just silenced. Gunny didn't break the stare he shared with the man, making certain his next words were heard. "Hurt her," he sucked in a breath, "fucking touch her, and I'm gonna put you in the ground," Gunny said, lifting his chin. *What the fuck is going on? Why are they here?*

"Obviously," the man gritted out, tugging his shirt up to expose a vest worn next to his skin. "You're still a little bastard, Lane." He dropped the hem of his ruined shirt and shook his head. "Kincade would be so proud. You coming with? My instructions didn't mention you other than to say she was bunked up here. Imagine my surprise when I saw your name on my orders."

Gunny dropped the empty gun and said nothing, just lifted his hands and laced his fingers behind his head in silent response, keeping his gaze intently locked on Woolfe's. There was no reading the man, he wasn't giving any indication of his next move, but, if they were taking Sharon and he had the chance to go along, he would take it, no matter the risk. He could hope they had tripped the alarm upon entry, which would mean the club would know something was wrong, but if Woolfe were here, that would be a questionable assumption to make. *He's always been a fucking ghost*, he thought. The man knew everything Gunny did about avoiding security systems and, given the past few years of him being entirely off the grid, he might even know more.

"Good boy," the former Marine Recon team chief muttered, unfolding to his feet, looming over Gunny, where he knelt on the floor. "You've got two minutes to dress." He stepped backwards, calling over his shoulder, "Girl secured?"

"Yeah, boss." The call came from a shadowy group of figures near the door, and as he stood, Gunny could see her naked form twisting in the midst of their group. Two of the men casually held her suspended between them, with what looked like a gag in her mouth. *Mine. Get your goddamned* fucking *hands off my woman.*

Thinking fast, he calmly said, "Let me dress her." Bending, he snagged his pants from the floor and pushed his feet into them, fastening the buttons with one hand. *If they put a mark on her*, his lip lifted in an unconscious snarl, *I'll fucking kill them all*. He grabbed his shirt from the foot of the bed with the other, tugging it on over his head, waiting on the answer that hadn't yet come. *Fuck, fuck, fuck.*

"Turn her loose." Woolfe gave the command and the men released Sharon. *Thank fuck.* She took two steps and silently launched herself at him, hitting his chest with such force it drove him back a half-step. *Not hurt, thank fuck.*

"Shhhh. I got you, baby." He soothed her with words as he tugged the cloth from her mouth. He kept a wary eye on the men in the room as he picked her shirt up off the nearby chair, peeling her arms from around his waist. "Shhhh." Gathering the material in his hands, he brought it over her head, and then helped her work first one then the other arm into the garment, pulling it down her torso. "I got you." Picking up her jeans from the dresser where he tossed them last night, he turned her in his arms. He saw her gaze dart past him to the group of men, panic beginning to twist her features, and he softly whispered in her ear, "Eyes on me, baby. One step at a time, you're doing great. Eyes to me; I got you."

He held the jeans in front of her, keeping his gaze steady on her as he coaxed her into the pants one leg at a time. "Shhhh." Deftly fastening the waistband closed, he sat her on the edge of the bed and handed her socks, setting her boots in front of her before putting on his cut and gathering his own socks and boots. "Boots, baby. Put your boots on." Balancing easily, he quickly pulled the socks on and had barely shoved his feet into his boots when she stood, taking the two steps to him and wrapping her arms around him again.

Arm around her shoulder, pulling her to him, he straightened slowly, cupping one of her hands in his, feeling her fingers thread between his automatically. "Who wants her?" He didn't actually expect a response, so he wasn't surprised when he didn't receive one other than a brusque head movement, indicating the open door.

Glancing around, he saw the four bodies scattered across the bedroom floor and a thought hit him when he looked up. "Not everyone got a vest, huh?" There was a groan from near the closet door, and he saw one of the men had their eyes open, chest still rising and falling with respiration. Staring at the man, he narrowed his eyes, because he seemed familiar. *Surely not*, he thought, looking closer and realizing it was Elkins, sucking in a harsh breath in surprise. *Motherfucker is still alive*, he thought, *like a fucking cockroach crushed beneath a boot heel, but still squirming towards the dark crack along the edge of the wall.*

"Woolfe," he said, turning his head to look at the man. "I need to clear my shit." Without waiting for a response, he moved in front of Sharon, lifting her chin with two fingers, bringing her eyes to meet his. "Baby, you're doing great, so good, baby...so good, but I need you here with me right now. You with me?" She nodded with shaky movements, trembling lips pressed tightly together in a flat line. *So fucking strong.* "You're going to step outside into the hallway, and you're going to cover your ears, baby. You're going to do that for me. I got one piece of shit to deal with here. You're going to give me a little space, and then I'll be right back with you, wrapped around you, yeah?"

She shook her head back and forth vehemently, hair flying out as it would when she danced, rejecting the idea without a word. *She can't see this.* He stroked along her jaw with his thumb, leaning forward to brush his lips across hers. "Baby, I know you're scared, and you're doing so good. But I got to take care of this." *What the fuck would Elkins be doing with Woolfe?* His head turned to look at Woolfe, and without thinking, asked the question running through his mind, "What the fuck were you doing running with a waste like Elkins?"

At the name, Sharon stiffened, twisting so she could see the bodies, and made a shocked noise when she recognized her ex-husband. Squatting in front of Sharon as he turned her away, blocking her view of the bodies, Gunny caged her chin in his hand, drawing her eyes back to him. "Baby, I'm going to make it so we don't have to think about him again. I have to, Sharon, you know I do. I promised you. You gonna be okay with that?" She stilled under his hands and her gaze darted over his shoulder to where Woolfe stood in the doorway, and then back to his face. Trapping her lips between her teeth, she nodded once decisively, and he said, "Okay."

He stood, looking at Woolfe, and had opened his mouth to ask him to keep her in the hallway, when she surprised him again, saying in an unsteady voice, "I am staying right here."

"Baby," he squatted down again to look her in the face, "you don't gotta do that."

She nodded. "Yeah, I do, Gunny." She reached up her hand and cupped his cheek in her palm. Leaning close to him, in a whisper that barely stirred the air around his face, she said, "I won't be afraid."

Looking at her, he realized those words meant more than in this moment. Witnessing this would wrap her around with the knowledge she would never feel the man's hands on her skin again. Never have to fear an ambush attack from him. Never look over her shoulder again. "Baby," he whispered back, "I get it; I do, but you watch me do this, and then I have fear." Leaning into her palm, he let her take the weight of his head, her wrist trembling with the strain. "You watching me kill your fucktard of an ex-husband and, make no mistake, that's my intent. You watching has the chance of curdling this thing we got here, baby. I don't want that to happen. It's one thing to know, but it's another to see with your own eyes. It ain't gonna be pretty, and you'll see that. Ain't gonna be easy, and you're gonna hear that. Because I ain't gonna let him go quick."

"Safe." Said without emphasis, the word still struck him like a blow. She had often said it the first few days after the attack, and he had proven the feeling and her belief in him every single time he had his hands on her since. She was safe with him, would always be safe. *Safe.* With a nod, he leaned forward and kissed her. Closed mouthed, but fiercely, he possessed her, marked her as his own to every man in the room. He admitted the ownership she had over him too, letting her curl her fingers around the back of his neck and hold him close. He tucked her head into the crook of his shoulder when the kiss had run its course, allowing her to comfort him with the feel of her skin on his. *My addiction.*

On a deep breath, he stood, already knowing what direction the next few minutes would take. She had explained about the pain in her breastbone, even where there was no bruising. One night, when the nightmares had woken him, he had spent a half-hour on the computer looking up erotic asphyxiation and breath control play. He knew what the bastard had done to her, and doing it to someone unwilling was as far from the accepted practice as rape was from consensual sex. Suffocation, not play, even if he would bet the bastard had enjoyed every last second of her gasping for breath, as he strangled her or used chest compression to limit her access to oxygen.

First time me being a big motherfucker is truly going to work in my favor, he thought as he stood over Elkins. The man had his hand clamped tightly on a freely bleeding wound in his neck. It looked like his bullet had probably nicked the carotid enough to kill the bastard, but damned slowly. *We'll speed this process up a bit*, he thought, lifting one foot and placing it squarely on Elkins' chest. The cockroach metaphor came to mind again and he grunted a laugh. The stunned look on the man's face pulled another dark chuckle out of him, and then he said, "Fucking sucks, don't it, knowing you can't stop me from doing this?" He watched the man's eyes dart back and forth, scanning the room, and he nodded. "I know who you are, Derek." His eyes fixed on Gunny's face in shock. "Yeah, I know every fucking thing about you. Know everything you did. I know you better than you know yourself, and I see what's going on there in your little cockroach mind. You're thinking you can't turn loose of your neck or you're going to bleed out." He nodded again, shifting forward slightly to give Elkins a little more of his weight.

He grunted. "Then I lean in on you, and now you start thinking that maybe the blood isn't that big a deal, because you need to get my size fifteens off your rib bones." He shook his head. "Ain't happening. Me knowing what I know? You know that ain't happening." He bared his teeth, "I know every fucking thing. You want this fast, you need to turn loose of the vein in your throat and accept the death staring down at you. Too fucking clean, but I'll give it to you just to clear my shit. You want it slow, want the giddy from hypoxia? Then clamp the fuck down on that wound, motherfucker. I got all the time in the world." He looked up and realized the mirror over the dresser was angled in such a way it let him see Sharon. He watched her standing there, near Woolfe but apart from him, her arms straight at her sides, hands balled, nails digging into her palms.

"That woman over there? The beauty that's been sharing my bed for weeks now? You ain't never going to have sweet like that again. Even if I was to step back and let you live." He paused for a moment, and then chuckled again, wincing as Sharon shivered when the noise rolled through the room. "Which I ain't, so don't get your fucking hopes up, but even if I did, you'd never have sweet like that again." He shifted, transferring more of his mass to the man's chest, feeling the creak of bones and cartilage beneath the sole of his boot. Staring at Sharon, he said, "Me? I got that sweet for the rest of my days, man. God, I love that woman." Glancing down, he saw the rigidity of Elkins' muscles, the beet-red face, mouth opening and closing like Eklund's did in the moments before his death in Iraq. *Huh*, he thought, and then tucked that away to look at later.

Looking back into the mirror, he found Sharon's eyes had located the vantage point, and her gaze was fixed on his mirrored face. On him, not Elkins. Him. Her eyes held steady as she stared at his reflection, her face open and trusting. She was telling him so much without saying a word. *I trust you*, she said. *I believe you will keep me safe. I love you.*

He nodded at her and waited for her response. When it came, indicating she was ready and, *please God*, would be okay with the outcome, he continued to hold her gaze, but shifted forward hard, hearing as well as feeling the greenstick fractures of Elkins' ribs as the cage protecting his rotten heart collapsed around him. The room was silent for a moment, and then Woolfe quietly said, "Jesus Christ."

Stepping back, he spared the body one glance to ensure the chest no longer rose or fell, and then he took the two strides that carried him to Sharon. He pulled her to his side, wrapping his arm around her shoulder and directing her towards the door, away from the bodies and blood...away from their bed, which until a few minutes ago had been the safest place she had known. Keeping up his one-sided running commentary, he said to Woolfe, "Hard to believe you'd stoop to this, betraying a brother."

***

Gunny paced, striding back and forth in the small space allowed by the chain tethering his hands, bound behind his back to the wall opposite the door. Separated from Sharon when they placed him in here, twice since then shouts had come through the closed door from the hallway, and once there had been a scream abruptly cut short. That voice had been male, *thank fuck*, or he didn't know what he would have done.

From the moment he recognized Woolfe in the bedroom, he had known they were fucked seven ways from Sunday, and had desperately taken the chance to kill him. Then, when the man hadn't stayed down from being shot point blank in the chest, he knew there was nothing else he could do, unclothed and virtually unarmed. The only fucking consolation was knowing one of the intruders he put down was Elkins. At least that motherfucker wasn't still breathing her air.

Sharon. That was the biggest question he had. What value did she have to draw in the kind of money he knew Woolfe garnered on a job?

He had known the man in the Marines, where he had a reputation for being the worst of the badasses. Assigned to different teams, they trained together often, but never went on the same assignments. Outside of training, they hung out some, mostly because Kincade was tight with Woolfe. After a shift in political leadership had changed so many things about their deployments and assignments, he knew Woolfe had separated from the military. Kincade had talked at length about him going private sector. They had both been amazed, because from the beginning, as a contractor, Woolfe was pulling in an incalculable amount of money, especially when he became known for taking jobs no sane man would accept. *Who wanted Sharon so bad they'd pay those kind of fees?*

Gunny heard a noise at the door and futilely spun that direction, even knowing the tether didn't have enough slack to allow use as a weapon against whoever was coming in. The door swung open, and he was shocked because it revealed not Woolfe, as he expected, but a large man with a leather cut that said President over his name, Fury, instead. For about the thousandth time that day, he thought, *What the fuck?* Not recognizing the man or the name, Gunny settled into a watchful, waiting stance, thinking if he could only lure the man close enough...

Then Fury stepped aside, and he saw a bound and blindfolded Sharon in the hallway behind him. "Baby," he said without thinking, wincing when she first flinched at his voice then lapsed into panic, twisting at the zip ties holding her wrists together. She was calling his name over and over, not able to hear anything over her own terror. Another man stepped into view beside her and all Gunny could do was shout, *"NO,"* and watch as he casually raised his fist, hitting the side of her head brutally, hard enough to knock her sideways and to her knees.

He felt a tearing pain in his wrists and shoulders, and vaguely heard a roaring noise, not realizing for a moment he was the cause, straining at his bonds and lunging towards the man standing so nonchalantly next to a now-sobbing Sharon. "Bitch absolutely won't shut—" The man's complaint to Fury was interrupted by the hard butt of a pistol upside his head in response, knocking him on his ass. Fury's patch in full view now, Gunny committed it to memory. *Diamante.*

"Stupid mother*fucker*," Fury gritted out, reaching down to grip Sharon's arms, ignoring her flinch as he lifted her to her feet, leaving the bleeding and unconscious biker lying on the floor. "Calm down, girl," he said quietly, gaze locked on Gunny's face, talking over the sound of Sharon's soft cries as she twisted and pulled against the restraints locked around her wrists. He held both her arms in one hand, saying gently, "You're going to hurt yourself, honey. Be still."

He pulled out a pocketknife, flipping it open, and Gunny held his breath in fear until it was folded and repocketed, her bonds snipped free. "Ain't no one gonna hurt you again, long as your man plays us right." She was silent now, and Gunny could see her shaking, see the trembling of her lips as she bit them in her efforts to be quiet. Fury rubbed her wrists, frowning at the marks he found there and Gunny clenched his jaw in frustration at the sight of his hands on her. *Mine.*

"What do you want?" Gunny ground out, confused at what Fury had said, *'Long as your man plays us right.'* He thought Sharon had been the primary target and he'd only been brought along because of his history with Woolfe. Now, it sounded like he had bargaining value. This was very good news, because he would be willing to gamble with his own safety much quicker than hers, any goddamned day.

Fury stepped away from a still blindfolded Sharon, scowling as he handed her off to another man in the hallway, and with a jerk of his head, directed her removal. *No, no, keep her here. Need to know...* Gunny kept his eyes on her until he could no longer see her, mutely watching the door. Staying silent was hard, but he wouldn't give these motherfuckers more information than they already had. They already had to know she owned him, had to see it in his frantic need to get to her...had to know he would do anything to keep her safe and whole. *Mine.*

He watched as yet another vested man hooked his hands underneath the arms of the one on the floor, walking backwards and dragging him out of sight. The heels of the man's boots scraped along the cement floor, bumping through the blood grooves leading to a central drain. *Compound*, he thought, recognizing the kind of layout the Rebels had in each of their main clubhouses. Isolation rooms with built-in restraints, easy cleanup after a messy interrogation. *What does the Diamante club want?* Ignoring the activity behind him, Fury pulled the door closed and said, "You and me got friends in common, Gunny. We also got enemies."

He paused here, apparently expecting a response, so Gunny asked what felt like an obvious question, given how he had been brought here. "Where's Woolfe?"

Shaking his head, Fury said, "He's been...unavoidably detained. Can't join us right now." Reaching up, he smoothed his beard, the paleness of his hand stark against the deep red. Leaning against the wall, it looked like he had settled in for a long chat. *Motherfucker.* Gunny closed his mouth firmly, sending a clear message.

Fury looked at him and nodded. "All right, I'll give you a little. We'll get a little give and take going; I'm fine with that idea. You have been looking into my business, and it is seriously jacking things up for me. I want you to stop, simple as that. I hear you're an honorable man. So, if you tell me you'll stop, well then I'm gonna take you at your word, turning you and the girl loose."

"What Diamante business am I fucking up? Only things I'm working are to sift out the connections between my club and Outriders. It isn't a secret we had trouble with them a few weeks ago. I'm merely making sure the piece of shit that lost itself in the wind doesn't make its way back to Fort Wayne. My brother Bear's old lady already had to put up with a fuckton of shit from the little bastard, and we want her clean shut of him." He stated these truths in a voice saturated with conviction, hoping to lull the man in case there were harder questions waiting in the wings.

"I'm aware of Mason's nephew, what he did...where he's not, and what that means for the Rebels." Not realizing the size of the bomb he just dropped, Fury continued while Gunny mentally reeled underneath the knowledge that the relationship between Mason and Shooter was known to this man, when the inner circle of the Rebels had only learned this information a day ago. "Got a vested interest in the same outcome, man."

"What business then?" *If I can figure the angle—*

"Got a profitable business in Kentucky; need your nose kept well clear of what I got going there." This was said in an agreeable, offhand tone, but Fury gave the lie to that with his steady gaze.

"Was only looking in Kentucky as it touched Shooter," Gunny informed him, but Fury shook his head.

"Stop blowin' smoke up my fucking ass, man. It was your gal who brought you down on us and I know it. Know what happened there, too. You just need to understand shit has been handled. I'm here to tell you *that* shit was dealt with in a terminal way. Those prospects didn't...make the cut, so to speak." He reached over, briskly pounding on the door with a closed fist. "I 'spect we're done here. From the look on your face, I hope so, at least. She's not been harmed, no more than you saw. And, my word on it, I'll deal with that shit, too. Fucking kids don't get the idea of honor, man. We fight that stupidity every single fucking day."

Gunny nodded and then shook his hands, rattling the chain as a silent reminder his agreement was coerced, and then finding himself grudgingly liking this man, he offered him an extra bit. "My oath to you, we have an understanding, Fury." They stared at each other for a minute, and then Fury nodded.

"Well, all right," he said, coming over and standing behind Gunny as he unlocked the chains binding him to the wall. Once freed, he stepped back, and the two men silently retreated from each other, quickly taking mirroring stances on either side of the room.

They brought Sharon to him then, and true to Fury's word, she had suffered nothing but the blow he had seen in the hallway. In that small room, smelling of his sweat and anger, he ran his hands over every inch of her he could reach, reassuring them both with a touch that they were okay. *Mine.* He whispered to her, feeling her fingers winding themselves into the shirt under his cut, "I got you, baby." She nodded silently, her face burrowing into his chest, and he felt her breath hitch with unvoiced sobs. Looking at Fury over her head, he said, "She stays with me," receiving an easy, agreeable nod in response. Their release was quickly organized, and hoping he wasn't making a mistake, he talked Sharon into accepting the blindfold again before they were loaded into a van and driven around for a half-hour.

Fury ordered the blindfolds removed, and Gunny looked out the windows as the van pulled into the parking lot of a diner he recognized. They were in Markle, a little village just south of Fort Wayne, and he looked at the glass windows on the front of the building as if they embodied safety. The shelter and security of friendly territory, nearly within reach. There were a few cars in the lot, but no one standing around, nothing out of place...nothing to indicate an ambush.

When the side door of the van opened, as if they did it every day, he and Sharon climbed out and turned to watch as the vehicle drove off, and he noted the plate number. *Nearly safe*, he thought, keeping one arm firmly around her shoulders, pulling her to his side. *Against all odds, twice in my life now, I've made it back*, he thought. *Oorah.*

Inside the diner, Gunny borrowed a phone and made a call, and less than twenty minutes later, another van drove up. They watched as Mason stepped out of it, walking into the diner as if he owned the world, his confidence going a long way in helping Gunny keep things together.

14. Soroicide

"What the fuck?" Gunny shook his head, looking at Mason and trying to decide which thing felt the most surreal—the fact he had been ambushed and abducted from his own home, or that a brother had betrayed the club in a way that ended in his permanent removal. *Betrayal.* He felt his heart race faster, saw his hands clenching into bloodless, white balls at the end of his arms, fisting tightly.

When they got to the clubhouse, he gently sent Sharon upstairs to a room, Ruby moving with her, arm around her shoulders in comfort. He had known Ruby nearly all her life, knew too well the history of abuse she carried, and in this moment, he prayed little sister was the right pick to care for his woman right now. They were both strong, survivors, but he knew from personal fucking experience how events like this could fuck with your mind, bringing up fears long buried, and he worried for both Ruby and Sharon. *My Rose of Sharon.*

"Yeah," Mason said, bringing his mind back to the moment, and he watched his friend scrubbing at the beard on his jaw. "Birdy fucked up one of the dancers. Hoss is sitting with her for now, but we hope she can shed some light on what the fuck he was doing." Birdy had been a member of the Chicago chapter first, then transferred to Fort Wayne a while back, about the same time Jase had come to town. He had been in the life a long time, coming to them from a friendly club out in Utah, Legends. Chief, one of Mason's friends, was president of that MC, and had vouched for Birdy's nomad status.

Gunny frowned, because beating a bitch wasn't reason enough to cut a brother. Censure him, fuck him up, then educate him on the way to treat a woman, yeah. Cut him, no. Kill him? Fuck no. This still wasn't quite adding up for him. There had to be more to the story than the man raising his hand to a woman, even one that belonged to the club; those pieces didn't fit together convincingly. He offered his opinion, "That can't be all."

Mason shook his head, leaning back, and Slate picked up the conversation. "He was sleeping with Manzino's sister. The dope dealer we fucking ran out of town, he finally raised his head again and sent his goddamn sister to ease his way. We picked Birdy up at the woman's primary operation, sitting and watching her minions cook up that meth shit." *Manzino*—Gunny felt his lips twist in distaste. That motherfucker had made the club's life hell for years, back when Bingo was president. He had connections out west, in Colorado, and the drug dealer wasn't above using them to add to the weight he tried to throw around.

It wasn't until Slate took over the chapter in Fort Wayne that they were able to shift the bastard off their own front porch. They had worked hard to push him and his enterprise out and away from Rebel properties to create a safe buffer zone around the clubhouse and businesses. Gunny still didn't know the full details of the deal that caused Manzino to pull way the fuck back, peddle his shit elsewhere. But, since it was about the same time Slate's little brother blew into town and ODed, he had an inkling things were linked by Slate and his past connections.

"Okay, that's enough to cut a rocker, but fucking put a brother to ground?" He shook his head. Shit *still* wasn't adding up. Beat a bitch, and then even sleep with a bitch who is attached to a club enemy, that shit was still not enough to warrant a bullet to the brain.

Bear spoke up then, and Gunny listened, knowing out of all the brothers, this man truly knew the pain of betrayal, because of what had happened to him at rogue Rebel hands in Iowa. "Motherfucker threatened the entire fucking club. Hatred and poison spewed from his mouth when he knew he'd been made. The man was a mole, but we don't know for who. He'd have killed us all without flinching, brother."

"God*damn*," he muttered, thinking hard. Wanting to confirm his knowledge, he asked, "We picked him up from Legends, that Utah club, right? When we picked him up, were we sure his leaving them was voluntary?"

"Don't fucking know anything for sure anymore, brother," Mason said, tapping his thumbs against the edge of the table. Then, backing up what Gunny already knew, he sighed and said, "But, yeah, he came to me from Chief with a high recommendation. I've already been on a call with him and the Legends officers; from the look on their faces, they were as stunned as I was to get the news." Myron was big into technology, and had forced Mason into using video chat a while back. They had all adopted it pretty quickly, because they found it helped to see the face of a man when you had to ask hard questions without enough precious time to get on location. *Fucking Myron and his toys*, Gunny thought, shaking his head.

"Fuck. That ain't good news, brother." He shook his head again, running the tip of his tongue along the inside of his teeth, and then said, "Let me tell you what went down with me. Don't know if it will tie anything together, but it is all fucking related to your discussion with the officers a couple days ago, Prez." He nodded at Mason, seeing the strained lines appear alongside his mouth at his words, hating he was the one to hand this to his friend. "I know you've had problems with Diamante in Chicago, heard about Watcher's problems out in Las Cruces." Watcher was the president of a club out west they had good relations with, the Southern Soldiers. From his digging, Gunny knew Watcher and Mason came from the same small town in Kentucky, and suspected their friendship ran deeper than anyone knew.

"Fury," he said, and saw recognition on Bear and Slate's faces. "Clearly you know this motherfucker's name. I did not, so his appearance in the cell where they were holding me was entirely a surprise to me. Fucking *shit*, I'm telling it all out of order. Let me start at the beginning."

He took a deep breath, forcing down the emotions that would cloud his memory, not wanting to screw up this debriefing. Leaning his elbows on the table, he gripped his hands together tightly, taking another deep breath and clearing his mind. *Begin at the beginning.* He knew that's what Kincade would say. "It was a crisp, coordinated insertion into the bedroom, with a flashbang followed by a rush attack. I grabbed my piece just before I was knocked from the bed, lined up and downed four targets. Shot the leader point blank, but he was vested, so the motherfucker stood back up. Elkins was one of the men I put down, Mason. Sharon's ex was in my goddamn *fucking* bedroom." He shook his head, trying to stay on track, because thinking about how Sharon had watched him kill the man pissed him right the fuck off. Motherfucker had a slow, painful death, and he could only hold onto her whispered, *I won't be afraid*, in blind and hopeful belief it also meant she would never be afraid of him.

"Team leader was an ex-jarhead, knew him from Force Recon. That man does not work on the cheap. He runs in rarified circles, so seeing him in my fucking bedroom was a jolt. His conversation indicated Sharon was the target, making me collateral, but I talked my way into the van with them. The compound was about twenty minutes from my house, give or take, so no real fucking idea where. That's almost anywhere on the south or west side. They landed us in Markle for the exfil, so I'd lean more towards the west." He ran his hand over the top of his head and then held it out, staring for a moment, idly watching it tremble. "Marines. *Oorah*." The silence in the room was deafening, the men all waiting for him to be able to continue. Another deep, cleansing breath.

"Separated us, secured me in a cell, and I waited. At least a couple hours, but not overly long, because they weren't trying to wear me down, weren't waiting for me to feel the need to talk, just…waiting, it seemed. The door opens, and in walks Fury, with a president patch on his cut. I couldn't see the club colors then, but he talked about Kentucky, Prez." He looked at Mason. "According to him, *I* was the one they wanted, which threw me, because Woolfe had sung a different tune. But, Woolfe wasn't there by then, so all I had was Fury. Either way, he focused on some business in Kentucky he claimed I was fucking up by asking around about Judge. Mason, I gotta tell you. I didn't know what the fuck he was talking about until he mentioned some trouble Sharon ran into down there."

"She danced at a club there before coming up here, had some problems that caused her to not work there anymore. 'Bikers,' her word, not mine, came in and demanded more than she wanted to give, threatened to rough up the bouncer on shift if she didn't comply. When she left there after her set that night, she didn't go back. Kept making her way north, and eventually wound up here. We all know what happened to her here with Elkins, so me finding him hooked up with Woolfe at the same time as they are all standing in my fucking bedroom where Sharon and I were sleeping is un-fucking-settling. Then, there's the strip joint itself. Prez, the club is called Shinedown."

Mason shifted and nodded, saying, "Owned by Shooter. I know of it." Already unstable, that answer pushed him into rage, because it hinted at things not yet uncovered, maybe important. Maybe touching Sharon. *Fuck.*

"Well, *I* didn't learn about the ownership until last night, so you might coulda shared, Prez." Squeezing his eyes shut, he fought to bring himself back under control. "Fury knew of the trouble she had, said he dealt with the prospects who caused the ruckus. He got me to agree to back off my investigation, unlocked the fucking chains, and proceeded to chat me up as if we were old friends. Saw the Diamante club patch and recognized it as a problem we've been dealing with on a bunch of fronts."

He opened his eyes, staring at Mason, "I got questions, man, because if Shooter owns the strip joint, why the fuck would Diamante be involved there? Why would Fury give even a half a shit about me asking questions about something that happened months ago at the goddamned club? Unless they swooped in after we dismantled Shooter's Outriders, but even that don't make a lotta sense. Hell, nothing about this makes sense, so I'm not sure why I think one little detail should." He shook his head. "Anyway, while we were waiting at the diner, I asked Sharon if she had seen any of the men before, but she was too shaken up to think. I'll try again tomorrow, but there ain't no guarantees. She's been through a lot, was finally finding her way back to goodness, and then this shit lands on us. Her only questions have been about the pups, and I had to tell her I didn't know."

"Pups are okay. PBJ has them right now." Slate nodded at his outrush of breath. "Brother, I'm sorry we weren't faster. Seemed all the shit hit the fan at once. Birdy fucking up Mercy, then ghosting. You going missing, leaving trash for us to clear. We made the Elkins connect, but that wound up muddying the waters a fuck of a lot, because it sent us looking the wrong direction. Jase...Captain dealt with Birdy, and we walked out after shit went down to find you had called and Mason was already on his way to pick you up." He flexed his fingers, popping the knuckles loudly. "Shit just kept hitting the fan, but we cleaned up things at your place, found the pups in a crate. All the bikes are there; nothing else was missing, only you."

"Good to fucking hear, brother," he said. There was a pause as all the men around the table tried to digest the information laid out between them. *Fist raised, Sharon falling. Mine. Fuck.* Pushing back the memories, Gunny sucked in a deep breath, blowing it out slowly, trying to bleed off some of the tension that seemed to have settled deep into his bones. He said, "I'm going to go check on Sharon. Gonna put us in my room here tonight. I don't want to spread the club thin by trying to argue going home. My fucking security will be upgraded. I already sent a text to Myron, and he's on it like white on rice." The men laughed humorlessly and stood along with him.

Headed to the door, he paused, turning to look at Mason. "Tonight or tomorrow, you tell me what you need, boss. I'm willing to keep on the shit in Kentucky, but damned if I don't feel obligated to stop. Fucking oath to a fucking stranger who let a man lay hands on my woman, but it don't feel right. I need to know what you need, and I need to fucking know what you know, Prez. Sharon got swept up in this because I fucked up asking shit, and you had information that might have made a difference. I'm willing to keep pushing, but I need what's in your head."

"No. We pause for a breath, brother. Should hear from our man out in Cali today; he visited Shooter already. Maybe he'll have an idea about Judge. Bear's got Eddie covered, so we'll let things rest a bit." Mason reached out, pulling him into a one-armed clench. "Love ya, brother. Fucking glad you're back in one fucking piece."

"Me too, man. Kinda fond of the undamaged me." He walked out and saw Jase sitting at the bar. Sighing, he tried to duck around him with no luck. Even frustrated and angry, he got it. He understood the man simply wanted to know his sister was okay. But right now, Gunny needed to be with her, needed her in his arms...needed to hear her say she wouldn't be afraid of him. Needed to watch her sleep without nightmares to believe they'd be okay. Then a thought drifted through his mind and he remembered Slate mentioning Jase stepping up and dealing with Birdy. They'd glossed over it somewhat, but he knew exactly what it had to mean, what it could mean for Jase...Captain. Knowing all this, he slowed and turned, facing him, willing to give him a moment, even as he denied him what he might need. "Not right now, brother. Mason or Slate can fill you in as they want, and I'll be glad to talk to you tomorrow, but I need to get to Sharon right the fuck now."

Jase's eyes were bright as they locked gazes, not holding the shadows he expected, and for this, he was thankful. Glad for Jase and DeeDee's sakes, but also for Sharon's. Finally, Jase nodded, his head moving up and down once, decisively, before he stepped back and gave Gunny tacit permission to keep moving. "Take care of her," he said softly and pointed across the room, and Gunny saw with a start that Sharon was waiting in one of the chairs, her eyes trained on him.

"You got it, brother," he said, turning on his heel and walking over to her. He squatted down, caging her chin in his hand and holding her gaze with his. His eyes fixed on the deepening bruise on the side of her face, and every muscle in his body clenched tight in anger. *Fist raised, Sharon falling to her knees, mouth open in pain.* Without smiling, he said, "Babe, let's go rest, yeah?" She nodded and he scooped her up, taking the stairs two at a time.

***

"Sometimes it helps to talk things out. Talking it through can let you fill in blank spots, keep a person from obsessing over details." He glanced over from where he was sprawled on the bed, looking at ease, as if nothing had happened to them tonight. When he carried her to the room, she opted for the chair, wanting the support, the feeling of security from having something at her back. She sat on the cushion now, curling into it, drawing her knees up to her chest.

She offered him a smile she knew was less than believable, then, without thinking, she quipped, "Smarty pants. How'd you get so knowledgeable about kidnapping trauma survivors?"

"Not kidnapping." His gaze fixed on a spot on the wall above her head. "Just trauma in general. Talking helps." He lifted the beer he held in his hand, taking a drink. "So does dope. The army is even using morphine on servicemen after a debriefing now. My doc said it helps move the brain from its hyperaware state. Breaking the hold early is good, and keeps the memories from cementing into place."

Shit, she thought. *How did I forget something like that?* If anyone would know, he would. "Okay. I'll admit I'm kinda freaking out."

He moved, uncoiling from the bed, and padded soundlessly to her side. He stared down at her for a long minute, then surprised her by folding down, kneeling on the floor. He was so tall his head was even with her chin, which made her smile. At the expression on her face, he reached out and wrapped his arms around her; they were hard and strong as he tugged her body towards him. She dropped her feet to the floor and he leaned against her legs, bending himself in half to rest his head in her lap. "Freaking out is allowed, baby. It was scary shit, Sharon. Every fucking bit of it was scary as shit."

Cradling his head in one hand, she slowly trailed her fingers across his scalp, feeling the rough stubble everywhere. He shaved his head weekly, and she never tired of watching him. His rituals, as important to him as Jase's were, choreographed movement self-assured and confident. Back and forth her hand went, caressing his skin, drawing comfort from the motion, from comforting him. Turning his face into her belly, he held her like that for a long time and she felt him slowly relaxing, their breathing coming into sync.

"I didn't know what was happening when I woke up." She spoke softly, and he made a quiet noise she took to be understanding. "It was loud and bright, like a really close lightning strike. Then something hit me hard, pushing past me, and you weren't beside me anymore. I couldn't see you, Gunny. I couldn't hear you. Baby, I couldn't find you."

She used her thumb to trace across his eyebrow. "It was so confusing. I didn't know if the house had blown up or what, and all I could think of was finding you, getting you out of there. Making sure you were safe." He drew a sharp breath at that, and she saw a frown cross his face. Using her fingertips, she smoothed it away, feeling the returned tension in his arms relax minutely.

"Someone grabbed my arm and I thought it was you." She paused, taking a breath and closing her eyes then opening them in a panic when all she could see behind her eyelids were the shadowy figures moving through the bedroom. Gunny must have noticed her reaction, because his hands moved, smoothing up and down her back, his cheek rubbing on her thigh. He took a deep breath, nuzzling her lap with his nose, and she breathed with him. "But it wasn't. It was a man with a mask on his face."

"A balaclava," he said quietly.

"Balacuntwaffle," she blurted, and he raised his head to look at her and laughed. That laugh was so loud and real she could almost run her fingers along the weft and weave of the feeling behind it. It was the first flicker of amusement, the first laugh, the first emotion other than anger she'd gotten from him since they had gone to sleep. Since she told him she loved—

"I like that. I won't ever think of them the same way, baby." He laid his head down, draping himself across her legs again, and gently urged her, "Keep going. Tell me."

"One guy, then two, then three, and then there were gunshots." She frowned. "Or maybe there were gunshots before the men." She paused and then shook her head, suddenly unsure. She recognized the quaver in her own voice as she said, "I don't know. Told you...it was confusing."

"Gunshots first. You were still on the bed. Guy tackled me and I rolled him off onto the floor, but I wouldn't have risked shooting if I hadn't been one-hundred percent certain where you were. You weren't in my line of sight, never in danger of crossfire." He said this so confidently she could do nothing more than nod.

It took her a minute, letting what he said sink in, and then she shook her head. "Well...of course, because everyone thinks of the risk of crossfire in their bedroom," she scoffed. "I was in the freakin' room.

They woke us up with a shot, honey. And my ears are still ringing, those gunshots were so loud."

"Yeah, they used a flashbang for entry, but I was awake a few seconds before they came through the door. So I had a chance to prepare," he said, cupping her ass with his hands. He scooted her closer to the edge of the chair and knelt in front of her, rising on his knees as he wedged his way between her thighs. From this position, he looked down at her face and she stared up at him. "But you're right; you were in the room, babe. I couldn't keep you safe."

"Pffffttt. Crazy ninjas wearin' balacuntwaffles on their faces? Who could have anticipated that?" The weak and trembling smile on her face faded when he didn't respond in kind. "Seriously, Gunny. It was scary, but it's over. Right? It's over?"

"Yeah, babe. After my talk with Fury, I think it's over," he said and lifted her, letting her wrap her arms around his neck as he carried her to the bed. After he had arranged them on top of the covers to his liking, he told her, "Keep going."

"Well...you were there, you know. I was naked in your bed." Heat swept over her at the thought of those men seeing her vulnerable like that, but she kept her head up, refusing to be ashamed. "You dressed me, kept me calm. Then they put you in a room and I could hear you yelling all the way down the hallway to the room they put me in." She smoothed the fabric of his tee over the hard, tense muscles of his chest, and then wanted to feel his skin under her hand so pulled it out of the waistband of his pants, flattening her palm on his stomach. "Wait, there was the van. Then the room. See? Confusing." He didn't say anything, only made another noise she took to be agreement, so she kept going.

"You weren't with me, but when you were yelling, you sounded so mad, but not scared, and that helped me keep it together." She sighed. "One of the men wasn't so bad; at least, he didn't seem like the rest of them. Got me a bottle of water and pressed it into my hands, made sure

I knew it wasn't already opened." She paused. "I mean…like I'd worry about being roofied after being freakin' jacked from your bedroom." She scoffed. "He yelled at one of the other men for talking ugly. I think he was the one who picked me up off the floor, after…" She paused and swallowed, feeling her lips turning down at the corners. Taking a shuddering breath, she blew it out softly, and then shaking her head, said quietly, "It scared me when you freaked out. Really scared me, because I didn't know…but you were so…I've never heard you like that. All I knew was suddenly I was on the floor, couldn't figure out what had happened, how I got there, at least until you were yelling about them hitting me. Then my face hurt, but you were still yelling." She moved her hand, tracing the trail of thick hair leading from his belly into his pants, and grinned when he grumbled and reached down to move her hand. She frowned when she saw the bruising on his wrist, gently touching the dark discoloration with one fingertip, wondering, *How did he get those bruises?*

"Yeah," he said with more than a thread of steel and anger in his voice. "Motherfucker hit you, because you were afraid. Fury, he must have been the guy who gave you the water, took care of him. Fury's also the one who cut the zips from your wrists." He trailed a hand down her arm, wrapping his fingers gently around her wrist and drawing her hand to his mouth for a soft kiss. "I could hear the fear in your voice, baby." Pressing her palm on his chest, he covered her hand with his and she could feel the pounding of his heart, at odds with his gentle voice as he said, "I couldn't get to you, wanted…needed. So fucking strong, Sharon. Watched you pull it together, watched you believe it would be okay. You are so fucking strong."

He stopped talking and she didn't fill the void, so they laid there in the dark and stillness of the room above the clubhouse. His breathing slowed, and she wondered if he were falling asleep, knowing she was so wired it would be hours before she could relax enough to drop off. Without thinking, she quietly asked him, "Did I ever tell you what I'd do when he'd beat me?"

He stiffened under her hand, and when she replayed her words in her head, she could have bitten her own tongue off. *He killed Derek for me tonight, took that on himself, and now I never have to worry about him. Not another single moment of fear*, she thought. Squeezing her eyes closed, she shook her head, feeling his arms tighten around her. His voice raw with emotion, he said, "Babe, he's not going to hurt you ever again."

"I know." She said this quickly, but until that moment, she hadn't remembered. She was so focused on what was happening right now that she somehow had forgotten *he* was dead. She saw his body, fallen gracelessly, one leg twisted under his torso, wide, white eyes staring up at the ceiling, motionless until he shifted his gaze to stare at Gunny. The flat, cold voice coming from Gunny, tone belied by the fury and pain in his face when she found his eyes in the mirror. Killing Derek took something from him. She knew that. But, she had likewise seen the breath Gunny took after that horrific sound filled the room, and she knew the grisly death also gave him something.

"I know he's dead." Taking a deep breath, she repeated slightly differently, "He's dead, I know." Another breath, echoed by Gunny's chest rising and falling. Softly, she continued, "But, I'm kinda like you; things stick with me. He can't hurt me now, but I remember what it was like. I don't remember every blow, or even every time he...there were too many. But I do remember the fear and emotion, the taste of the panic and terror in my mouth when I knew it was coming. That fear would get so big it pushed me out, so after a while, I found I had a room in my head."

He made a noise and she paused, but when he didn't say anything, she continued, "I made a room in my head only I could lock. Then, when he'd start, I'd visualize myself rushing inside, crashing the door closed behind me, and see my hands twisting the lock. Then I would stay there until it was safe to come back out.

"You sounded so angry at what was going on, what had happened. I knew you'd figure things out. I didn't need my room, Gunny." She pulled his tee up farther, nuzzling his hot, smooth skin and resting her cheek on his bare chest. She teased herself with small, feather-light kisses, and darted her tongue out to lick at his nipple. "Then you got quiet and they walked me up the hall. I heard you call me baby, and you sounded so afraid. I couldn't see you, but you seemed so scared. That was the most frightening thing—you sounding scared."

"You hold that power, babe," he said softly, his hand cupping the back of her head and holding her tightly. "My life...you are my life, Sharon. My obsession, my love. If anything happened to you, I don't know what I'd do. My Rose of Sharon. *Mine.*"

"I feel the same way, Gunny." She picked her head up, pushing back against his hold, and he gave her the space she wordlessly demanded. She slid over to rest on his chest and propped her chin on her crossed wrists. "I love you so hard. I do, honey. I love you." She sucked in a breath, lifting her head in panic at a memory. "The pups?"

"Pups are okay. And, I love you right back, babe. Love and need you. You can be afraid, just not of me. I'll always do my best to keep you safe, Sharon. My Rose of Sharon." He soothed her, his hands stroking across her skin over and over as she rested her cheek on her hands, feeling the powerful swell and dip of each breath he took in. He moved, slipping his hands up her arms to grip her biceps, effortlessly pulling her up so he could kiss her.

Relaxing into him, opening for his kiss, she gave him all the horror, fear, and pain, feeling him take it in and return that energy back to her as confidence and love. After a minute, she pulled back, staring into his eyes. "So what happens now?"

He rolled them, moving to lie beside her, reaching with one hand to cup her face. "Now you let me love on you, babe," he said, before leaning in to kiss her again.

***

"Diamante out of Lexington called, brother. Got a message downstairs for you." When those muffled words came through the wood of the hallway door, Gunny woke fully, carefully shifting Sharon off his chest and nestling her onto the pillow, pulling up the blanket to cover her bare shoulder.

"On my way," he called quietly, listening as the sound of leather soles hitting the floor echoed and diminished, the footsteps moving away from his door. Twelve hours since their release. Twenty-four since they were taken. Forty-eight since he gave Mason his gift and ate dinner at Bear's house. As he rolled out of the bed, he looked down at Sharon quietly sleeping, her hands tucked underneath her cheek. He reached out and threaded his fingers through her hair, pushing it back off her face so the bruising was clearly visible. *Fist raised, Sharon falling sideways to her knees, mouth open in an unheard scream.*

He glanced across the room towards the door, catching sight of himself in the mirror. Hazel stare intense, he was looking over Sharon's shoulder, hand caught up in her hair. He was angry at the mark of her injury, at the proof he hadn't kept her safe, and the rage that still filled him was evident on his face.

She had given herself to him last night, letting him take what he needed from her body, from the knowledge she was alive and safe, with him. He'd eaten her until she came on his mouth, hands stroking and touching, fingerfucking her hard and fast. Using his tongue and the edge of his teeth to pull her over the cliff, catching her before she hit the bottom and bringing her back up again, feeling her clench around his fingers, hearing her breathlessly call his name. *Safe.*

Knee nudging her legs apart, he'd settled between her thighs and used his fingers to spread her open, angling the head of his cock and sinking inside, not giving the first goddamn he was bare. Now, standing here beside her, he remembered thinking one word while he slid into her, that single syllable beating at his brain. *Mine.*

The reflection of his face had changed with these memories, hard lines softening. He had needed his hands on her, and once seated deep inside, rolled them, and pulled her onto his chest. On his back, levering his heels into the mattress, rocking up into her again and again, he'd felt her move against him as his hands stroked her back and sides where she lay draped over him. Palm cupping a breast, his other hand sliding into her hair, he'd tugged her head to bring her mouth down on his, and fucked her deep, sweet and gentle until she came again, trying to infuse his love for her into every movement. Then he rolled her to her back and moved over her, keeping his torso lifted by planting a forearm in the bed. *Precious. Loved.*

Hand between them, hips working his cock in and out of her pussy, he thrummed her clit with his thumb, eyes focused on her face, their gazes locked as they gave each other what they needed. Chin down, he remembered watching her come, following her a second later, their eyes never leaving the other. The passionate intensity of the experience something that would remain etched on his mind. *So fucking strong. So beautiful.*

Cleaned up and snuggled into his side, about ten minutes later she had fallen asleep with a smile curling the corners of her mouth. Not a flinch or whimper marred her sleep; from what he could tell, it was deep, and dreamless. *Mine.*

For him, most of the night had been spent unsleeping. He kept twisting the events around in his head, tracing the facts back and forth, trying to find the kink in the stream.

Now, getting ready to go down and see what kind of fucking message Diamante had left for him, he found his mind wouldn't leave things alone, continuing to tease along the edges to find the pattern.

Elkins hooked up with Diamante. Sorting through the bag Deke brought him last night, he pulled a clean tee over his head, tugging it down his chest, and absently smoothing it across his stomach. *Diamante hooked up with Shinedown.* Digging in his boots, he pulled out the dirty socks and tossed them across the room, pulling a clean pair from the bag. His brain still rolling things around as he balanced on first one foot and then the other to pull them on. *Shinedown belonging to Shooter.*

Stepping into his jeans, he drew them up his thighs and palmed himself, tucking his cock into a comfortable position in the fabric. His mind kept working, pushing and pulling at the pieces to try to find an identifiable shape. *Shooter is Judge's old man.* Sliding sock feet into his boots, feeling the little thud as his heels seated firmly in the worn leather. *Judge taking Eddie back to the Outriders.*

He picked up his cut, slipping his arms through the holes, settling it comfortably across his shoulders. *Shooter has always played long games; he's proud of his plots and plans. Judge...what about Judge? Where is he? Then there's the Outriders. Shooter. I'm back to Shooter.* He paused, staring at himself in the mirror again. *Outriders.* Something he uncovered recently about that club pecked at his brain...about how Shooter took it over from his old man. What happened when he took it over, same time as Mason reworked the Rebels?

He was turning towards the door when the connection hit him, and he bolted from the room, turning back only to pull the door closed with exaggerated care, locking it from inside with one last glance at Sharon. She slept on, her demons purged in their conversation last night, at least some of them. He knew there would be more, from what was done to her, as well as from what he had done, but they had made a substantial start last night, and now she knew she could bring anything to him and he would take it all.

In the main room, he scanned the members seated around on the couches and chairs, looking for...*there.* Catching Mason's eye, he tilted his head to the office door and got a chin lift in response, quietly making his way to the office to meet him there.

"What's up, brother?" Mason asked, closing the door as he came inside.

"Utah." He saw Mason scowl and shake his head, so he continued, "Justice Morgan, Shooter's old man. He went missing in Utah, and as far as I could find out, no one ever located the body. Birdy comes to us from Utah, with a hatred of you that goes so deep the man is willing to die for a chance to take down your club. It's the only thread I find, but it's not small, boss. I kept tracking things back, but continued to get hung up on the Outriders. Sharon to Elkins, Elkins to Diamante, Diamante to Shooter through Shinedown. Then there's Judge to Outriders, Outriders to Utah, Utah to Birdy. Make a call, Mason. Something's sticky up there."

"Fuck. That's thin, brother." Mason shook his head, leaning one hip against the desk.

"No thinner than the threads that took me to Shinedown. No thinner than the drug dealer's sister being Chismoso's aunt. And Chismoso being president of the Diamante's Chicago chapter our good friend Bones has had nothing but trouble out of, and that same drug dealer's sister—Manzino's sister—is balling Birdy, who's the exact motherfucker we're discussing right the fuck now. Utah. There's something here, Mason. It centers in Utah." He nodded, dragging his palm across his scalp.

Taking a deep breath, Mason looked at him with an expression he couldn't identify, and then walked around the desk, sitting heavily in the chair there. "Utah," he said flatly, and Gunny nodded again. Mason sighed, and then said, "Deacon is the missing piece, brother. He was trying to make some kind of deal with Shooter, back before we made our trip. Then, the last I knew, Deacon was headed up to Provo. Provo is where the Legends are based. And, fuck me running, but Provo is where

Birdy came from. Utah." He thrummed on the edge of the desk with his thumbs. "Less thin, looking at it from that direction, wouldn't you say?"

Pressing his lips together, Gunny frowned, looking down at the toes of his boots. He let his mind turn this information over, holding it up against what he already knew to find the fit. Deacon was Mason's old president, upended from the club and tossed aside like trash when the Rebel Fiends became the Rebel Wayfarers. Shooter was a Fiend under Deacon's reign, so there was a clear connection there. And the hate? Hell yeah, there would be a fuckton of hate for the Rebels and everything they stood for, because from where Deacon stood, he would believe the club had been stolen from him. He would hate Mason with every fiber of his being. "Provo," he tried the word out, hearing it slip from his lips like a promise. Nodding, he said, "Lots less thin. We haven't seen the last of Judge, Prez. I feel it in my bones."

"Yeah, I know. Boy's got a hard-on for me. Was told he's calling me 'Club Killer' for what we did to the Outriders. He'd have proudly murdered his own sister, but has the balls to label me a killer."

Still distracted, Gunny said, "Sororicide."

"Latin for killing one's sister," Mason said in response, and Gunny froze.

"Boss. Oh fuck, boss. Hoss told me Fury called, woke me, but I missed it. Then I got stuck in my head." He shook his head. "I got a feeling, Prez. Fucking shit, man. Call Memphis. Call Bethany, man. Get your sister on the phone," he said, watching as all the color fled from Mason's face and he pulled out his phone with a curse.

***

Mason scrubbed at his face with his palm, thinking, *Goddamn it, I want a fucking cig.* He looked up and out the window, seeing for a moment the spreading branches of the trees in the family holler in Kentucky, and not the skyline of downtown Fort Wayne. *Bethany,* he thought and shook his head. He hadn't seen his baby sister in far too long, not since before Carrie Sosa came to Chicago and dropped off his boy, Chase, nearly two years ago. The person who answered the phone at Iron Indian Records, where she worked, said she was traveling, scouting a band, but he would pass along the word her brother wanted to hear her voice at the first opportunity.

A memory of his father filled his mind and he let the thoughts roll without guidance, seeking recollections from the past. He had been about seven, which would put the timing about a year before his mother came home for the final time, the last few months he had her before she was gone again. During all the years she was missing from their day-to-day, mostly his daddy had turned hard and brittle, toughened to the point his shell was as impregnable as a turtle's, but this was a memory of soft.

"You turn it this way," Daddy said, demonstrating with the willow stick in his hands as Davy watched intently. "Then you whittle the top of the whistle off flat, like this. 'Cause when we put the bark back on, you gotta give the air somewhere to go or it ain't gonna work." His hands deftly worked with the knife, the edge of the blade plucking and trimming, notching and cutting the soft wood, forming something out of nothing in front of Davy's eyes.

"Now, we put the bark back on." His daddy matched actions to words, lining up the sheath of bark they had removed earlier with the end of the whistle and gently twisting it back and forth to seat it in place. "Gotta get it just right. Can't force it, or you'll split the bark, so you work it easy to get it back in place." His big hands, the deep creases of his knuckles and palms seamed with the dark beauty he chased underneath the mountain, lifted the whistle to his mouth. "Then you do the easiest thing in the world." He pursed his lips and blew into the end of the willow branch, creating a soft, melodic, monotone whistle. He varied the force of the air, and the sound danced up and down the scale, like lightning scattering all throughout a thunderhead poised at the top

of their mountain. He paused and looked down at his son with a soft smile. "You breathe and it lives."

Mason shook the memories from him, twisting in the chair to look down at the desktop. He knew Gunny had hold of something in what he had presented earlier, because from what he could see, all signs were indeed pointing back to Provo and Deacon. Shaking his head, he softly said, "Can't force it." Thoughts of Willa flooded his mind, and he leaned back deep into the chair. He had taken her to Slate's wedding, had wooed her since with soft words and smooth touches, phone calls and day trips on his bike. He had been patient with her for a while now, waiting for the right time. He would see her today at Jase and DeeDee's, show her what it meant to be his when they were around people who were also his. Nodding, he stood, agreeing with his long-dead father on something at last. "Can't force it. But I sure as fuck can coax it along."

***

Gunny felt Sharon tremble and glared at Hoss. "Hold on a second, *brother*," he snarled, bending to put his mouth next to Sharon's ear. "Baby, let's go to the kitchen for a minute." He knew DeeDee was in there, and he also knew as soon as she saw Sharon, she would pull her close. Her girls were hers, and this included his woman. Sure enough, his hold on her was quickly preempted, and she was put to work making food for the crowd gathering to help with move-in day at Jase and DeeDee's new place. It took a fuckton of fuel to keep a bunch of big men going, and he saw dozens of sandwiches in progress on the countertops behind the women.

He stalked out of the kitchen followed by Mason, managed to ditch the man by peeling him off on a piece of furniture that needed to be taken upstairs, and then went hunting Hoss. There was still no love between the two men. For as long as Gunny had known him, they rubbed each other the wrong way, but this—his behavior today—might be just about the final straw.

"What the fuck were you thinking, bringing up something like that in front of Sharon?" He leaned in close and gritted his teeth. "Did you conveniently forget she was taken and held not long ago? In time still best counted as hours, not days? That she was taken from my bed in the middle of the night? Or, maybe you forgot she had to watch me wipe her ex from the face of this earth, and then be held, bound, and blindfolded until Diamante decided to cut us loose? My woman is dealing with shit you can't fathom, *brother*. Leave her the fuck out of any conversations you want to have about people missing and just shut the fuck up."

Straightening, he was surprised at the look of remorse on Hoss' face, feeling somewhat mollified when he heard a quiet, "Fuck, man. I'm sorry. Was a shit move on my part. Soon as I saw her face, I realized the audience. I wanted to get your take on what I'm thinking. I value your opinion, brother."

"Now, what the fuck was so important about Willa?" He put his shoulders to the wall next to Hoss, scanning the room automatically, the urges to identify danger less now than a year ago, but still present. He found it somewhat odd this most recent episode hadn't triggered a stronger response in him, but over the past days, he had decided to accept the lack of panic as a gift. *Fist raised.*

"I think she's gone. Eddie was asking about her yesterday, so I had a prospect take a quick run. Her apartment is buttoned up tight." Hoss shook his head. "Want to tell Mason, but I don't have anything concrete to say. Woman might be on a trip for her job, or might have gone downstate to visit her folks. Or she might be gone, which is what my gut tells me, but I don't have anything in hand to support that."

"Then don't say anything. Let the man soak up today. It isn't often he gets to simply be with us without some kind of fucking politics getting in the way. Drama is a fucking killjoy, and maybe the bitch will show up before he has to leave. Give it a few, brother." He nodded, and then felt a twist in his gut. "Which prospect did you use?"

"Hurley." Hoss nodded. "He's turning out pretty good. Steady and sharp, boy does as told without making a stir. He's about nine months into it, but I like him so far."

Gunny sighed. "He's fucking young."

"Yeah, they're all fucking young, but the desire is in his gut. Can't deny his want-to, and he applies himself." Hoss shrugged. "He's good to have around for Chase, too."

Chase, Mason's seventeen-year-old son, had been sent to Fort Wayne with Tug months ago, and depending on the day, was either staying at the clubhouse, or in Tug's apartment. Mason had made Tug responsible for his boy, and Tug took the charge seriously. The boy wanted to patch into the club in the worst way, but Mason had decreed he would have to wait another year. "Yeah, probably good for him to see what kinda hell prospects catch from us. Fuck, we all know if he does decide to patch in, he's going to get the worst of anyone, because ain't any one of us gonna want to be seen playing favorites. Most of the brothers will sway too far the other way, I bet."

Hoss lifted his chin in agreement. "You know you're right. He's been playing guitar with Slate's little brother and Bear some. You heard him yet?"

"Nope, but DeeDee was talking about how good he was the other day. Benny's been a good influence on him, appearances to the contrary." He laughed, because Slate's brother had wound up in Fort Wayne through a series of bad decisions his brother rescued him from. It was funny to think of him being a positive influence, but he was about a year sober now.

"Boys say the bar's packed when they're on the ticket. People must be finding something they like." Hoss shifted, and then asked, "Hey, man, you want a beer?"

Surprised by this offer, a sarcastic rejection was on his tongue, but he held it, saying instead, "Sure do. You know where they're keeping the cooler?"

"Backyard, next to the big-ass grill Jase bought." Hoss laughed. "Come on, I'll show you."

***

Sharon had hung out in the kitchen with DeeDee for a while, helping with sandwiches and drinks. If she was honest, it was more hiding out than hanging out. When Rebel members would come in, she screened her face behind the curtains of her hair, watching them out of the corner of her eye. It seemed like she spent the past few days trying to hide from herself, too. Trying to forget what had happened.

They had been back to the house a couple of times and everything looked normal, but she found herself anxiously looking around corners. There was new carpeting in Gunny's bedroom, and the holes in the walls were gone, patched and painted out of existence. But, she couldn't forget what had happened in that room. Even though she hadn't said anything to Gunny yet, through the stench of the paint fumes, she thought she could still smell the thick, hot, copper scent of blood. It smelled like fear to her, and caused a feeling that caught at her heart in her chest, reminding her of the moments she thought Gunny was hurt...or worse. They were staying at the clubhouse still, hadn't yet been cleared to go home for good, which was a mixed blessing. On the one hand, she didn't have to face those fears quite yet, but it also meant they were living in the clubhouse, where all the members hung out.

Their pups—his pups, she reminded herself—were staying with PBJ, one of the club members he was friendly with, and she found she seriously missed playing with them. Mostly, she simply hated being around so many people all the time. Before, when she worked, she had his quiet and calming house to go back to when she was done, when her set was over. Now, the clubhouse was a beehive of activity, and there were entire families who had moved into those walls for safety. Deke was one thing, because he had introduced himself to her as Gunny's friend, but the other members were more difficult to categorize. Except for Mason, who, even if she was still trying to figure him out, she knew Gunny loved like he loved Deke, which made her trust him.

Another member walked into the kitchen and she dropped her head again. All these men wearing black leather reminded her of the ones who had taken them, who had hit her, had hurt Gunny—

A hand closed on her arm and she desperately tried to shove away, drawing in a frightened breath, jerking at the iron hold on her wrist, pulling and twisting to get free. "Shhhhh, sweetheart," she heard as arms wrapped around her shoulders, pulling her back, the familiar voice cutting through her panic.

She was nearly sobbing as she turned in his arms, throwing her arms around his neck. "Ace," she said, hearing the tears thick in her own voice. "God, I'm glad it's you."

He answered an indistinct question from the doorway leading outside then steered her towards the interior door, pushing her before him without a word, ignoring her protests. She glanced around the living room, glad to see they were alone. She had time for only a quick yelp as he pushed down on her shoulders, seating her on the floor in front of the couch. She ducked her head when he swung a leg over the top of her, settling onto the sofa behind her. "What are you—" He put his hands on her shoulders and pressed, his thumbs rotating into the tense muscles there. "God," she moaned, and he laughed.

"Don't let Gunny hear you making those noises, sis. You're my sister, but he forgets sometimes," he teased, using the heel of his hand to work the muscles just underneath her shoulder blade. "You're tense, sweetheart."

"Well, yeah, who wouldn't be, with a house full of bikers?" she shot back and felt his hands slow, and then continue the firm massage. *Shit, these are his friends too, not only Gunny's. I need to remember that*, she thought. "You are all scary, scary dudes." Trying to play off her earlier statement, she twisted her neck to glance back and laughed, but then lost her smile and tucked her chin down at the look on his face.

"DeeDee said you were going to ask her a question earlier, but got interrupted. What did you need, Sharon?" His tone was even, but the hurt she had seen hovered in the background of his voice.

What she had been going to ask DeeDee was not something she wanted to say to her brother. For one, he wasn't an old lady, with the responsibilities carried by being in a relationship with a club member. From what she had seen and heard, first at the dinner party at Bear and Eddie's place, and then at the clubhouse these past days, her riding on the back of Gunny's bike put her in a position she hadn't expected. The association with him warranting her respect she hadn't earned. Jase might understand; he was always big on making your own way. But, she knew he wouldn't have any idea about protocol for telling a man he was—

She slammed the door on the thought, twisting the lock firmly. Instead, she chose to address a different question that had pressed in on her all day. "Does it seem weird that these people are nice to me?"

His hands paused again, and then his fingers found a knot and rubbed hard at it until it eased, before moving on, seeking the next tight muscle. In a quiet voice, he asked, "Weird how? And nice how?"

"You know. Like today, people have been kind to me. They don't even know me, so why would they be nice? Why would they go out of their way to try and talk to me?" She knew she wasn't articulating this very well, but maybe he would get it. She hoped he would understand without digging, and then be able to help her map her path in this group of people. "DeeDee I get, because she's awesome, and loves you, and is the best boss ever. But, everyone else? I just don't understand."

"You belong to Gunny, and these men are his brothers. I'm his brother, sweetheart. That means you belong to us, too. You're surrounded by family here, Sharon. They want to get to know you, to show respect to Gunny through their interactions with you. Family to him, and you. And, their women are his family too, just as much as you are mine. More, maybe, because they don't keep secrets." Ouch, that hurt, but it was an earned dig, and she had to own the sting. She hadn't been honest with him for a long time, ever since the day she found out he was going to Russia to play hockey and asked her if she would be okay. She had looked him full in the face and lied that day, telling him she was excited for his opportunity and, of course, she was going to be okay.

His fingers found a particularly sore spot and she hissed, trying to move away, but with a hand on her shoulder, he pulled her back into the pressure and eventual relief. "So, tell me again; in this current scenario, why wouldn't they be nice to you?"

"I'm only some chick who works in the strip joint—" she started her response, but stopped abruptly when his hands tightened painfully on her shoulders.

"You're so much more than that, Sharon," he whispered, his mouth near her ear. "You're beautiful and strong, so fucking strong. Talented, because, baby sister, I've seen you dance, and you belong in front of people. Yours is an art that needs an audience. Maybe not the one you have right now, but I see you on stage somewhere. You're poised and intelligent, and you have so much fucking love in your heart. So much to give, and giving that love makes you happy. I think only you could have found a man like Gunny and fallen in love with him." His hands cupped her shoulders and he shook her lightly. "Wake the fuck up, sis. You are not just some chick. You're so much more than what you believe."

He pressed his lips to the side of her head, and there was a deep rumble from across the room. She knew what she would see when she lifted her tear-filled eyes. He was padding across the room towards them, his gaze fixed on her face. Squatting down in front of her, Gunny reached out and replaced Jase's hands on her shoulders with his own, frowning over her head at her brother. "You fucking made her cry, brother," he said in an accusing tone, sliding his hands up the column of her neck. Wiping the tears from her cheeks with his thumbs, he cupped her jaw and lifted her face to his, softly kissing her lips. "You okay, babe?"

She nodded, leaning her forehead against his, eyes open and staring at him. *My family.* "I am now."

***

"Fuck." He gritted the word into the phone from between clenched teeth, already moving and grabbing his cut. "I'm in the wind, brother. I can be there in ten."

Sharon made an inquisitive noise from the bed and he paused, looking down at her. At least when she was taken, he had been beside her. For good or bad, he would have known what happened to her as it happened. If what he just heard were true, then Prez wouldn't have the same solace. "Sleep, baby. I'll be back soon as I can." She mumbled again, and he pulled the door of their clubhouse room closed, locking it behind him, moving to the stairs with long strides.

In the main room, he found Slate and Tug, knowing from the easy look on their faces that what he held would be news. Un-fucking-welcome news. *Fuck*, he thought. Nothing to do but rip the fucking bandage off. This would be hard for Slate to hear, because of what had happened to Ruby, but they had to be there for Prez.

"Mason called," he said, barely getting two words out before Slate's phone lit up. Turning to Tug, he continued, "He thinks Willa's gone. Said shit's not right at her place. He wants some brothers to come give it a look-see, figure things out. Hoss had the same thought yesterday, ran Hurley out there. No joy. So we know her place has been buttoned up at least that long."

From Slate's conversation, it was clear Mason had called and was filling him in on the few known details he had already gone over with Gunny. The three men shared a glance, and Gunny asked, "Lockdown?" At Slate's nod, he pulled his phone out and tapped a group message then called a prospect over and instructed him they were about to be descended upon by members and their families. Slate pulled out his wallet, flipping the chain out of the way. He balanced the phone on his shoulder, talking to Myron now, getting him to cast his talented, electronic net. He pulled several bills out and pressed them into the prospect's hand, muttering, "Groceries. Get a cage; Ruby will text you a list."

Off the phone, Slate looked at Gunny, and then turned to Tug. "Organize shit, Tugboat. Get my woman and babies here, brother." Without another word, the two men walked outside and slung legs over their bikes, kicking them to life and rolling off the lot within five minutes of Mason's first call.

15. Utah

"Clear," he called, pitching his voice to carry, moving from room to room inside the small building. There was nothing of note in the rooms he was set to check, and he came back to the central area. Seeing several men clustered near a door, he walked over, standing next to Watcher. He had come to like the president of the New Mexico Southern Soldiers in the past few hours, having finally met him when their planes landed in Provo. The group of Rebels hadn't been ahead of him by much, so the wait wasn't overly long, but you could nearly see Mason's skin crawling, because they had to stand around for thirty minutes as he deplaned.

He listened as they discussed what they had found, which wasn't much more than him, and then Bones, president of the Skeptics MC in Chicago, quietly said he found a tape. Skeptics had supported the Rebels for as long as the club had been around, and Bones was known to be a good friend of both Mason and Slate. It was difficult to read his expression, but you couldn't mistake his tone when he said it was in everyone's best interest that Mason never see the contents of the tape, and how he said it, made Gunny's blood run cold.

Things had been moving so fast over the past twenty-four hours it was enough to make his head spin. Actually, over the past ten days. First, Mason hadn't been able to contact his sister, but only in a semi-worrisome way, just her doing her job, but being out of touch. But then Willa went missing. Missing, or had bolted, leaving everything behind. Trying to decide which path she trod without knowing her mindset was debatable, and also worrisome, but they didn't have anything concrete. Nothing to point to and say bad things were afoot.

Then, two days ago, they found out Mica left for the airport, but failed to arrive at her destination. Out here, in Provo. The very place where so many of his thin threads led. Gunny shook his head, and then hearing a commotion across the room, lifted it to see Mason standing in front of a man. With a shock, he recognized him, one of Mason's own blood. *Motherfucker*, he thought. It was one thing to wonder if, or even to believe the man would be capable of something like this—with that thought, he cut his gaze to the closed door, hiding a body inside the sealed room—but another thing entirely to see the evidence with his own eyes.

Hoss stepped up beside him, saying in a quiet voice, "I got prints heading into the woods. Bare feet, small, looks like three women, moving fast. I'm gonna go see if I can find them, brother. Could use your help."

With a nod, he followed him outside, glad to finally have something specific to do. They were about a hundred yards away from the building when a gunshot rang out, and he saw only the smallest hitch in Hoss' step. "Motherfucker got everything he deserved," he said quietly, and saw Hoss' head move in agreement.

***

"You think he's gonna get past this?" Gunny voiced the question quietly, looking down the body of the plane to where Mason sat.

"Yeah," Hoss said, just as quietly. "He's a tough motherfucker. He did what he had to do, same as he's done all his life. At least he did the deed quick and clean. I suspect the only regret Mason's going to have once he knows for sure what went down in that compound will be the single decision to do it quick. If someone had given me the chance to get at Birdy, I'd have done him slower. Motherfucker put his hands on Mercy, fucking beat her to hell."

Gunny nodded. "I know what it's like to watch someone you love hurting like that. When Sharon was hurt, it damn near killed me. I didn't know then I loved the woman, but I knew I couldn't stand to have her hurt, needed my hands on her. Had to know she was okay."

Hoss scoffed. "Fuck that noise. I don't fucking love that woman. I've fucked her, but so has half the club, man. She's a good woman who didn't deserve anything Birdy did to her. I hate she's hurting like she is now, and wish there was a way to make things right for her that wouldn't end in blood. But she ain't mine, motherfucker."

He laughed, looking over at Hoss. "That's good news for Deke, then. I think he's been sweet on Mercy for a while, but been holding back, because he thought you were tapping that pussy in an exclusive way. I'll pass on the good word, brother." With a start, he realized for the first time he had called Hoss his brother and meant it. He looked around the plane at the men scattered on the seats and knew he would not only die for any of them, but now he could truly count them his friends, too. *Feels kinda good*, he thought, and then snorted silently, because only he would be backwards enough to get some good out of this kind of cluster.

16. Visitors

Nearly a month later, Gunny stood in their kitchen and smiled to himself at her full-blown rant. He had just given her what he thought would be a nice surprise, but she had worked herself into a frenzy in moments. He had seen the pleased expression she wore for a bare second before she swept it away with her frenetic energy, so he knew his efforts had made the right impression. He would do anything to make her happy.

"I can't believe you're flying her up here without saying anything to me." Sharon flipped him an irritated look, picking up another dog toy and placing it in the half-full basket she carried in her hand. "And she's bringing Kitt? That's crazy. He's never flown. She always said the reason she drove everywhere with him was because she might be able to get him on the first flight of a trip, but once he knew how small and close the inside of a plane could be, the return one would be questionable." She laughed, looking at the dogs following close behind her. "Your pups crack me up; they only want the toys when I'm cleaning."

Gunny paused what he was doing and looked at her with a slight frown. Her phrasing bothered him. "Our," he corrected her, and then went back to loading the dishwasher, glancing around the kitchen to see if there were additional tidying tasks waiting for his attention.

She looked up at the wall clock with panic on her face, and then turned back to him with a scowl. Scolding evident in her tone, she said, "Dammit, don't do that. I still have three hours before they land."

He laughed and walked over to her, shutting the dishwasher door with his foot as he stalked past. He reached out and grabbed her by the waist, pulling her tight against his chest. "Our pups, not an hour, Sharon." Nuzzling the side of her head, he said again, "They are *our* pups." She went still, her body stiff, and he frowned, because her reaction wasn't what he expected. "Babe?"

"What do you mean? They are your pups; this is your house." She swept her hand out. "Your things. Your place. Your pups." She shrugged.

Turning her in his arms, he smiled down at her, shaking his head. "No, baby. Ours. You're mine, but everything else here is ours." He watched her eyes move, tracking from his eyes down to his mouth then back up, looking at him steadily, as if she were expecting to see something other than what was on his face. He repeated himself, wanting her to understand, "You are mine. You'll agree to that, right?"

She nodded, and he continued, "Then it means I'm yours, unless you don't want me." With a small smile, she shook her head, and he pretended to misunderstand her, pulling a sad face. "You don't want me?"

"Smarty pants," she teased. "You know I do. I love you."

"And I love you, Sharon. What's mine is yours, baby. For as long as you'll have me, and probably even after that, because I can't stay away from you." He leaned down, capturing her mouth with his in a soft kiss that left her breathless. "I love you, babe."

***

I should have known, he thought, watching the woman step from the escalator and walk across the airport lobby towards Sharon, who was jumping up and down in her excitement. Dark hair framed a round face, and eyes he knew to be green hid behind glasses. She was pulling a small suitcase and checking behind her on the progress of a tall, thin boy who was far more interested in whatever he held in his hand than his surroundings.

The airport greeter offered the arrivals a cookie in welcome as they walked through the metal archway into the public portion of the airport. The moment they were past security, Sharon had her arms wrapped around the woman, molding herself so tightly to her that you could barely have gotten a whisper between them. The boy looked up and a flash of a smile crossed his face, and he patiently held up his hand, palm first. Soon enough, she unwrapped herself from the woman and turned to the boy, and he pushed his palm towards Sharon, giving that same, brief smile when she performed some complicated handshake with him. She lifted her hand and apparently asked him a question, because he frowned in response, but then nodded, squeezing his eyes tightly closed while Sharon ruffled his hair. He tolerated her touch for a moment then jerked his head back, his shoulders drawn in slightly, apparently the few seconds of contact all he could tolerate.

Sharon linked arms with the woman, drawing her over to where Gunny sat waiting, and he watched for the moment when the woman, Vanna, recognized him as he had her. Her mouth dropped open for the barest of seconds, and then it closed as she drew her lips into a broad smile. He unfolded from the uncomfortable metal bench, standing straight and looking down at the uplifted faces of the two women.

"Lost Lane," Vanna said, reaching out a hand and pausing until he nodded, then gripped his arm with her strong fingers, and he reached up and covered them with his own, extending the contact. The similarities to the private dance Sharon and the boy had stepped through were not lost on him, and he smiled at her as she told him, "Never thought I'd see you again, son."

"Peepers," he said, and saw Sharon looking between them in confusion. He never told her about his encounter with the angel on the trail, the woman who jarred him out of his own head and put him on the path to where he was now. "Looking good, woman," he said, reaching out to pull her into a tight hug.

Glancing down at Sharon's perplexed but pleased expression, he grinned and said, "Long story, babe. Good news. You and me? We got friends in common."

***

Over the next week, he watched Sharon as she visited with Vanna and loved on Kitt as much as he would allow. She was so light and happy with the boy, so open...loving. The two of them played with the pups until they all fell into the grass in a pile of sweaty skin and fur, exhausted, dozing in the sunshine. The day before the pair were supposed to go home, he sat with Vanna at the outside patio table, watching as his crazy woman danced through a water sprinkler with the dogs and boy.

Vanna cleared her throat and he glanced her way, seeing she was looking at him with a serious expression. "Yeah?" he asked, sipping his coffee.

"She said Elkins isn't a problem now. What does that mean?" Ignoring the shouts and barking from the yard, she kept her eyes on him, her gaze steady.

"Means he ain't a problem for her ever again." He shrugged.

"Don't fuck with me, boy. Tell me straight out." Her attitude pulled a laugh from him and he leaned back, putting his feet in a chair seat opposite, pushing it backwards with a scraping noise until he found a comfortable angle.

"Don't ask for what you don't understand, Peepers. Just know she's safe." He gestured to the backyard. "And happy." He turned his body to face her, holding her gaze. "And loved."

"I had a friend once," she said, and he laughed again, interrupting her.

"Just once? Damn, woman, what a miserable life to only have one friend." With a shake, he realized that until Sharon danced into his world, a miserable life was exactly what he had. Deke had been his only friend for a long time, but then things had changed. She had changed him.

"Boy." She shook her finger at him. "I had a friend who did something for me, took care of a problem I had. Back in Texas, Blackie took care of me, taught me I was worth something. He's a good man, a good friend. I've kept track of him through the years, tried to keep the connection open, which means we still exchange calls and texts. I knew when he lost the love of his life, and then when he got her back. Now, he's married to that same good woman. He and his old lady have a half-dozen kids. But, for me, when I needed one, he was a God-sent miracle who took care of my problem, much in the way I believe you took care of Sharon's. You can't shock me, Lane."

She turned in her seat and looked out at Sharon and her son, and he twisted and watched too, seeing the sunlight slanting through the water and creating bright flashes of color, leaving sparkling droplets on smooth, soft skin. "I think you are that woman's miracle, and I thank you for making her feel like she does. Safe, and loved." She nodded and glanced back at him. "She's right for you, too, you know. You're a very different man than the one who handed me a mug full of coffee in the shallow light of morning. The man I met that day was afraid...of so much. Now, you...I don't know how to explain it, but now you seem settled and happy."

He slowly nodded, eyes tracking Sharon. "I am."

***

"Are you sorry you didn't go home with Jase?" Gunny asked casually as he reached out with a pair of tongs, testing the doneness of the burgers on the grill. They needed a minute or two more. He picked up one of the speakers on the table, turning up the music. Passenger was singing *Keep on Walking,* and he liked this song.

"No, he needs this time with the folks. He'll have a hard enough time making Dad understand why he's quitting hockey. They didn't need me there as a distraction." She set the plates on the patio table, handing him a beer as she opened one for herself.

"Hmmm," he hummed noncommittally, glancing over in time to see her surreptitiously toss a piece of hotdog to Tank from her seat in a patio chair. He looked, and Rocky was already swallowing and licking his lips, obviously the first recipient of the contraband goods. "Babe," he scolded, rolling his eyes. "You feeding the pups again?"

"Only a little bite," she said. Standing, she walked over to him and leaned against his shirtless back, resting her head on him. "You smell good," she said, sniffing.

"What do I smell like?" He used the tongs again to lift a burger, deciding it might be done enough for him. "Medium okay with you?"

"Yeah, sounds good. You smell like..." she sniffed again, "like apple wood and leather," she said, planting a hard kiss against his back and he grinned, setting his beer down and turning around.

Tugging her into him, he intended it to be a quick lip touch, but as always, his hunger for her took over, and they were both gasping for breath when he broke it off. "Goddamn, baby," he murmured, mouth against her ear. "Mmm, yeah. You make me..." he dragged his fingers under her shirt and up her side, lightly pinching a nipple and pulling a gasp out of her, "make me wanna fuck you," he finished and turned her around, pulling her back against his bare chest, his hands going to her stomach and the waistband of her pants. He unfastened the button, pushing his hand inside, down into her panties, sliding his fingers along her heat, slipping his middle finger deep into her.

She arched her body, pushing her shoulders backward, reaching up and locking her fingers behind his neck. Bending down, he grinned against the side of her head, because she could barely reach. He pushed her pants down, taking her panties with them, then his palm was covering her pussy and his fingers worked in and out of her quickly while he listened to her rapid breathing. "God, you are so fucking wet, babe," he said, using the edge of his hand and one knee to force her legs farther apart, widening her stance as far as the jeans around her ankles would allow.

Pushing his hand deeper between her legs, he let his fingers roam in between her ass cheeks, fingertips finding and circling her tight entrance, hearing her gasp when he touched her there. Slipping his thumb shallowly in and out of her pussy, he teased and circled the pucker of her asshole with a fingertip. Holding back, he waited until she threw back her head in frustration to press into her in both places, moving slowly. "Yeah, you like me playing with your ass, babe," he said softly. "I know you do. So fucking hot."

He thrust his pelvis forward, grinding his erection into her through the fabric of his jeans. "Feel what you do to me? How you make me want you? *God*, baby. Take off your shirt, Sharon. Bend over, baby. I want to touch you, yeah? Place your hands on the seat of the chair in front of you," he ordered, taking a deep breath as she complied. The position put her head lower than her hips, and he was granted a view of her beautifully rounded ass leading to her spine, a sensuous sway to her back as she arched her head down.

"Be still, baby," he murmured against the skin of her lower back, kissing down her body as he stooped behind her. Squatting on one knee, he rested his hands on her thighs, tugging them apart to expose the reddened lips of her pussy more fully. Stroking inside her with two fingers, he drew her wetness back and upward, circling around her asshole, and was rewarded with a low groan from her. Nuzzling between her legs with his mouth, he lapped and licked at her, fingers and thumbs continuing to work both her pussy and ass, pressing deep inside her then withdrawing, working both hands in tandem.

He teased her to the edge of pleasure and then eased back, repeating each motion countless times, hearing her hiss in displeasure and frustration again and again. Her legs were beginning to quiver and shake from the strain of continually tensing and chasing her orgasm, only to then have that release denied. Her softly voiced sounds of desire made him smile, even as his mouth was still eating at her, his tongue darting and brushing from her entrance where his fingers thrust inside, up to her clit, which was engorged and sensitive. "Love going down on you, baby," he murmured. "Fucking love my pussy. Edge you all day. Eat you all day."

Nibbling and pulling at her with his teeth, he nipped her clit sharply, and then pressed his tongue flat against her, repeatedly licking from clit to asshole, working his tongue around his fingers, pushing her up and over, finally allowing her to come. He felt her clench down on him as she came hard, his tongue moving up to flick rapidly back and forth on her clit, drawing out her climax.

Standing, he opened his pants using one hand, the other still thrusting and circling fingers deep inside her. He slowly stroked a hand down his length, circling the base of his cock with finger and thumb, gripping hard and hissing between his teeth at the pounding of blood inside. "You ready for me, babe?" he asked, adjusting his stance to line the head up with her pussy, inching in slowly. "You want my cock? You want me?"

"Yeah," she panted, rising on her toes in anticipation of his first plunge into her.

"Then take me," he said, standing still, legs spread wide, head thrown back, and teeth gritted. *Fuck, she's hot*, he thought. *Come on, baby, fuck me with that pussy. My pussy. Fuck me. Yeah, mine. Me only...* His thoughts became chaotic when she pressed backwards, impaling herself on his cock so quickly he felt the rough drag of her inner walls against every inch of his dick before her wetness made him slick and slippery.

For several backwards thrusts of her hips, he stood still, letting her take what she wanted from him. She was rising and falling on her toes, pushing back with her ass and then grinding in a small circle when he was deep. *Goddamn*, he thought, *she's fucking amazing. Mine.* Vaguely, he heard the music change, the sounds of Fink's *Perfect Darkness* rising and falling.

"Babe," he growled. "You need to get ready. You got about thirty more seconds to take yours, and then I'm fucking you for mine." She groaned loudly, and he was suddenly glad his house was isolated from his few neighbors by both a tall fence and distance, because he would have to kill any man who saw her like this, abandoning her inhibitions, lost in passion. *Fuck*, he thought, *this is my pussy. Mine. She ain't never getting away, won't allow her to leave.*

Reaching his hands out, he flexed his fingers, releasing them from the tightly clenched fists they had been locked into since she first slid backwards onto him. Smoothing his palms up her back, he ignored the silvering scars and slowly stroked up the long muscles on either side of her spine. "Gunny," she called, breathlessly, "please." Curling his fingers around her sides, he cupped her breasts for a moment, squeezing and teasing her nipples before slipping his hands back down to her hips as he moved against her. He made the slow circuit three times, speeding the pace of his hands when he snapped his hips forward, meeting her backwards thrusts, the loud slap of their flesh filling the air around them.

Settling one palm on her waist, he wrapped the fingers of his other hand midway across her belly, brushing a finger down to press hard against her clit, then thrummed it rapidly, feeling it harden again under his ministrations. Bringing his other hand backwards on her hip, he stretched his thumb out until he could reach her anus. Still lubricated from his earlier play, he pressed his thumb slowly inside, pushing past the ring of muscles, then smoothly stroking in and out.

"Goddamn. Love you. Love this ass, baby," he whispered, gaze locked on where they were joined, on his hand, where his fingers were gripping her cheek, fingertips digging hard into her flesh. Seeing his thumb tucked into her tight heat, watching his wet and shining cock slipping in and out of her silken core. "My woman. Baby, you're mine, always. Mine. My pussy," he gritted, bending his knees slightly to thrust upward and into her, driving hard and fast. "Mine. *My* Sharon," he roared, feeling her clenching around him, her loud cry undulating as she came. He could almost feel the sound like a caress on his skin, flushed with the knowledge he brought her to this place filled with mindless, wordless pleasure.

Bending forward, he covered her with his chest, his teeth finding the flesh over her shoulder blade, biting and tugging. His hands kept moving her back and forth, even as she came hard with him deep inside her. Before she could finish, he straightened, pulling out of her and lining his cock up with her anus. Without a word, he pushed forward, and felt her shiver as he relentlessly pressed inside her there. Slippery with her wetness, he slid the head of his cock in without much resistance and then stilled, head thrown back, nearly undone by the tightness and heat that surrounded him.

He brought his hand up, wrapping his soaked fingers around his cock, sliding that lubrication up the length until his knuckles bumped firmly into her ass, then moved his hand back to her pussy, teasing and stroking her as before. He knew the full width of his cock would be harder for her to take, would require her participation to keep it painless. With his fingers slowly sliding alongside and strumming her clit, he told her, "Breathe, babe. Push back, pressing out, baby. Take me in."

She did, and he let her set the pace of this initial penetration, holding back fiercely, even as every fiber of his body wanted to plunge deep inside her ass, fucking her wild and fast to chase the orgasm he denied himself before. Gently rocking his hips, he withdrew by small measures and pressed back inside, deeper every time, repeating the motion, but keeping it slow. "Baby, talk to me," he said. "Tell me, Sharon. My Sharon. You okay?" This was his first full penetration of her ass. Up to this point, it had only been fingers and thumbs stretching and teasing her. Now that he was in there, he wanted to make sure this was pleasurable, wanted to take her without pain, especially given her injuries only months ago.

"Yeah, it burns a bit, but God it feels good. You feel good, Gunny. So full, God. Don't stop," she pleaded breathlessly, and he saw her arm move, felt her fingers join his at her pussy, her hand sliding underneath his so he was grinding her fingertips against her clit along with his.

"Oh, babe. Aw goddamn, I ain't gonna last long, baby. Can you come?" He threw back his head again, taking deep breaths while keeping the steady, deep, slow pace he set. *Heaven Knows* was playing on the radio now, and the driving beat of The Pretty Reckless song helped him stay slow. Randomly, he thought, *That's it; give every stroke a two count, no double-time. Keep it gentle. Make it good. Slow and steady. Make it the best for my Sharon. My woman. Exquisite woman. Mine. Make it good.*

"I don't think so, baby. But it feels good, don't stop." Her voice was stronger and he smiled. She was mistaken. *She'll come with me in her ass. I just need to...* He shifted his hand from her clit to her opening, feeling his sac slapping against the back of his hand as he pressed two fingers deep inside her. Matching the rhythm he was using to fuck her ass, he wasn't surprised when after only a few strokes, he felt the first tightening flutters inside her pussy.

"Yeah, baby, just like that," he urged, hearing her gasp. "Not gonna last. Baby, come for me…come around me…clamp down on me." The music changed again, the fast-paced *Band of Brothers* from Hellyeah began and he grinned fiercely, fingers moving faster in response to the beat. *Take her over the wall. Push her. I'm gonna make her come.*

She groaned and pressed backwards hard, pushing him deep and holding there as she came, more gently than before, but still a climax she hadn't expected. He smiled victoriously, thrusting deep with his fingers and holding there, the movement of his hips still sliding his cock in and out of her ass. "All right, babe. We found yours. Now. My turn," he said, panting as he sped the pace and pulled his fingers out, moving both hands to her hips.

He was tugging and pushing at her again, controlling the angle of his penetration and the depth of his thrusts to provide the greatest pleasure, and within a couple minutes, he was there, right fucking *there* with her. Tucking his chin to his chest, his gaze wandered her torso from where her ass jumped and jiggled with every plunge he made into her body. Grinding deep, he felt the heat from her thighs on his, the softness of her body giving to his needs, and he clenched his ass and drove deeper, drawing small circles with his hips. He looked up the slope of her back, gaze tracing along the muscles and curves to where her face was half-turned, hair draped over one shoulder. She stared back at him, an unreadable expression on her face, but her eyes were deeply hooded with satisfied passion. Seeing her like that dropped him over the precipice, freefalling as his cock exploded inside her.

He leaned over her, reaching out to grab at the table and support himself, breathing hard and fast, sweat dripping off his nose and chin onto her skin. He thrust into her at uneven intervals, the muscles of his stomach jerking as the sensations assaulted him. She shifted her hands from the chair to the table, folding her arms on the edge between his hands and propping her head on them. Covering her, he framed her arms with his, threading his fingers together. Dropping his head to the middle of her back, he wiped the sweat-slick skin of his scalp back and forth before coming to rest with his cheek pressed to her spine.

"Babe," he whispered, feeling his cock slowly soften inside her, knowing from the uncoiling feeling that it would be dropping out of her soon if he didn't withdraw. "Fucking amazing," he said, softly kissing the marks he left on her skin. "You okay?"

"Better than okay," came her answer and he smiled, lips moving across her skin.

"Burgers are burnt," he said, sniffing. "Gonna hafta call for pizza."

She laughed, and he joined her, trailing kisses across her back again.

***

The pups were growling and she lifted her head from the pillow, cautiously looking around the room. Nothing seemed out of place, but her stomach clenched, remembering the last time she woke unexpectedly in this room. It was still dark out, only a little light leaking in around the blinds. She reached over and picked up her phone, squinting for the time...nearly three in the morning. *What could have them stirred up?* she wondered, and then Gunny spoke from the darkness, saying clearly, in a voice thick with anger, "Fuck you, Kincade."

The whole bed jumped and she twisted around to look at him in surprise, barely making out the deep frown on his face in the weak light. His lips moved, and it looked like he was talking, but she couldn't hear anything. "Baby," she whispered, reaching out a hand, gasping when he swatted it away.

"You didn't fucking kill everyone. Leave me the fuck alone, bastard. You don't get to tell me how to feel." This was less distinct, more of a mutter, and she pushed up onto her elbows so she could see him better.

A little louder than last time, because his dream—combined with the continuing chorus of growls in the background—was unnerving her, she called his name. "Gunny? Baby, wake up."

"Fuck. You. I said fuck you." His mouth twisted, then he shocked her by shouting, "Kincade, get the fuck down. LZ is overrun; we gotta fall back." He thrashed to one side, then back to his back, pressing his head into the pillow. Breaths coming fast and hard, he yelled, the terror in his voice stealing her breath, "Kincade, brother, Porter's done for. *What do I do?*"

She sat on the mattress, pulling the sheet up to cover her breasts. Lips pressed into a thin line, she stared down at him. Every muscle in his body was coiled, ready to strike, tendons in his neck standing out like blades from his skin. Fear and anger were rolling off him in waves and Rocky whined, a frightened sound, then both dogs fell silent. "Gunny," she said loudly. "Wake up. Please, baby, wake up."

His head twisted towards her, and she saw with relief his eyes were open. Taking a deep breath, she leaned in to place her hands on his chest, but the moment her palms touched him, her wrists were bracketed by unbreakable bands of steel. He gripped her arms and twisted, pushing her underneath him, his weight crushing down on her. "Gunny, baby...let me go." With a little scream, she struggled, pulling and pushing to get away from him, but he held on, staring down at her with a deep frown.

"Gunny," she pleaded, barely able to push the word past the tightness in her throat, the dogs now barking loudly in counterpoint to his heavy, rasping breathing.

"*Fuck,*" he yelled, throwing himself off her and to his feet, his back thudding against the wall with such force she could swear the timbers within the plaster groaned. He stood like that for a moment then turned without a word and stalked into the bathroom. With trembling arms, she pushed herself to the top of the bed, taking the covers with her.

Leaning against the headboard, she drew in a shaking breath, wondering what she had just seen, and who the hell Kincade was.

17. New roles

"Gunny!" He heard Sharon's breathless, panicky voice. She had never sounded like that before, and it startled him. Opening his eyes, he found her sprawled beneath him on the bed, his fingers wrapped around her throat. In horror, he released her and saw the dark red marks in her skin matching the spread of his fingers. He knew he had been only moments from crushing her throat in his sleep. Her voice came again, but she lay there with her eyes closed, skin a sickly, sallow gray. Kincade's voice called from beside his ear, asking him what he had done. Reaching out slowly, he cupped her cold face in his palm, the chill felt there burning him, causing him to jerk backwards, rolling from the bed.

Staggering, he leaned against the wall with shaking legs, unable to take his eyes off his life lying there on the bed, unmoving. His Rose of Sharon. His love, gone.

"Gunny." He heard his name and opened his eyes. He was sitting up in bed, covers pooled at his waist. When he saw her kneeling in front of him on the bed, it stripped him of breath. She wasn't dead. She was alive. "Baby," she said, reaching out to put her warm—thank God, they were warm—hands on either side of his face. "You were having a nightmare."

Still panting, he felt sweat cooling on his skin, raising goose bumps all over his body. Reaching up, he covered her hands with his, holding the precious warmth to his skin and nodded, still unable to speak. It had been a week since the first dream, and he continued to dream about Kincade nearly every night, but this one...this dream held a terrifying twist. What if he... *No, I would never hurt her.*

"What was the dream, baby?" She moved closer to him, crawling into his lap and pressing her body against his, letting his arms wrap around her. She did this every night he disturbed her sleep like this; covered in sweat, yelling himself awake, she still got as close as she could to him, the skin to skin contact calming his heartrate. Nestling into his chest, he felt the vibration as she began to hum, the familiar Faker tune nearly bringing a smile to his face.

"Just a bad dream, baby," he whispered and drew in another broken breath, letting her sing him back to sweet. "Just a dream." The smile still failed to make its way onto his features, and he knew his mouth twisted with grief he prayed would never become real.

Later, he lay next to her, head propped up on his hand, and watched her sleeping. He had done this so often when she was hurt, using his eyes to caress her when the touch of his hand would have brought pain. Tonight, it was himself the touch would hurt; the memory of her dead in his bed, even if the vision was only in a dream, was too much to put behind him.

"What if I hurt her?" he breathed out, putting words to his worst fear, something he had wrestled with ever since they had been together, since she agreed to move in with him, agreed to stay, agreed to be his. He knew there had been episodes when he couldn't remember whole swaths of time, sometimes losing entire days, but the last one that bad had happened years ago. "What if I get bad again? What then?" She moved restlessly beside him and he stroked his hand up her arm, fingers curling around her shoulder as she sighed, the corners of her lips turning up into a smile at his touch, even in her sleep. *My Sharon.*

Jase is back from Canada, he thought, not sure where his mind was going. *If this is the start of an episode, she can move back in with him.* The moment the thought crossed his mind, he clenched his eyes closed tightly. *No, no, no. I can't lose her.*

Then hike your ass to the doc, he heard, and turned his head, expecting to see Kincade standing there, as he had often been before. No Kincade, nothing to see but the pups, Rocky with raised head looking at him accusingly, as if he knew Gunny was thinking about setting her aside. *I'm hearing dead people again*, he thought then mentally shook himself and laid his head next to hers. Closing his eyes, he reassured himself, *Everything will be okay. Everybody has bad dreams.*

***

"There's still Shooter," he reminded Slate, and got a scowl in return.

"I fucking know Shooter's still out there. He's tucked away for now, and what we've gotten so far is he's not holding Prez responsible for his spawn's stupidity." Kicking the door closed, he stalked around the desk, throwing himself into the chair. "Man fucking kidnapped four women, five if you count Eddie as the first one. Man was fucking stupid."

"I'm just saying Mason's still got shit to sort out. I've got a feeder in Kentucky, and from the information he's sending me, it sounds like Fury's settling in for a fight. What we don't know for sure is with who. We already know he's got ties to Shooter, so it's a logical jump to wonder if he's looking this way." He shook his head. "I know I don't always make sense, Prez, but when things don't sit right, I pay attention. And brother, something in Kentucky isn't sitting right."

"Okay," Slate said, tipping his head back to look at the ceiling. "I'll talk to Mason tonight; he wants to have a fucking video chat with the fucking chapter presidents. I'll bring it up to him when we're done with church." Looking at Gunny, he narrowed his eyes and asked, "Good enough?"

"Yeah, thanks." Gunny sat for another minute then sighed as he unfolded to his feet.

"You doing okay, brother? Looking tired. Actually, you look like shit." Slate's eyes flicked up and down, then he said, "You're stressing. Things good, man?"

"Good as they get anymore," he said, stalking out and closing the door on more than the room.

***

She grinned at him, saying in a mocking tone, "So you're probably wondering why I asked you here today."

Deke laughed, tipping his head to the back of the room. "No warder today?" He reached into the cooler and pulled up a brown bottle, water beading on the surface of the glass.

Shaking her head, she made a face at the proffered beer. "Got any juice? Maybe apple?" He looked at her as he closed the cooler, but left the room and went to the clubhouse kitchen, coming back with a container. He shook it at her with a grin and then poured a tall glass of iced apple juice. Pushing it across the bar, he watched as she picked it up with a smile, taking a small sip, then a larger one when the tart, sweet flavor hit her. "God, that's good," she said, and he laughed.

"Where's Gunny?" He pressed her, but she wasn't ready to go there yet, and tried to deflect.

"You mean Anthajelous? He's at home slaving away in the garage, I suspect." Picking up her juice again, turning slightly away, she barely managed to keep a straight face.

"Anthajelous? What the fuck, you renamed him? Disallowed, woman. No fucking way. Hell, that ain't never gonna fit on no patch. Fuck that noise." He laughed as she intended, so she twisted and grinned at him.

"Well, I thought was kinda important to acknowledge the truth." She paused, twisting the glass between her palms. *Wait a beat. One more...* "See, here's the thing, Deke. All the women see him and they jealous he's mine." Head down, she grinned at the bar top, waiting. *Give it a second...*

He threw back his head and laughed hard, reaching up to wipe at his eyes with the back of one hand. After a minute, he quieted and sighed, then repeated, "Anthajelous," before winding down to silence. With another humor-filled sigh, he shook his head, asking her, "So why are you here, Sharon?" He stashed the juice in the ice bucket then walked around the bar and sat two stools down from her. She had a questioning look on her face when she studied the space between them, and he laughed again. "You know what your old man will do if he comes in to find me snuggled up next to you. I like my face arranged as it is," he said, and she grinned.

"Okay," she said then paused. "All seriousness now, because I have questions, Deke. You told me to call you if either me or Gunny needed you, and I think he needs you. I have questions about things that came before me, but I'm not trying to jack with your friendship. I don't want you to tell me anything you aren't comfortable talking about. That's the first rule. Because you're his friend, not mine." At a noise from him, she paused again.

"Sharon, I'd like to think we *are* friends," he said with a frown, tilting his head to look at her.

"Okay, maybe we're friends. But...you're his friend *and* brother, and this is me trying to respect that relationship. But something's wrong, Deke." She let him see her worry, knowing he would understand. "He's been having nightmares. Bad ones. Awful ones. Or, at least he was. Now, I don't know for sure, but from how he looks, I think he still is."

"Why don't you know if he's still dreaming?" He turned away and looked at the bar top and she winced, glad he wasn't looking at her, because this was hard to admit.

She whispered, "He's not sleeping with me anymore. The first night, the first dream, I thought he was awake, but he wasn't. When I touched him, he reacted and then woke up because of that reaction, and I think he scared himself." She rushed to reassure him, "He didn't hurt me, nothing at all like that, but he...reacted to my touch." Swallowing hard, she continued, "It took a few days, a few more dreams, but he stopped sleeping with me. And now, I don't know if he's even sleeping at all. He's always out in the garage, working on the bikes. I found him dozing, sitting upright on his stool out there the other morning. I think he was at it all night long. But, his dreams, Deke, they are scary...were scary. Whatever...just plain scary."

"Scary how?" She caught his gaze in the mirror over the bar and held it. He needed to understand how strained and on edge his friend was, and she didn't think Gunny would be the one to tell him. She knew now this was why Deke had come to her before, why other members had extended the same offer, to come talk to them if Gunny needed them.

"He talks in his sleep when he's dreaming. When it's a bad dream. Then, when it's terrible bad, he yells and makes the pups growl. That's where we were...before he stopped coming to bed." Licking her lips nervously, she decided to go for broke and asked, "Who's Kincade?"

His head came up with a jerk and he quickly twisted to look at her. "Where'd you hear that name, babe?"

"From Gunny. He talks to Kincade in his sleep. Yells at him, too. Tells him to eff-off a lot." She tried to laugh and failed. She repeated the question, his reaction reinforcing her feeling this was important. "Who's Kincade?"

"Dude was in the Marines with Gunny. I think they went through basic on Parris Island together. They were close, good friends. He was tight with the whole team, but he and Kincade were more like brothers. Kincade was team lead on their last mission." He watched her when he said this and she felt herself flinch, and then she slowly nodded. She knew Gunny was the only one who came back alive from that mission, the one where he had been shot, the one that took his friends.

"What's he say? When he talks to Kincade, what does he say?" The anxiety in his voice wasn't forced; it was there plain as day. What she was telling him, what she had shared, had his attention, because like she thought, it wasn't good. His worry for his friend validated her own feelings, and she felt her hands begin to shake, wrapping them tightly around the condensation-covered glass in front of her.

"Mostly gibberish, but sometimes I can make out words or sentences. Lots of eff you's and arguing about who has the right to be responsible for what happened, or what's happening in the dream. Deke, I'm scared for him, but him not coming to me...that's terrifying. It's the first time since he found me that we've slept apart." Tipping down her chin, she stared at the bar, gathering her courage. "Why do you think he doesn't want...me?" Those words hurt so badly to say she covered her mouth with one hand, holding in a sob.

"Little one, I don't think it's that. Have you tried talking to him?" She nodded. He leaned over, reaching out and smoothing his palm up and down her arm, soothing her. "Babe, you gotta try again."

18. Never leaving you

Standing with her forehead against the wall, she waited for her music to begin. It killed her to think this might be one of the last times she'd dance here. She liked the club, liked the vibe DeeDee brought to everything, but if things worked out with what her dance instructors suggested, she wouldn't be able to stay on here, at least not taking the number of sets she danced now.

She had begun taking lessons again weeks before, mostly because she missed the structure of the time spent in the studio, but also because she loved learning and growing. She liked the feeling of being better when she walked out of the teacher's presence than she had been going in, and both of the instructors she engaged were encouraging her to look towards another stage, much as Jase had. There was a cattle call coming up for a local theater company, and she decided this morning, even with the upcoming change in her life, she would be throwing her hat in that particular ring. It was time to fly.

Tinkling notes of a piano sounded, followed by a fast, rhythmic drumbeat, and she reached out, pushing open the door. Head high, she sashayed around the stage, timing the music to hold and pause at the end so she could look across the room to where she knew he would be standing, where he always was when she danced.

Lifting one corner of her mouth in a small smile, she slowly removed one shoe, sliding the sole of her bare foot up the inside of her leg and straightening it behind her, bending her knee in a deep plié. Bringing that foot back to the ground, she performed the same movements with the other leg, turning to transition to a tour jeté, and winding up with her back against the pole.

I love you, she thought as she climbed the pole, feeling safe, because Gunny was here watching over her as he had done every day since she walked through these doors. Even before she loved him, he watched her. Was watching her still.

I will always love you, she called in her mind. The music swelled and she twisted through a complex series of movements choreographed to look effortless, but Gunny knew how much it took out of her, how hard it was to make it look so easy. Like her whole life, she tried for years to make things look natural, even while dying on the inside. For him, she could do this one more time. A hundred times. A thousand, if that was what it took to make him look at her with desire again. *I will never leave you*, she promised.

She spun around the pole, seeing the upturned faces, hands twitching in laps or mouths open in silent need. Looking back to Gunny, she locked gazes with him, willing him to see how much she wanted him. *I'm afraid*, she thought, arching backwards into a spiral down towards the stage. *I'm scared of being without you, of losing you. Don't pull away.*

I need you, she cried, collapsing to the floor at the end of the routine. When she stood, breathing hard, he remained impassively against the wall, unmoved by her dance, by her unspoken pleas. If one dance didn't do it, she was willing to go again and again, dance until her feet bled for him, until he knew how much he meant to her. *I'm not going to leave you*, she promised again, looking at him.

Lifting her chin, she forced down the tears and moved around the stage, accepting money from strangers in exchange for a few seconds of her undivided attention. *Like DeeDee loves Ace, I love him—* Her thoughts were interrupted by a rough hand grabbing her arm, pulling her towards the edge of the stage. Shocked by the unexpected touch, she ripped her gaze up to see an unfamiliar face, suit coat-clad shoulders, tie tugged loose. A businessman out for an evening's thrill. In the next second, a rumbling snarl sounded from across the room and she jerked frantically at where the man held her captive, trying desperately to get away before Gunny—

***

"Get your goddamned fucking hands *off* her, you asshole," he roared, heaving the table over on top of the man who had grabbed Sharon's arm. A scream cut short and he twisted to see Sharon backed up against the pole, one hand across her mouth. She turned and ran from the stage, and he looked back down at the man on the floor, cowering with a spreading stain of piss on the front of his slacks. "You were going to tip her, right?" Chest tight with fear and rage, he asked this in a forced, steady tone, holding out a hand for the twenty the man still clutched. "That's why you put your fucking hands on her, right? I'll pass it along to her with your thanks." He reached down, plucking the money from the man's suddenly slack fingers, and turned to stride backstage to find Sharon and make sure she was okay.

He looked in the first place he could think of, but she wasn't in the dressing room, and he felt an electric stab of panic. Scanning the room again, he turned back to the hallway and began a systematic search. But she wasn't anywhere he could find, not the storeroom or the bathroom, and he stood stock still in the back hallway, listening and thinking. She couldn't have left the club, because she had ridden with him today. He had a thought and flicked his earpiece, and suddenly her voice filled his hearing, granting him the ability to take a full breath for the first time since the bastard up front had tried to manhandle her. The sound jolted him into motion, and he quickly headed for the office.

"—don't know what to do." What sounded like a sob echoed through his head, and he listened more carefully, his rapid steps slowing. "He won't sleep with me, hasn't for days. I love him so much. I need him to understand I'm not going anywhere. I won't leave him simply because he's struggling, and he needs to know I'm not afraid of him. I love him. He might have scared himself, but he didn't frighten me. But if he's struggling like he is, then how do I tell him *this*, when he can't even stand to touch me anymore? What if this is something that tips him farther?" She sniffed and he heard a mumble, realizing she had to be on the phone, knowing he would hear the full conversation otherwise.

"Well, no. What am I supposed to ask him? Hey, Gunny? Do you remember how we used to hump like bunnies? You know, that fun thing we did together? So, what happened to that?" A trembling laugh and another pause. He wished he could hear the other person, wished he knew who she was spilling her fears to instead of him. *Be honest, man,* he thought. *She's not saying anything that isn't true.*

"No, I was all set to ask DeeDee how she'd handle it, but then Slate and Ruby came in with the babies. I just don't know what to do, Ma." It was her mother on the phone. Jacque and Kenny Spencer, her parents, had come down for a visit not long ago, and she had talked to her mother for the first time in years. "How do I tell him?"

Another pause, then he snorted with laughter, because he could almost hear her rolling her eyes. *Picking up bad habits from DeeDee,* he thought humorously, and then froze when the meaning behind her next words finally hit him. "Oh, stop it, I'm not being dramatic. We never talked about kids. I mean, what if it's not what I think and instead of staying away because he's afraid he'll hurt me, he's simply tired of me. If he doesn't want me anymore, then what do I do? I would never put him in that position; we never even talked about the possibility. If he doesn't want me, then why would he want this?"

Staring straight ahead, he saw his hand come up and his knuckles rap on the solid wood of the door. Through his earpiece and through the door, he heard, "Sec, Ma. Yes?"

"Babe," he called, "you okay?"

There was a hesitation, and then she said firmly, "Yeah, I'm good, Gunny."

Still on his side of the door, he leaned his forehead against it, once again finding himself hating that barrier between him and her. He wanted his hands on her, wanted to hear what she needed to tell him. Wanted to shout how much he loved her. Instead, he said, "Okay, babe. I'm here. I'm going to be right here when you are ready."

19. Knotted ends

"The man who found himself in my house, in my goddamned, fucking bedroom. Man who put his hands on my woman, taking her to a place she didn't deserve to be. Man who crated my pups? That man don't deserve to live, and I'm only here out of courtesy for who you were, and what you meant to Kincade." Gunny hadn't spoken until his ass was firmly in the chair across the table from Woolfe. He hadn't trusted himself to touch the man, to speak to him without a firm barricade between them. "You draw attention from me and my brothers the way you have, and shit will rain down on you and yours, unless you give me enough of a reason to settle things another way."

"Kincade would be proud of you, Gunny." That name from his mouth took him by surprise for a moment, and then it pulled him back to Parris and beyond, back to when he had been Gunnery Sergeant Lane Robinson. Woolfe took an easy breath, twisting slightly in his chair to lean his elbow across the seat next to him, relaxation written in every muscle of his body. Woolfe did not fear this meeting, did not fear him. Gunny's gaze flashed around the diner, not seeing any clear backup stationed anywhere. "Nope, I came alone. Nobody here but me and you," the man said, then flicked a hand towards the plate glass window, "and your shadows."

Looking outside, he shouldn't have been surprised to see his brothers seated on their bikes across the street. Pipes backed up to the brick wall of the building, every face tilted his direction. Shouldn't have been, but he was, which meant he wasn't paying attention. Turning back to Woolfe, he asked, "Who?" This was the one question he wanted answered from this meeting, because he knew from his informant in Kentucky that the paper on Sharon hadn't been the Lexington Diamante's contract, nor was it Shooter's. That left a hell of a lot of unknowns, and he didn't fucking like unknowns.

"Your man's step-daddy," Woolfe said, and then tapped a fingertip against the table, straightening to face him fully. "I don't know who the girl is to him, but he wanted her. I got all kinds of shit for bringing you along; seems your reputation precedes you, and he would have much rather I ended you there, but you know how sentimental I can be." He shrugged lightly, one corner of his mouth tipping up into a sardonic smile. "My one good deed, it seems." Then he pretended to think, laying a finger alongside his nose. "No, two good deeds, I brought you the dung heap that was your woman's ex-husband." He pointed at Gunny. "That was fucking twisted, man. I get it; I've seen some of the videos he posted, but your method? Fucking twisted."

Here, Gunny stopped breathing, because he didn't have the faintest idea what Woolfe was talking about. *What fucking videos?* he thought, but the man kept talking over the torrent of thoughts pouring through his mind. "And they are fucked up, so I get it. But you squashed him like a fucking bug, scraping him off the bottom of your shoe and walking away with the prize curved into the crook of your elbow. Righteous fucking Gunny, man. Kincade would be proud you protected her like you did."

"Makin' sure I got this straight." With some effort, Gunny brought his thoughts back to the present, dragging them away from the horrifying images of some fuckers getting off on the pain Elkins brought to Sharon on a regular basis for all the time she was with him. "You saw my name on your orders, and came into my house anyway. You didn't pick up the phone, make a courtesy call." Woolfe made a noise and Gunny nodded. "Oh, I get it too, man. You knew you could only be successful with that shit in an ambush, so making a call to me would have made your job harder. But you fucking knew it was me, otherwise you wouldn't have brought eight men for one woman and the stupid sap who shared her bed. Yet, still you came, bringing your fucking army, and you brought it to my house. My bedroom. My woman." He gritted his teeth and took a breath before continuing. "You brought that fucking dung heap to the woman he had tortured for a long time, expecting...what, exactly?"

"Wasn't expecting anything, Gunny." His tone was too bland. There was something here. His thoughts turned back to the night they entered the room, the muzzle flash of a gunshot.

"Not everyone got a vest. Am I right?" Gunny saw the minute tightening of the skin around Woolfe's eyes and knew he had found it. "Of the eight men, I took out four, the first ones into the room. Elkins was one of those. You knew first entrants would be targets, but you didn't give them a vest. You saw the videos," *fucking shit*, "before you came in...wanted me to be the one to do him. Because you couldn't. Not without..." he stared at Woolfe for a minute, "...not without pissing off someone you didn't want to piss off. My man's step-daddy? You're deep into that shit, aren't you? What do they hold on you, man?"

Now it was Gunny's turn to sit back in his seat, lounging across the table from the man, projecting a look that was relaxed and loose. "It's been a lotta years since I saw you last. Makes me wonder, man, exactly what changes life has brought your way. You got a wife?" Another flash of tightness, there and gone. "Kids?" The prod bought a flare of Woolfe's nostrils, unable to contain his physical reaction to sudden fear. *Manzino*. "The Mexican club Mason and Slate had a hand in cleaning up, the old Machos had a corridor through Colorado." Woolfe's head jerked back and Gunny drew a quick breath of satisfaction at bringing things together. "Colorado. Because someone's resurrecting those connections, aren't they? My man's step-daddy, you mean Mason, and you're talking about Shooter's old man. Utah."

"You always were a smart fucker," Woolfe said admiringly, and Gunny shook his head.

"Not smart enough," he said, catching the manager's eye and jerking his head towards the door into the kitchen. "But I know when I've gotten all I'm gonna get. No good deed goes unpunished, right?" He watched the man gather up his employees and usher them into the back. "My woman." Woolfe stared at him, understanding dawning on his face. Gunny sighed. "You put your hands on Sharon. My Rose of Sharon. I'm a man of my word, Woolfe. Told you what I'd do, you went right on ahead, did that shit anyway." He shook his head, lifting his hand from his lap, carrying the weight he had been holding there, revealing his intent here at the last. Leveling it calmly, he said, "That shit simply cannot stand."

***

Walking out of the diner, he was unscrewing the small metal tube from the end of his gun when he passed the prospects headed inside. With a hand on Hurley's arm, he quietly said, "Manager cooperated, so there ain't nothing to clean up but the trash." He waited for the nod of understanding before he turned loose and let him walk inside. Continuing across the street, he lifted a hand to Deke and Hoss, scanning the rest of the brothers who had shown by their actions that they had his back. Memories surfaced of the first night he met the club, seated with Winger and Bingo, watching as without being asked men left to assist one of their members, because they had his back. Full fucking circle.

He nodded, moving to his bike. No surprise, Deke had parked next to him and was waiting there. "You good, brother?" He heard the question and lifted his gaze to meet Deke's.

With a startled snort, he said, "Fuck no, I'm not good. That was Kincade's friend. A jarhead I served beside for more than one deployment. The man fucking betrayed all of that when he went into my house. I ain't good with that."

"Not what I meant, brother, and you know it." He was taken aback by the scolding tone in Deke's voice and he frowned.

"I found out what I needed, and more than I wanted. I see the next stone in the path, Deke. We just gotta get there." Pulling out his phone, he held down a button and said, "Dial bean counter." Deke barked a laugh as the phone rang, and Gunny flashed a grim look at him. "I'm not good, brother." Myron answered the phone, and with Deke listening, he told him about the videos Woolfe had mentioned, eyes fixed on Deke's face, watching as it fell into harsh lines when the full understanding of what he meant settled into place.

"Fuck." The bleakly whispered word filled the air around them, even as Myron uttered much the same from his place in Chicago.

"Yeah," he said shortly, swallowing hard to push past the pain of knowledge he never wanted. "Can you find them? Find the account and delete them?"

"Goddamn right, I can do that, brother. Anywhere they exist online, I'll wipe them out. Does Sharon know about this?" Myron's quiet confidence and resolve was contagious, settling Gunny, and he felt his shoulders lower as his muscles loosened.

"No," he said. "I don't think she knows anything about this. She knew he had a camera, and talked about live sessions, but not videos, so I'd like to think she doesn't know anything. I'm gonna want to keep it that way."

"You got it, brother," Myron reassured him. "I'm on it right now. Priority number one, man. I'll let you know when everything is purged."

"Obliged," he said, and Deke gave a short laugh as he disconnected the call.

"You are a country motherfucker at heart, aren't you?" Deke reached over, resting a hand on his shoulder. "We need to talk about Sharon, brother. Meet you back at the clubhouse?"

With a nod, he turned away, straddling his bike. He sat there for a moment, watching as one of the prospects pulled a van up to the door of the diner. Seeing Hurley drag a bag through the room and then pause to wait for the other man to come back in from outside. "Yeah, brother. I'll meet you there."

***

They had seated themselves at a table far from the bar, away from the pool tables, and hopefully free from any chance of interruption. Deke's gaze never wavered from his face once Gunny started talking. "I nearly killed Sharon in my sleep." Deke took a breath, but he powered on, wanting to get it all out there. "I woke up and had her under me, about two seconds from putting my hands on her neck. Now, if I lay next to her, I can't let myself sleep. I'm too afraid of what I might do, what I might wake up to if I lose myself in a dream. I went back to see the VA doc, wanted to see if this was fucking PTSD fucking with me yet a-fucking-gain. He agreed as how it probably was, and he got me hooked back up with a talking doc, and you know how much fucking fun that is for me." Deke snorted and made a motion with his hand to continue. "They want me to take something to help me sleep, but I'm afraid to take it. I can't take the risk, because what if it puts me too far under to control myself? What if I hurt her?"

Shaking his head, Deke asked, "Did you hurt her, or did you not?"

Absently, he shook his head, remembering the fear on her face that night, the sound of the dogs growling at him...*at him*. Because he was the greatest threat in the room, even with what had gone down before, he was the worst the house had ever seen, and even his pups knew it.

"Not, but it was a near thing. From the feeling in my gut, I could tell. From the fear on her face, I could tell she knew it, too." He picked up his beer and took a drink. "You know the kind of reactions I've had to meds in the past. Some of them work, some of them don't, and some of them fuck with me in ways unexpected and strange."

"She's worried about you." With those four words, Deke had his full attention. "She came to talk to me, man. She's worried, and afraid because she knows something is up. I don't think she likes you putting this distance between you and her. In fact, I know she doesn't, because she's wondering what she did to turn you off like a switch." Gunny remembered her words to her mother on that phone call, the words that made his heart beat faster with equal measures of fear and excitement. *We never talked about kids.*

"She's pregnant," he said quietly, and didn't miss the lack of a smile on Deke's face. "Yeah, in all this, she's pregnant." He scrubbed at his face. "Everything I could ever want is all wrapped up in those two fucking words, but what if I hurt her and she's carrying my baby? What if I do something and it gets ended because of me? Why would she want a kid with me, the fucked up man who can't stand to see his hands on his woman now, because all he sees is the possibility of bruises left behind? Of gray skin and slack muscles? I'm so fucked up, man...why would I want to wish this on anyone, much less the woman I love?"

"When's your next appointment?" Deke asked quietly.

"This afternoon." He looked at his phone. "In about two hours."

"I'm going with you," Deke said confidently, and Gunny laughed.

"My security blanket again, brother?" He asked the question lightheartedly, hoping to bring a smile to Deke's face.

"Whatever you fucking need, brother." The response was so steadfast and true he had no answer.

***

Repeating her words from a few days ago back to her with a broad grin, Deke jokingly asked her, "You wondering why I asked you here today?"

She laughed and nodded, noting with a twitch of her nose he had a glass of apple juice waiting for her. "I'll play along, Deke. Why did you ask me here today?" They were seated side-by-side at the bar, a move she also didn't miss, as it made a statement about something; she was just unsure of exactly what.

"Talked to Gunny," he said without preamble, and she drew a quick breath. He continued, "He's seeing his VA doc again. This is a good thing, little one. He reached out for help on his own, because you were right; he scared himself shitless that night. I talked to the doc with him, and what I found out is he's not lost in himself like he would have been in the past. These kind of episodes would draw him into himself, but that isn't happening here. The doc said you anchor him. You keep him rooted in the now, so he doesn't get as lost in the then. With everything that happened to you with Elkins, what happened to both of you when all that shit went down in your house, all the fucking shit we've got running rampant in the club...shit you don't even know about, and, fucking trust me, it's best that way. But, the doc said it's no wonder all the stress had brought on the issues he's seeing. But this round seems different; he's anchored, little one, and he ain't going anywhere. You need to give him time to sort through his shit, to find his way to the other end of it. You told me once if he tired of you, you would cut him loose, and this is *me* telling *you* that ain't what's going on here. He needs you. You...since the first time he laid eyes on you, he breathes easier when you're in the room."

She sat still for a moment, taking in all he had said. Gunny was seeing a doc who said she was good for him. Out of everything, that was what she latched onto. That was her knot. "He needs me." Deke nodded in agreement at her brief statement. "I need him, too." Forcing down a sob, she licked her lips, pressing them into a thin line for a moment. Once she felt she could speak without breaking down, she told Deke,

Gunny's best friend, reassuring him as best she could, "I'm not going anywhere. He's worth anything I have to do, any battle I have to fight to keep him. I love him."

He nodded, reaching out to stroke her hair behind her ear, tugging lightly on her earlobe as he said, "Everyone sees it, Sharon. That love shines from your face every time you look at the big bastard. You keep my number handy, little one. Call me if you or Gunny need anything; my offer will always stand."

They had chatted for a few more minutes before she left. It seemed Deke was looking for something else from her, something he needed in order to be comfortable with letting her leave, so she gave him smiles and conversation, gently reassuring him she wouldn't be abandoning his friend—she wasn't going anywhere. Now, she was sitting in the car Gunny had given her to use when he couldn't be around to haul her butt on his bike. Chin down, she rested the top of her head against the steering wheel, thinking about the conversation she had on the phone with Vanna just now.

"If you love him, then you're making the right decision," her friend had told her. *"Life with him might not be easy, but if you love him, then you're right, and it's worth the struggle. Love is always worth it, sweetie."*

Nausea swelled in her throat, filling her mouth with bitter saliva, and she swallowed with difficulty. Not limited to the mornings as advertised, the sick feeling accompanying her pregnancy could come on her without warning at any time of the day. Hand resting low on her belly, she closed her eyes, thinking about the urgency of the sound filling the doctor's office earlier that morning. The rapid, echoing *thup-thup-thup* confirming what she already knew had drawn tears to her eyes, and her hand clenched into a fist now, still longing for Gunny's holding hers. That solo visit had torn her heart in two, deeply afraid it was the first of many, but now she had hope it wasn't her future after all. She was reaching for the keys in the ignition when a soft rapping came from the window beside her head, and she looked up to see DeeDee smiling down at her.

Returning the smile, she flipped the keys on and rolled down the window. Reaching in, DeeDee cupped her face and looked at her intently, the smile having faded from her lips. "Is everything okay, sweetheart?"

She lifted her hand, covering DeeDee's with her own, holding that warmth and tenderness to her skin as she responded honestly, "No, but it will be. I'm headed home. I need to go talk to Gunny."

"You're okay to drive?" The caution in her tone wasn't lost on Sharon, and with a shudder, she remembered how DeeDee's husband and daughter had been killed, the inattentive new driver swerving into them, killing all three.

"I am," she said emphatically, and nodded. "I'll call you later, okay? I want to have lunch or something."

She didn't miss the surprise that crossed DeeDee's face, but it was rapidly followed by a pleased excitement, and the smile she got from DeeDee was so broad and filled with joy she wondered why she had ever doubted this woman liked her. "I'll be waiting. If you don't call me, then I'll call you. Promise." With a quick pat on her cheek, DeeDee moved away, walking to where Jase waited for her at the door to the clubhouse. Sharon lifted a hand in a careful wave and got a typical over-the-top Jase response, as his waving of both hands looked more like jumping jacks than a goodbye.

With a grin, she started the car and drove home, not even noticing that for once, she hadn't called it Gunny's home.

20. Feels like flying

"Gunny?" She called his name from the garage like a question and he walked towards the door with a grin. She had barely gotten home, and had probably seen the new scoot and wondered what he was up to this time. Eve To Adam was playing over the speakers, Taki Sassaris singing about focusing on the only thing that mattered, which for him was Sharon, and he paused for a moment, thinking the words were perfect for this moment, his woman, because they were each other's safe refuge, and he would follow her anywhere. *Shut Out the World* could be their song, he noted, the corners of his lips curling up at the thought of dancing with her to this music while people who cared about them both looked on, witness to one of the most important moments in his life.

I sleep, but my heart waketh: it is the voice of my beloved that knocketh, saying Open to me.

"Yeah, babe?" It had been nearly a week, and she still hadn't spoken to him about her fears, or anything else. He and Deke had gone to his appointment together, and thanks to his pushy friend, he had gotten some of the answers to questions he couldn't even articulate. It had been one of the most productive conversations he had in a long time.

All Gunny wanted to know was if the doc felt he was a danger to Sharon or the baby, and the man had rushed to reassure him that clinically, he was long past the acute stage of his PTSD, and practically, he already knew this about himself. The doc reassured him he had been managing his behaviors for a long time now. And even though various things could still trigger a reaction or an episode, he had known for the past couple years that things were evening out, and his actions supported the change, his reflection in the mirror showing a near-normal person for the first time in more than a decade. He still had a lot of work to do, a fuckton of it, but with Sharon as the reward waiting him at the finish line, he would suffer any amount of effort to get there. *My Rose of Sharon.*

With that powerful knowledge tucked into his pocket, over the past week, he set out to quietly make changes, wanting to ease her fears and bring them back to where they were before. He hadn't allowed another single night to pass without her beside him in bed, and each eventless waking brought him closer to assurance that he could get them through this. His nightmares hadn't left completely, but now the fear they evoked was muffled, muted by the medicine, and even the pups were sleeping through the night again.

He made it to the door of the garage, ducking his head through the doorframe to see her staring at the bike sitting to one side, sidecar unmounted and placed on top of the workbench. "Yeah, babe?" he repeated and grinned as she swung her gaze to him.

"What is this?" She flung a hand at the offending bike, and he smiled more broadly.

"Sidecar," he said and went back to the kitchen, moving to the counter and putting the song on repeat, then picked up the knife he had laid down when she first called him. Cutting vegetables into strips, he was sorting them into piles, dropping them into the baggies and sealable bowls he set out for this purpose.

"Gunny?" She asked this from near the door, leaning a hip against the cabinet and watching him with curiosity.

"Yeah, babe?" he deliberately repeated his words, knowing it would eventually make her crazy.

"What are you doing with a sidecar? And, what are you doing in the kitchen? Are those...is that celery?" He wondered for a moment if he should be offended at her tone of astonishment, but then he decided to simply go with it.

"Yeah, vegetables. Making some snacks. Sidecar is a project, a relatively new one. You know how much I like projects." He kept cutting and sorting, seeing the tip of her tongue dart out and wet her lips. "You hungry, babe?"

He had noticed she was losing weight, and now he understood why, realized she must have been hiding the morning sickness that had stripped her skin of its luster, and packed the bags he had seen under her eyes. His psych had put him in touch with an obstetrician, and he kept that appointment too, finding out ways to make food that would be easier on her system. They now had a pantry full of crackers, vegetable and chicken broth, applesauce, and electrolyte drinks.

"Maybe a little," she ventured, and he tossed her a bag of freshly cut apple slices. She caught them and turned the bag in her hand as she asked, "Who's the sidecar for?"

"Me," he said, turning back to his cutting board, grinning down at his hands when he heard a crunch followed by a breathy little hum of appreciation.

"What do you need a sidecar for, baby?" She still had apple in her mouth when she spoke and he looked up, watching as she examined one of the slices with what looked like surprise. "These are good, Gunny."

"I figure I've got a little while to get the sidecar finished," he said, keeping his eyes on her. When she flicked her gaze up to meet his, he stared into her face, willing her to ask him how long.

"A little while?" She licked the side of the next apple slice and he grinned, because it was something Kincade had always done, claiming if he licked something, then it was his. It was good to think of his friend with something more than sorrow. Sharon had given him that, along with so much more.

"Yeah, I probably have a couple of months before it needs to be finished," he said, his hands working to close the bowls, stacking them preparatory to putting them into the refrigerator. He was watching, so he saw her head come up, eyes boring into him now.

"You know," she whispered, taking a reflexive step backwards, her involuntary reaction twisting something in his chest. He needed to reassure her, make sure she knew this wasn't just welcome; it was a fucking miracle, and he would treasure her for giving him this too.

"So fucking happy, babe," he said, giving her a soft smile. "You know what this means, right?"

"You know?" This was a question, and he answered with a nod.

"Come here, Sharon." He held out his hand and saw her look at it with something like awe in her face. "This means you're mine for always. Stuck with me, babe. Come here, lover." He waited patiently for her to react, and when she reached out her trembling hand to place it in his, he took a deep breath, so filled with love for her that it was like flying.

The End (of this story)

THANK YOU FOR READING *GUNNY*!

Thank you for reading *Gunny*, book #5 in the **Rebel Wayfarers MC** book series. This particular character, Lane Robinson, tried desperately to take over *Jase*, the previous book, but I persevered and was able to convince him his story was worth waiting for, and promised him a standalone book.

Inspiration for this character is drawn from a variety of sources, including a young man I met on Knobstone trail in Indiana in the spring of 2014, and a recently separated vet who was gracious enough to grant me several interviews to talk about the hard topics of coming home accompanied by the demons of PTSD.

Post-Traumatic Stress Disorder is very real, and many people don't realize the existence of the condition is not restricted to soldiers returning from dangerous deployments. PTSD can be present in the abused spouse or child, as a result of a car accident or other trauma, or, as was my case, a single parent of an explosively reactive special needs child.

For more information, talk to your health care professional or contact one of the following sources:

National Mental Health Association

2001 N Beauregard Street, 12th Floor
Alexandria, VA 22311
703-684-7722
www.nmha.org

National Institute of Mental Health

Public Information and Communications Branch
6001 Executive Boulevard, Room 8184, MSC 9663
Bethesda, MD 20892-9663
866-615-6464 (toll-free)
www.nimh.nih.gov

National Center for PTSD

802-296-6300
Email: ncptsd@ncptsd.org
www.ncptsd.va.gov

GUNNY'S PLAYLIST

I've put together YouTube playlists of music both mentioned in the book, and used during writing and editing. Want a peek into the mind of me? Be sure of your decision, it's not always normal here!

Gunny's playlist: bit.ly/gunny-playlist
Sharon's playlist: bit.ly/gunny-sharon-playlist

ABOUT THE AUTHOR

Raised in the south, MariaLisa learned about the magic of books at an early age. Every summer, she would spend hours in the local library, devouring books of every genre. Self-described as a book-a-holic, she says "I've always loved to read, but then I discovered writing, and found I adored that, too. For reading...if nothing else is available, I've been known to read the back of the cereal box."

Also by MariaLisa deMora

Alace Sweets

A dark thriller, this book is not a light read. Filled with edge-of-your-seat suspense, this intense story commands the reader's attention as it drives towards the explosive ending. Alace Sweets is a vigilante serial killer, with everything that implies and is sure to trip all your triggers. Be ready.

At seventeen, Alace Sweets turned a corner in her life, taking the wrong shortcut home from school.

Resisting the harsh knowledge her attackers will never be made to pay for their actions, Alace takes a stand. Justice must be served, and if fate's scales are out of balance, she's determined to set things right as best she can.

When the laws of men fail, the rules of Alace prevail.

5-Star Reviews for Alace Sweets

"deMora has a superb story-line and exceptional character development. All of her characters have such depth that will intrigue the reader..."
~Turning Another Page

"Hot, sweet, dark thriller."
~Beth D

"It will keep you on the edge of your seat and give you chills."
~Escape Reality Book Blog

"Disturbing, haunting, sickly; yet hot, sexy and heart racing!"
~Amanda L

"From the first page [deMora] pulls you into the world she has created and you do not even try to escape..."
~Little Shop of Readers Blog

"A must read for all those dark, gritty romance fans out there."
~Sweet & Spicy Reads

"You will find yourself so drawn into the story that the outside world is blocked out and your locking the doors and turning on all the lights."
~Danena F

"Don't judge me for bonding with a vigilante serial killer, she's more than what she does."
~iScream Books

"Thrilling...chilling...full of suspense, nail biting edge of your seat excitement."
~Tracey H

"Every time MariaLisa deMora picks up her pen (or opens her computer), she creates characters you want to believe in."
~Gail S

"Intriguing dark storyline, beautiful love story and nail-biting conclusion, what more could a reader ask for?"
~Manda M

"This book takes you a dark and twisted ride that is gripping..."
~Renee Entress' Blog

"This book is dark and gritty and I literally had to take a day off from reading it because it's that intense."
~My Girlfriend's Couch

"This is my favourite book so far from this author ... I recommend this book if you enjoy dark romantic thrillers."
~Cheekypee Reads and Reviews

"There's not enough stars to give this book and 5 just doesn't really do it justice!"
~DeLane C

"I couldn't put this book down from page one! Tried to stop & go to bed but couldn't sleep thinking about Alace and got up & finished the book."
~Debbie M

"MariaLisa DeMora, wordsmith that she is, made this a story of the enlightenment of a woman and finding love in a life where she has had none."
~Kat W

"Whatever deep dark trench [deMora] pulled a character like Alace from should be revisited again and often."
~Confessions of a Serial Reader

ADDITIONAL SERIES AND BOOKS

Please note that books in a series frequently feature characters from additional books within that series. If series books are read out of order, readers will twig to spoilers for the other books, so going back to read the skipped titles won't have the same angsty reveals.

Rebel Wayfarers MC series:

Mica, #1
A Sweet & Merry Christmas, short story #1.5
Slate, #2
Bear, #3
Jase, #4
Gunny, #5
Mason, #6
Hoss, #7
Harddrive Holidays, short story #7.5
Duck, #8
Biker Chick Campout, short story #8.5
Watcher, #9

A Kiss to Keep You, novella #9.25
Gun Totin' Annie, short story #9.5
Secret Santa, short story #9.75
Bones, #10
Gunny's Pups, novella #10.25
Never Settle, short story #10.5
Not Even A Mouse, short story #10.75
Fury, #11
Christmas Doings, #11.25
Gypsy's Lady, #11.5
Cassie, #12
Road Runner's Ride, novella #12.5

Occupy Yourself band series:

Born Into Trouble, #1
Grace In Motion, #2 (TBD)
What They Say, #3 (TBD)

Neither This, Nor That series:

This Is the Route Of Twisted Pain, #1
Treading the Traitor's Path: Out Bad, #2
Trapped by Fate on Reckless Roads, #3 (TBD)

Other Books:

With My Whole Heart
Alace Sweets
Hard Focus

More information available at mldemora.com.

www.ingramcontent.com/pod-product-compliance
Lightning Source LLC
Chambersburg PA
CBHW051525260626
47170CB00003B/786